DOG SAVE THE KING

LTUE Benefit Anthologies

Trace the Stars

A Dragon and Her Girl

Twilight Tales

Parliament of Wizards

A Hero of a Different Stripe

Troubadours and Space Princesses

Dog Save the King

For Glory and Honor (forthcoming, 2026)

Tales from the Silver City Saloon (forthcoming, 2027)

OTHER WORKS BY JALETA CLEGG

Dark Dancer

Autumn Visions (collection)

Brain Candy (collection)

Llama Tell You a Story . . . (collection)

Soul Windows (with Frances Pauli)

Waiting for Elephants (collection)

ALTAIRAN EMPIRE SERIES

Nexus Point

Priestess of the Eggstone

Poisoned Pawn

Kumadai Run

Cold Revenge

Jericho Falling

Obsidian Tears

Chain of Secrets

An Indecent Proposal

Phoenix in Flames

Redemption

AS EDITOR

Wandering Weeds: Tales of Rabid Vegetation (with Frances Pauli)

OTHER WORKS EDITED
BY JOE MONSON

DOG SAVE THE KING

EDITED BY

Jaleta Clegg and Joe Monson

HEMELEIN PUBLICATIONS

Dog Save the King
LTUE Benefit Anthologies, volume 7

Edited by Jaleta Clegg and Joe Monson
Cover Designer: Joe Monson
Interior layout and design: Joe Monson
Proofreader: Marny Parkin
Managing Editor: Joe Monson
Publisher: Heather B. Monson
Published by Hemelein Publications, LLC., hemelein.com

First Hemelein printing, February 2025
10 9 8 7 6 5 4 3 2 1
ISBNs:
978-1-64278-055-0 (trade paperback)
978-1-64278-056-7 (ebook)

Library of Congress Control Number: 2024936487

To Sue Ream.
Thank you for all your support over the years.
We miss you, your after-parties, your dogs, and your love.

Contents

A Rare Love, Unfeigned

Joe Monson

Dogs have been "man's best friend" for a very, very long time. They appear in some of the oldest drawings and written works. Canines have been used as beasts of burden, protectors, entertainers, and even (sadly) food in some cases. These faithful companions have helped shape our world, possibly more than any other type of animal on this planet. Anywhere humans are found, dogs can be found, even in some of the most remote corners of the Earth.

Sue Ream loved dogs.

Ask practically anyone who knew her, and one topic that inevitably came up was her dogs. She had many different dogs over the years, but the one I remember seemed almost as tall as me (not really, but it sure seemed that way). Kenjo was enormous, nearly three feet tall at the shoulder! I wouldn't have been surprised if he had wolf DNA. Small children could have (and possibly did) ride him like a horse. And he was the friendliest dog on the planet.

Kenjo always loved the after-parties Sue held at her home because so many people from the symposium committee came by and visited with Sue. He would happily go from person to person seeking head pats and ear skritches, cycling through the crowd multiple times by the end of the festivities.

In addition to loving her dogs, Sue contributed a lot to the world. She served in the military. She taught creative writing and English classes at Brigham Young University for decades (from the late 1960s into the 1990s), and students loved her wit, imagination, and humor. I wish I had been so lucky as to have a class from her, if only so I could have gotten to know her better.

Thankfully, she spent a lot of time helping out the committee of Life, the Universe, & Everything, taking care of guests and volunteers alike. Her house and Betty Pope's house were just down the street from each other, and committee members and guests were a constant stream between the two on Saturday evening following the end of the symposium.

So we dedicate this volume to Sue. These stories are ones we think she would have loved, all about dogs saving the day and being, well, dogs. Dogs are overflowing with love, which is likely why Sue loved them and they loved her so much. I'm sure she's having a grand old time in heaven with all of her dogs. I can't imagine it any other way.

Thank you for all the love and support through the years, Sue. We can only hope to achieve half the kindness you showed us over the years.

Joe Monson
February 2025

LONG LIVE THE QUEEN

DAVID HANKINS

"T he King is dead. Long live the King."

The automated fold-space transmission cycled through my sluggish Canid circuitry, informing the Imperium of their new monarch, and reminding me of my failure. King Cyrus's body was still warm beneath mine, rank with the coppery tang of blood. Hypersonic bullets had pierced us both. My friend, my king, was dead. Xavier, Cyrus's twenty-five-year-old son, was king now.

I raised my head. Articulated metal ears twitched, and I scanned the room with sensors far more powerful than those of the extinct Belgian Malinois hound I resembled. Bodies littered the well-appointed bungalow's living room. Four Imperial Shìwèi Guards slumped by the main entrance, monofilament Jiàn swords clutched in their hands, bodies tangled with a half-dozen assassins. Two more assassins I'd dispatched lay sprawled across a once-white couch. Queen Ximing Luo lay crumpled in the corner under Shelby, my fellow Canid Guardian.

Shelby did not respond to my neural query. An assassin's bullet had pierced the core processor. A spike of sorrow slid through my circuitry. I would miss Shelby's dry humor. The sparkle of her mechanical blue eyes when she teased me. Shelby had been a ruthless guardian and an insatiable flirt.

Expensive art hung on natural wood-grain walls. Simple arched doorways led to bedroom suites and the kitchen, and two broad glass doors opened to a veranda that overlooked a manicured lawn. The wild jungles of Mallora-9 lay beyond the grass, a distinct line separating civilization from the towering canopy. This was supposed to be a secluded planet. Safe for a royal getaway that had been years in the planning.

Clearly, an enemy had been planning as well. Who that enemy might be, I hadn't a clue. Court politics were not my job. Protecting the royal family was.

And now only two remained.

A directional beacon told me that young King Cyrus was in the jungle, two hundred fifty-seven meters away, and running at a heading of zero degrees. Due north toward the spaceport at Palma Base.

Distant screams pricked my sensors followed by the unmistakable recoil of a hypersonic rifle. The screams cut off abruptly, along with King Cyrus's beacon.

"The King is dead. Long live the Queen."

Damn it!

I surged to my feet, then nearly collapsed. Red hydraulic fluid leaked from the bullet holes in my flexi-armored side. I directed combat repair subroutines to seal the hoses. Diagnostics said that I'd lost two-hundred sixty-three centiliters of fluid, dropping my effective strength and speed to fifty-two percent. No stronger or faster than an actual Malinois hound.

It would have to be enough.

Thirteen-year-old Princess—no *Queen*—Cassandra's beacon blared through my sensors. The only survivor of the imperial family was in her bedroom closet.

Voices and footsteps approached the veranda. "Find the brat," a man's rough voice said. "We don't get paid unless we get them all."

I took two tentative steps, testing my hasty hydraulics repairs. They held. A squad of seven assassins blended out of the jungle, reactive camouflage fatigues bending not just light, but infrared, radio, and x-ray as well. My sensors saw only blurry outlines.

That was Imperial Marine tech. How had assassins gotten it?

The blurs flowed across the manicured lawn. I ran for the bedroom suites, cutting in front of the open doors.

"Shit!" the man yelled. "One of the Canids survived!" Footsteps pounded onto the veranda.

My rubber-padded paws were silent on the red tiles as I sprinted down the hallway. "Queen Cassandra!" I tried to yell, but nothing came out. Belated diagnostics informed me of a damaged verbal modulator.

I dropped my snout and head-butted her bedroom door at the end of the hall like a battering ram. A shower of wooden splinters sprayed across Cassandra's canopied bed. My paws kept perfect traction on the tile, and I turned a sharp left toward the closet. The thin closet door didn't even slow me.

I crashed into the walk-in closet and came eye-to-eye with Cassandra, new queen of the Chino-Persian Imperium, and absolute ruler of three-quarters of known space. Small but fierce, like her mother, she wore white pajama shorts, a shirt festooned with dancing flamingos, and an expression of terror. A Shìwèi's small pistol wavered in her two-handed grip. The young queen screamed and pulled the trigger.

Thankfully, she missed. Her sea-green eyes bulged when she recognized me, and Queen Cassandra dropped the pistol.

"Sasha!"

She threw her arms around my flexi-armored neck. Her short black hair felt silky smooth to my surface sensors, though tinged with salty tears.

I spun toward the door. In a motion practiced since then-Princess Cassandra was old enough to walk, she lay across my back, hooking her feet into stirrups I extruded from my hips. Her hands gripped matching handles that extended from the forward edges of my shoulders.

The assassins burst into the bedroom, reactive camouflage making them look like humanoid-shaped water bubbles.

Water bubbles that moved with deadly intent. Water bubbles that stood between us and the nearest exit, a picture window beyond the bed that overlooked the bungalow's side lawn.

I sprang toward the nearest assassin. A rifle-shaped blur spun toward us. My titanium teeth clamped onto the barrel, and I wrenched it from his grip as my forepaws hit his chest.

One-hundred-fifty kilos of enraged Canid Guardian—and fifty kilos of terrified royalty—smashed the assassin to the floor. My claws dug in, and he screamed. I leapt right and slammed a shoulder into the next assassin, who dropped to a knee.

Were I alone, I could have killed them all with teeth and claws. I was designed for close combat. But protecting Queen Cassandra took priority.

We rebounded left into another assassin, knocking him onto the bed. I leapt for the window. It was closed, but not armored. Queen Cassandra and I crashed through in a shower of glass.

I hit the lawn at a dead run. Twin yellow suns burned in Mallorca-9's sky, making the shadows of the nearby jungle seem that much darker. The perimeter markers at the edge of the lawn were dark. Someone had disabled the force fence.

More shots echoed behind us. Hypersonic rounds whizzed past. I jinked left and right to make us harder to target as I bounded for the jungle. Queen Cassandra held on, shifting her weight with mine. She'd loved riding me when she was young. Though she was a bit big for it now, the years of practice were finally paying off.

We flew past the perimeter markers, and verdant darkness wrapped around us, moist leaves slapping my face as we barreled through. I stopped jinking and just ran, letting the dense jungle hide us from our pursuers. They gave chase but were no match for me. Even at fifty-two percent speed, I outdistanced the assassins within minutes. I had no destination in mind, only distance. Only one burning imperative driving me forward.

Protect the queen.

AFTER HALF AN HOUR OF RUNNING, I stopped at a tight grove of broad-leafed trees that resembled palms, their sharp pink leaves erupting from knobby trunks every meter or so. It was dark as twilight under the dense canopy, but my sensors indicated no predators nearby. I squeezed into a small space between the clustered trunks.

The queen slid from my back and collapsed onto a soft mat of moldering leaves. Her face was blotchy and streaked with tears. Queen Cassandra leaned back against a knobby trunk and met my gaze, sea-green eyes clouded with worry.

"My parents. Are they dead?"

I nodded, guilt hunching my shoulders.

"And Xavier?"

I nodded again.

Queen Cassandra drew a shuddering breath and wiped her eyes. "Thank you, Sasha," she said, voice rough, "for saving me. I know it's your job, but . . . thank you." Her voice cracked and for a moment I saw not the monarch of the Chino-Persian Imperium, but a girl who'd just lost everyone she loved. She looked small and frail.

I bowed my head, acknowledging her thanks. Queen Cassandra's eyes narrowed. "Why aren't you talking?"

Were she an adult, I could have communicated directly with her implant, but the privacy restrictions for a minor's implant required direct contact for digital communication. I looked pointedly at the four bullet holes in my left side. Two-centimeter-wide entry wounds dimpled my smooth flexi-armored skin, a tight shot group that had pierced several, but not all, of my critical systems. The exit wounds on my right side had merged into one large hole whose ragged edges curled outward like ripped cloth. King Cyrus's dried blood coated my right side. Some of that blood had worn off onto Cassandra's flamingo pajamas.

Her lips pursed and she fingered the exit wound. I noticed that she was careful not to touch the blood. "I think I see the problem. There's a loose connector. Um . . ." She cast around, then grabbed a leaf whose tip had a needle-sharp point. Then she leaned in and poked around my insides. I let her. Not because she was my queen—though that would have been enough—but because she was studying cybernetics in school. And she was good at it.

Something crackled inside me, and Queen Cassandra leaned back. "Okay," she said. "Say something."

I tried to say, "Thank you, Your Majesty," but all that came out was a gruff crackle that sounded distinctly like, "Woof."

"Woof?" she repeated.

"Woof."

A girlish smile blossomed on her face. "Now you sound like a real dog!"

I wanted to grump about that. I was not a dog. Dogs yip and whine and lick their own butts. I was a highly decorated Canid, a killing machine perfected for the tunnel warfare of Argus-4. Canids are full sentients with free will, so after the war ended, I volunteered as a Canid Guardian for the royal family, where I'd served faithfully for five generations. I was not a dog!

Yet, the light in Cassandra's eyes and the joy in her voice cooled my annoyance. "Woof," I said again, and even—to my shame—wagged my tail a bit.

Queen Cassandra giggled.

Right. We were safe, but not for long. I may have outpaced the assassins, but if they had Imperial Marine fatigues, then I calculated with a ninety-seven percent certainty that they had other restricted tech and could track us.

Unfortunately, I also calculated with eighty-six percent certainty that this assassination was an inside job. Too many layers of security had obviously failed. Where was the orbiting battle cruiser on overwatch? The battalion of Imperial Marines who should have swarmed in to protect the royal family? No, this was *definitely* an inside job. I raised my calculations to ninety-five percent certainty.

Which meant that the assassins had access to our internal networks.

My gaze snapped to Queen Cassandra's left forearm. To the lump hiding her bio-cybernetic implant.

And her beacon.

Queen Cassandra followed but misinterpreted my gaze. She rolled her eyes. "Of course! I'm such an idiot. I'm so used to talking to you that I forgot we could link." She placed her left wrist against the right side of my head. Her implant—a learning model that grew as she did—connected to my internal network.

<*Your Majesty, time is short. We must deactivate your implant.*>

"What?" she jerked back, breaking the connection. I understood her response. Without her implant, she'd be helpless, unable to interact with even the simplest technology.

But she'd be alive.

I leaned forward and placed my temple against her wrist again. Her skin was warm, sweaty from the humid jungle heat. Her pulse raced.

<*The mercenaries can track your beacon.*>

"But what about the Marines? How will they find me?"

<*We've been betrayed. I don't know who to trust. I can deactivate your beacon with my embedded spoofer,*>—a remnant and now-illegal bit of tech from my days in the Canid Corps—<*and then we'll have to run again.*>

Queen Cassandra bit her lip. "Where?"

<*Palma Base and then off-planet. Your throne awaits you on Xi'an.*>

Her expression tightened, but she nodded. My plan had holes you could fly a battle cruiser through, but she trusted me. Her mother's determination solidified in her eyes. The determination of a queen.

Queen Cassandra set her jaw and broke our connection. She held out her wrist. I placed my left paw on her forearm, covering the bulge of her implant, and pressing her arm to the jungle floor.

<*I'm sorry,*> I said, though she couldn't hear me, and punctured her skin with my claws. The spoofer embedded in my left paw connected to her implant.

Queen Cassandra jerked as though she'd touched a live wire, and in a way, she had. I pressed hard, keeping her forearm pinned to give the spoofer time to fully fry her implant and beacon. She screamed.

Abruptly, the scream cut off, and Queen Cassandra collapsed to the moldering leaves. I retracted my claws and sniffed at her. She was alive but unconscious. I listened for any telltale remnant of her beacon but heard only digital silence.

I gently gripped Queen Cassandra's wrist in my jaws and dragged her from our hiding place. Once free, I positioned her body so that I could wriggle under her. It wasn't easy.

The whine of antigrav overhead caught my ear, and I froze half-under the queen. I looked up, but jungle canopy blocked my view. The approaching craft grew louder, circling.

Friend or foe, I couldn't tell.

I wasn't waiting around to find out.

Queen Cassandra regained consciousness within a few minutes. She slipped off my back and ran barefoot beside me. We could have made better time with her riding, but this gave me the agility to defend her, should the need arise. She rubbed at her wrist as we ran, at the dead lump of her implant.

The jungle air was heavy, humid, and full of sound. Avian calls, insect chitters, and the constant rustle of life-and-death struggles hidden behind dense foliage. The rich cacophony of jungle life varied only slightly from planet to planet.

We angled north and westward around the compound where Queen Cassandra's family had been assassinated. King Cyrus had bought Mallorca-9 with the sole intent of making it a royal getaway. The planet had clustered islands more than continents but boasted all the environments one might desire in a vacation. Soaring mountains, pristine beaches, and mysterious jungles. King Cyrus had built several vacation homes on Mallorca-9. Palma, where we were, was the largest island and boasted the only spaceport. Palma Base served as both an administrative hub for the planet and barracks for the Imperial Marines who'd failed to protect their king.

My plan was simple. Reach Palma Base, steal the automated royal courier ship King Cyrus always kept handy, and get Queen Cassandra to her throne on Xi'an.

We traveled in relative silence, following game trails through dense jungle. As we crossed a fast but narrow stream, Queen Cassandra finally spoke.

"Do you think the Argusi are behind the assassination?"

I paused long enough to look back and shake my head. Please. The spider-like Argusi had been restricted to their planet since the war. Besides, they weren't a cunning race. Just extremely violent. No, humans had plotted this assassination. I resumed my easy lope, leading us uphill between near-ferns with broad purple flowers.

Queen Cassandra huffed and followed, bare feet making squishy sounds in the soft soil. "It doesn't matter, I guess. I'm not taking the throne."

I stopped dead in my tracks.

What?

I turned and cocked my head, expression intentionally quizzical. Queen Cassandra cocked an eyebrow.

"Don't look at me like that, Sasha. I never wanted the crown. That was Xavier's job! There's a reason I'm studying cybernetics instead of politics. Machines make sense. People baffle me."

I shook my head. "Woof!"

"No. I'm not the queen you want. Not the queen the Imperium deserves. Aunt Priam is next in line after me. She can have the throne."

True, King Cyrus's sister was quite the political animal, but she wouldn't be a benevolent ruler. She was too self-centered. Too cunning . . .

Realization surged through my circuits. Duchess Priam was the cunning mastermind behind today's massacre. Only one more death and the throne was hers. And Queen Cassandra wanted to just *hand* her the crown?

I growled. Well, I ground my damaged voice modulator in a mechanical semblance of a growl. Queen Cassandra narrowed her eyes.

"Don't you growl at me. I may not want the crown, but I am your queen. For now."

I stopped growling and trotted back down the hill to her, sliding a bit in the soft dirt. We stood near the burbling creek, staring at each other. How to make Queen Cassandra understand that her aunt wanted her *dead*?

"Woof," I said, frustrated.

She cocked an eyebrow and folded her arms, looking every bit the queen she didn't want to be.

My sensors picked up the click of a scrambled comm's burst transmission. My head whipped back the way we'd come, ears perked. I couldn't discern sounds of pursuit over the stream and the jungle, but if I'd caught the edge of a transmission, then they were close.

Fear cracked Queen Cassandra's determination. "The assassins?" she whispered, placing one hand on my flexi-armored back.

"Woof," I said in a matching low tone. I jerked my head and pointed my snout up the hill. She scrambled up past me, grabbing near-ferns to pull herself uphill. I followed, keeping myself between my queen and her pursuers.

Protect the queen. Right now, that meant surviving to reach the Imperial Capital on Xi'an . . . where Queen Cassandra would run straight into her aunt's arms. And to her own death.

Somehow, I had to convince her of the truth before that happened. Before my queen died.

MALLORCA-9'S TWIN SUNS HAD SET, and evening was heavy in the sky by the time we reached the outskirts of Palma Base. Four hours we'd trudged through the jungle. Via aircar, it would have taken under ten minutes. Queen Cassandra no longer looked regal—more like a wrung-out rat, her bare feet cut and torn. She was muddy, bloody, and drenched with sweat. But she never complained.

I didn't look much better. One of my repaired hydraulic lines had popped an hour earlier, weakening my left foreleg before I could seal it again. I lost another ninety-eight milliliters of hydraulic fluid, leaving me with a choice. Either reduce all motor functions to twenty-seven percent—no faster than a slow human walk—or reroute hydraulic fluid from my left foreleg entirely and assume a heavy limp.

I chose the limp.

Palma Base looked like a beehive that had been kicked. Troop carriers sped across the spaceport's tarmac, carrying Imperial Marines to a line of waiting CP-35 Transports whose antigrav engines revved with a high-pitched whine. Sirens wailed, adding to the noise. A bulky supply trawler—a civilian model—at the tarmac's northern end was the only ship not bustling with activity. Its crew sat amid half-unloaded crates, looking bored. Grounded, no doubt, because of the emergency.

My internal comm picked up a cycling announcement.

"Attention: detain or disable all Canids. Marines, report to emergency stations. Attention: detain . . ."

Duchess Priam was setting Canids up for the assassination.

And why were the Marines only now scrambling? This beehive should have been kicked four hours ago!

We skirted the Palma Base's western edge, stopping behind the last fighter hangar we reached. The hangar that—assuming my data was correct—should hold the automated royal courier. Palma's rocky coastline lay to our left, just beyond the grounded supply trawler. The roar of crashing surf was muted behind the whine of CP-35 engines and the blare of the siren.

Because the planet was supposedly a royal preserve without sentient threats, physical security was limited to a force fence to keep out local wildlife. But Canids were built for infiltration. We were the only reason Imperium forces had finally broken through the Argusi's devilishly clever defenses inside Argus-4's intricate cave networks.

I lifted my left paw with my teeth to place it on the force-fence post. My claws extended and the embedded spoofer went to work. Five seconds later, one section of force field flickered out even though the fence control systems still thought everything was secure.

We crept onto the base like refugees and sprinted twenty meters for the hangar. A door on the hangar's left side was unlocked, so we slipped inside. A cluster of utility benches and tool cabinets greeted us along with the noisy bustle of scrambling fighter jets. Queen Cassandra put her hands over her ears, and I bit the hem of her shirt to pull her down behind a cabinet. I popped open the cabinet's door and motioned her inside. She looked quizzical but didn't argue. Once she was hidden, I scanned the hangar.

It was massive, as are all such structures, and painted light military gray. The wall to our left shimmered with an adjustable forcefield in lieu of sliding doors. Its lavender hue indicated it was currently permeable. Four small but fierce-looking Imperial Fighters rested in cradles, bristling with weaponry. Ground crew, humans and a mix of other Imperium races, scrambled about conducting preflight checks. The nearest fighter got a thumbs up from a crew chief and lifted from its cradle with a whine of antigrav. It slid through the permeable forcefield.

Beyond the fighters sat the courier. It was long and sleek: ninety-two percent foldspace engine, three percent living quarters, and five percent everything else that made couriers the fastest ships in the galaxy. Not the most comfortable, but we didn't need comfort. We needed a ticket off Mallorca-9, and that thing was fully automated.

A growl made me spin. "Sasha, you traitor!" A small Canid flew out of a cabinet beside the door. He looked like a bulldog, small but heavy, and slammed into my side. We crashed into the cabinet hiding Queen Cassandra. She squeaked from inside.

My attacker scrambled onto my back, metal teeth snapping at my neck while claws dug at my armor. I twisted and bit one of his forelegs. I could have ripped it out if I was at full strength, but instead I twisted to pull him off my back and slam him into the floor. Unused to my dead left leg, I overbalanced and landed on my side. I recognized this bulldog: Kim, a former member of the Canid Corps who'd become a mechanic when I'd become a Guardian. We'd never gotten along.

Kim kicked me hard in the chest with both hind legs.

<Stop!> I sent via neural link, shaking his foreleg in my teeth.

"You killed the king!" He twisted and snapped at my neck. I had to release him to dodge aside. Kim's bite was like a hydraulic press. If he got my neck, it would be all over. "And now they're blaming the rest of the Canids!"

<We're being framed! I tried to save King Cyrus.> Pain twisted through my processors. *<This isn't just an assassination. It's a coup.>*

Kim circled me, growling. "How much did they pay you?"

<I'm not the enemy!> I glared at Kim. He was bullheaded and a pain in my ass, but he was honorable. I made a decision. *<I need your help saving Queen Cassandra.>*

Kim glanced around. "The queen, were she here, would only need saving from *you*."

The cabinet behind me clicked open and Queen Cassandra poked her head out, short black hair swinging to frame her face. Her glare was fierce. "Leave my Guardian alone."

Kim's brown mechanical eyes widened, and he bowed his head. "Your Majesty, forgive me. But Sasha is a trai—"

"Sasha is my Guardian and my friend. He saved me from the assassins." She climbed out of the cabinet and sat beside me, arms wrapped around her bare knees. She leaned toward me. "Do you trust this Canid?"

"Woof." I nodded, then glanced around the cabinet at the hangar. No one was looking our way. They hadn't heard our struggle over the whine of the antigrav engines. A second fighter had departed and the third was lifting off.

"Woof?" Kim sneered. "What are you, some lapdog?" He stepped forward to sniff at my side and grunted. "Oh, your voice modulator's damaged."

<Really. I hadn't noticed.>

Kim sat on his haunches. "You wanna be sarcastic, or do you want me to fix it?"

I shook my head. *<No time. Why didn't the Imperial Marines come to the bungalow four hours ago? Why are they just now scrambling?>*

"Comms went out. When they came back up, someone was screaming that you and Shelby had assassinated the entire royal family."

<You didn't hear the fold-space announcement that the king was dead?>

Kim's eyes tightened, but he shook his head. "Not until the comms came back up a few minutes ago."

<We need to get Queen Cassandra off-planet. Duchess Priam is behind the coup, and I don't know who else she's suborned. The Queen will only be safe once we're back on Xi'an surrounded by Kingsguard.>

Kim's gaze flicked skyward. "Duchess Priam is here. She's on the battlecruiser."

Damn. I'd hoped to slip off-planet unnoticed, but if Duchess Priam was in direct control, she'd shoot down anything departing atmosphere. We were trapped.

"Aunt Priam is here?" Queen Cassandra's eyes lit up, relief evident on her young features. "Take me to her!"

Kim met my gaze with a curious tilt of his head. "She doesn't know?"

"Know what?" Queen Cassandra asked.

Kim nodded toward me. "Sasha says your aunt is behind the coup. Considering all the crap that's gone wrong today, I'm inclined to believe him. Someone powerful is behind this, and Duchess Priam is next in line for the throne."

Queen Cassandra's eyes went wide. She shook her head. Her voice was quiet and disbelieving. "No. Not Aunt Priam. She wouldn't."

The hanger grew quiet, and I glanced around the cabinet. The last fighter had departed, leaving only the Imperial Courier at the far end. Ground crew gave each other high-fives and filed toward the hangar's far exit. I eyed the courier, an idea forming.

<Okay,> I said to Kim. *<You'd better patch me up. I need to talk directly to my queen. And then, I need your help with something much more delicate and painful.>*

"Yeah? What?"

<I need to kill Queen Cassandra.>

THIRTY MINUTES LATER, Kim and I watched from inside the hangar as the courier sped into the darkening sky. Queen Cassandra's beacon called to me, fading with distance as the courier rose on powerful antigrav. Once it cleared atmosphere, the courier could activate its fold-space drive and jump to Xi'an.

It never made it that far.

The battle cruiser, a dark blur in the starlit sky, fired a single particle beam at the courier. The particle beam thickened and twisted through the atmosphere, throwing off waves of energy that looked like Aurora Borealis. Yet, even diluted by atmosphere, a particle beam was a powerful weapon, and the courier was unarmored.

It exploded.

The automated fold-space transmission cycled through my Canid circuitry. "The Queen is dead. Long live the Queen." It was done.

I turned at footsteps behind us. Cassandra—queen no longer—stepped out of a small latrine, cleaned up and dressed in mechanic's overalls that were too big. She'd rolled the cuffs and was cinching the waist as she approached. She stopped and glanced skyward. Debris rained down, splashing into the ocean north of the Palma Base. Cassandra drew a shuddering breath.

"You were right, Sasha. Aunt Priam did want me dead."

"I'm sorry," I said with my freshly repaired voice modulator. "Are you ready?"

Cassandra nodded and stepped onto the unlit tarmac. Kim and I followed, me limping heavily on only three legs. My left foreleg, which Kim had removed, was somewhere among the falling debris. The spoofer embedded in my paw had done its job mimicking Queen Cassandra's beacon and giving Duchess Priam the chance to assassinate her way to the throne.

It wasn't a far walk to the supply trawler. The lounging crew glanced up. This was the most dangerous part of my plan, the part whose variables I couldn't predict. A middle-aged man rose to greet us. He was tall with dark skin and a tight haircut. A former Marine's haircut if I didn't miss my guess.

He extended a hand. "I'm Captain Midcoh. You are?"

Cassandra shook his hand. "In need of a job. I'm trained in cybernetics." She didn't mention her dead implant. "My Canid companions are a mechanic and a security specialist."

The captain eyed us, cocked an eyebrow at my missing leg, then nodded. "I was just telling my First Mate that we could use a cyberneticist, wasn't I, Liam?" He glanced back at a large, heavily tattooed man who lay sprawled across three crates. Liam had wild blonde hair and spoke with a heavy New-Irish accent.

"Oh, aye. And a mechanic Canid, too. Need someone who can fit into tight spaces. Not so sure what we'll do with a three-legged security dog, though."

I glared. "I'm not a dog." Liam chuckled and gave me a "gotcha" smile like we were old friends. I added, "I have other skills that might prove useful."

"I'm sure you do," Captain Midcoh said, a half-smile quirking his lips. He waved toward the boarding ramp at the back of his ship. "We'll depart in a few hours once things settle down. Liam will get you settled." Liam heaved himself up.

Cassandra nodded regally, and we followed the First Mate.

We were on the ramp when Captain Midcoh exhaled heavily and swore under his breath. No one else heard him, but I was a Canid Guardian. I glanced back. Had this been a mistake? He caught my gaze and then gave the slightest of bows. His voice was soft.

"She is safe. Long live the Queen."

Daciana's Pack

Christina Tang-Bernas

The story begins with a prince, as these stories so often do.

A clamor started up outside King Gregory's bedroom. "Prince Xander, you're back," came a muffled voice. "Let me announce you to the—"

"No need," the familiar voice replied, distracted and amused in equal measures, before the door slammed open, followed by the sight of the tall man tromping in. The large brindled wolf by Gregory's feet grunted and heaved himself up, padding over. "Father, are you still awake? Hello, Rommel, old boy," the dark-haired young man said as he bent to pet the wolf. Rommel pranced from side-to-side at Xander's feet, tongue lolling, tail a-blur in a fit of overexcited wagging.

Gregory's eyes scanned his son from the top of his wind-ruffled blue-black hair to the soggy patches on his clothes where his cloak hadn't shielded him from the day's snowfall to the well-worn boots and thick fingers digging deep into Rommel's fur. Twenty-two years old was a good look on him, half-boyish glee, half-budding wisdom.

"I was waiting up for you." Gregory leaned back in his chair. "Come. Tell me about your patrols."

Xander straightened, immediately serious, launching into a full report of his regular tour of the surrounding lands, a task he'd taken up since he'd come of age and been officially declared Heir.

"Oh, also," he finished. "Daciana's Pack has been particularly restive the last few months. The town guard has reported multiple sightings of wolves at the edge of the forest and along the perimeters of some of the outlying farms. One even ventured all the way to the town gates, a big white wolf. Which is strange, considering how elusive they are. The guardsmen almost caught it too."

A chill snatched at Gregory's spine. "Is that so?"

"The old ones, the more superstitious ones, have been telling me that change is upon us. That—" Xander paused. "Father, you would tell me if anything was wrong, right? With you. Or with anything else."

"I would," Gregory said. "If there were anything wrong." He unclenched his hands. "It's good they didn't catch the animal. You know no harm is to come to the wolf pack. There's a reason it's the symbol of the royal family."

"I know," Xander said. "But it won't matter much, Father, if livestock starts to go missing."

"No, not them," Gregory said. "Other wolves maybe, but not that pack."

"Are they so different?" Xander hesitated, before forging ahead. "You seemed so sure just now."

"You know the stories."

"Well, sure," Xander replied. "That they're immortal, the chosen mates of Daciana. The only pack consisting of all alphas. And even though the pack has both males and females, that no one has ever seen a wolf pup. But those are just tales, all explained away easily." He laughed. "Don't tell me you believe them also."

"Tales last for a reason," Gregory said.

Eyebrow raised, Xander stared. "Never knew this side of you. Father, you've been holding out on me."

Gregory waved his son away. "Don't mind me. I'm an old man who's stayed up too far past his bedtime."

"Then I'll take my leave." Xander sketched a short, untidy bow, the door banging shut behind him.

Gregory winced and stared at the closed door. It was at these times he particularly missed the late Queen Lydia. His wife always seemed to know exactly what to do, and he'd floundered in the wake of her passing. Thankfully, his subjects were kind enough to not mention it within earshot and loyal enough to pretend all was well.

Rommel chuffed, nudging his master in the direction of his waiting bed.

After a sleepless night, Gregory summoned the High Priestess.

"I'm not ready," Gregory burst out, when the stately woman had ensconced herself in a leather armchair.

To her credit, she didn't even have to ask what he meant. "Daciana's Pack seems to think otherwise."

"Oh yes, and wolves would know better than myself about my own readiness."

"It's your choice. Daciana would never force your hand. It's not Her way. Besides, are you so self-centered as to believe it's all about whether you're ready?"

"Can it not wait? Another year?"

"What would another year change?"

Gregory closed his eyes, needing something, someone to ground him. As if summoned by his thoughts, Rommel leaned heavy and warm against his thighs. His hand began its automatic ministrations behind the wolf's ears. Then he stopped, staring down at the animal huddled against him.

"And if I choose not to do this?" Gregory asked. "If I stay and let things take their natural course?"

"You already know what will happen. It was all explained to you when you first ascended the throne."

"Remind me."

"If you choose not to go through with the winter solstice ritual, you will live a normal lifespan and so will Rommel," the High Priestess said, as if by rote. "And when you both pass, Xander will be alone."

"But—"

"What do you want from me, Your Majesty? Do you want to be convinced to go ahead with the ritual? Or to be convinced against it? I have no preference either way. I work Daciana's will, but do you think She is so weak as to not be able to do what She needs to do despite any choice you might make? It is you who must decide which consequences you are willing to live with in what remains of your life."

Gregory swallowed down the words lodged in the back of his throat.

"Father," Xander said as they supped together a week later. "Are you all right?"

"Yes, of course," Gregory replied, automatic.

"Because I just told you we'd been invaded, and all you did was sip your soup," Xander said, peering into his father's face. "You've been distracted. And Rommel keeps following after you like a hairy shadow."

"I'm fine," Gregory insisted. "Too much on my mind, that's all. We haven't really been invaded, have we?"

Xander stifled a smile, before sobering. "Anything I can help with?"

"Not necessary."

Xander's expression creased. "I can help, you know. Whatever it is. I think you've taught me well enough by now, and I've been going on patrols and had no complaints. You can trust me."

"It's not that, Xander. I know you're very able."

"Do you? Sometimes I wonder."

Gregory looked at his son, at his perpetually mussed hair, the patch of stubble he must have missed while shaving that morning, and the ink stain marring the cuff of his shirt. He's still so young, Gregory thought, images of child-Xander over the years layering over the slumped figure across from him, before dissolving away. "I do trust you."

"I'll know it when I see it."

"And I love you, son. I know I should say it more often. I forget, without your mother here to remind me."

Xander's face softened. He nodded. "Don't worry. That's one thing I'll never forget."

Gregory breathed in. Wood smoke. Roast beef. Rommel's damp fur. That hint of musty ozone that crackled in the air on both ends of a thunderstorm. He knew what had to be done.

He stood in the courtyard on the morning of the solstice, eyes tracing the mortar between the stones. Rommel leaned against his legs, warm and almost-comforting.

Xander held the reins of the horse, looking up at his father.

"I may be late tonight, but I'll still be back in time for the end of the solstice," Gregory said.

"Okay, I'll make sure things run smoothly."

"I'm sure you will." Gregory smiled, even as tears pushed their way to the corners of his eyes. He saw the High Priestess standing behind his son. She met his eyes with an understanding gaze and nodded. She would explain everything to Xander, as she had once explained everything to Gregory when they had once both been young long ago. He clasped his beloved son on the shoulder, committing the feel to memory.

Rommel ran with an easy gait beside the horse as they rode past the outskirts of the main city and into the surrounding farmlands. When they arrived at the edge where grass shifted with suddenness into tangled woodland, Gregory slid to the ground and peered into the gloaming darkness. The trees of the ancient forest loomed above him. He wasn't often here; there was no need in this mostly deserted area. But whenever he was, he was always awed by the sentience hovering among the rustle of leaves and the rich loam. Rommel butted his head against Gregory's thigh.

He sunk to his knees and looked into the wolf's golden eyes. Gregory had thought about what he wanted to say to his faithful companion, who had supported him his whole life in so many different ways, but nothing really sounded quite right. "I—I wanted to say thank you for being so good to me, for choosing to stay by my side all these years."

The coarse fur bristled under his hands. Rommel whined and pushed Gregory's chest with his broad flat head. "I don't want you to go either," Gregory choked out. "By Daciana, I will miss you."

Wolves started appearing from behind the trees, ghostly wisps that solidified into golden eyes gleaming under the moonlight. Rommel turned his head to watch them, then looked back at Gregory.

Gregory knew if he wanted Rommel to stay by his side all he had to do was grab ahold of his ruff and tug in the direction of the castle. They would go home together, and nothing would change. But would it be fair? Not only to his faithful companion, whom he would condemn to the short lifetime of a normal wolf instead of the immortality awaiting him in the forest, but Xander as well.

Daciana's Pack had deemed Xander worthy and ready, no matter how illogical and silly it may seem to others, just as they had once deemed Gregory ready. What did it say about him if he refused to believe the same of his only child?

He swallowed. Then forced his hands to release. "Go on, Rommel."

The wolf took a few steps toward the forest, then the same number back. Gregory nodded at him, then took a forceful stride backward. "Go on now," his voice cracking on the last word.

A white wolf trotted up to Rommel, their noses touching. They circled one another, and it seemed to decide something. Rommel tossed a last look back at Gregory before disappearing into the forest. The pack melted away into the gloom, except for the white wolf.

And then, something Gregory hadn't said in a very long while rose in his throat. "Goodbye, Father," he whispered.

On shaky legs, Gregory mounted again. The white wolf turned and moved in another direction. Gregory swallowed and turned his horse to follow. Soon a narrow path through the forest appeared, shimmering slightly in the glow of the rising moon of the longest night.

He didn't know how long he rode but eventually found himself in a hidden clearing set with a wide ring of white stones and a large bonfire in the center. Gregory knew that he would only ever see this place this one time, this hidden sacred heart of his kingdom.

The other white-robed priestesses stood waiting for him. One detached herself from the whispering group, her dark brown hair piled high on her head. "Are you ready?"

"I will be," Gregory said.

"Are you willing?"

His hands clenched and unclenched. "Yes."

Her head inclined. As one, the other priestesses surrounded him, pulling his clothes away and tossing them into the fire. The dark-haired priestess returned to stand before him, a large brush clutched in one hand, a pot of shimmering dark-blue paint in the other. "Then let us begin."

He shivered as the tip of the brush settled on the round of his shoulder. For a moment, it stayed there, unmoving. Then it slid down his arm.

Instead of cooling as the air touched it, the paint warmed wherever the priestesses laid it along his body, the curve of his flank, the lines of his back, the space behind his knees, burning hotter and hotter, burrowing deeper and deeper, until his legs buckled, and he fell, the world blurring around him into a mass of color and light and movement.

THE WOLF WATCHED as the man walked in the room. He knew this man with his night-black hair and the smell of wind clinging to him. But something was wrong. This man was not-happy. The wolf sidled when the man approached, wary of the not-happy feelings shimmering off him.

The man extended a paw in his direction. The wolf hesitated, but he remembered loving this man, so he stepped forward and dipped his nose to it, the familiarity of the scent filling his head and sinking down into his chest.

Yes, he thought, yes.

The wolf sighed and rested his head on the man's knee. The not-happy feelings wavered, then dimmed. A broad hand came up to card through the wolf's ruff.

"Fath—," the man said, then swallowed. "Gregory," the man said, then. The wolf recognized this particular set of sounds to be his name.

I am yours, the wolf thought. And you are mine.

The King's Road

Dale Parnell

At the highest point of Enlais, looking down over the vast and sprawling city, stands the Mourning Tower. At its summit, the Black Bell—forged twelve hundred years ago by the first king of Enlais, Pietr. On the day of his death, the Black Bell rang out exactly thirty times, once for each year of the King's reign, before being silenced with a heavy, thick shroud.

And so it was that the Black Bell would only ring out across the city of Enlais on days of great mourning. To have the bell sound at your death was considered the highest honour. All the people of Enlais would stop and bow their heads in reverence at the solemn chime. As the last ringing strike echoed down the narrow winding streets, the people of Enlais would speak the final prayer, a million voices calling out to the heavens as one to bid the newly deceased fair travels on their journey through the Dead Lands to their final resting place:

To the forests
And the mountain pass
To the raging rivers
That flow too fast
To the full moon's glare
To the scarlet rose
To a secret longing
That nobody knows
Now night, and tears, and endless sleep
And the Watchman's call
From my master's keep

Today, as the sun climbed the eastern face of the Shattered Mountains, the Black Bell sounded and the city wept. King Aris, the city's kindest and wisest monarch in living memory had died, and the chimes of the Black Bell rang louder and longer than ever before. For sixty-two years King Aris had watched over the city and its people. He had protected them from the greed and the violence of the northern tribes and had fostered peace and trade with the cities of the west.

Aris was more than their king, he was a father, brother, and son to every man, woman, and child of Enlais, and they loved him, just as Aris loved them all in return.

As the sixty-second chime rang out, their voices joined as one and they sang the final prayer, their words filling the valley and drifting across the sea to the furthest corners of the known world and beyond. King Aris had passed into the Dead Lands, and the journey that lay before him was his alone to make, his fate his own to decide.

ARIS AWOKE SLOWLY, as if from a deep, consuming sleep, light and sound coming to him gradually. Sky, blue and clear, sat above him, framed by the outstretched arms of towering bher trees, their solid, wide trunks reaching nearly five hundred measures high, their fine, evergreen leaves dancing this way and that in a strong southern wind.

He lay in the middle of a grassy clearing, somewhere in the forest. His first thought was that he had been thrown from his horse, although surely his attendants wouldn't have left him alone had that been the case. Glancing about the clearing, Aris could see no sign of anyone. The deep, shaded forest offered no sound other than the wind and the leaves.

Aris stood, his mind racing to remember what had happened and where he might be. Taking a deep breath to calm himself, Aris marvelled at how clear his chest felt. His arms and legs felt strong also, his back straight, and his mind sharp. His hair was thick and long, and his hands were no longer grey and wrinkled, spotted with dark brown smudges. He was a young man again, barely twenty, feeling as tall and vibrant as he had on the eve of his coronation, over sixty years ago. It was a dream of course, beautiful and cruel, to give an old man back his youth, however intoxicating the sensation.

As Aris stood pondering his options, a sound at his back made him turn on the spot. Standing a little way off, and staring directly at him, was an enormous grey-haired dog. It stood as tall as a dray horse, its snout as long and pointed as a wolf's, its huge paws as large as a battle shield. Aris took a step backwards, keeping his eyes fixed on the creature, who dropped lazily into a sitting position while staring at Aris with a quizzical look.

Aris risked a quick glance about the clearing, looking for a way out through the packed trees and searching for any more hounds but finding neither. He returned his gaze to the dog, and the two of them remained poised in silence. After a few moments the dog sneezed, the sound ricocheting through the clearing and startling a flock of distant birds, who lifted up from the tree tops to noisily fly away. The dog shook its huge head, its ears flapping wildly, before emitting a second, albeit much quieter sneeze. It lifted a massive paw to its face and rubbed it across its nose, and once satisfied, returned to its more dignified position, looking back across the clearing to Aris, a fat, pink tongue lolling from the left side of its mouth.

The whole performance left Aris somewhat confused, and though the creature's size was unmistakably formidable, he couldn't help but feel that the dog meant him no harm.

"Hello there," Aris said, his body relaxing.

The dog tilted his head and emitted a grumbled, rolling sound in reply, its voice deep and resonant yet containing no hint of aggression.

Aris took a step forward, holding his arms out and trying to make his own voice sound as calm and reassuring as possible. "Where did you come from?"

The dog gruffed a reply, once more flicking his huge head from side to side, this time to disturb a small bug that was buzzing about his face.

Aris continued taking small steps towards the massive dog. He had kept dogs as a boy, not anywhere near as large as this one, but they had all been hunting breeds. Aris recognised the same look of intelligence in the creature's eyes, a degree of understanding and tolerance that working dogs have for their master.

The dog remained perfectly still save for the occasional flick of its head to dissuade the insects, and it watched as Aris drew level. Sitting on its hind quarters, the dog was at least two measures taller than Aris, and it lowered its head to look down at him. The clearing had grown warmer, the air feeling close, and the dog was now panting, its breath splashing against Aris' face. This close to the creature, Aris once again felt his heartbeat quicken. The dog's mouth was huge, the jaws lined with pristine white teeth, each one as sharp as a cook's knife. Aris sidestepped to the left, keeping his gaze locked on the creature's gleaming teeth, and slowly raised a hand towards the dog's flank. The dog continued to watch Aris, but still didn't move as his hand made contact. Its fur felt softer than Aris expected, and its huge chest moved in and out with each quick breath.

"That's not too bad, is it," Aris said, stroking the dog's flank in long, slow movements.

The dog's head moved forward, dropping down so that it sat face to face with Aris, who froze in place. The dog inhaled deeply, its nostrils flaring as it breathed Aris' scent in, and without warning or preamble, it stuck out its tongue and licked the side of Aris' face, tickling his ear and wetting the hair on one side of his head. The dog grinned and sat back, its head cocked to one side, its huge, pale brown eyes shining brightly.

"That wasn't what I was expecting," Aris said, wiping the saliva off his face. "But it's better than the alternative, I suppose."

The dog barked once in reply, and Aris returned to stroking its long, grey-haired side.

"Now I just need to find out where you came from and where I am," Aris said. "There will be people out looking for me I expect. Although I doubt I will be able to explain how I appear to be sixty years younger. Or you for that matter."

Aris continued to stroke the dog's side, its soft fur passing through his fingers, and he found himself staring up into the dog's wide, brown eyes. They really did shine, catching the bright sunlight of the clearing perfectly, and yet there was some-thing behind the bright gleam. A truth, sad and somehow inevitable, that Aris felt creeping into his thoughts. Memories drifted back to him—the city of Enlais, its people, and a lifetime of protecting them. He had been an old man, strong yes, but waning, spending his last days in his chambers, his closest attendants at his bedside until finally . . .

The dog bowed its head, its huge eyes closed, and Aris's arm fell to his side.

"Is it true?" Aris asked.

The dog gruffed a low reply, opening its eyes and looking down at Aris gently.

"And so these," Aris said, turning slowly and sweeping his arm out to indicate the forest surrounding them, "are the Dead Lands."

The dog barked a reply.

"And you, my friend," Aris said, turning back to the dog. "Who are you?"

The dog barked, loud and clear.

"Dog?" Aris asked, more surprised by the reply than he was by the fact that he understood it. "Your name is Dog?"

Dog stared down at Aris, grumbling a mumbled reply.

"No, that's a perfectly fine name," Aris said, holding his hands up in apology. "Dog it is then."

Aris reached up to give Dog's ear a scratch. He knew what he had to do—his people had told stories of the Dead Lands for centuries, of the journey that you had to make to earn your final reward. Faced with the reality of it, however, Aris couldn't help but feel apprehensive. The journey was said to be a hard one, a way to test a person's worth. Those who found the journey too hard became lost, their memories fading, their spirit doomed to wander the Dead Lands forever, never finding peace. He looked around the clearing again, the tall lush grasses giving way to a solid flank of trees, the forest full of uncertain gloom.

"I don't suppose you know the way?"

Dog gruffed.

"Haven't you been here before?"

Once more, Dog grumbled a reply.

"I see," Aris replied. "So what do you suggest?"

Dog flicked his great head from side to side and then slowly stood, dipping his head to stretch out his long back and front legs before returning to his full height.

Aris looked about the edges of the clearing for some sign of a path, or at least a way through the densely packed trees. He missed it the first time, but circling back around he saw it. Not a path exactly, but at the eastern edge of the clearing stood two huge bher trees, their trunks marginally farther apart that the rest. It wasn't much, but it was a way out. Aris took that to be as much of a sign as he was going to receive. He looked over his shoulder at Dog and nodded once before the two of them set off, leaving the clearing behind and disappearing into the forest.

They walked in silence a while, weaving between the trees, wading through waist-high ferns that blanketed the forest floor. More than a few times Aris tripped on thick tree roots that protruded above the rich-smelling soil, whereas Dog seemed to pad his way through the forest with ease.

Gradually the trees thinned, the spaces between trunks widening and the flora at their feet becoming more varied. The breaks in the canopy above allowed sunlight to reach them, and after the cool damp of the forest, Aris welcomed the warmth. There still wasn't any sign of a path or road, but Aris began to feel a tickle at the back of his mind, a flicker of something approaching certainty that he was headed in the right direction. Dog kept pace with him, padding silently at his side, neither leading nor following as they made their way.

"Is this what you do?" Aris asked, turning to Dog. "Accompany people on their journey?"

Dog regarded Aris a moment, his huge paws pushing through the tangle of grasses and weeds with ease. He barked once, the sound travelling across the quiet landscape.

"Why not?"

Dog gruffed, chewing consonants between his massive jaws.

"I may have been king, but I hold myself no higher than any man or woman of Enlais," Aris replied.

Dog stopped walking and stared at Aris, another low, rumbling growl coming from deep within his throat.

"Forgive me, my friend," Aris replied, holding a hand up to his chest and bowing slightly. "I am happy you are here. It is just that I am not sure I warrant your company."

Dog barked, his voice lighter this time, softer.

"Thank you," Aris said.

They set off once more, following a gentle slope downwards. As they left the forest behind them, the view opened to show a wide, green country. In the distance, at the southern horizon, stretched a blue-black mountain range, its peaks capped with brilliant white snow. Towards the northeast, a hazy glistening shimmer of ocean, a ribbon of green giving way to bright azure sky that extended up and above the world, as high and awesome as any cathedral ceiling the great city of Enlais could offer.

"I had not expected the Dead Lands to be this beautiful," Aris said.

Dog barked, exhaling through his palm-sized nose in a single huff.

"I don't know," Aris replied. "But not this."

The slope of the hillside continued downwards towards a wide valley through which snaked a narrow river, its clear water sparkling in the bright sunlight.

"We should head that way," Aris said, pointing towards the river.

They walked on, side by side, Aris admiring the scale of the new world he found himself in, and Dog simply content to be out in the open air.

IT TOOK LONGER to reach the river than Aris thought, distances didn't seem to work quite the same way in the Dead Lands, and the sun was setting by the time they reached the sandy riverbank. Aris had also started to feel a change in himself. As they made their way down the long, slow slope, he had felt the first twinge in his knee. His whole body felt heavier, bigger than when he first awoke in the forest clearing. Reaching the river edge, Aris peered into the clear water, the last of the retreating sunlight just enough to see by. The face that looked back was nearer thirty. His features were fuller, hints of lines forming around his eyes, the first flecks of grey showing in his long, dark brown hair. His chest was broader, his limbs sturdy and strong. This was the strongest he would ever be, and for a moment he relished the memory. But the feeling was fleeting, and the truth added a new sense of urgency to his journey.

"I'm aging, aren't I?" Aris asked Dog.

Dog sat a little way off, watching Aris. With the fading sun at his back, Dog's impressive stature was even more formidable. He gruffed, chewing the reply in a low grumble.

"How long do I have?"

Dog barked.

"I see. And if I don't make it in time?"

Dog considered the question, fixing his gaze on Aris, before looking away over his shoulder towards the far side of the river. Aris followed his stare, not sure what he was looking for. Despite the warmth of the evening, Aris felt a chill travel down his neck, and he shivered against the sensation. Over the river on the opposite bank, faint, ghostly figures drifted into view. They moved slowly, some stepping to the edge of the water and staring into the dark water, others milling aimlessly along the bank, their movements slow and melancholy. Aris tried to focus on one figure in particular, but each time it came into focus something shifted and the figure blurred, like watching people move through the fog that would sweep in off the sea at Enlais in the depths of the winter months. They were wraiths, lost souls still searching for their path through the Dead Lands, still looking for their final rest.

"I am sorry," Aris whispered, as a single tear ran down his cheek, dropping sadly onto the dark red velvet of his tunic.

A movement at his side broke the spell. Dog lowered his huge head and nuzzled Aris, who reached up his hand to stroke Dog's grey face.

"Thank you, my friend."

Aris composed himself, watching the figures over the river moving away, before looking up and down the winding river. A small quiet instinct pulled him downstream, so he turned east, as the last rays of sunlight played on the underside of billowing clouds. With Dog at his side, Aris followed the river as it wound along the valley, heading towards the distant ocean.

A FULL, bright moon climbed the night sky, providing enough light for Aris and Dog to follow the river. The chalk-white face of the moon goddess reflecting in the dark water was their constant companion, illuminating silver flashes of tiny fish that darted beneath the water's surface. From time to time Aris saw the wraiths, lonely figures wandering through fields or high up on the surrounding rises. Whether they perceived Aris and Dog or whether their passage was of no consequence, Aris couldn't say, but they continued without incident or confrontation. For Aris, that was enough.

After a time the river widened, the flow picking up pace until it was a raging torrent, the sound of rushing water filling the air. They continued to follow the river, crossing smaller, shallow tributaries as they came to them. Aris felt his legs tiring, and in a few of the more powerful tributaries, he lost his footing, banging his shins against sharp rocks on the river bed. His boots were soaked, and his feet rubbed against the creaking leather. As the first hint of dawn crept into the eastern sky, Aris was wet through and exhausted. They turned a final bend in the river, then fought their way through sharp, tangled brambles that spilled over the riverbank. Aris stopped, his breath laboured, his chest tight. He turned to Dog, who's wet fur clung to all four limbs.

"Now what?" Aris breathed, bending over with his hands planted on his knees. He sucked in a lung full of damp air, then coughed against the effort. He pulled himself upright and took a few steps forward, edging towards the sheer drop that lay before them, the river tumbling over the edge of a wide, deafening waterfall that ended somewhere beyond a cloud of mist a thousand measures down.

Aris sank to the hard ground and pulled his boots off, pouring water onto the ground, watching as it seeped into the porous rock. Dog paced to the edge of the cliff, peering down before carefully retreating backwards and falling onto his haunches.

"That's what I thought," Aris said, rearranging his long, tattered cloak underneath his body before laying down on the stone to catch his breath, his eyes squinting against the climbing sun.

They rested a while, steam rising from Aris's boots as they dried in the warm morning sun, the constant roar of the waterfall reminding Aris of their situation. He slept a few hours, and when he came to, the sun was high in the sky. He sat up and looked around. Dog was stretched out on a patch of scrubby grass to his left, his eyes closed, the slow rhythmic rise and fall of his huge chest indicating he was asleep.

Aris pulled his boots on, then eased his stiff body up, stretching his arms over his head to stretch out his sore back. The river here was too fast and churning to show his reflection, but Aris knew without needing to be shown that he had grown older still. His knees and back ached with the effort of the night's long journey, and though they still held some of their strength, his hands felt weaker, less nimble.

He ambled to the edge of the river and crouched on the bank, dipping his cupped hands into the ice-cold water and splashing it over his face, running his fingers through his hair and easing the ache in his neck. He didn't feel thirsty, but he brought his cupped hands to his lips, relishing the sensation, letting the cold wake him fully. When he stood and turned from the river, Dog was awake, stretching out his massive frame and growling in a low bass rumble.

"And a good morning to you," Aris said.

He moved towards the cliff edge, careful of the loose stone and soil that cracked and fell. The land rolled out towards a distant, hazy horizon on each side, and Aris could see other, similar waterfalls tumbling over the edge and dropping down into oblivion. The cliff itself was sheer in every direction, with no sign of a way down. Yet Aris knew this was the way he must go. Whatever instinct had brought him this far felt even stronger now, and he knew that his journey was almost at an end.

Dog padded over to stand at his side, staring down into the void. The churning vapor coming off the waterfall obscured the bottom of the cliff. As Dog shifted his footing, a chunk of dry earth slipped, causing his massive paw to shoot forward over the cliff. Dog howled, crawling backwards as more dirt and stones fell away. Aris threw his arms around Dog's chest, pushing backwards until they toppled onto the hard, rocky ground. Dog harrumphed as he tried to disentangle his long, bony legs from underneath Aris. When they finally freed themselves, they sat a moment, Dog panting heavily.

It was impossible. How was Aris expected to climb down? Or was it a leap of faith? Was he meant to simply dive from the top of the cliff and trust the pool at the bottom was sufficiently deep that he would survive? Could the dead die over again? His mind flashed back to the wraiths they had seen wandering hopeless and lost the night before. There were fates worse than death. Failure in the Dead Lands meant eternity in perdition. Aris had not come this far, had not lived the life he had, to falter at the final step. He pulled himself upright, brushing dirt and grit from his clothes before gingerly stepping towards the cliff edge.

"I have to find a way down," he said, not turning away from the vast open expanse of sky.

Dog grumbled, chewing fat round letters between his huge teeth.

"I know, my friend," Aris replied, turning to Dog. "But I won't leave you here."

Dog barked, and a passerby would have been forgiven for mistaking the sound for laughter.

"No," Aris replied, unhooking the clasp at his neck and removing his long cloak. "I'm going to carry you."

"Are you ready?" Aris asked, bracing himself face down on the hard ground, his legs dangling over the edge of the cliff.

Dog barked, and shifted against the makeshift sling that circled underneath his body and up around Aris's shoulders.

It had taken some work and a few moments hunting to find a sharp-edged rock that would tear through the heavy material, but after careful cutting, tearing, and a liberal application of the best sailors' knots that Aris knew, he had transformed his cloak into a length of crude rope that he fashioned into a long sling. It took several attempts to find the best position that would support Dog's weight evenly without causing too much discomfort. With his back pressed firmly against Dog's flank, Aris fed the free loop of the sling up and around his chest and shoulders, leaving his arms free.

When Dog's full weight dropped onto his back, Aris let out a muffled cry and forced himself to take small shallow sips of air as he crawled backwards towards the cliff drop. As he lay braced to make the final push, Aris thought that maybe this was the worst decision he had ever made. He coughed into the dirt, sending a fine cloud of dust up into his face, his chest wheezing with the effort.

Dog grumbled, his view nothing but open blue sky.

"Too late, you're coming," Aris breathed before heaving himself backwards, his body dropping over the edge of the cliff. His feet scrambled until they found purchase, and he dug the ends of his boots in tight, easing the top of his body over the hard edge of the cliff. As they reached the tipping point, gravity took over and Dog's massive frame slipped over the edge, the sling drawing tight across Aris's body. He gripped the cliff as firmly as he could, his knuckles turning white. He took two deep, slow breaths, then carefully shifted his weight, moving one foot out and letting his leg drop down, searching for the next foothold. When he found one, he lowered his body over the edge of the cliff. His hands moved over the ragged cliff face to find suitable handholds.

"There," puffed Aris, straining against gravity, keeping his body pressed as close to the cliff as he could. "That wasn't too bad."

Dog whined, fighting the urge to kick his legs.

"It isn't meant to be easy . . ." Aris breathed, moving his way methodically down, step by step, hand hold by hand hold, "that's the point of the journey."

And so they continued, Aris straining as he climbed downwards, Dog's four limbs dangling loosely in thin air.

THE WAY WAS HARD GOING, but Aris was determined, focusing his attention on the rocky spurs at his feet, testing their strength, planting his feet carefully, deliberately. After several hours climbing, Aris felt his arms and legs going numb. He blinked away sweat, misjudging the distance to the next foothold and his left foot slipped. Aris grasped hold of a granite outcrop with every ounce of strength he had. As the loose material fell away, Dog barked, his voice echoing off the solid cliff face.

"Are you sure?" Aris cried.

Dog barked again.

Aris loosened his grip, trying to push his face away from the razor-sharp rocks that threatened to slash his cheeks. They dropped barely two measures, far enough for Aris to feel his heart hammer in his chest. He let himself slump to his knees, dropping low so that Dog could get his feet down on the ledge and brace his body. Aris's head slumped down; his arms held slack at his sides. His back and shoulders burned, the muscles in his calves and thighs tight and aching. He took a moment to catch his breath, and then lifted his head to stare back up the cliff face. It was midday, and the sun was almost directly above them. He couldn't see the top of the cliff, and the ledge didn't feel wide enough for him to risk turning to look down.

"I'd say about half way, wouldn't you?"

Dog grumbled a long, low reply as he shuffled his feet on the shallow ledge. When he was in position, Dog braced his body so that Aris was between his body and the cliff face.

"Thank you, my friend," Aris said, lifting a tired arm up and across his body so that he could stroke Dog's flank. He felt the press of Dog's rising chest, and through sheer exhaustion, Aris fell into a deep and dreamless sleep.

IT WAS late afternoon before Aris awoke. As he stirred, Dog shifted his massive paws so Aris could stretch out his stiff legs. They had a few good hours of sunlight left, and while Aris didn't relish the thought of more climbing, he knew they couldn't stay on the ledge. He shifted position so he could see first the leftmost edge of the ledge, then the right, carefully studying the cliff face for the best way down.

"That way," Aris said, shuffling across the ledge, letting Dog find his footing until they were at the lip. Aris pulled his feet underneath his body then carefully pushed upwards, taking the weight of Dog's body as his paws lifted off the ledge. Pressing the front of his body flat against the cliff face with his hands held above his head, Aris side-stepped a fraction before reaching out his right foot, finding a suitable foothold before leaning out with his right hand extended. With one final breath, Aris pulled his body away from the ledge, his left foot finding a hold, his left hand following suit. It was easier than crawling over the cliff top had been, but was still terrifying. Aris tried to push the fear to the back of his mind, concentrating on the rhythm of his movements; right leg, right hand, left leg, left hand, crawling backwards down the cliff face as the relative safety of the ledge edged further and further away.

THE ROAR of the waterfall had been a constant, almost reassuring friend, but as they continued, Aris noticed the sound was growing louder. The air felt damper, the rock face slick with moisture. Dog growled, and Aris felt the rumble from his body pressed against his back more than he heard it above the sound of the waterfall. The cloud of mist he had seen from the very top of the cliff was right at their feet. That meant the climb was going to get even more dangerous. Worse than that, Aris's strength was failing him. His legs were weak, his hands grey and mottled, the skin of his palms slashed and scarred by the sharp rocks he clung to. He didn't know how much longer he had, how much longer he would be strong enough to climb, and a single, frustrated tear fell down his cheek.

Hanging limply from his back, Dog seemed to sense Aris' panic, and he howled against the roar of the waterfall.

"No!" Aris screamed. "I will not let you go."

Grimacing against the pain burning in his hands, Aris lowered his foot, searching for the next foothold, the black rock shining slick in the fading sunlight. His foot slipped and his grip gave way. Aris and Dog tumbled from the cliff face, piercing the white cloud of churning mist to disappear from sight.

THEY FELL THROUGH THE AIR, cold vapor stinging Aris's eyes, all thought and feeling abandoned. He closed his eyes, not through fear, but acceptance of his fate. He had done what he could, he had tried for as long and as hard as he was able and no man, king or peasant, could offer any more than that.

THEY HIT the water with a thunderous splash, dropping into black, freezing water that felt like Death's own grip. It was cold and dark, but more important, it was deep and free of boulders and knife-sharp rocks that Aris feared would meet them. Aris beat his arms, trying in vain to pull them to the surface. For a moment, he believed that this—after everything—would be his end. Suddenly, he felt his body jerk upwards as Dog's powerful legs kicked against the water, pushing them towards the broken halo of sunlight playing on the surface, back towards a last, final hope.

Dog's massive head breached the surface. He paddled them to the nearest bank, clawing his way up the wet mud before chewing through the sling that tied Aris to him. Aris spluttered as he hit the ground, the impact knocking the water out of his lungs, forcing a fresh breath in. His chest heaved as he brought up the last of the water, each wet hacking cough shaking his frail body. Dog shook himself violently, whipping the water out of his soaked fur. He padded to Aris's slumped frame, nudging his arm with his snout, emitting small mournful whines. Finally, Aris lifted a shaking arm and patted Dog's head, gaining a grateful lick in return.

"Let's not do that again," Aris wheezed, pulling himself to a rough seated position. He tried to stand but his legs wouldn't support his weight and he slumped back into the mud; Dog crouched at his side. Grasping hold of the grey hair on Dog's back, Aris eased himself upright again, leaning on Dog for support, his head swimming. He was spent; his body bruised and battered by exhaustion, and he felt every single one of his eighty years. Holding on to Dog, Aris led them away from the pool, across a wide meadow towards a copse of delicate fey trees, their branches glistening with small pale flowers, the sweet fragrance drifting on the warm evening breeze. At the edge of the copse, one of the elder fey trees had fallen, and—drawing level with the smooth trunk—Aris stopped, patting Dog's back.

"This will do," he said, easing his body down with a soft groan. He looked up to Dog, a grateful smile spreading on his serene face. "I wouldn't have gotten this far without you. Thank you."

Dog mumbled a reply, dropping to a seated position beside Aris.

"It was indeed, my friend."

Dog turned a few times, then dropped to the grass at Aris's feet, resting his head on his huge paws, letting his eyes fall closed. Aris watched him a while, then turned his gaze upwards, content to watch the sky darken, greeting each newly appearing star as a long-lost friend, still enamoured by the beauty the Dead Lands offered. The moon's silent face climbed steadily in the sky, illuminating the wide meadow, the soft fey blossom shining like jewels. As the moon reached its zenith, Aris closed his heavy, dry eyelids. He was weary, a tiredness that whispered for him to let go, to forget.

He opened his eyes slowly, gazing up at the moon, smiling at her beauty. He blinked away watery tears, and for a moment he was sure he saw movement, shadowy and tall as mountains. He was dreaming, that was it, for the figure standing before him was a giant, as tall as the eldest bher trees, clad in a long cloak of midnight black and carrying a staff that—for the briefest moment of perspective—appeared to be topped by the moon itself, a pale, shining orb lighting the stranger's path across the dim and endless Dead Lands. The vision resolved itself, the edges becoming firmer, the body solid and real, while at the same time the figure shrank in stature. It moved forward, its strange gaze locked on Aris, until at last it stood before him, silent and watching. He was taller than Aris, taller than any man he had known, but lean with it, his pale thin fingers grasping the tall wooden staff at his side, his long, black cloak dirty and frayed at the hem, as if the stranger had been walking for centuries.

"You are well met, Aris, King of Enlais," the stranger said, his voice soft.

Aris bowed low from his seated position, his curiosity regarding the stranger's arrival not outweighing his manners.

"You have me at a disadvantage, sir," Aris replied. "If we have met before I am afraid your name has slipped my mind."

"We have never met," the stranger replied, bringing the staff around in front of himself and gripping it with both hands, leaning his weight on it. "But I do know you."

"May I ask your name?" Aris asked.

"I rather wondered if you might guess?" the stranger replied, a wry smile showing briefly.

Aris beheld the stranger. Despite his appearance from the night sky, Aris saw nothing remarkable about him now. His cloak was worn, his staff marked by age and wear, and his face, though pale, held a semblance of kindness and sympathy. And yet there was a sadness also, a great and long sadness that Aris knew had been with the stranger all his days.

The stranger watched Aris for that moment of realisation. It was different with each person; some would know him straight away while others would never admit it to themselves. But most would come to know him, sooner or later.

Aris looked up finally, and the stranger nodded once.

"What of Dog?" Aris asked, looking down at his sleeping companion. "Are you his master?"

The stranger smiled warmly, comfortably. "Dog has no master," he replied after a beat. "He is my friend, as he has been yours."

Dog raised his head and yawned widely. He hefted himself up, shaking his grey fur out. He looked to the stranger for a moment, his great long tail swishing from side to side. Then he turned to Aris, stepping forward to nudge his hands with his huge snout.

"And I shall miss you," Aris said, stroking Dog's head and scratching behind his folded ear.

Dog mumbled once, pushing his head into Aris' hand, who smiled in thanks. Dog padded over to the stranger's side, sitting on his hindquarters, and the stranger reached down to greet his friend.

"What happens now?" Aris asked.

"You have crossed the Dead Lands, Aris, King of Enlais. You have journeyed a second lifetime, and you have come before me as your true self, with memory, courage, and honor intact. Your peace is earned. Go well, Aris."

The wind stirred, catching fey blossom in its gentle hands and dancing across the plains to the distant seas. High above, the charcoal sky sang out with a hundred thousand stars, serenading their moon goddess, and bidding welcome as a new soul joined them in the heavens.

The wind died, and the stranger's cloak hung still once more. He looked into Dog's upturned face and gave his ear a reassuring scratch, then took up his staff.

Dog gruffed, flicking his head.

"I know," the stranger said. "Me, too."

They stood a while, listening to the night sky, before the stranger set off across the meadow, his long steady strides stretching as his form grew once more, taller than mountains, taller than thought and memory, courage, and hope.

Behind him, Dog stood watching the sky, his low, rumbling howl carrying across the empty meadow. And then he was off, chasing the stranger to run at his side, the wind blowing freely through his fur, the scents of all the worlds laid out before him to explore.

To Fix

Rick A. Pearson

Soks couldn't have known why
He'd been taken away from the young prince he loved,
And a life of luxury up high, and now found himself in a pile
Of biomechanical waste that reached ever so high,
But not yet close enough to the stars Soks now gazed up at.

Had it mattered to the prince
That Soks had an organic heart and mind of his own?
Perhaps that was the problem—that he loved to run wild—
As the latest model of bio-dog companion that had replaced him
Was AI-controlled.

Soks still wore the red socks that gave him his name,
On his four metallic pads that so annoyingly
Chinked on the floor, to the chagrin of the prince's parents.
But he couldn't move his limbs—deactivated
By the uniformed men who'd taken him away.

A redundant fixer-bot's restraining bolt had malfunctioned,
Hopped feebly over the junk and found its missing leg,
Catching sight of Soks' rolling and roaming eyes.
Despite being thrown away,
The robot's desire to fix remained.

The fixer raised Soks up before
Looking up at a sentry drone that shone
A white light on them, bathing and blinding.
The scampering droid darted away with Soks,
Over decay and into the night.

Police bots wielding EMP batons pursued the fixer
That clutched Soks tightly, into the woods,
Until a circle of six bots formed
All around them, growing tighter, nearer.
The fixer caught sight of Soks' blinking bolt button and hit it.

Soks sprang out, slicing through half of the ring
Of police bots, defenceless against
The metal maw
Of the biomechanical canine,
Tearing through throats of wires and plastisteel.

The remaining police bots
Charged,
Heading for the fixer,
Metal arms raised high,
Ready to bring their batons down.

The fixer was struck down,
Disabled.
Soks sprinted at the police,
Leapt into the air,
Landed and crushed them.

The bots writhed, limbs broken,
Strewn about.
Soks took the fixer in his jaws and
Dragged it away, the weight
Straining the muscles in Soks' mouth.

Passing through dense, endless woods
Until they reached a derelict building,
Headed inside,
Soks dropping the fixer on the floor.
Now still and silent, no longer whirring.

Obsolete and defunct,
Soks curled up beside
The fixer's stone-cold frame, hoping
To warm it as relentless rain lashed down outside,
Making the night colder and colder.

Soks awoke to the sound of light rain pattering
On the roof, and the fixer upright, standing before him.
Soks leapt up and slapped it in the face with a tongue like ham.
The bot had fixed Soks, and Soks had returned the favour.
And yet, neither had a purpose.

The fixer had nothing to fix, Soks had no prince.
But the fixer knelt down—its old, worn knees creaking,
And placed its cold, compassionate hand on Soks' head,
Its receptors sensing brain and heart—life and love to give and receive—
And realised that there was a lot more fixing still left to do.

OF POTIONS AND PINECONES

HANNAH MARIE

Adelaide gazed out the window of the carriage. The heavily wooded road upon which they traveled was woefully bereft of lurching minotaurs. The trees did not hide any goblins or wights. In their three-day journey, they had not come across even a moderately dangerous highwayman, though the last innkeeper had seemed rather ingratiating. *Too* ingratiating. And a bit sweaty. *Guilty*-sweaty.

"I still think we should have—" she began before her betrothed cut her off.

"He had just finished chopping wood, Ada," Prince Griffith said from across the carriage. "And we were the first customers to stay at the inn for the past week. No need to torture confessions of conspiracy and treason out of an honest man making an honest wage."

"Honest?" Adelaide snorted and folded her arms. "He charged me three coppers for a mug of ale."

Griffith turned the page in his book. "Only because you smashed the mug against the fireplace after." His eyes flickered to hers, crinkling in amusement at the memory. "Three coppers was a fair price, I'd say." He turned back to his book.

Adelaide examined her betrothed. He sat sideways on the opposite bench, one arm propped against the cushioned back, hand holding his book. His tunic and trousers were, as always, spotlessly clean, his nails trimmed, his hair shiny and caught in a queue at the nape of his neck. The royal seal emblazoned in garishly bright gold embroidery on his chest matched the gold latches on his brown boots and the belt around his waist.

He dressed well, Adelaide had to admit. Like the prince he was. Even if he wore a potato sack, he would catch her eye. With large brown eyes, high cheekbones, a square jaw, and a dimple in his cheek, he had been the target of many attempted betrothals. But he had accepted Adelaide's suit.

Of course, her having a big sword and using it to save him and his kingdom helped make the other ladies look like a bit of a limp biscuit. But it was still a shock that he had agreed to marry her. And even more than that, it was mind-boggling that he actually loved her.

She grew warm at the thought. He said it now and again, and Adelaide would sometimes mumble an approximation back. It wasn't that she didn't love him back. She did. Quite fiercely. But expressing the softer emotions had always been a bit of a pickle for a girl raised on daggers, fisticuffs, and swordplay.

But she tried. And she had a sneaky suspicion that he knew that she tried and would be willing to wait for their golden jubilee, if that is what it took for her to say "I love you" in a clear, unflinching tone.

Griffith turned another page in his book. He fairly devoured the things. The title declared it to be "The Properties and Use of Medicinal Herbology: The Science of Herbs."

Adelaide suppressed a snort. Science. Black magic, more like. She'd take a wizard with stars dangling from his hat any day over a dour-faced, pinched-nose scientist. Magic made sense. Everyone knew that the moon sent clouds to make it rain. Not, as Griffith had once explained to her, the "evaporation" and "condensation" of water. She would know if water was flying upward in the sky. She would be able to see it, wouldn't she? She saw the rain coming down, so she should be able to see it going up. It stood to reason.

Science was madness.

"I can hear you glowering at me, love," Griffith said, not looking up from his book.

Adelaide's face heated at the endearment and her eyes darted to Lady Bumble, their chaperone. She sat quietly next to Adelaide, embroidering pretty flowers along a length of cloth. Lady Bumble's eyes filled with humor and she smiled down at her work. Her dog curled in the remaining space on the seat, his head in her lap, a puddle of drool wetting her dress as he slept.

Adelaide tugged at her ear, attempting to reduce their burning. Very well. If Griffith could say "love" in front of Lady Bumble, then Adelaide could try a pet name as well. There were just the three of them in the carriage, plus the dog, so it was a perfect place to try. After all, she couldn't be humiliated in front of her betrothed, her good friend, and a dog, could she?

Adelaide cleared her throat. Lady Bumble looked up, her round, cheerful face settling into an encouraging expression. Adelaide's mind raced, and then she caught hold of a phrase in the swirling depths. She brought it to the surface.

Adelaide smiled what she hoped was a loving smile and spoke. "You look very handsome today, you sultry minx."

Griffith's eyes widened and shot to her face. At her side, Lady Bumble drew a short breath. For a long moment, the carriage was silent save for the dog's snores, and the sound of the carriage wheels rolling over the unpaved road.

Several emotions crossed Griffith's face, too quickly for Adelaide to catch them all, but she was gratified to see red tint his cheeks and ears.

"Why, thank you," he said finally, his voice strangled in the back of his throat.

Adelaide nodded. Endearments did that to her, too, so this was to be expected. "You are welcome," she replied gravely.

Lady Bumble coughed suddenly and buried her face in her embroidery, shoulders heaving.

Adelaide patted her on the back, concerned. "Are you well?"

She looked up, tears in her eyes. "Quite well. Thank you, dear."

The carriage stopped and Griffith looked out the window. "We're here."

"Oh, thank Grundel." Adelaide shot to her feet and whipped open the carriage door, startling the dog awake and whacking the approaching footman off his feet and into the dirt.

"Oh, I do beg your pardon," she said, stepping down from the carriage, and hauling the footman to his feet. "Are you all right, Eddie?"

The footman winced as she slapped at the dust now coating his sleeve and back. "I'm well, Your Highness. Thank you."

Adelaide nodded. "Excellent."

"I did try to hurry," Eddie said to the remaining occupants of the carriage.

"It's fine, Eddie," Griffith replied. "My love is always eager to stretch her legs."

Love. There it was again. Adelaide's ears burned, but she turned and bravely ignored the embarrassment as she said, "Please help Lady Bumble and my sultry minx from the carriage, Eddie. Thank you."

The footman's mouth dropped open. Before she could die of embarrassment, she strode away.

"Lady Bumble, would you be so kind as to—" Griffith started.

Lady Bumble hid a chortle and nodded. "I'll talk to her."

THIS WAS a proper wizard's cottage. Adelaide surveyed the structure from the front. It had stone walls, a thatched roof, wooden door, and glazed windows. But thyme creeped between the steppingstones, an owl perched on the chimney, and a little red gremlin snoozed in a flowerpot beside the door.

Lady Bumble's dog caught sight of the gremlin and moved to investigate.

"Oh, no, Winston, leave it be." Lady Bumble stooped and gathered up the dog in her arms.

Because he was not a small dog, he dangled from the armpits, furry belly swinging and back feet tapping the dirt as Lady Bumble attempted to maneuver him away from the gremlin. His floppy ears perked and he began to whine as she marched him to the side.

Winston, Adelaide thought, was a wonderfully regal name for a dog that chased his own tail for amusement and widdled while balancing on his two front feet, like the world's most unemployable acrobat. But Lady Bumble loved the beast, and so Adelaide tolerated the brown and white mongrel.

Griffith knocked on the door of the cottage and the gremlin cracked open an eye.

"He's out back," the creature said, its mouth cracking wide to reveal sharp teeth. "But he's expecting you and the cottage is open. Go in."

"Thank you," Griffith replied politely, and eased open the cottage door.

Adelaide, Lady Bumble, and Winston followed.

As expected, the interior of the cottage looked nothing like what the exterior promised. The wide entrance spilled into a large, stone-floored receiving room, crammed full of plush chairs and couches, side-tables, and, to one side, a large chalk-board upon which scribbled letters seemed to dance and sway. A circular staircase wound around the room to the floor above and continued even further. Adelaide peered upward and guessed that the cottage had at least five floors, maybe even six. In fact, she would wager that from the top floor of the wizard's cottage, you could see the whole forest and into the next kingdom.

Somewhere beyond the furniture, a chime sounded and then a door swung open, bouncing against an armchair and ricocheting back closed. A hand caught the door before it could shut and pushed it open again, this time with a little less force and more caution. The armchair squealed as the door edged it out of the way.

"Ah ha!" The wizard said, entering the room. "Prince Griffith, my favorite nephew!"

"He's not wearing a robe," Adelaide hissed at Griffith.

Griffith rolled his eyes. "He's the best—and only—wizard around, Ada. I promise you, he is no scientist." He moved to meet his uncle halfway across the room.

The wizard picked his way through the tables and chairs and couches, weaving and bobbing like a fishing lure in the waves, and pulled Griffith into a hug, slapping him forcefully on the back.

"Welcome!" His voice boomed in the space. "Welcome to my humble abode."

He wore a large-brimmed, pointed hat with several stars stitched onto the brim, but, Adelaide noticed, he also wore an apron and rubber boots. She surreptitiously examined him for other signs of scientific practices.

"And your lovely bride!" the wizard declared, marching over to bow over Adelaide's hand.

She narrowed her eyes suspiciously as he straightened.

"Uncle Izra, may I present Princess Adelaide Marchessa von Brumstrup," Griffith said, dodging an ottoman and a pile of books to stand next to her. "We are here to formally request a blessing for our marriage."

Wizard Izra beamed, clasping his hands together. "Of course, my boy! I have been preparing one all week, ever since the messenger bird arrived. It's ready and waiting for you now. I know you are eager to be wed. No need to delay, eh?" He winked at Adelaide, who scowled back. "It's upstairs, if you'll just follow me."

He turned and nearly ran over Lady Bumble.

"Oh!" she exclaimed, dropping Winston to all four paws, and caught the wizard by his arms.

"Oh!" the wizard exclaimed, and exploded in a flurry of small, pink birds.

Lady Bumble screamed.

"Ah. Okay, yes," Adelaide said, nodding. "He's a wizard." She lifted the now-vacant hat to see a pile of clothes on the floor.

Lady Bumble screamed again, and Winston barked wildly and chased the birds flying around the room, knocking over piles of books and jumping on the furniture.

Griffith huffed out a breath. "Uncle Izra!"

The birds chirped and flew up the stairs, followed closely by Winston. They heard a door slam and a startled yelp.

"I say," Izra's voice floated back down the stairs, but the words had a squishy quality, as if they were being spoken through the small crack of a door. "Would you be so kind as to meet me on the third floor? And, uh, Griffith, will you please bring me my clothes?"

THE THIRD FLOOR held the wizard's workshop. Herbs hung from the ceiling, a cauldron bubbled over the hearth, and rows and rows of glass vials crowded for space on the table in the middle of the room. A tall bookcase stood at one end, crammed full of books and scrolls. Another bookcase, short and squat, stood at the other, filled with jars of powders, bugs, and—Adelaide bent to read the label—frog's teeth.

"I do beg your pardon for startling you down there, Izra," Lady Bumble said, her eyelashes fluttering.

The wizard tugged at the collar of his shirt and a blush crept up Izra's neck to stain his cheeks. "Oh, no, not at all. Not at all. I just didn't expect to see you. Er. There. Here. How are you, Madeline?"

Lady Bumble smiled, "All the better for seeing you."

"Er, wonderful. Wonderful. DON'T EAT THAT!"

They all jumped, but Izra pointed at Winston, who held a dried lizard in his mouth.

Deciding this was the most interesting thing to happen on their trip so far, Adelaide darted over to the dog, who began to chew the lizard as fast as he could. Adelaide straddled the dog, forced open his mouth, and withdrew the slimed lizard. Winston growled and she growled right back.

"Oh, thank you, my dear." Wizard Izra said as Adelaide dropped the lizard in his outstretched hand.

"I'm so terribly sorry. Was it valuable?" Lady Bumble asked.

The wizard shook his head. "Not at all. But it is very cursed. I'd hate for the small fellow to have unbearable fetid flatulence the rest of his days."

They all stared at Winston, who stared back with a vague, doggy expression of semiconcussed happiness. He licked his nose, scratched his ear, and then let out a small, distressing *poot*! If the smell had a color, then the air would have turned a sickly brown-green.

"Ah," Izra said, opening the window. "We may have been too late there."

"No, no," Griffith sighed. "He just ate some cheese again." He bent and scooped the dog into his arms, holding him like a baby. "I'd best hang on to him just in case he gets into real trouble."

"Good idea, lad," Wizard Izra said, gesturing to the vials on the table. "I've been working on a few experimental potions, and I'd hate for the little chap to get ahold of something he shouldn't." He rubbed his hands together. "Now, for your blessing, eh?"

"Yes, please," Adelaide beamed.

He certainly *was* a wizard and she knew, just *knew*, that his blessing would bring them something wonderful for their marriage. Blessings of health and happiness were common, but she hoped for something a little more interesting. Like a dragon. Or the ability to swim underwater without holding their breath. Or maybe they would instinctively know where to find the best strawberries. Or perhaps—

The door to the workshop slammed open with a roar and a troll shoved his way inside.

Lady Bumble screamed, Adelaide shouted, Winston barked, Griffith yelled, but the noise didn't deter the troll. Tufts of cotton poked out of the troll's ears, muffling his hearing. He grinned widely at the room at large and reached for the wizard.

"Now see here!" Izra shouted as he was scooped up from the hearth and thrown over the troll's shoulder.

Cursing the lack of swords, spears, and maces in the workshop, Adelaide rushed the troll. He was only seven feet tall. That was nothing at all. If she could get to his head, then—

But the troll saw her coming and swung his arm, connecting with her midsection and throwing her backward across the table. Glass crunched beneath her as the vials broke open and she slid backward, landing heavily on Griffith, still holding the dog.

"Are you all ri—" Griffith tried to say.

The table flipped over, covering them in potions and glass.

The last thing Adelaide heard was Lady Bumble's scream.

ADELAIDE OPENED HER EYES. It felt as though someone had just licked each side of her face.

Griffith stared back at her with a wide grin, his tongue lolling out of his mouth. "It worked!" he crowed and jumped backward. He stomped in a small circle, glass crackling under his boots, and waggled his hands above his head, his hips swaying back and forth. "We did it! We did it!"

Warm breath huffed in her ear and she turned her head to see Winston staring at her. At least, she thought it was Winston. He had the same floppy brown ears, the same short, brown-spotted white fur, and the same long snout and pink nose. But the expression on his face looked . . . human.

Hello, Adelaide, Winston sighed.

The words entered directly into Adelaide's brain without bothering to go through her ears.

Adelaide sat up. "What in the world . . ."

She did a quick sweep of the workshop, noting the smashed potions, the overturned table, and the very pretty, pink-blossomed tree growing out of the center of the room. As she watched, the tree twisted around, the branches and flowers shifting to form a face.

"Lady Bumble?" she whispered.

The tree nodded, managing to shrug in a manner that conveyed both resignation and annoyance at the lack of shoulders. "Welcome back, Adelaide. You were out for quite some time." Her voice blew like the wind, carrying the scent of sweet flowers and the promise of spring.

Several drops of Izra's sleeping potion fell into your mouth and knocked you right out, Winston said at her side. *We weren't sure if you were going to wake. But Lady Bumble suggested we try . . .* He trailed off and pointed his snout at Griffith across the room, who was now sniffing the bubbling cauldron with extreme interest.

Adelaide stood up and shook the glass out of her skirts. It tinkled on the floor while her mind raced madly. "You tried the kiss of true love?"

Well, we tried the kisses *of true love. My kiss didn't work and Winston's kiss didn't work, so we thought if we* both *kissed you, then it might work. And it did.*

Adelaide paused to stare at the dog. "Griffith?" she whispered.

He nodded, a whine crawling out of the back of his throat. *It seems that we were doused with one or more of the experimental potions and now I am in Winston's body and Winston in my body.* He threw his head back and howled.

Adelaide blinked at him.

After a moment, he stopped, and pawed at his nose. *I'm sorry. I just . . . felt the need to do that for some reason.*

Winston-in-Griffith's-body bounded over. "Are we howling? I can howl. Watch." He threw back his head. "Aaawooooo!"

"Gah! Stop!" Adelaide threw her hands over her ears.

Winston smiled but stopped howling. He stared at her, and she stared back. It was Griffith's face, but it wasn't Griffith. She had never seen such a simple, joyful expression on his face before. He looked as if he was just happy to be alive.

She nudged the glass at her feet.

Which, of course, he should be. They should all be happy to be alive after that troll attack and the mixing of potions. They were lucky Lady Bumble was only a tree and not a rage-filled banshee. They were lucky that Griffith could still communicate his thoughts as a dog. They were lucky Winston was—

"Throw it." Winston pressed a stick into her hands. "Please? Please, throw it."

"Great Grundel's tears," Adelaide cursed and heaved the stick across the room.

It landed atop the tall bookcase and Winston scampered after it.

We have to find him, Griffith said, his doggy eyes narrowing with determination. *Izra can reverse the effects of the potions. I can't marry you like a dog! And Lady Bumble can't remain a tree! Winston certainly can't rule in my stead! Look at him!*

They turned to look at Winston, who ignored the overturned chairs and was currently jumping in place, trying to fetch the stick from the top of the bookcase.

And I'm sure you want to get back to normal, too!

Adelaide stared at him. "Normal? What happened to me?" She whirled around, looking for a mirror. "Am I hideous?"

No! No, nothing like that! Your hair just turned a lovely shade of . . . of . . .

"Blue, dear," Lady Bumble provided.

Yes, blue. Griffith repeated. *A lovely shade of blue.*

Adelaide tried not to be disappointed that she hadn't been turned into a fire-breathing dragon or a ten-foot-tall giantess. She glanced down at her braid, noting the deep sapphire color, before tossing it over her shoulder. Hair color was immaterial. There was a wizard to rescue.

"Well . . ." she put her hands on her hips. "I'll go rescue him, then. The troll couldn't have gotten far, not in this daylight. You two stay here and I'll be back in—"

I'm going with you! Griffith said and barked for emphasis. *I can't let you go out there all on your own.*

A warm, fuzzy feeling curled up under her heart at his words. "One last adventure, before the wedding bells, then." Adelaide nodded. "Very well, but I won't have time to craft you armor or a sword to hold in your mouth, so you'll have to stay behind me."

Griffith bared his teeth. *I'll manage just fine.*

"Oh, do hurry," Lady Bumble sighed. "According to Izra's notes, some of these potions are permanent if not reversed by midnight on the third day."

"Wah!" Winston shouted.

They turned to see him halfway up the bookshelf, having finally figured out how to climb it, and now it tipped forward, threatening to dump him and all of its contents on the ground.

Adelaide darted over and grabbed him by the back of his collar, hauling him off the bookshelf and onto the floor. "No, Winston! You are in my sultry minx's body and you musn't hurt it!"

Winston twisted his face into a smirk. "Hur hur. Sultry minx," he chortled.

"You had better take him with you," Lady Bumble said. "I won't be able to protect him as a tree and it would be terrible if he got into trouble. The little dear."

Adelaide paused. "Couldn't we lock him up somewhere or perhaps ask the guards to watch over him?"

Griffith shook his head, then shook it harder, then paused and scratched his ear with his back foot. *I'm afraid the guards and coachman have been turned into butterflies, the horses into garden gnomes, and poor Eddie is occupying the well as a newt. And I don't trust him to be locked up on his own. Do you?*

Adelaide tapped her lips. "Hmm. You may be right. He does have fingers and opposable thumbs, now. Could get him into trouble in a wizard's house." She turned on the dog occupying her betrothed's body and shook a finger under his nose. "Now listen to me, Winston. You're coming with us, but you have to obey me and do exactly what I tell you. Do you understand?"

Winston cocked his head to one side and smiled. "Absolutely. I love walks."

Adelaide nodded. "Lady Bumble, we will return as soon as we can. Will you be all right here on your own?"

The tree rustled its blossoms. "Oh, yes. It's actually quite pleasant to be grounded and listening to the breeze."

"Excellent." She turned and snapped her fingers at Winston. "Let's go."

Winston snatched something out of the wreckage and ran out down the stairs. "Let's goooooo!" he yelled.

Oh, hurry, Adelaide! Griffith shouted, darting past her down the stairs.

"So eager!" Adelaide called after him. "We have at least three days. Plenty of time!"

But Winston grabbed the dried lizard! Griffith said from the floor below. *And he's in* my *body! What if I get the fetid flatulence?*

Adelaide ran after them.

AFTER WRESTLING the dried lizard away from Winston, Adelaide hurried over to the carriage. Four stone garden gnomes squatted in front of the carriage, where the horses used to be, and another six gnomes lay scattered across the yard. Six butterflies in various hues of blues, oranges, and pinks flitted from the gnomes to the carriage and back again.

"How in the world did this happen?" Adelaide asked, raising her skirts to her knees and belting it in place. She looked from the butterflies to the gnomes and back again. "The guards and horses weren't in the workshop."

Behind her, Winston stood at the doorway of the cottage, muttering a low growl at the gremlin.

Best guess? Griffith said at her feet. *The troll had a magic user cast spells from the tree line.* He nodded his head at the edge of the clearing. *Then once the guards were neutralized, the troll strolled in unchallenged. A single troll wouldn't dare approach six armed men, but six butterflies? No problem.*

Adelaide looked down at the soft ears and shiny fur. "Did you . . . Is your hair . . Did you brush your fur?"

As a human, Griffith would often make a small "ahem" or "aha" when he was embarrassed or didn't know what to say. Now, as a dog, the noise was significantly different.

"HOURK!" Griffith cleared his doggy throat.

Adelaide jumped back, startled, then bent to look him in the face. "Are you well?"

I do beg your pardon, Griffith said, looking appalled at the sound. *I had Winston comb out his—I mean* my *fur while we were brainstorming how to wake you. It seemed to keep him calm and occupied.*

"Hmm. And made you look very handsome, too." She ruffled his ears and he drew back.

What's our plan?

Adelaide opened the carriage door and flipped open the seat. "We track down that troll and get our wizard back, so we can get you back into YOU and Winston back into HIM."

She rifled around and withdrew a large, oiled leather package. Unwrapping it, she withdrew her emergency travel stash. It consisted of one sword, one dagger, one short bow with extra string, twenty-five arrows in a hip quiver, five throwing knives, two hunting knives, and a skin of water. It also held one vest and a pair of trousers.

Ada! Griffith said, colors of chastisement in his voice.

Adelaide turned as she slipped the vest over her bodice. "What? Too much?" She laced the vest shut, slipping the throwing knives into the various pockets.

I thought you were going to leave your weapons at home!

She blinked at him. "We agreed I would leave my *best* weapons at home. This is only my second-best sword and my fifth best bow. Besides, what if I had left them home, then where would we be?"

From the cottage, Winston let out a high-pitched shriek and drew back from the gremlin. "It bit me!"

"HOURK!" Griffith cleared his throat again. *I don't really scream like that.*

Adelaide nodded. "Of course not."

And it was true. Even while facing a dragon, Griffith had not wailed like a cat stuck at the bottom of a well. But Winston seemed to find alternative ways of stretching his new body's vocal chords.

"Winston!" Adelaide called. "Get over here!" She snapped her fingers and pointed to the ground in front of her feet.

This is so embarrassing to watch. Griffith ducked his head.

Winston fairly galloped over, his arms swinging, queue of hair whipping up and down like a ship tossed on stormy seas, and knees fairly kissing his chin as he brought his feet high off the ground.

"I thought it was a squirrel, but it wasn't a squirrel," Winston began as he dropped to the ground on his haunches, looking up at Adelaide. "It doesn't have any fur, but it does have a tail, so I thought, hey! It's a squirrel. But then it yelled at me and bit me, and I've never—"

Adelaide held up a hand. "Winston, stop!"

The dog-man's eyes widened and he drew his lips into a quivering frown.

For some inexplicable reason, Adelaide felt bad and wanted to pat him on the head and tell him he was a good boy.

With herculean strength, aided by Griffith's narrowed eyes, she resisted.

"We're going to leave in five minutes. The troll is probably half a day ahead of us, but we can catch up if we hurry. But there'll be no stops. So if you have to go . . um I suggest both of you . . . er, go . . . er, potty before we head out."

"Can do!" Winston replied and jumped to his feet.

Uhh . . . Griffith said as he watched his body hurry over to the nearest tree and attempt to do a handstand.

Adelaide rolled her eyes and turned back to her weapons. "Griffith, my sultry minx, please be a dear and instruct him on the use of the garderobe."

As a general rule, trolls were tall, wide, and prone to swinging their arms when they walked and ran, so the trail was not difficult to follow. Broken branches and split bushes marked the direction the troll had taken. Footprints the size of Adelaide's head imprinted the detritus littering the forest floor. She crouched to examine the footprints and noticed that the left footprint was deeper than the right, indicating that the troll still carried Izra on his left shoulder. The gait was uneven, as well, which meant that the troll was unaccustomed to carrying such large burdens. Good. That would slow it down.

She rose to her feet. "We'll need to hurry if we are to catch up."

At her side, Griffith barked his assent. *The scent is still strong. They can't be far ahead. Let's go!*

He pushed past her and hurried down the path, his nose to the ground, tail wagging like a flag.

Adelaide pursed her lips as she followed after him. Was it her imagination, or had he seemed excited? A little too excited? Was her betrothed having fun? As a dog?

This was . . . concerning.

She quickened her pace. The sooner they rescue the wizard, the sooner everything can go back to normal. And then they could get their blessing, be wedded, and live—

"Ow!"

Winston crashed into her, knocking her to the ground.

Because she was lithe, limber, and athletic, Adelaide slipped free of his tangled limbs and jumped to her feet. Because Winston was still unused to operating two arms and two legs, he flopped around on the ground like a landed fish. Rolling her eyes, Adelaide hauled him to his feet.

He beamed at her. "Look what I found!" He held out a pinecone nearly the size of his hand.

Adelaide moved to grab it and he drew back.

"No! Don't touch it! It's mine." He tucked it against his chest like a baby, then held it out again. "Just look."

"Ok. It's very nice. But we have to go." She reached for his arm and he pulled back again.

"But, LOOK at it," he almost whined. "It's new and pokey and sticky and it smells like—" he brought it to his nose and took an exaggerated whiff, "—a *thing* and cleaning solution and dirt!"

Adelaide paused, the memory of her first introduction to Griffith passing through her mind. Then, he had been shackled to a throne, a royal puppet for a devious dragon, and yet he had been proud, fierce, and intelligent. His noble features and clean, shiny hair were new and exciting for a girl that had been taught the healthy benefits of dirt baths. His starched collar and blindingly white sleeves were styled just so, with a pair of boots polished to a mirror-like finish. Adelaide remembered seeing the reflection of her wide, awe-inspired eyes in those boots as she was forced to kneel on the ground. She remembered the sun glinting off his crown, lighting his head in a halo of light. She remembered thinking that this man had a god-like visage and was the most handsome man she had ever seen.

Here, now, in the forest, as she stared at Winston in her love's body, she realized that no, it wasn't Griffith's looks that held her heart. Winston had the same face, the same hair, the same body, but the wry smile, quick-wit, and intelligent eyes were missing.

It came as a slight shock to realize that Adelaide had fallen in love with Griffith's mind. Not his body.

She took a step back and looked Winston up and down.

And certainly not *this* body, with the torn sleeve and sap-sticky hands and a bundle of leaves sticking out of his collar.

"Winston . . ." she started, then paused as his face broke into a wide smile.

"Yes? That's me! Yes?" He scooted closer and bent his frame so he could rub his head on her arm and look up at her.

"Uh, no." She gently pushed his head away. "Look, Winston, this is very important. We have to find Izra—"

"The man who smelt of cabbage and birds."

"Er. . . yes, the wizard, so we can get everything back the way it was." She tried for some positive reinforcement. "You did such a good job finding that pinecone. Such a good boy." She reached out to pat his shoulder.

He growled and jumped back, guarding his pinecone. "It's mine!"

She tried not to sigh. "Do you think you could use those same skills to find the wizard?"

He looked down at his pinecone dubiously. "Well, I don't know. I just found this. I'd have to track the wizard."

"Yes! Good! Let's go find him!" Adelaide clapped her hands. "You can do it! Yes, you can!"

A grin spread over Winston's face, his eyes widening in joy, and he began to wiggle his posterior. "I suppose . . . I suppose I could! Yes! Let's go!"

He whooped and took off running down the path.

Adelaide dusted her hands. "And that's how you do it."

She followed Winston through the bushes.

And then she realized that Griffith was out of sight.

GRIFFITH HAD STEPPED off the path.

Adelaide stared at the paw-prints in the mud incredulously. He had been scampering after the troll for nearly twenty minutes. The spacing of his paw prints over the troll's footprints showed he had been running, and the small drag marks were most likely his nose, held to the ground. Then he veered left and *stepped off the path*.

"Griffith!" Adelaide called into the trees.

Nothing.

Feeling a little silly, she whistled, high and piercing. "Griffith! Come!"

About twenty feet into the trees, something rustled, and then a pheasant burst into the air. Adelaide threw an arm out, ready to catch Winston, but she needn't have bothered. Winston lay in the middle of the troll's path, arms flung wide, eyes closed, mouth open, and breathing heavily.

Sensing no danger, the pheasant settled on a tree branch, its glittering eyes peering at them through the leaves.

Adelaide wasn't surprised at Winston's exhaustion. He had spent the last twenty minutes darting back and forth, from tree to bush to rock. He had sniffed, poked, licked, and tried to eat nearly everything he had come across. He had dropped his massive pinecone in favor of a small leaf, and then abandoned that because he found a rock the width and length of his forearm. And when that had proved too heavy to carry for more than three minutes, he broke a branch off a tree and brandished it like a sword, until that too was dropped.

She toed him in the side. "Winston, get up. We've lost Griffith."

He opened his eyes and squinted at her. "Griffith? He's gone? Where did he go?"

Adelaide pointed. "That way. Come on."

He groaned and pushed himself to a sitting position. "I thought we were tracking the troll and the wizard. Hey!" He jumped to his feet. "What's that?"

He barrelled past her and jumped at the pheasant, which startled, winging higher into the tree.

"Hey!" Winston shouted at it, exhaustion forgotten. "Hey! What are you? Hey! Hey! Hey!"

Adelaide watched him for a moment.

Yesterday, she had been worried about dying of boredom on this trip.

Now, watching her friend's dog in her betrothed's body jumping and yelling at a bird in the tree, she wanted to go back and kick herself in the head.

"I'll learn to treasure the boredom," she muttered as she stomped over to Winston. "I promise, I will." She grabbed his arm. "Hey!"

He grinned at her. "Hey!" he replied.

"Argh! No!" She grabbed his head. "No, Winston, look at me. We need to find Griffith. We need to find him now. Are you going to help me, or should I tie you to this tree?"

Winston's eyes dulled a little at that, and he whined in the back of his throat.

"That's what I thought." She released his head and shoved him. "Now let's go." She clamped a hand on his arm and tugged him down Griffith's trail.

Winston hunched over as he walked, and Adelaide resisted the urge to slap him. Dirt crusted his entire back, from the head to the bottom of his heels. Griffith would have a fit when he saw what the dog had done to his clothes.

Winston huffed, stealing glances at her over his shoulder. "I don't like to be tied up." He sniffed.

Adelaide tried not to feel guilty, but it was hard. Winston used Griffith's beautiful brown eyes like a master, widening them and glancing at her beneath the long lashes. She felt the vague urge to hug him and give him a biscuit. She resisted.

"I won't tie you up, Winston," she sighed. "But we need to keep together." She looked down. "And I just lost Griffith's trail."

"Hey! I can track him!" Winston said, brightening. "I am a dog, you know. With the keen senses of a hunter!"

Adelaide shook her head, backtracking to find the paw-prints. "No, I don't think that's a good idea."

"But I can!" Winston insisted. "I can use his scent!"

She sifted through some disturbed mulch, finally locating a partial print in the dirt. "Fine. Track him." Another print marked the ground just beside a fallen log. Was Griffith still running?

Winston lifted his nose in the air and took an exaggerated sniff. "Ahhh, yes. Good. Now, what does he smell like?"

Adelaide looked up, surprised. "You don't know? You've been with him all day."

Winston raised his eyebrows. "Oh, I know! He is my favorite!"

She shook her head. "You don't know, do you? Because you are in HIS body and you don't have YOUR senses anymore."

Winston managed to affect an offended air. "I can track him by scent. If only you'll tell me what he smells like."

Adelaide paused, her cheeks heating. How to describe Griffith's scent? She never dreamed she would be required to describe how her betrothed smelled.

"He smells like . . . paper and leather and . . ." She closed her eyes as she struggled with the description. "A sunny day on the grass, with bees buzzing and a butterfly flitting from flower to flower. And lilacs. Just a hint of lilacs."

She opened her eyes to see Winston biting his tongue while he scanned the trees above him.

"Were you listening?" she demanded, suddenly angry and embarrassed and frustrated all at once.

"Lilacs. Got it." He grinned and bounced on his feet, sending his hair flopping. "I've got it! He's this way! Follow me!"

Winston took off through the trees, whooping.

Adelaide shouted after him, but he didn't stop. She checked the tracks and saw that Winston was more or less running in the same direction as Griffith's paw-prints.

"Wait for me!" she hollered. "I can't lose you, too!"

"Hey! Hey! Hey!" Winston called back. "I can smell him!" He lept over a fallen log, rounded a small boulder, and disappeared from view.

Adelaide chewed angrily on the curses on her tongue and followed.

She rounded the boulder and screeched to a halt.

Three very large men stood in front of a fire, over which a plucked bird turned on a spit. They each wore leathers that had been mended multiple times. Rather than indicating the state of their financial status, the mended leathers stated to those that knew how to read them, that these leathers had been stabbed multiple times and *had survived*.

"Well, well, well," one of the men leered. "What have we here?"

Adelaide scanned the clearing. Griffith was not present, though she thought she spotted a tuft of white fur caught on a branch. Winston was, again, flat on his back, with one of the men pressing a foot against his head, and a sword pointed at his belly.

"It wasn't Griffith," Winston whined. "I think it was the chicken."

Adelaide sighed and unsheathed her sword. "It was definitely the chicken."

A NATURALLY PEOPLE-LOVING DOG, Winston struggled with the finer points of fighting.

In his dog body, he never, ever bit anyone, for fear of the dreaded "bad dog!" and bop on the nose. Every now and again, he would accidentally jump on someone and knock them over, or perhaps whip his tail exuberantly enough to leave bruises, but he never tried to actively hurt someone. His canine policy was to lick and grovel and use his puppy dog eyes to his advantage.

This policy, as it turns out, was not very effective in a human body.

"Ow!" he shrieked as the flat of a sword slapped him on the shoulder.

"Stop lookin' at me like that!" the thug growled and slapped him on the other side.

"I'm sorry!" Winston whined, real tears blurring his vision. "Why are you hitting me? I'm a good boy!"

The man swung a fist and knocked him to the ground. Winston rolled with the blow. "How cruel!" He curled into himself and whined again, high and loud.

"And stay down!" the thug smirked, aiming a boot at his head.

It caught Winston on the face, knocking him out. He went limp, legs and arms slack.

The thug moved to approach Adelaide from the rear.

Adelaide held a sword in one hand, her dagger in the other, and wielded both with ease. Like an extension of her arm, the sword swung around to slice the stomach of one thug, while her dagger parried an attempt from the other man's sword. She braced against his weight, flipped around, and jabbed at the third thug.

"Haha!" she crowed as she knocked his sword from his hand.

He growled and dove at her.

Twirling, she avoided his grip, and booted his backside as he went past. He fell into the first man with the sliced leather.

"HaHA!" she said again as they fell to the forest floor in a tangle of arms and legs.

The remaining man used her distraction to grab her from behind, pinning her arms to her sides.

"Who do you think you are?" the man snarled, his breath foul enough to curl her hair. "You try to take on the Grimson brothers? Trying to collect our bounty?"

Adelaide bared her teeth. "Bounty, eh? I was going to do it for free, but now that I know money is involved—"

She jerked her head backward, pleased to feel her skull crunch the large and very breakable nose. The man's grip loosened, and she stomped on his instep. He howled in pain as she tore away, slamming the hilt of her sword into his temple. He dropped like a tree.

Eyes blazing, grinning like a berserker, Adelaide whirled on the other two men. They rose to their feet, scowling, and cautiously spread apart.

Adelaide balanced on the balls of her feet, her sword and dagger held at the ready. They would try to attack her from both sides, a fairly common tactic. Too bad that she was not a common swordfighter. Her blood fairly sang in her veins, eager for the sound of steel to fill the air.

"What do you want?" the man on the left growled.

"I'm looking for my betrothed. He's a brown and white dog with a long tail and floppy ears." The tip of her sword and dagger followed each man as they circled her. "You haven't seen him, have you?"

"Uh . . ." The man circling her left paused and cocked his head. "A dog?"

"Yes, a dog!" Adelaide replied, teeth bared.

He squinted at her, shadows of concern crossing his face. "Your betrothed is a . . . dog."

Adelaide dropped her arms. "Yes, he's a dog. There was a magical accident and he and a dog swapped bodies. What do you not understand?"

"Okay, so . . ." he scratched the back of his neck. "That's not really possible. I mean science tells us—"

"A scientist!" Adelaide howled and lunged with her sword.

He jumped backward to avoid being eviscerated and stumbled on some loose stones, falling into a waiting bush.

Adelaide turned her attention to the remaining Grimson brother. "And you? A scientist too? One that perhaps stole my betrothed?" She dashed across the clearing.

"Maybe we did see him," the man snarled, holding his sword at the ready. "And maybe we ate him."

Adelaide's grin turned feral. "You had better pray he is still alive or—"

The man's eyes darted behind her, widening in shock.

Even as she turned her head to look, Adelaide berated herself. This was the oldest trick in the book. She had employed it herself on many occasions. And now she fell for it.

But she had to look.

She had to.

Griffith might be standing there.

And so she turned her head and took her eyes off of one of the thugs.

Griffith was not there. Of course he wasn't. Just like she knew he wouldn't be.

She expected the blow to the back of her head, but it still hurt. Fortunately, the second blow knocked her out, so she didn't feel any more pain.

ADELAIDE AWOKE TIED TO A TREE.

In her experience, this was one of the more pleasant ways to wake up, directly after waking up face down on a horse, and just before waking up hanging upside down from one ankle. Of course, she would have preferred to wake up in her own bed, but she wouldn't complain. Not when she did, after all, wake up.

Whoever these thugs were, it was clear they weren't murderers.

"Oh, you're awake. I'm so scared!" Winston whined from the other side of the tree.

Adelaide tilted her head back and squinted through the leaves. "How long have I been asleep?"

She felt his shrug through the ropes wrapped around her waist and shoulders.

"A good long while," Winston said. "I was getting worried, and Alfie suggested they try to wake you, but then you started to snore, so Bruno and Carl convinced him to let you sleep."

"You know their names?" Adelaide whispered. "Did you all have tea while I was unconscious in the dirt?"

There was a slight pause, and then Winston's voice skittered around the tree trunk. "Well, no, but they did give me a bit of chicken after I cried for a while, so that was nice, and—"

"Winston!" Adelaide hissed. "The stars are out and I can see the moon!"

"Ah, yes," Winston replied cheerfully. "So they are!"

"I mean," she growled through gritted teeth, "that it's nearly midnight. We have only two more days! We've lost the troll's trail, we've lost Griffith, and we are tied to a tree!"

"And that's . . ." Winston's tone wavered as he searched for the correct word, ". . . bad?"

Adelaide strained against the ropes. "It's very bad!"

The tree creaked, the ropes sawed against her stomach, and on the left side of the tree, the knot tightened with a small squeak. Adelaide felt the corresponding give in the rope. The churning in her stomach eased slightly. The rope was looser than it should have been, but it was still too tight to wriggle out of.

"Winston!" she whispered. "Can you reach my knife if I swing my leg around the tree?"

"Oh . . . um . . ."

She paused. "They took it, didn't they?"

The ropes tightened as Winston slumped in shame.

She huffed a breath out through her nose and leaned to the right to examine the campsite. Two of the three Grimson brothers slept on the ground, curled around the glowing embers of the fire and the remains of their roast chicken. The third brother sat on a felled log, idly tossing a dagger into the air and catching it again. Moonlight glinted off the blade and Adelaide recognized it as her third best dagger. At his feet, a pile of weaponry reflected back the starlight and the fading fire. Adelaide's palms itched as she recognized her bow, her knives, and her arrows.

"My weapons," she whispered.

"But!" Winston said, his voice high and chipper.

The man tossing the dagger paused and glanced across the clearing. Adelaide let her head fall to her chest, hoping that in the dark, he wouldn't be able to tell she was awake.

"You still whining back there?" the man called.

"Say yes," Adelaide hissed.

"Yes!" Winston replied obediently.

The man chuckled and returned his attention to the dagger.

"But what," Adelaide whispered.

A grunt, the sound of bark scraping against leather, and a leg, encased in trousers and a calf-high boot curled around the trunk.

"I think there's a knife in here. They didn't bother to search me. I don't know why."

Adelaide pursed her lips for a moment. "I'm sure they had their reasons."

The leg raised higher. "You see, there's a cleverly concealed sheath sewn into the boot right here and I—" he broke off with a yelp that was quickly followed by a groan. The leg went limp.

"What happened?" Adelaide demanded. "Winston, what's wrong?"

"I-I-I pulled a . . . muscle." His voice held tears. The leg disappeared back to his side of the tree.

If she could have, Adelaide would have dropped her head in her hands. Instead, she rolled her eyes. "Winston, can you reach the knife?"

"I can try."

The tree shuddered and the ropes pulled against Adelaide's stomach and chest.

Just on the other side of the fire, the bushes rustled. The conscious Grimson brother paused in his knife-tossing and stood up, peering into the darkness.

Every monster Adelaide knew raced through her mind.

Minators roamed the woods, though they were more active during the day. Hydras usually kept to the ocean, but they would venture inland if they were hungry or breeding. Chimeras and basilisks sometimes banded together, when they weren't fighting each other, and the Grimson brothers would feed a pair for a week. Hobgoblins were small, but plentiful, and loved to hunt at night.

The thug walked toward the moving bush, then jumped back as something growled.

And with the full moon, a werewolf might be searching the forest for something to prey on.

"Winston!" Adelaide hissed. "Give me that knife right now!"

The rope pulled tight as he struggled to reach his boot. Adelaide kept her eye on the Grimson brothers and the rustling, growling bush.

"Carl, Alfie." The upright thug—Bruno—nudged his brothers awake.

The bush exploded and Bruno screamed as small, furry shapes leapt into his face.

The other two brothers jumped to their feet, swords swinging. In the glowing embers of the fire and the light of the moon, the small creatures jumped into the air, attacking the men as they screamed.

Adelaide smiled grimly.

Hobgoblins. Only fifteen or so, but that was more than enough to take down a full-grown man. The other two wouldn't be far behind, and here she was, tied to a tree! They would feast on the men, and then come for her and Winston. She strained against the ropes.

"Winston!" The time for subtly had passed. "Do you have the knife? Get the knife!"

The rope dropped away and she fell to all fours.

Hurry! Griffith's voice bloomed in her mind like a rose. *They won't distract them for long!*

"Griffith!" Adelaide cried and dropped her arms around his fuzzy neck. "You're here!"

He nosed her to her feet. *Let's go! Follow me!*

He darted around the tree, Adelaide close on his heels. Winston lay on the other side of the tree, flailing with the tangled rope. She tore the rope off him and dragged him to his feet.

"Come on!"

They followed Griffith through the forest, his white fur easy to see in the bright moonlight and against the dark foliage. He led them through thick underbrush, past tall, bristly pines, and across a creek, before he finally stopped.

We're safe.

Adelaide braced herself on her knees as she caught her breath. Winston threw himself on the ground, then crawled to the creek where he lapped noisily at the water. Griffith, in the dog body, curled his lip at the sight, then seemed to sigh.

"I hate to break it to you," Adelaide panted, "but those hobgoblins can still track us. We're not as far away as I would like."

"Poor Alfie," Winston burbled in the creek. "To die like that."

Griffith's face broke into a doggy grin, lips pulled back, tongue lolling to one side. *Hobgoblins? No, no, no, I just convinced some jackrabbits to help.*

Adelaide's mouth dropped open. "Jackrabbits?"

Yes. Griffith nodded proudly, ears flopping. *Those men will be fine.*

"Have you *met* a jackrabbit?" Adelaide asked. "Those men will certainly NOT be fine."

Griffith wrinkled his nose. *Well, they won't DIE.* He plopped down on his haunches and scratched his neck with his back foot. *They will be bruised and battered, but they'll be ok. Jackrabbits couldn't possibly cause that much harm.*

Adelaide stared at her betrothed for a long moment. "I left my *sword* back there!"

I am sorry about that. Griffith lay on his stomach, crossing his front two paws. *Do you want to go back and get it?*

The sound of fuzzy feet the size of trout kicking the ever-loving-HECK out of three full grown men filled her ears and she shook her head, shuddering. "No, I've got your knife." She tossed the blade skyward before catching it by the handle. "That's all I need."

Winston stumbled over to them, his front dripping with water, completely soaked. "I'm hungry."

Griffith eyed his body. *My tunic is completely ruined.*

Winston looked at his chest, shrugged, and wiped his hands down his front. Dirt, mud, small twigs, and now water played a hand in destroying the delicate quilted silk and gold embroidery. The dragon was barely visible, and only if you knew it was there.

"Dinner?" Winston whined.

Griffith shook his head. *I'm sorry. I haven't got anything to eat.*

"Could have had a jackrabbit," Adelaide muttered under her breath.

But Griffith's dog-enhanced hearing caught it. He scowled at her as well as a dog could scowl. *What happened to you? I was tracking the troll, then turned around and you were gone!*

The stress of the night caught up with her and Adelaide scowled back. "Ask Winston about his stupid pinecone!"

Winston immediately perked up. "My pinecone! Yeah! It was brown and long and spikey and felt like how celery tastes and—"

"And when we went to follow you, your tracks led off the trail!" Adelaide twirled the knife through her fingers in agitation. "You left us behind and then you deviated from course. The troll went that way—" she pointed with one hand "—and you went THAT way. We were supposed to be following the troll to rescue your uncle. NOT dashing off into the woods to make nice with jackrabbits of all things!"

I WAS looking for the troll!

"Hey." Winston's voice wobbled with tears. "Are you guys fighting?"

"You were OFF the trail!"

That's because I smelled— Griffith broke off, a stricken look crossing his canine features. *I . . . caught the scent of a squirrel, and I . . . chased after it.*

"A squirrel!" Winston squealed. He clapped his hands and squatted next to Griffith. "Tell me more about this squirrel!"

Griffith's ears pinned back as his eyes widened. *I chased a squirrel, Ada. I chased a squirrel! What is happening to me?*

Winston scooted closer, leaning in close to Griffith's face. "The squirrel. Did you catch it? How was it?"

Griffith ignored him and stared at Adelaide. *Ada . . . I think I'm . . . losing myself.*

Adelaide's stomach turned around and tried to bury itself in her spine. She knelt in front of him. "Lady Bumble said we have until midnight on the third day."

She said some *of the spells have until midnight on the third day. Not* all *of them. What if this one only has until midnight tonight?* He tilted his head to peer through the trees. *What if I only have a few more minutes of being ME?*

Adelaide shook her head. "No, no, that can't happen." She smoothed her hands over his face and pressed a kiss to his nose. "I won't let it."

He flicked out his tongue to lick her chin. *I will always love you, Ada. Always.*

Adelaide blinked away tears and buried her face in his neck, clutching him tight. Above them, the moon inched closer and closer to midnight. Time was running out and there was so much she hadn't said. She hugged Griffith close, hoping that he understood everything she couldn't say.

"What are you doing?" Winston asked, pressing his face against theirs.

"Gah!" Adelaide jerked back.

Griffith rolled backward, gaining his feet and snarling.

"Winston!" Adelaide shouted.

He sat forward. "Yes?"

It's past midnight, Griffith said. *I'm still me. For now.*

For now. The words echoed through Adelaide's mind as she led them beneath a pine tree, its branches brushing the ground like a woman's skirts. Griffith was dog-shaped, but he was still Griffith. For now. She cleared the space beneath the tree of any rocks and large sticks, then began raking the pine needles into a pile. And as the three of them huddled together on the bed of pine needles, the words beat against her eardrums.

She closed her eyes, hugging Griffith close, and didn't cry.

For now.

THE STREAM HELD FISH, which meant they got breakfast. The small fire Adelaide managed to coax into existence browned the eight trout filets nicely.

I found the trail. Griffith trotted around their pine tree, a bundle of wild carrots in his mouth. *I followed it a ways and it ends at some old ruins.*

Adelaide retrieved the wild carrots and washed them in the stream behind her. "Was the troll at the ruins?"

Griffith followed her to the stream, where he lapped at the water. *I didn't go in very far, but it smelled like troll. And Izra. And another person.*

"The scientist?"

Griffith raised his doggy eyebrows. *A who? You can't possibly think that a scientist would attack a wizard.*

Adelaide dropped the carrots at the edge of the fire, then poked them toward the heat. "I was thinking about it last night. Who else would want to attack a wizard? A person that hates magic. A person who doesn't believe it's real. A scientist."

Griffith tilted his head. *Ada, a scientist does* believe *that magic is real. Because* magic is a type of science.

Adelaide laughed.

But Griffith continued. *Science is the study of natural laws, and all magic does is take those laws and bend and twist them a little bit. Like what happened to your hair.*

Adelaide was hoping that he wouldn't notice, but her hair wasn't in the best shape. The sapphire blue braid was now less of a braid and more of a fuzzy, knotted rope decorated with twigs, leaves, sap, and no small amount of dirt. She had caught sight of herself as she fished, and saw that it even fuzzed around her head, like a blue halo.

Could magic turn your hair blue? Of course, and it did. But science could also do it. It's the same result, following the same laws, just from different ends.

"You sound like my Aunty Deb," Adelaide snorted. "And she wore rubber pants."

Because . . .

"Because she experimented with dangerous chemicals and didn't want to get her trousers stained. Or eaten," Adelaide said. "She was insane. As are all scientists."

I beg to differ. Griffith used a paw to drag a carrot out of the fire. He propped it between his paws and crunched.

"Besides," Adelaide said, removing the fish from the fire. "Science can't explain what happened to you and Winston. Or to Lady Bumble and the rest of our party."

Griffith's eyes watched the fish, drool pooling at the corner of his mouth. *That's true, but science is also exploratory. I'm sure that, given enough time, the right scientist could explain how it happened.*

Adelaide pulled two filets off their stick and placed them on a bed of semi-clean leaves. "I'll save you the time, because I know how it happened."

Don't say—

"Magic."

Griffith sighed.

"Now, let's eat so we can get out there and rescue Izra." She pushed the two filets beneath his nose. "Where's Winston?"

Griffith gulped down one trout. *He's foraging.*

Adelaide paused, fish halfway to her mouth, and narrowed her eyes. "Foraging for what?"

Winston crashed through the bushes across the stream and splashed over to their side, his tunic gathered together like an apron. "I'm here! That smells good. Can I have some?" He plopped down and scooped something out of his tunic. "Here, I got this for breakfast. I thought it was so tasty, but also itchy, like eating a fuzzy caterpillar."

Adelaide picked up the red berries and sighed. "Winston, did you eat this?"

He scratched at his neck, where a red rash bloomed at his collar, making its way up to his jaw. "Yum!"

Griffith stared at his body. *Winston, I'm allergic to bramble berries.*

Winston crunched a carrot. "Good thing you didn't eat it, then. I ate it and it was delicious. But this carrot is so much better. But the berry—"

Adelaide put her head in her hands. "Let's all just eat—not that!" She swatted another berry out of Winston's hands. "The sooner we rescue Izra, the sooner we can get back to normal."

For a given amount of normal. Griffith muttered into his fish.

THE RUINS MUST HAVE BEEN a castle once. The outer curtain wall had completely crumbled, with just a few square-shaped stones in place. The inner curtain wall was missing entirely, leaving its gate leaning to one side, embarrassed to be all on its own. The footprint of the main hall stretched long and wide, filled with stones that must have made the walls. One tower stood tall and lonely against the wreckage of the remaining buildings.

And in what could loosely be called the courtyard, a troll sat in front of a fire, carefully roasting a pile of chestnuts. On the ground beside it, an orb glowed softly. The troll picked up the orb, held it to his ear, nodded, then spoke, the words rumbling across the orb's surface. Then the troll put the orb down and cracked open a chestnut, popping it in his mouth.

"Okay," Adelaide whispered as she crept back to Winston and Griffith. "It's definitely the same troll. It's got the same spiral fingernails."

They had hiked through the forest and now sat in what must have once been the moat surrounding the castle. Trees had grown through the watery mud, their roots snaking beneath the water to sprout yards away. Stones from the castle littered the ground here and there, their flat surfaces providing easy stepping-stones to cross, but they did have to step in the thigh-deep water now and again. Though calling it "water" was being generous. The mud and water mixed to create a cement-like slurry that dried grayish-brown and flaked as they walked.

Did you see Izra? Griffith asked, then immediately snapped at Winston. *No! Stay!*

Winston froze in place, one foot in the air, one arm in front, one arm behind, like a ballerina ready to take flight. His rash had eased slightly, but only because Griffith had made him bathe in the stream and then instructed Adelaide on how to make a paste out of curly root flowers and wild lavender.

Adelaide glanced at him, then decided it was in her best interest not to ask questions. "Griffith, I'm going to ask you to take care of the troll. If you bark and dodge and weave—"

But Griffith was already nodding. *I can distract the troll, and maybe even chase it off, if I can bark loud enough.*

"Winston, you'll stay on the treeline and act as a lookout."

Winston dropped his foot to the stone and straightened. "Lookout?"

Adelaide nodded, attempting to inject some confidence in her voice. "It's a very important job. If anyone sneaks up on us, you bark really loud. Not now!"

Winston shut his mouth and nodded.

"And I'll take care of the scientist," Adelaide said. "Let's go."

They crept forward. The swampy water gave way to mud that squelched beneath their feet, and also splashed as Winston fell face-first into it.

Don't. Griffith said as Adelaide went to help him up. *He did that on purpose.*

Winston rolled in the mud, coating every available surface of his clothes and skin with the thick, gray water.

"Ahhh," he sighed, then struggled to his feet. "Much better."

Adelaide glanced at Griffith. Griffith glanced at Adelaide. They both turned and walked away. Winston squelched after them.

They paused at the tree line.

"Here we go," Adelaide whispered. "Everyone remember what to do?"

Yes, Griffith said, intent.

"Yes." Winston started to shake, flicking mud into the air. "Look. LOOK! Do you see that?"

"The troll?" Adelaide asked.

The fire? Griffith asked.

"The BALL!" Winston roared and charged out of the trees.

Aghast, Adelaide watched him run full-tilt and slam into the back of the troll. The troll rocked forward, nearly tipping into the fire. Winston peeled himself from the troll's back. A perfect impression of his form remained on the troll's skin, like a tattoo made of mud. Winston snatched the glowing orb and held it aloft.

"Ball!" he shouted. "It's mine!"

Change of plans, Griffith shouted, and darted forward.

The troll roared, then pressed hands to his ears as Griffith approached, barking madly. He lurched to his feet and chased after the mud-covered dog-man. He swiped at Winston, who danced out of reach with the orb.

"HahaHA!" Winston tossed the orb from hand to hand. "Mine!"

It wasn't exactly the plan, but the troll was occupied. Adelaide dashed across the courtyard. Knife held in hand, she opened the door to the tower and crept inside.

STAIRS SPIRALED UPWARD.

Footsteps hurried downward.

Caught halfway up the stairs, Adelaide paused on the landing, knife at the ready. Wizard or scientist, she would take them captive and demand the release of Wizard Izra.

She tried to ignore the shaking tip of the knife. She had handled a dragon, for crying out loud. She could handle a single person. So why was she nervous?

A little voice in the back of her head whispered that she was nervous because she had so much more to lose. When fighting the dragon, Adelaide and Griffith either won or lost, together. They survived or didn't, together. But now, if Adelaide couldn't rescue Wizard Izra, Griffith would be a dog, leaving Adelaide alone with Winston, who didn't seem to get any more human, no matter how long he spent wearing Griffith's body. And trapped in a dog's body, Griffith had . . . what, six, seven years to go before his body gave out?

Something like paralyzing fear threatened, and Adelaide beat it down.

The footsteps were almost on her.

She retreated into the shadows, ready to defeat the enemy.

Feet pounded the steps, rounded the landing, and Adelaide pounced. "Gotcha!"

A figure in a wizard's hat screamed at Adelaide's descending knife.

Adelaide froze in shock, the tip of her knife barely touching the top of the pointy hat.

It was a child, with two long pigtails draping down her back. In a dress and apron, with dirty bare feet, the girl could be no older than six or seven. The round face beneath the wizard's hat screwed up in fear and she began to cry.

In the apron pocket, a small head poked out and Wizard Izra looked up. He wore what looked like a small toga made from a handkerchief.

"Oh, Adelaide!" His voice was as tiny as he was. "How lovely to see you! Pardon my appearance. My clothing didn't shrink with me. Is Griffith with you? And oh, my, what have you done to your hair?"

THE TROLL LAY on the grass in the fetal position, hands pressed against his ears and eyes squeezed shut. Griffith stood at his head, barking and barking and barking, while Winston stood a few feet away, howling as he tossed the now cracked and dull orb from hand to hand.

The girl tore away from Adelaide's grasp and ran to the troll. "Trojo!"

Griffith stopped barking and stared. Winston continued howling.

Adelaide strode over and snatched the orb out of the air. "Winston, stop!"

He yelped, then reached for the orb. "Mine!"

"Sit!" Adelaide commanded.

He might be wearing Griffith's body, but years of obedience training took hold of his haunches and he dropped to the ground.

"Stay!"

He whimpered, but obeyed as she walked over to the girl.

"Hello, Trojo," Adelaide said to the troll. "I'm sorry about all of this."

The troll rolled to a sitting position and cautiously dropped his hands from his ears. "Hurt."

Adelaide exchanged a glance with Griffith and sighed. "I know. I'm sorry. We promise not to make any more noise."

"Oh, Trojo!" the girl cried and wrapped her arms around his neck.

The troll returned the hug, standing and holding the girl against his chest.

What is going on? Griffith demanded.

All eyes turned to the dog and Izra popped his head out of the apron again. "Griffith, my boy! What has happened to you?"

It was your experimental potions. Winston and I switched bodies, Ada's hair turned blue, and Lady Bumble turned into a blossom tree! Griffith growled, his hackles rising. *And now I'm losing myself! I'm turning into a dog. Can you fix us?*

Wizard Izra's tiny face screwed up in regret. "I'm sorry, Griffith, but if you and the dog were doused in the potion I think you were, there's nothing I can do."

Adelaide's heart shattered. She fell to her knees and opened her arms. Griffith huddled against her chest, his chin resting on her shoulder, and she sobbed into his neck.

I'm so sorry, Ada, he whispered. *I will love you forever and ever until the end of my days.*

Adelaide cried even harder. Words jumbled themselves on her tongue and she stuttered a few convoluted phrases, but everything she wanted to say, *needed* to say, got lost in the maelstrom of emotion.

"Griffith!" she managed to cry.

He licked her cheek. *I know. I know. I'm so sorry.*

Strong and mud-crusted arms surrounded them as Winston wrapped them both into a hug.

"Why are we crying?" he asked, then opened his mouth, squeezed his eyes shut, and bawled. "Why? Why are we crying? Ooooooh! Noooooo! We're crying!"

"Er . . ." The tiny voice broke through their crying. "Perhaps I could have phrased that better."

Adelaide's sobs cut immediately to hiccups and she looked up. "What?"

Izra clung to the girl's pocket and looked at the huddled group, concerned. "I can't do anything to change it, but Griffith and Winston can."

What? What can we do? Griffith disentangled himself from the group hug and turned to his uncle. *I'll do anything.*

Izra spread his hands wide. "I created this potion to allow people to change places with their pets so they can experience their pet's life to better understand how to improve it. To reverse the effects, all you have to do is touch noses."

Griffith tilted his head, ears flopping to one side. *That's it?*

Izra nodded. "I needed to make it simple."

Nothing about this has been simple! Winston! Griffith barked and turned.

"Yes! That's me!" Winston crawled over to Griffith.

Without any hesitation, Griffith pressed his doggy nose against Winston's human nose.

Adelaide expected lights, sparkles, something. But instead, they both blinked slowly, as if they each were just waking up from a bad dream.

"Oh, dear," Griffith's body moaned, and slowly fell over.

Winston's body stumbled backward, before flopping over on his side.

"Oh, we should have waited," Griffith's body said from the ground.

Adelaide dropped beside him and took his dirty, crusty face in her hands. "Griffith, is that you?"

"Oh, great Grundel," Griffith groaned. "Everything is dirty. Everything. I have mud in my . . . er, everywhere. Oh, we should have waited until we got him cleaned up."

"It is you!" Adelaide fell on his face, kissing him all over, despite the mud. "My sultry minx is back! It's you! I love you so much!"

He laughed, returned her kisses, then pulled a face as he tasted mud. "I really, really need to bathe."

A small voice said, "Ahem."

Griffith and Adelaide looked up to see the girl staring down at them, and a blush staining Trojo's trollish cheeks.

"You can use our bathtub, if you want." The girl pointed at the tower.

Griffith rose to his feet, clicked his heels, and bowed. "Thank you, my lady. And who might you be?"

The girl smiled beneath her hat, revealing two missing front teeth. "I'm Emiliana. But you can call me Emily. I've been cursed. I have to stay at the tower until true love finds me."

EMILY TOLD her story over a light snack of stale crackers, roasted chestnuts, and more bramble berries.

One year ago, while searching for food on the streets Emily had broken into a laboratory and accidentally found a beaker filled with shiny pink liquid. Hungry after two days of begging on the streets, she drank it, and it transported her to this crumbly castle. The scientist who made the potion appeared once, with Trojo in tow, to explain that the chemicals mixed together to create a potent spell that even the greatest scientist couldn't undo. And apparently, it was her own fault for breaking into his lab. ("Scientists!" Adelaide sneered.) But he left Trojo there to take care of her, along with the orb through which he could communicate. And he promised to send several eligible young men along in ten years or so. And so Emily was forced to remain at the tower until true love found her.

"But that's ten years!" Emiliana said from where she sat on the floor next to a snoozing Winston. "I can't wait ten years. And I don't need a man to rescue me!"

"That's right!" Adelaide agreed, pumping her fist.

Griffith smiled and patted her hand. After his bath, he had burned all of his clothing and fashioned a toga out of the paisley curtains that used to separate the lab from the main area of the tower. "That is right. You saved me, not the other way around." He pressed a kiss to her cheek.

Adelaide blushed, cleared her throat, and pretended she wasn't embarrassed.

"And then Trojo told me about Wizard Izra." Emily pulled the tiny wizard out of her pocket, where he had been chewing on a small piece of cheese. "And I asked him to go bring him here."

"This tower used to belong to the scientist," Izra said, gesturing to the tables loaded with beakers and chemicals and potions. "Emily here did a magnificent job of mixing together a few spells, one of which accidentally turned me into this diminutive figure you see before you. And don't worry, mine will wear off in another twenty-four hours or so."

"And the others must have turned our guards, horses, and footmen into the gnomes, butterflies, and newt," Griffith said, nodding.

Emily ducked her head. "I'm sorry. I didn't know what else to do."

"You've done so well on your own," Izra said, patting the girl's hand. "I'm sorry Trojo didn't kidnap me sooner."

"And have you found a way to break the curse?" Adelaide asked.

Izra shook his head, his tiny wizard hat spinning slightly. "It's a pretty standard curse, but the terms are ironclad. Without true love, she's stuck here."

"For another ten years? At minimum?" Adelaide growled, waking Winston.

The dog peered at the girl, then Adelaide.

She pointed at the troll. "What about Trojo?"

Emily draped an arm over Winston's neck and leaned against the dog. "We tried. He can carry me to the swamp, but that's it."

"It seems that because Trojo was brought here at the behest of the scientist, he is excluded from the terms of the curse," Izra explained. "It's masterful, really. The scientist closed all loopholes. I'm sorry about your blessing." Izra turned to Adelaide and Griffith. "I don't feel I can leave the poor girl now that I know what is going on."

Griffith replied, but Adelaide didn't hear it. Her attention was on Winston and Emily. The girl was completely comfortable with the dog, and Winston appeared to be besotted. It probably helped that Emily kept feeding him crackers, but Winston's eyes never left her. And when the girl ducked to reach for a chestnut, Winston took the opportunity to lick her chin.

"What about the dog?" Adelaide asked suddenly, interrupting.

"The dog?" Izra parroted. "What about him?"

Adelaide glanced at Griffith to see understanding dawn, but she explained. "Winston loves everyone. He even loves the thugs that took us captive in the woods. He surely loves this child enough to break the curse."

"It could work," Griffith said, nodding.

"I don't know . . ." Izra said, skeptical.

"We could at least try," Adelaide said. "What do you say, Emiliana?"

The girl bent to kiss Winston on the head. The dog responded by covering her face with his tongue. She giggled.

"We can try," she said, wiping her face with her sleeve.

Adelaide eyed the dog. "What do you say, Winston? Do you love this girl enough to break her curse?"

Of course, Winston said, his voice strange and familiar all at once. *I love everybody!*

"Ah, yes," Izra said as everyone looked at the dog in shock. "I forgot to mention that the potion has some side effects."

EARLY THE NEXT MORNING, with one hand on Winston's collar, Emily walked past the swamp and broke her spell.

Everyone laughed and cried, even Adelaide, who then immediately set course for Izra's cottage. The journey back to the cottage was quicker and less adventurous than their trip out, but they still had to manage Winston.

Winston, happy to be back in his dog body, darted back and forth across the forest, sniffing everything he could put his nose on, and narrating his experience for anyone who cared to hear.

From her perch on Trojo's shoulders or carried on Griffith's back, Emily kept up a constant stream of chatter that rivaled Winston's. She was excited to finally be free of the tower, excited to see the forest, and excited to see Izra's cottage.

"A real wizard's cottage," she sighed happily. "Not a scientist laboratory. Yuck!"

Adelaide agreed.

It came into view around dusk.

The gremlin hung by its tail from the thatched roof. "Welcome back," it said as they approached.

The gnomes were still in place, four in front of the carriage, the other six scattered around the yard. The six butterflies flitted around Adelaide's blue hair and a newt crawled out of the well to grin.

Still tiny, Izra jumped down from Adelaide's shoulder and hurried into the cottage.

"I've got just the thing to help!" he called from inside.

They followed him into the cottage, to see him frantically combing through the wreckage of his workshop. Winston ran over to Lady Bumble and barked happily.

"Oh, Winston! You're back!" The blossoms turned toward Adelaide. "How was he? Did he behave?"

Adelaide glanced at Griffith. "Yep."

"He sure did," Griffith agreed.

The blossoms bent toward the dog. "Good boy, Winston! Good widdle boy!"

I was a good boy! Winston shouted at the top of his telepathic lungs.

"Oh my!" Lady Bumble's blossom eyes widened in shock, and then a smile split her face. "How amazing!"

"Found it!" Izra shouted, holding up a vial. "Here it is—oh no!"

With a loud pop! his spell broke and he rose to his full height, completely naked.

Lady Bumble screamed.

Wizard Izra screamed and ducked behind her wide trunk.

Lady Bumble screamed again.

Emily laughed and pointed.

Adelaide took the girl by the hand. "Griffith, I'll just let you, er . . . we'll be downstairs."

BY THE NEXT MORNING, everything was back to normal. Potions were reversed, spells were broken, and everyone was back in their normal bodies.

For a given amount of normal.

Adelaide still had sapphire blue hair ("It will just have to grow out," Izra said) and Winston could still "talk" to anyone who cared to listen. Right now, he was rattling off every stick he could remember to the gremlin, who nodded and asked follow-up questions.

Lady Bumble and Wizard Izra had come to an agreement of a romantic nature, and both agreed to adopt Emily and Trojo, both of which would benefit from some schooling in both manners and magic.

Lady Bumble gave Adelaide a hug. "I'll see you at the wedding."

Adelaide smiled and nodded. "Absolutely. And please keep everyone here out of trouble." She didn't intend to, but her eyes drifted to Winston.

Lady Bumble nodded. "I certainly will. Nothing to worry about. You take care of yourself and your sultry minx."

Adelaide blushed, having heard the explanation for that particular endearment three days too late. In his position at the door, Eddie smothered a laugh. She scowled at him but allowed him to help her into the carriage. Like a lady.

Griffith hugged his uncle goodbye and pocketed their blessing. Adelaide had examined it very carefully the night before and was surprised to find herself relieved at its contents. Instead of aquatic abilities or a gorgon, their blessing was a small device that allowed them to record memories. They could use it to tell their story to their children and grandchildren.

It was perfect.

Griffith hugged Lady Bumble and entered the carriage, settling against the squabs next to Adelaide.

They waved goodbye and the coach and company trundled down the road.

Griffith put an arm around Adelaide and pulled her close. "That was quite the adventure."

Adelaide nodded. "I'm glad it's over."

He kissed her temple. "Me too."

They rode in silence for a moment, enjoying the rocking motion of the carriage, the breeze through the open windows, and the comfort of each other's company.

After a few miles, Adelaide looked at Griffith and asked, "Should we get a dog?"

BAD DOG

FRANCES PAULI

The hellhounds were born in the witching hour under the dark of the moon. Nothing indicated that the litter would be unusual. The bitch whelped easily and in absolute silence at the exact stroke of midnight.

Three pups escaped the womb, slick and wriggling, before the minute hand shifted. Three perfect pups, black as ink and as hairless as a stone. Their mother sniffed each in turn and knew them in that instant. She turned her muzzle to the sky, to the round shadow of the empty moon, and opened her lips to howl.

The pain shivered through her again. Her nose dropped, stunned, to her trembling abdomen. The clock had shifted, and yet, she felt the unmistakable pressure that was birth one last time.

Thirty-five seconds after the witching hour, one fat, smoke grey pup slid into the world with a grunt. Though near-black and as hairless as its kin, its difference glared up at her. Pale and glassy, the white lozenge between the tardy pup's ears shone like a light.

The pup whimpered, but she ignored it, too hypnotized by the horror of his white spot. He grunted and shivered and started to whine before, at last, her nose fell close and she claimed him with a sniff and, when his tail wagged fiercely, a quick cuff of her paw.

"Hellhounds do not whine," she said. But then, hellhounds are always born on the stroke of twelve . . .

HATACH STOOD over the hare's carcass and snarled. The pack's lead female, Javani, and her young cronies slunk back into the shadow, eyes glowing and still fixed on his dinner. He didn't want it, and would eventually relinquish it to their snapping jaws. What mattered was the timing.

If they ate his food, it had to be because he'd grown tired of it, because it displeased him. His status and his life depended on that. Still, Javani tossed off a final growl before she backed away. That one coveted more than his meal.

Hatach stared her down. He put the force of his dominance into the look, and when she averted her gaze, he lay pointedly across the dead hare. It stunk. His sensitive nose found death offensive. Javani knew that. She sensed his difference, and she fully meant to exploit it.

His size had spared him an early death. Hatach had fought for the milk his mother might have denied him. He'd fought his littermates, and he fought his pack mates as well, proper hellhounds who saw their chance in the single white spot on his brow, who mistook it for weakness.

Before the upstarts could make another bid, the heavy scent of brimstone reached the pack. The Master approached his dark kennel. He drifted across the black stones as only a Demon King could and came to a fluid halt in front of Hatach, pack leader, head hound. The Master spared no words for the rest of the pack. He paid them no notice, but he nodded to their leader and smiled, "Well done, Hatach."

It was this moment for which Hatach lived, though he ground his teeth against the urge to wiggle, to make some noise that might indicate his pleasure, his eagerness to serve. It was enough that the Master noted and approved. He had a fat hare as his proof. What more could any hellhound crave?

Hatach stifled the old feeling that something was missing. They'd done well, his pack, and he swallowed that other urge and bit into the hare he didn't want.

HE SMELLED the intruder before he heard her. The pack slept, and Hatach, restless and unwanted amongst them, patrolled the Master's grounds. The thief was good. She hadn't made a sound at all when the wind shifted and he caught her scent.

His lip curled. He crouched and drifted toward the kitchens. His charcoal skin blended with the shadows and his nose twitched at the familiar odor: human. Humans had no place here.

Something rattled inside the back entrance. Hatach crouched low outside the door, just beyond the sliver of light. It spilled from a doorway that should have been barred at this late hour. He heard muttering from inside and crept forward. His smooth belly pressed against the flagstones and his muscles bunched, ready to spring in an instant.

The door sat open enough to allow his narrow frame access, but as he slipped around the obstacle, his body froze mid-step. He could see the thief squatting beside the Master's huge stone oven. Her back faced him, completely vulnerable to attack. One lunge and he could take her down, serve his king and secure his place at the head of the pack.

Something in the air stopped him. His nostrils flared and itched for it. Meaty. It smelled of smoke and grease and something sweet. He salivated. His tongue rolled inside his mouth. Something thumped behind him.

The woman spun around to lock eyes with him. Her gaze held steady, but he read the hint of fear behind it.

"Well," her voice purred softly. The sweet smell came from one of the many bags she carried. "Aren't you a pretty thing?"

His lips curled, exposing his deadly teeth, but the thumping resumed from the doorway. He risked a look and stared at his own tail. It thumped again and again, as if proud of the little rebellion. Hatach considered biting it.

"Hey boy," the woman's voice called his attention forward again, but before he could bite *her*, she tossed something at his head. He ducked and let it smack to the floor beside his paws. The smoky scent wafted from it in ripples. Hatach refused to look.

"Don't you want it?"

His lips curled. He should have growled, but his tongue had started rolling again. He feared opening his mouth would release it completely.

The woman smiled at him. "Go ahead." She turned her back on him, ignored the threat he posed and reached one greedy hand into the Master's silver drawer.

Her audacity infuriated, but the scent of the sweet meat boiled in his head as if she'd cast some spell to immobilize him. He had only one option. His muzzle lifted to the ceiling and he let out a long howl.

The thief swore and stood up. Before he could tear himself from the bacon's hold, she waved one finger in front of his nose.

"Bad dog!" she said and bolted past him into the night.

Bad dog. Shame flooded his senses. He ran through black trees, his pack at his heels and his foe in full flight before him, but the words pounded in his ears. *Bad dog!*

His breathing came harshly, each chanted "bad dog" stabbing somewhere deep in his chest. He'd left her treat to the dust and the mice, but somehow her words had managed to poison him. *Bad dog*.

Javani ran at his hip. Her shorter legs churned to keep even, to prove her worth as his second, or perhaps, his replacement. The pack heaved forward as one, black and deadly and silent but for the correction screaming inside its leader's head.

The forest thinned as they approached the stream. The woman's scent swirled here, thickened where she'd paused to catch her breath, to plan her hopeless escape. Hatach sang to the sky, and his pack answered. Their howls would warn her, remind her that she'd never live to see the dawn. *Bad dog*.

He snarled and the hounds surged forward. They milled along the bank, nose down, hunting for the key to their quarry's movements. Javani splashed ahead. She leapt the deep section and took position on the far shore, tracking, sniffing her way along the mud.

It was too direct, too obvious. His thief was better than that. Hatach knew as much, but when Javani's nose pointed skyward and she howled her success, he kept his little secret to himself. *Bad dog.*

She'd be nearby, high up, perhaps, waiting for them to take the false trail, waiting to slip away behind them. Hatach drove the pack across the water in Javani's wake. He nipped at heels and growled encouragement to follow the lead bitch, take the scent, all forward! He even ran a pace or two amongst them before turning and dropping to his belly in the weeds.

His eyes fixed on the stream. His nostrils opened and his breathing stilled to near nothing. Hatach melted into the night and waited.

She dropped from a tree, landing on the ground not four steps from where the pack had crowded moments before. The water separated them, and the human's nose was no match for his. Her eyes could never find him in the darkness. Still, Hatach imagined that she stared right at him. He heard her voice say, "bad dog." He smelled the bacon in her pocket.

His tail moved. The grass rustled, and the woman leapt away. Hatach stared at his rump. His tail fluttered. Hellfire! He'd chew the damned thing off if it did that again.

He crossed the stream and tracked her back through the trees. She followed the length of water upstream toward the cliffs and the cataract that marked his Master's border.

She was good. He'd known it right off. Beyond the cliffs, the Demon Kings held no sway. If she made it to the top, the hellhound pack would never follow. Hatach followed. He shadowed her steps and kept his breathing and his tail silent. He could take her before she climbed the falls.

THE WOMAN WAITED for him at the base of the cliff. She sat on a rock and watched him emerge from beneath the forest's shade.

"Ah." She sighed. "It's you again." She put her lips together and made a high-pitched noise. She slapped her thigh a few times and then shrugged.

Hatach took a step forward. His lip curled.

"What I can't decide—" The woman stood and glanced up at the wall of stone. The water roared out over the river, but Hatach followed her eye and saw the path she wanted. "Is whether you're so intent on getting your jaws around me or this." She flicked her hand and a lump of bacon sailed away to the right.

His eyes didn't flinch from her. He didn't even twitch.

"Ah," she said. "I was hoping it was the bacon." Her voice held displeasure. Her words dripped with disappointment.

Hatach lowered his head a touch. He advanced another step. Over the crash of water he heard a distant howl. Another followed, nearer, louder. The woman's head snapped in that direction. Hatach whined. His tail, perhaps at last awed into obedience, tucked tightly under his belly.

"It's all right." A heavy pressure settled on his head. An electric shock jolted through him. The woman's hand rubbed his brow, lifted and patted him on the head once, twice. "It's all right," she said.

He skittered away from her, away from the contact that left him feeling hollow and needy. Another whine broke free before he could swallow it. What had she done to him?

He heard the pack behind them in the woods. Javani would have found the trail by now. Their trail. The woman pulled a metal hook from her pack. It dangled a coil of heavy rope. The pack's howls neared and the woman spun the grapple. She flung it toward the cliff's rim.

Hatach stepped closer. He could take her now. It would be easy to do it now.

The hook caught, and she tested it with a mighty pull at the rope. She looked at him once before she started up. She cast a glance at the dark and the sound of the pack and then she winked at him and smiled.

"Good boy," she said. "Good dog."

She leapt into the air at the same instant Javani burst from the trees. The woman kicked against the rock and climbed fast, her arms scrambling along the rope. Javani snarled and streaked forward. She launched from four strides away and flew like a skinny missile at the thief's dangling legs.

Hatach caught her mid-leap.

They crashed against one another and fell into a snapping tangle of teeth and muscle. They rolled together to the base of the cliff, and both came up bleeding. Hatach growled and stood his ground. Javani circled, snarled the word "traitor" to the pack.

Confused, the hellhounds froze and watched the exchange. Hatach was still pack leader for the moment. He didn't count on that moment lasting very long.

"Turncoat!" Javani snapped. "*Dog*."

Hatach growled and lunged at her, forcing her to dance. If he could keep her at bay and distract her from the thief scrambling up the rock face, the woman would make it to safety. If only he could hold them that long before they understood. After that, the pack would take him for sure.

He listened to the woman's progress, but his eyes remained fixed on Javani. The female lowered for a spring, slid to the left then the right. Her teeth flashed as she snapped. Her tail whipped. She lunged, and he met her head on. His jaws found the skin of her neck, but she twisted away. Her front paws raked his side, scratching his bare skin, leaving jagged white trails.

"Traitor." She spoke to the pack now, though her attention held on Hatach. "He's helped the thief! He's turned on the Master."

Hatach lowered until the grass brushed his belly. He heard the throaty growls as the pack crept closer. A wall of stone stood at his back. A river roared to one side. Javani and the pack were everywhere else. He snarled and watched them come. Let them come. He heard the woman's words. *Good dog*. What more could a dog want?

He bared his teeth and waited for them all to spring.

Fire shot past his shoulder. It rained from the sky, landing between Hatach and Javani. They both cowered away from it, but when the second bolt fell, Hatach glanced upward. Something above was dropping fire around him. He turned to the wooden shaft flaming against the grass and saw it for what it was—help.

Still he pressed his body tighter to the stone. Two more arrows fell, ringing him against the cliff face, a dotted wall of flames between him and the pack. He saw Javani's face pass behind the fire, in and out between the lines as she paced. Her eyes glowed with hate and triumph.

The first arrow already sputtered when Hatach felt a brush at his flank. He whirled in place, had no room to maneuver otherwise, and found a metal hook hanging at his side. The grapple spun slowly, reflecting the fire's glow. From above, a long whistle called.

Hatach barked. The pack froze at the sound. He did it again. Bark. Bark! His tail thumped wildly, narrowly missing the fire. He hardly noticed. The grapple slowed and he stepped over it. He slid his shoulders between the spines and laid his front paws across the metal. One hook cradled his chest. Another curled under his flank.

Hatach looked through the fire at the hellhounds and barked again. The line pulled. His front paws lifted from the grass. Javani leapt through the flames. The grapple surged up the cliff, and he saw the hound bang into the wall below him. Her jaws already snapped as she spun, turned her muzzle up and jumped for his hind end.

He banged into the cliff as the rope shortened. The stone face passed quickly. Hatach used his paws to keep his body steady in the hook. He shifted his weight and tried to keep from spinning, from bumping the rocks again.

The frenzied pack snapped and howled, but they were far below now and out of range. A soft voice called from above. "Good boy. Good dog." The grapple stopped moving, and he was lifted up by hands that smelled of bacon.

The thief set him on the grass and turned back to the rope. She retrieved her grapple with a parting glance toward the distant sound of howling. Hatach watched her roll the rope into a coil. He watched her fold and store the metal hook once more. He waited.

When she stood and turned to face him, he let the wiggle loose. His tail thumped before he thought to stop it. The woman smiled and took a step in his direction. She reached out with one hand. Hatach whined.

"What the hell is that?" A new voice growled behind her, deep and male. A man stepped from beside the cliff. He wore a case filled with arrows and carried a bow, but he scowled at Hatach.

"It's a dog." The woman's hand settled between his ears. Her fingers brushed at the white spot. "It's *my* dog," she said.

"But it's a—he's a—" The man waved the bow in their direction. "You *know* what he is."

The humans faced one another. Hatach understood. This was her pack, and she fought for him. He stifled a snarl and waited for the match to be decided. Eventually, the man folded. He shrugged and turned away from them.

The woman's fingers scratched Hatach's head. She dropped into a squat beside him and they shared a good long look before she nodded. She knew what he was.

"You're a good dog," she said. "Aren't you, boy?"

Hatach wiggled. He barked softly, and she patted his head again.

"All right, Good Boy." She reached one hand into her pouch and dug around. "Let's try this again." Her hand retrieved the smoky meat. She waved it, and the scent swarmed between them. "You want some bacon?"

Hatach barked. It started somewhere near his toes and rolled up and out of his whole body. His tongue rolled freely, spilling from his open mouth. He wiggled. The woman dropped the meat in front of him and he dove on it. He couldn't hear her chuckle over the wild thumping of his own tail. *Good dog.*

Princess Victoria & the Monsters or the Money

Angelique Fawns

Victoria hugged her knees in the cabinet under the sink in the condemned condo unit, her breath came in harsh gasps. Two wiry mongrel puppies, Bacon and Butter, were squashed against her thighs. Boots thumped down the hall outside, the rotten floorboards creaking in protest. This was the first time the Enviro Cops had entered the forsaken building. She tried to swallow, but her mouth had gone completely dry. Why were they here? It's not like anyone cared about a missing sixteen-year-old ex-monarch.

When the new order ousted her family, they fled back to Britain. She stayed with her dog Gus. No dogs allowed on the plane. No dogs allowed anywhere.

She'd been living on the fringes for almost a year now. Her little apartment was an oasis hidden in the Newest York's wasteland of abandoned real estate. Most squatters lived in squalor, but Victoria had retrofitted the place with cast-off furniture, bright pillows, and a generator. An attempt to create the comfortable, loving home she'd never had. The palace was always cold and formal. Like her parents. All she wanted was a safe place to live with her beloved pets.

All three shivered in the fall air leaking through the hole she'd cut for the sink's cistern. The dogs squirmed and looked at her with liquid brown eyes full of confusion. Butter flinched as someone pounded on the door, but Bacon's tail beat a rapid tattoo on her hip.

Victoria cupped her hands over the puppies' muzzles, sweating despite the chill. "Hush guys, maybe this is just a routine patrol. Why can't they leave us in peace?"

With a crash, the door was kicked in and Victoria whacked her head on the pipe she was hunched under. Sharp pain bloomed in her skull, and a whine escaped from Butter. She tightened her hand on his nose.

Peeking through the cabinet door, she saw two cops slink into her apartment. Both bulky and awkward, they had rifles slung over their shoulders. She swallowed down a burble of vomit.

This wasn't a routine patrol. They'd never entered her apartment before.

"Janet, you check the closet." The man took a quick look into Victoria's bedroom and bathroom. "All clear."

"Closet looks like the bottom of a donation box, but it's also clear," Janet said.

The two relaxed as they began searching the living room.

Janet puffed out her rosacea-mottled cheeks and picked up one of Victoria's handmade candles. "Harold, can you believe this dump?"

Harold knocked a row of dog food cans off a shelf. "She's living like an animal. Can you believe she used to be a princess? Now she's a mutt. Just like those disgusting fleabags she's hiding."

Janet bent over to read some of the tomes Victoria had in her bookcase. "The little urchin has veterinarian textbooks in here."

Harold spat on the threadbare Persian carpet. "Another infraction we can haul her in for. Paper books? When was the last time you saw those?"

Janet shrugged and threw the book on the rug. It made a squelching splat landing in the snot gob.

Victoria bit her lip to stop herself from screaming at them to leave. Those were treasures. She had to break into a library museum for the books. And she'd traded a week's worth of stolen tofu for that rug.

Janet put her hands on her ample hips. "Are you still moon-lighting for that reality show?"

Harold nodded. "Selling pretty runaways is good business. Imagine if I scored a runaway royal?"

Janet sniffed, judgment coloring her words. "You know most of them die, right?"

He shrugged. "What do I care? It pays for that black-market booze you like to guzzle."

Janet rubbed the broken blood vessels on her nose. "Princess Victoria, come out and surrender."

"She's probably rounding up more stupid dogs." Harold kicked over a pile of scavenged wood.

Anger crawled up Victoria's spine. She needed that wood for the days she couldn't steal enough gasoline to keep her generator running. She shifted and her necklace, a chain holding a dog whistle, swung and hit the bottom of the sink pipe.

Butter and Bacon's ears pricked up. Victoria's chest tightened. If the cops heard that tinny ding . . .

Janet crouched to pick up a rock from her pile of painted tombstones. "Would you look at these? Our girl is an artist." The rock was big enough that the cop needed both hands. Each was painted with the name of a dog or cat already lost to extermination patrols. There were over twenty of them.

"More like a punk if you ask me," Harold said with a snarl.

Victoria exhaled in relief; they hadn't heard the ping under the sink. She tucked the orange whistle under her sweater. It was her lucky charm, reminding her of Gus. The big mastiff had been her hero, once protecting her when someone had tried to kidnap her. Back when people carried about the monarchy. He'd lost an eye but saved her life.

Janet turned the large piece of granite over in her hands. "Gus" was etched in calligraphy. "This is exquisite. Look at the painted flowers."

Victoria squeezed her puppies, tearing up at the memory. Bacon, the size of a football, yipped in protest and wiggled out of her grasp. The furball busted the cabinet door off the one remaining hinge and ran straight at the patrol officers.

Janet dropped the rock and swung her rifle off her shoulder. "I got this."

Victoria's heart froze. She couldn't watch another pet die. The fluffy mutt ran right for the cop, his little legs scrabbling on the splintery floor. Bacon sniffed at Janet's boot, his tail wagging.

Janet kicked at the puppy, who growled and tried to play with her toe. "I'm going to shoot my own foot off if I fire."

Harold raised the butt of his weapon. "Here, I'll whack him on the head."

Anger flushed Victoria's cheeks. Bacon gave short, excited yips, thinking this was a fun new game. As the heavy end of Harold's weapon dropped, Victoria grabbed her dog whistle and blew a short, hard puff.

The high-pitched sound was inaudible to humans, but Bacon danced and spun toward the sound. Harold missed the dog's head by inches.

Janet aimed her weapon. "Now I got you."

Victoria had spent years hiding from the authorities, but this wasn't going to happen. Not today. Not like this. She wouldn't cower under a sink and watch Bacon get shot or clubbed to death.

It was "go" time. She gathered all her bravery and mixed it in with her outrage.

Butter yelped in astonishment when she scrambled out from under the sink cabinet. She ran on all fours, like a war horse, straight at Harold.

"What the heck." Harold aimed his gun at Victoria.

Janet dropped her rifle and reached for his arm. "Harold, don't shoot the girl. Money remember? Plus, do you want to risk being the guy that shot the princess?"

Harold flicked his eyes at his partner and hesitated. "No one cares about the royals. In fact, most people hate—"

Victoria plowed into Harold's gut with her head. The startled cop made a strangled "whoomp" and collapsed. Bacon narrowly avoided being squashed when the heavy man fell. The terrified dog skittered under the couch.

Butter yipped and scurried from the kitchen cabinet to join Bacon hiding behind the stained sofa.

Victoria blew her whistle again. This time with two short puffs. The pups beelined for the door and ran for the hiding place she'd prepared for them in an old dumpster in the alley. There was a store of food and toys there. Enough for three days.

She charged after the dogs. When she tried to leap over Harold, he grabbed her ankle. She would have crashed to the floor, but Janet caught her and wrenched her arms behind her back.

"Princess Victoria, you are under arrest for violating the domestic pet laws."

Her guts turned to ice as the handcuffs bit into her wrists. She was in a lot of trouble.

THIRTY MINUTES LATER, Victoria rubbed her forearms while sitting on a red leather couch. The cuffs had left angry lines on her skin. She pressed her lips into a thin white line. This place was not a cop shop. High ceilings held stage lights dangling from the rafters. There was a murmur of voices, like the muted roar of a stadium crowd. It was furnished with comfortable chairs, movie posters, and photos of famous actors on the walls.

The cops had talked about kidnapping "pretty runaways" for a reality show. Nausea rose in her throat. Hadn't Janet said something about most of the kids dying?

Victoria wasn't alone in the room. She caught the eye of a good-looking teen sprawled across from her on another couch. He had tats of dragons lacing up his arms and was wearing a ridiculous neon green costume. It was cut high on his arms and short on his hairy, muscular legs. A long sickle earring, Death's scythe, dangled nearly to his shoulder.

She nudged his calf with her foot. "What are you in for? A fashion offense?"

He gave her the middle finger.

A stunning middle-aged woman with cheekbones like razors strode out of her office in a red ballgown. Her blonde hair was piled high on her head in an elaborate bun.

"So someone found the missing princess?" She smiled with a mouth full of veneers and zero genuineness. "I'm Rissa."

Despite the churn in her gut, Victoria straightened her spine. "Nice beehive on your head. Why don't you buzz off and let me go!"

Rissa rolled her heavily mascaraed eyes. "That's not an option, but you're one very lucky young lady." She plucked at one of Victoria's dark curls. "Harold didn't lie; you are gorgeous, even with the facial scar. Our audience is going to love you. A real princess on our show. Royal redemption."

Victoria jerked her hair away from Rissa's fake nails. "Touch me again, and I'll bite you."

"Spicy!" Rissa laughed. "You are going to be perfect for *The Monsters or the Money.*"

The blood drained from Victoria's face. She'd heard the promos on her satellite radio, hardcore rock music under a deep "voice of god" announcer:

We're putting justice in the hands of fate!

The only reality show where offenders determine their guilt or innocence.

They choose . . . The Monsters or the Money.

Winners open the door to a life of riches. The losers get the death penalty.

Streaming Fridays at 8:00 Eastern on GAME TV.

Victoria felt her consciousness swim. Black dots spotted her eyes.

"Why should I cooperate? I'm probably going to die anyways. I'll take my chances with the legal system."

Rissa's eyes hardened. "This is your chance to avoid prison. There is a lot of hate for your family. You'd probably die in the first week there. Here you could win enough money to buy anything you want. Maybe even an exemption for your illegal pets."

Victoria's jaw dropped. A tiny flicker of hope bloomed in her chest. "You can get exemptions for domestic animals?"

"The rich can get exemptions for everything."

"Do I get a choice in this?"

Rissa flicked her fingers at her. "Of course, you have a choice. You can go to jail and wait several years for your trial. I hear you left two cute puppies behind."

Victoria felt a flash of rage. "What do you know about my dogs?"

Rissa leaned in, nose to nose. "Play my game and maybe you'll find out."

She sighed and nodded. "I'll play."

The boy on the couch gave a harsh laugh. "Welcome to my nightmare. A princess? More like pathetic." He stood up and cracked his fingers.

Victoria noticed he was a few inches shorter than her five foot eight but lean with muscle. He resembled a cobra, his body tight with tension. His neon suit showed every ridge and bump.

"That's Randolf. You'll be competing against him." Rissa frowned at Victoria's torn jeans. "We have to get you changed."

Rissa held out a shiny green suit. It was like Randolf's but had a skirt instead of shorts.

The skirt would hardly cover her butt. Victoria put her hands on her hips. "I'm not wearing that!"

Randolf sniggered. "No tiaras and gowns here."

A tinny voice blared out of Rissa's headset. "And we are live in five."

Red rose in the cheeks of the show host and she snapped at Victoria. "Non-negotiable. Time is up. Put it on or I'll bring security out here to do it for you."

Victoria's face also went red. "Whatever."

She took off her clothes—ignoring Randolf's amused expression—and pulled the body suit over her head. "I'm so skinny, there's nothing to show anyways." She took care to tuck her whistle under one spaghetti strap.

Rissa ushered the two of them through a heavy metal door under an ON-AIR sign.

The roar of the crowd made Victoria flinch. She could feel sweat dribbling down her armpits. People were jammed into stands around the large studio. Randolf followed her into the spotlight. A blue pond, the size of a backyard pool, twinkled several feet from them with a swing hovering from the rafters.

Victoria relaxed a little. It looked fun, not fatal.

There was a table on the other side and a huge maze covered in paper-mâché stones. A cheesy sign blinked in neon lights on the façade: CAVE MAZE.

A trendy piece of music swelled throughout the studio and Rissa rose out of a trap door on a silver pedestal. Rissa waved one arm magnanimously. "Welcome to *The Monsters or the Money!* This reality show puts justice in the hands of the offenders! Our contestants today are a boy who has lost his way, and real-life princess who has been found! One of them will face the Doors of Destiny, and the other will be judged a little sooner."

Victoria's stomach lurched. What did "judged a little sooner" mean?

The crowd hooted in approval. A huge spotlight snapped on Randolf. He gave the crowd the middle finger. They jeered and threw popcorn from the stands.

Rissa laughed, egging the spectators on. "Let's meet our first player. Randolf Smith was arrested yesterday for selling drugs to school children."

Boos emanated from the stands, as the music turned into a tribal beat.

"Today we find out if he is guilty or innocent!"

Victoria covered her ears as the decibel level of the screaming crowd increased. The spotlight clicked off Randolf and illuminated Victoria.

Rissa's voice cracked as she yelled over the noise. "Our second player was arrested just this afternoon! Princess Victoria was found hiding illegal pets!"

Gasps from the stands, and the audience quieted. One deep voice from the first row cut through. "Way to go, girl!"

Rissa continued her intro, "She isn't even pretending she's not guilty. The princess believes the law banning her dogs is unfair. She thinks she is above the law!"

The host looked around expectantly, waiting for the audience to react as they did with Randolf. Rather than boo, a slow clap started near the heckler. The studio erupted into raucous applause. The spectators got to their feet, pounding and clapping.

Rissa paled, and rushed on, "Well Victoria, it looks like you have some support here. Let the challenges begin! First, our contestants face the Piranha Pond."

The tribal beat transformed into a fun sea shanty and the crowd took their seats. Blood and chum fell from the rafters and the deadly fish turned the surface of the pond into frothy bedlam.

Victoria felt her knees get weak and she gagged at the rotten smell. Scratch fun, the pond was fatal. The swing swayed gently in the middle of the pond.

"Have you watched the show?" Randolf whispered into her ear. "I'm a superfan."

She shook her head and watched the sharp teeth of the piranha tear into the fish guts. Blood pumped in her ears.

"The object is to get across the pond without falling in. Looks impossible unless we work together." He gave her a lopsided grin.

Victoria looked into Randolf's blue eyes. "Why would you help me if only one of us can win?"

He charmed her with a smile. "If you watched the show, you'd know that everyone makes alliances at the beginning. Besides, if we make it to the end, maybe we can both win. You take me home as your prince."

"Is that possible?" Victoria felt hope bloom in her belly.

Randolf did a few stretches, limbering up. "This show is famous for doing the unexpected. You never know."

She took several shuddering breaths. "The swing looks solid, but it's too far to reach."

"They change the challenges every episode, but I've seen something like this. We can tackle this together."

Victoria gulped, and then nodded.

Randolf clapped his hands. "Okay, you launch me, and I will grab the swing. I'll ride it across and then throw it back toward you. It should swing close enough for you to grab it easily."

Victoria hesitated, not sure she should trust him. "Why don't I go first?"

His eyes flashed with annoyance. "I'm slightly smaller than you are. Better hurry, the longer we take to do this, the harder the challenge becomes."

She shrugged, once again, there wasn't much of a choice for her. "Alright, let's do this." Victoria bent down on one knee and cupped her hands so he could step on them.

"On the count of three?" Randolf asked.

"Yup. One Two Three!" Victoria launched the skinny teenager into the air.

He caught the wooden bar effortlessly and swung up onto the seat. He pumped his legs back and forth, trying to get the swing moving. His toes were only a foot or two above the sharp teeth of the fish.

The sea shanty was replaced by the sound of a ticking clock. Every three minutes, the swing dropped closer to the pond. Randolf's sinewy muscles strained like a snake gearing up to strike. He picked up enough torque to make it to the other side and dropped to the ground.

The clock stopped and a celebratory trumpet bugled.

Randolf held the swing above his head and a nasty grin pulled his lips.

Victoria chewed her cheek uneasily. Why the evil smile? Randolf better hurry if she was going to make it across. The swing was much closer to the water now.

Victoria waved at him. "Send it over!" She rocked back on her heels, ready to make the leap.

Instead of pushing the swing back, Randolf unhooked his scythe earing. He used the sharp edge of the jewelry to cut through the rope. Victoria's hands flew to her mouth. It only took him another moment to cut the other side. The seat fell to the ground beside him.

"You backstabbing bastard!"

Randolf gave her a salute. "Sorry sweetheart."

Randolf jogged toward the tunnel under the "Cave Maze" sign, leaving Victoria alone and trembling on the other side of the pond. There was a table by the entrance with two headlamps. He put one on his head and disappeared through the narrow opening.

Rissa's voice boomed over the studio. "Randolf has begun phase two, leaving his competition behind."

Victoria's knees trembled. This couldn't be the end already.

VICTORIA LOOKED AT THE CROWD, not sure what was supposed to happen now. Without the swing, there was no way around the water.

An intense audio sting thrummed as the lights dimmed. The musical drone ignited a headache behind her temples. This didn't look good.

Rissa spoke into her microphone. "Looks like we need to call in our executioner. Randolf will be continuing his trials alone and Princess Victoria has been judged GUILTY."

A man dressed in black, face hidden by a hood, strode over with a handgun. Victoria's breakfast rose in her throat.

Victoria tried to plead with him. "This is fake, right? You have rubber bullets in that gun."

The executioner raised his weapon and Victoria looked frantically for an exit or a weapon. Her stomach was threatening to puke up whatever bile churned in her gut. The studio audience hushed, and she squeezed her eyes shut. Her brain screamed at her to do something. Anything. She wasn't dying on this cold stage.

Before she could reconsider, she jumped into the pond. She expected frigid water, but the pool was lukewarm. Her back itched, waiting for the bullet.

But nothing happened.

Rissa said, "This is unexpected. Our princess chose the pool of piranhas."

The audience cheered and the lights brightened back up as a piece of light pop music began.

Victoria took a shuddering breath and hoped the school of piranha wasn't hungry. Her skintight costume was as good as a bathing suit, and she swam the breaststroke, fighting the urge to kick frantically.

What did her books on animal behavior say?

Piranhas were attracted to movement—

So, the less she disturbed the water, the better her chances of making it to the other side.

The water smelled brackish, but she wasn't feeling any nibbles on her skin. The audience went nuts, cheering as she glided through the water. She smiled and increased the tempo of her swimming. She was going to make it!

The studio music changed again, and the famous soundtrack to a shark movie reverberated through the studio.

Rissa said, "Let's make this more interesting."

A deluge of chum fell from the rafters. The smell was appalling. Ancient fish, rot, and spoiled meat. Victoria gasped as the slimy pieces whacked her head and surrounded her body in a pool of blood. The piranha frothed, finding her, and points of pain needled through her body. The tiny teeth tore into her legs, arms, and back. The other side of the pond was still yards away. Her brain seized with panic. If she died right now, what would become of her puppies? Squeezing her eyes shut, she forced herself to think.

It would take 300 to 500 piranhas approximately five minutes to strip the flesh from her bones, and they preferred their meat dead. There might only be 100 fish in this pond and the fresh guts they'd just dumped on her were an easier meal.

Taking a deep gulp of air, Victoria dove deep, leaving the chum and piranhas on the surface. She thrust her arms and legs trying to dislodge the few fish that were still attached to her skin. Her lungs burned and her skin stung as if bitten by a thousand wasps. She swam along the bottom of the pool until she bumped up against the plastic side. She hauled herself onto the concrete, bleeding from dozens of small bites.

The crowd went wild, chanting her name, "Princess Victoria! Princess Victoria!"

Rissa shouted over the clamor, "Victoria may be back in the game. But can she catch Randolf, who has a considerable head start?"

Heroic music pumped as Victoria grabbed the remaining headlamp and staggered into the maze. A sliding door slammed shut behind her, and the sound of the studio disappeared. Black dots swam before her eyes. She passed out two steps into the dark corridor.

THE SHOCK of hitting the cold concrete startled her into consciousness. She crawled up the rocky walls, pulling herself up with both hands. If there was still music playing, she couldn't hear it in here. It took her eyes a few minutes to adjust to the gloom.

She shook her hands and jogged on the spot. If they thought they could kill someone who'd survived not only the royal family but the worst of Newest York streets, they were sorely underestimating her.

Blood dripped down her thighs and back, but no arteries were nicked. The maze felt claustrophobic with the ceiling grazing her head. Cameras mounted at regular intervals reminded her of the TV viewers and live studio audience watching her every move. The corridors were twisty and dark, so she flicked on her headlamp.

She soon became lost, taking turn after turn until panic crawled up her spine. She was soaked in sweat, the salty dampness making her wounds throb. It felt like she was going in circles.

With one trembling finger, she touched a piranha bite and smeared an arrow of blood on the floor. At least she'd know if she came this way before. She continued this way, stopping at every junction to paint a new arrow. Frustration gnawed at her belly when she fought her way back to a place she'd just come from. She continued to paint her arrows but was running out of tunnels to try. Her imagination conjured up all sorts of horrid creatures lurking around each corner.

She gasped when a figure stumbled toward her. He was wearing a headlamp, and the light blinded her.

"Randolf, you rat, is that you?" His sharp earring glinted in the light from her lamp.

Randolf came to an abrupt stop. His eyes were red and bloodshot. "Damn. Victoria. Die already." He sprinted down another corridor.

Victoria jogged after him. "Randolf! Get back here you loser, I'm not done with you."

He ignored her, disappearing into the gloom.

The speakers crackled. "What's a cave without stalactites?" Rissa's voice tinkled with glee.

Brown spikes shot out from the ceiling. Victoria gasped as one brushed her cheek.

"Ouch!" Randolf yelped from somewhere ahead.

The brown spikes retracted. The whooshing sound turned her blood to ice. She hunched low where the stalactites didn't reach. This strategy wouldn't work for long. Her quads were screaming and with each thrust, the spikes reached a little further.

Victoria took turn after turn, hyperventilating. Every time she rounded a corner, hoping it would lead her out, she saw one of her blood arrows. She was still going in circles. Each corridor was a loop, always leading back to the middle.

She stopped and swallowed a sob. Each path was marked with a blood arrow. She'd tried every corridor. Her mouth was pasty and her throat so dry it hurt.

Why hadn't she passed Randolf again? There must be a trick here.

At the pond challenge, she'd gone through it rather than over it. Could she go through the maze walls? There was one wall that was solid. Every other wall had a tunnel cut into it.

She ran her hand over that wall until she felt a lever. The thin wand was painted to blend perfectly. She pulled on it and an invisible door slid open into a dark passage. Away from the series of connected loops. She shivered with relief. The ceilings were higher in here and torches lined the walls. Her spirits warmed with the dim gleam coming from the propane flames. Added to the light from her headlamp, that sense of being lost in the dark was gone.

Victoria gave herself a mini pep talk. "You got this. You will see Bacon and Butter again."

With renewed energy, she trotted down the black corridor. She slowed when she saw a thick mat of bats on the ceiling. She remembered another chapter of her exotic pet medical books.

Bats are nocturnal animals and like to sleep in dark areas. However, they can be attracted to light because it draws insects, which they like to feed on.

She flicked off her headlamp, leaving herself in just the low glow coming from torches. A male scream reverbed further down the tunnel.

Rissa's voice echoed through the maze. "Randolf has just discovered that in every cave you will also find bats."

Victoria turned the corner. Randolf rolled on the ground while swiping at a cauldron of the flying creatures. Her lips turned up in amusement. Bats rarely attacked people. Randolf was overreacting.

"Help me!" Blood dribbled down his forehead. "The damn things are biting!"

A veiny black creature flapped at Victoria's face, and she felt tiny teeth shear off the top of her ear. Alarm fired in her brain. These weren't your everyday normal bats. Had they genetically enhanced them for the show?

She dropped to her hands and knees. "Turn off your headlamp."

"What?" Randolf gasped.

"They think your light means food."

Randolf ripped his headlamp off and smashed it into the ground. They waited silently for a few moments, Victoria silently praying she was correct. Her hair was brushed a few more times by leathery wings, but then the bats settled onto the ceiling.

Randolf, his voice raspy from screaming, said, "Tough and smart, aren't you?"

He edged closer. One hand abruptly closed on her wrist and another scrabbled for her throat. Randolf lunged forward, throwing Victoria to the ground. His hips were heavy on her stomach, his fingers tight around her throat. His other hand joined the first and Randolf squeezed.

Victoria writhed beneath him. She tried to knee his groin, but only caught one hip. The pungent smell of his sweat made her gag. Hunching her shoulders, she drove her head up into Randolf's chin. He yelped and released her.

She flicked on her headlamp and pulled it over Randolf's head, leaving it hanging backwards like a garish necklace. The bats fluttered off the ceiling, a few circling downwards.

"Nice try," Randolf scrabbled behind his head to turn off the light.

Victoria thought fast.

High-frequency sounds mimic the spectro-temporal patterns of bat echolocation pulses, thereby enhancing the bats' ability to detect and localize prey.

Victoria untucked her dog whistle from her shoulder strap and gave it a blow. More frenzied bats flew off the wall. The tunnel was teeming with them. Victoria ducked and ran, leaving Randolf behind shrieking in rage.

Her heart lifted when she saw a tunnel out of the maze. She'd never been so happy to see unnatural lighting. Scurrying on her hands and knees, she stumbled onto the stage as a metal door clanged shut behind her. The bright lights hurt, and she put her hands over her eyes as she focused on the next challenge.

SHE BLINKED at the fenced pit, realizing she was almost at the end of this insane game. It reminded her of a mini gladiator coliseum, with a dirt floor, and stands filled with overly excited spectators. All eyes were focused on the ten enormous screens hung strategically throughout the studio.

Randolf was banging on the exit door of the maze, bleeding from multiple bat bites. He looked like a war survivor, bathed in the green glow of infrared footage.

Rissa rose from a platform beside her. "In a stunning comeback, Victoria is our finalist, and she will face the Doors of Destiny. What will she choose? The Monsters? Or the Money!"

The audience cheered. "Victoria! Victoria!"

Victoria bit her lip, hesitating before she walked up the ramp into the caged arena. "What will happen to Randolf?"

Rissa winked at her. "Our executioner has entered the cave maze. Randolf has been judged GUILTY."

The music ramped up and a suspenseful drone put Victoria's nerves on edge.

On camera, Randolf raised his hands and sunk to his knees when the hooded man approached. Victoria stiffened in disbelief as the white blast left the end of the weapon and the few remaining bats scattered. The sound of the gunshot reverberated through the studio as the audience gasped in glee. Randolf twitched a few times, then lay still.

Victorias bladder loosened, and she choked down vomit. They killed people on this show? For real? She'd half believed it was all fake, but Randolf looked truly dead. Disbelief screamed in her brain and tears welled in her eyes. The screens faded to black and then she saw herself, brightly lit, ten times over.

A new piece of music, urgent and fun, signaled the segue into the final challenge.

Rissa covered her microphone and hissed at her battered player. "Walk, Victoria. Move to the arena." Victoria limped up the ramp. The dirt coliseum was surrounded by a chain link fence. Her ears rang with the intense chanting coming from the stands.

"Victoria. Victoria. VICTORIA."

The gate slammed and Victoria stumbled into the deep sand. The arena was the size of a high school gymnasium. The far end of the space boasted two plain wood doors.

"This is the moment we've all been waiting for. Princess Victoria will determine her own destiny. Fate will judge her innocent or guilty. If she opens one door, she will be rich and go free. If she chooses the other, heinous monsters will rip her to shreds. Princess, your judgement is now! Will it be the Monsters? Or the Money?"

The crowd cheered, stomping on the stands.

The music flowed into a tense piece underlaid with a ticking beat and the audience quieted. This was the moment they'd been waiting for.

Victoria's breath came in ragged gasps as she looked at both doors. Blood pumped in her ears, and she had to fight to stay on her feet. Her eye flicked back and forth. The doors were identical in size, design and color. Heavy wood, carved and ancient. If she selected the correct one, she would be rich for the rest of her life. Rissa had said there were exemptions for the rich. She would have enough money to take care of her dogs.

Her hands trembled and she froze. After surviving the Piranha Pond and the Cave Maze, how could she choose? She had nothing left.

Rissa's voice rang out from large speakers on the edge of the caged arena. "In a show first, Princess Victoria has thirty seconds to pick a door and her choice will determine her guilt or innocence! Royal redemption, right here on national TV!"

A spotlight snapped on, punctuated by a loud sound effect, and illuminated the Executioner on a platform above the two doors. He had a sniper rifle trained on her. His eyes looked like portals to hell, shining from the holes in his hood.

Victoria was dizzy. Only thirty seconds to determine her entire future?

The spectators screamed out their choices. Some yelled "left", others "right." Their screaming faces looked like one enormous blur, spitting gibberish at her.

"Ten more seconds Princess Victoria, or we choose for you," Rissa said.

Both doors looked the same and blood roared in her ears. The audience, Rissa, and the entire studio disappeared, reduced to a hum of confusion. As she stood there, in what might be the last moments of her life, she had some regrets.

She regretted running away from the palace with her one-eyed dog, Gus. She regretted hiding in fear in her apartment. If she could do it again, she would have fought. Her family used to have some pull in this country. She should have organized a protest with other pet lovers. They eventually killed all the animals anyway. What did she accomplish? Nothing. It all came down now to chance.

She raised her trembling arm and pointed to the one on the left.

Rissa's voice cracked with excitement. "The decision has been made."

The music stopped. The studio was in complete silence.

The left door creaked open. Victoria crossed her fingers, and the audience held its collective breath.

In what might be the last minute of her life, a sense of calm washed over her. She was Schrödinger's cat. At that exact moment, she was rich and free. She was also dead. She was both and neither.

Harsh, throbbing metal music rang out over the studio and the peace was shattered. Five enormous creatures bounded into the arena. Nightmare mega dogs. Their ears were tiny triangles, their tan and black bodies layered with muscle. The largest beast paused, lowering his head and raising a ridge of spiky fur along his spine. The other four lined up behind the alpha in a V formation.

The audience gasped and Victoria's blood ran cold.

She blinked.

These monsters were dogs that had been genetically enhanced. More muscle and sharper teeth. But still *Canis lupus familiarus.*

The lead dog had a dime-sized dot on his nose and was missing one eye.

Just like Gus used to have.

The enormous mastiff growled, saliva dripping off his teeth. She stepped back and then froze. Victoria would recognize that rumble anywhere. When she was targeted by kidnappers, Gus's warning growl saved her life more than once.

There was no recognition in his eyes. Brief joy curdled into despair. How could he forget her? He advanced a step, showing another inch of fang.

"Gus? My sweet boy." Victoria bent on one knee and reached a hand toward the pack.

Gus advanced, the hair on his back standing straight up. The other four dogs fell into formation behind him. Her knees trembled but she fought to keep her voice strong and calm.

Whatever they had done to enhance the old battle dog's DNA, she would still recognize him anywhere. "It's me. Who's my good dog?"

Gus growled, his head tilted to the side, his shorn ears flicking.

Lowering her voice slightly, so she sounded authoritative but not threatening, she said, "Stand down, Gus. It's okay."

Dogs react aggressively to fear. The pack would follow the lead of the alpha. Her only hope was to convince Gus that she was still his alpha.

The dogs were less than four feet away. Her mouth dried and a roar began in her ears. This couldn't be the end. Torn up by her own beloved Gus?

Her eyes met Gus's deep brown one. It was cold. None of the eager familiarity he used to have.

Rissa drew a deep, theatrical breath. "And Princess Victoria has been judged GUILTY."

Gus tensed his muscles to leap . . .

She was dead. Unless Gus remembered her training. Victoria's trembling fingers found the whistle and she blew it.

She was too late.

Gus launched. Victoria pinched her eyes shut and waited for those oversized teeth to tear into her neck.

She should have fought when the laws first came in. She should have—

Big paws struck her shoulders and the air rushed out of her lungs when she crashed to the dirt, hot dog breath on her face.

Tears filled her eyes as she thought of Bacon and Butter shivering behind the dumpster. Resigned, she waited . . .

Ominous drumming, like something from a deranged tribal sacrifice, increased in volume.

Teeth did not rip out her jugular. A rough tongue lapped her cheek. Gus whined and coated her face in kisses.

The dark music stopped. There were a few awkward moments of silence and then a sweet melody with heart-wrenching riffs swelled.

Victoria sat up and threw her arms around the dog's neck. "Gus, I can't believe it's you!"

"Go Princess!" and "How sweet," came from the audience. There was even some crying. Gus whined and wiggled his docked tail in uncontained excitement. The other dogs were confused, walking in circles. A bitch gave a hesitant growl and advanced on Victoria. Gus snarled and leaped at the dog, nipping at her ear. She slunk back to the other three dogs. They all settled on their bellies, tails wagging slowly.

"You know what they say about our game show. Expect the unexpected. Princess Victoria has been judged GUILTY. Our monsters are malfunctioning. It's time for the Executioner."

The music broke off mid-ballad and the tribal drums returned as the spotlight illuminated the man on the platform. He raised his rifle again.

Victoria released Gus's neck and stood beside him with one hand on his head. She remembered the heckler at the beginning of the show. Confusion and muttering came from the stands.

She cupped her hands. "I picked the correct door! I won my dog back! I am NOT GUILTY!"

Someone called from the stands, "The princess was judged, and she won. No fair."

"Give her the monster dog," a woman said.

A chant started slowly and grew to a rousing cry. "Let her live. Let her live. LET HER LIVE."

The Executioner dropped his rifle to his side.

Victoria raised her fists in the air and the crowd roared in approval.

Rissa appeared on the platform beside the confused man. The screens swapped footage from Victoria and Gus. The host and the hooded shooter filled all ten TVs. The two seemed unaware that they were now on the live feed.

Rissa whispered into the Executioner's ear, and he pulled off his mask.

It was Harold. Victoria's jaw dropped and she clenched her hand in Gus's fur.

The audio rang out softly into the arena. "We are going to have a riot here if we execute her." Rissa looked down from the platform, pointing at Victoria.

Harold snarled. "I got her here for you, it was up to you to control the game."

"Shut up, that's not helpful. This is live TV. Think fast," Rissa said. "Our viewers are bloodthirsty morons. We need to find something dramatic to end this episode."

The audience went silent, the sea of white faces awash with shock. Victoria drew her shoulders back and felt something she hadn't in a while.

Hope.

VICTORIA CAUGHT the eye of a woman with a complicated chignon and appalled expression. She looked educated and refined. Victoria raised her arms in a questioning manner.

"What the hell kind of nonsense is this?" the woman called out. "We aren't morons, and this game is rigged."

Rissa looked in horror at the screens and saw the closeup of her own face. She blanched and hustled off the platform with Harold. The audience exploded in shouts. They flung popcorn, candy, and pop cans into the arena. Some stalked out of the studio.

One man leaned over the railing and tossed a business card. "Give me a call Princess Victoria! I'm a lawyer."

A woman in a beret did the same. "I'm a journalist. This is the story of a lifetime!"

Others followed and bits of paper joined the rain of paraphernalia littering the arena.

Victoria dashed around, gathering them, and tucked a few into the hem of her costume. The monster dogs were eating the snacks and yipping.

Victoria took a deep breath and looked at the faces of the crowd. They were on her side now. She was going to save her dogs. All of them.

Rissa reappeared at the edge of the fenced area and the spotlight found her. Harold was a few feet behind her. She forced a smile, and her voice rang out over the speakers. "Princess Victoria has been judged NOT GUILTY."

The crowd cheered and chanted. "Victoria, Victoria, VICTORIA."

Rissa, flustered, her face bright red, continued, "Furthermore, let's congratulate our new Monster Handler! We are offering the princess a job on our show! Do you accept?"

Victoria looked down at Gus, his eyes soft and happy, his tongue lolling out. Could she ask him to kill hapless victims accused of trumped-up crimes? Give the command week after week? She would be no better than Harold and Rissa.

She forced a smile. "Yes! I accept! On one condition. Can I go home and get my pups Bacon and Butter?"

Rissa looked uncertain and glanced at Harold.

He hoisted his gun. "I wouldn't let her. Keep the urchin locked up here."

The crowd changed the chant. "Let her go. Let her go. LET HER GO."

Rissa shrugged helplessly. "Princess Victoria will be allowed to get her puppies!"

The crowd roared in approval. The studio was complete mayhem.

Rissa whispered in Victoria's ear. "At least this will be ratings gold. Go home and get your puppies. Harold will take you."

"I'm not going without Gus." Victoria squeezed the old mastiff's neck, and he gave a low growl.

"Okay . . . be quick!"

Rissa motioned to someone behind the scenes. The theme music signaling the end of the show rang out and the audience, satisfied now, filed out.

Someone called the other monster dogs back into the den, but Gus stayed with Victoria. She gave the dog's head a pat and followed Harold out of the studio. She gulped when Harold gave her a sly wink.

Victoria felt her chest tighten as the black van rolled in front of her decrepit building. The last time she had been in a vehicle with Harold, he had delivered her to reality show hell. She was still dressed in the ridiculous skintight costume, but Gus's head on her lap was keeping her warm. A muzzle secured his jaw, a heavy chain apparatus Harold insisted on before he'd let the dog into the van. Her heart soared looking at the broken windows and garbage on the front walkway. She never thought she'd see this place again. The ugliness outside hid the comfort and beauty of her home within.

"Do I need to come with you, or can you get your mutts on your own?" Harold peered through bars into the back of the van from the driver's seat.

"I can get them."

"The big dog stays here."

Victoria quietly unhooked the straps of the muzzle on Gus. "Okay."

Harold unlocked the rear door and quickly shut it before Gus could follow her.

Victoria paused and looked up into Harold's cold dark eyes. "I suggest you let my dog out."

"Go, before I shoot you right here." He patted the gun on his hip.

Victoria blew her dog whistle and Gus leaped through the back window. The glass shattered as the enormous creature burst out, knocking one of the doors right off its hinges. He landed on Harold, the metal muzzle clanking off his scarred face. The big man slammed into the rusty metal fence separating the apartment building from the sidewalk. A low ominous growl accompanied the saliva Gus dripped on the shocked man's face.

Victoria knelt over him. "Harold, unless you want me to tell Gus you're 'guilty', I suggest you listen very carefully."

Harold's face was swollen and red. His voice squeaked from the pressure of the dog's paw on his throat. "Okay. Whatever you want."

Victoria grabbed the gun out of his holster and slid it out of his reach on the cracked sidewalk. "I'm going to handcuff you to this gate so you can think about how you've treated us folks on the fringes." She pulled Harold's handcuffs off his belt and secured his wrist to the metal fence. "Think of it as the royal treatment."

He jerked as though he was going to resist but lay still when Gus barked a warning.

Victoria kicked the metal fence. "I think that'll hold." She leaned over Harold. "I'm going to leave you here for a bit."

Harold's eyes widened and he screamed, "Help! Someone!"

Victoria laughed and brought her finger to her lips. "Hush, Harold. Do you think anyone in this neighborhood is going to help you? This can be our little game. How long will you survive before one of your own patrols finds you? Or will a local gang get here first? Good luck."

Victoria pulled Gus off Harold and walked to the alleyway without a backward glance at the quietly sobbing cop. The big dog danced happily at her heels. They stopped by a rusty dumpster.

"Bacon! Butter!" The two puppies came squealing and wiggling from their hiding place.

Victoria scooped the pups under her arms and felt her belly warm with happiness.

"Let's go home, guys."

They took the fire escape stairs up to the apartment. Victoria cried tears of happiness as they crawled through a window. She loved her home. Gus leaped on the couch and plopped his enormous head on a pillow. The puppies scrambled up next to him.

Victoria joined them and let deep contentment and exhaustion wash over her. This was her dream, to be home safe with her dogs. She was too tired to take off her bloody, sweat-stained costume, but she did peel off the business cards stuck to her skin. She lined them up on the coffee table.

A few had random names and phone numbers. One was a law firm. "The Goodall Group. We Fight for Your Pets."

"Looks like we might have some supporters? Right, Gus?"

She stroked his enormous, battle-scarred head and smiled. She had her best friend back, and better yet, he was a killing machine. It wouldn't be easy to take her again. Victoria knew she had some hard work ahead of her. She would have to find a new hiding place for her little family of misfits. Sooner rather than later. If Harold got loose, they'd come after her.

She ran her fingers over the cards. She would find others like her. If she could win a game show on her own, imagine what she could do with help. She vowed to make Rissa open a "Door of Destiny".

She'd never used her infamy as a royal before, but maybe there were loyalists still hidden in the country. Animal loving loyalists?

All three dogs cuddled close. Princess Victoria felt her soul soar. Time to start her own game.

SCHROEDINGER'S DOG

LEE ALLRED

I f you select for uncertainty, you *get* uncertainty," Adjunct Professor Collier
Leach temporized to an angry dean with all the unctuous ingratiation of a man
possessing a thousand dollars' worth of unaccounted for equipment just when a
thousand dollars was missing from the departmental petty cash box.

The equipment in question was an oversized kennel cage completely covered in
scrap cardboard, a few breadboarded circuits affixed to the inside of the cage, and a
cheap Radio Shack wireless mic. Leach stood strategically in front of a metal cylinder
stenciled with a yellow trefoil that the Radiation Lab hadn't reported missing yet.

"And Schroedinger chose for uncertainty at every stage of his thought experiment," Leach continued. "Trigger, mechanism, target, observation. And that's where
he made his irreducible mistake."

Leach cued his mic and said "Black" into it. There came a series of rapid thumps
against cardboard from inside the cage—something hitting the cardboard walls—
then a click of a button. The metal cylinder emitted a high-pitched whine like that of
a magnetron. A tinkle of breaking glass followed, a hiss of gas, then a flash of light—

—and tenured Professor Collier Leach stood proudly before a precision-tooled,
custom-built enclosed kennel-apparatus, part of the million-dollar grant he had wran-
gled for the department. A stenciled metal cylinder lay attached to the roof, a gift
from an appreciative Radiation lab.

"Observation affects results, and Schroedinger somehow overlooked that first
observation—thus only observation—occurred not by the scientist outside the box,"
Leach told the very attentive dean who hung on Leach's every word, "but by the
living creature within. A creature that is the epitome of chaos and uncertainty—the
cat. Willful, obstinate uncertainty."

Leach spoke into a state-of-the-art lavalier microphone affixed to his collar.
"White," he said.

Again, a series of rapid thumps against the side of the enclosed kennel and a click of a button. The cylinder whined like a magnetron again, only this time there was no tinkle of glass, no hiss of gas, only a larger flash of light—

—and Professor Collier Leach, holder of the Collier Leech Chair for Advanced Quantum Physics, sat comfortably in the sky box of what had been the university's football stadium. The football team had long since been disbanded and the stadium given over to Leach to keep the school's Nobel Prize winner happy. A worshipful dean who "oohed" and "awed" with sickening regularity listened as Leach deigned to explain the experiment he was about to conduct. The stadium's floor—what had once been a grassy field—was filled with hundreds—thousands—of kennel-cage apparatuses.

"But," Leach pontificated in a stentorian voice Orson Welles would have envied, "suppose you select for *certainty*? Suppose with an absolutely certain inside observer, you could choose whether atomic decay happened or not depending on whether that observer pressed a white or black button. Further suppose that you could marry this certainty of atomic decay with quantum entanglement. Why, you could reorder the universe to your personal whim provided you conducted your experiments in a series of prescribed patterns!"

Leach's finger lightly caressed the execution key on his computer console. "Of course," he said, "you would need to chose a completely faithful, loyal, and obedient embodiment of certainty for your observer inside the box, the antithesis of a cat."

Instead of speaking into a mic, Leach pressed the execute key. A meticulously planned pattern of recordings—Leech's voice saying either "black" or "white"—flashed to the interior speakers of kennel cages covering the field. The kennels were in fact quantum duplicates of the same kennel cage and their occupant quantum duplicates of the original as well.

Thousand of quantum duplicate tails wagged, *thump thump thump*ing against the kennel sides. An earsplitting whine of a thousand magnetrons fired, followed by tinkling glass and hissing vapors and—

—Emperor of the Known Universe Collier the First sat relaxed upon his regal throne. He looked out over his imperial throne room.

The dean stood in the back, mingling with the rest of the courtiers. In the front ranks were the emperor's attendants of a more personal nature, beautiful women clad in the scantiest of garments.

To the side of the throne sat a gem-encrusted pet carrier of solid gold. The Emperor fingered open the latch, and the wet nose of a tail-wagging golden retriever pushed the door open. The utterly dependable agent of certainty lay down at the emperor's feet and looked up at him with eyes that were mahogany pools of warm love, absolute love. Eyes that would ignore reality to observe the universe however his master wished it seen, as long obeying earned a *skritch* of the ears, a pat on the head, and an affectionate "Good boy!"

THE BODY-BORROWER

EMILY MARTHA SORENSEN

Tasha opened her eyes to see the kitchen ceiling. She blinked, as this wasn't where she'd left from. She was lying flat on her back on the kitchen floor, instead of in her bed.

She looked suspiciously over at the room's other occupant.

"Angel," she growled, "have you been borrowing my body again?"

The large, shaggy puppy pawed the ground innocently.

"Are you trying to get caught?" Tasha demanded. "You know Mom's trying to breed a familiar. You know you don't belong in this world. And you're the one who begged me to not let her find out!"

Angel whimpered and put her paws over her eyes.

Dogs were impossible to reason with. Tasha got up off the floor and muttered to herself. She was covered in doggie biscuit crumbs, which were kept on the highest shelf so Angel couldn't reach them. There were also lots of dangling loops in her sweater, so probably the puppy had been pulling on them excitedly with her fingers.

"Look," Tasha said sternly. "Let's review the ground rules again . . ."

"—the opportunity of a lifetime!" Sorkan Rena's voice trilled through the front door. There was a hubbub of voices following after her. "I've got a litter of brand new kittens that will just—oh, hello, Tasha darling."

Tasha nodded at her mother and the gaggle of excitable women following after her. Her mother was a charlatan of a witch, but that didn't stop other wannabes from hanging on her every word and traipsing through the house every day. None of them actually had magic, but they were all hoping the right familiar would change that.

Tasha had magic, unlike her mother. They came from a long line of witches, but magic often skipped a generation or two. Sometimes she thought her mother envied her more than she loved her. And it wasn't even like magic was fun all the time. Magic homework on top of normal homework took so much time out of her days.

No real witches came near the specialty pet shop her mother ran out of the basement, but the wannabes often bought pets from her. There was one woman who Tasha knew for a fact now had fourteen parakeets, five piranhas, and four cats. How she kept the cats from eating the fish and the birds was a mystery.

Tasha's mother kept hoping to capture a real familiar so that she could start breeding them, since magic ran in animal families as well as human ones. But familiars tended to be wily and prefer their freedom to being somebody's pet, particularly a human who had no magic of their own and wanted to have a familiar for the purpose of borrowing theirs.

So the closest Tasha's mother had ever come to breeding a real familiar was one annoying tomcat who could sneak out of any cage. Which, cats being cats, proved nothing.

The gaggle of wannabes headed downstairs, and Tasha heard their excited giggles rising up from the basement.

"Ooh, what kind is that? I love those markings!"

"Is this the one that's always escaping from its cage?"

"Do you have lovebirds?"

"Ohhh, did you stop carrying piranhas?"

"Ouch! That cat clawed me!"

Tasha snickered and looped her finger through Angel's collar. The constantly escaping cat wasn't fond of the wannabes.

"C'mon, puppy," she said, leading the dog upstairs.

A shriek of excitement came from the basement, and a bidding war started between two gullible women. It seemed Sorkan Rena was trying to pass off exotic lizards as baby dragons again.

Angel's tail wagged, and an excited image of chasing kittens popped into Tasha's head.

"No," she said sternly.

She settled down on her bed, lying on her stomach, and tried to concentrate on her homework. The yells and squeals from downstairs were familiar by now. After the "baby dragons" were sold, there would be the trained birds. Then the dogs, then the cats.

And at the very end, for wannabes who hadn't yet bought anything, there would be the rodents. Sorkan Rena never mentioned that she didn't even try to breed them for magic and in fact used them as cat feed.

Angel placed her drooly jowls on the back of Tasha's knee and whined. Wistful images appeared of an idealized forest scene. There were three siblings who smelled like mischief, and one runt always whimpering. There was the strong scent of fatherly protection, and the warm taste of motherly fur. Home. Warm. Love.

Tasha yelped and yanked her leg away from the dog drool.

"Angel!" she hissed. "I know you want to go home. But I don't know how to get you there! I'm sorry, but until you can explain exactly where the portal is, you're stuck here!"

Angel whined and looked at her with pitiful eyes.

"Don't look at me like that," Tasha said with annoyance. "Do you know how hard it was to convince Mom to let me keep you as my own pet? Hard! Do you know how much work I had to do to make sure you flunked every magical test she put you through? Lots! And then I had to promise that I'd take you as my only birthday present, even though I knew you'd be leaving as soon as possible anyway!"

Angel's toes pawed the ground. She whimpered.

"I know, I know," Tasha sighed. "I want to help you find your family. But I don't know how you got to this world, either. If we can just find the entrance . . ."

Her voice trailed off. They'd been searching everywhere in the neighborhood for weeks. So far, no dice. She was beginning to wonder how far Angel had wandered since crossing into this world.

At least one thing was sure: the portal couldn't just close. Once someone went through a portal one way, it wouldn't close unless that person or animal went back through it again. Or died.

It was a fact of portals that was either incredibly convenient or incredibly annoying, depending on who you asked. Personally, Tasha was glad of it right now, though when she was a fully licensed witch and had the authorization to make portals to go out and gather things like dragons' toenails, well, then she might not be so glad about the fact that the wide-open portal could let things like wyverns or dire wolves into her house. Especially since you couldn't close a portal until all of the animals had been sent back through.

For right now, though, it was a good thing.

"Tasha!" her mother called from downstairs. "I need some feed for the dragons!"

Tasha groaned and heaved herself off her bed. That was code for "these ladies aren't as gullible as I thought, and they want to see the lizards breathe fire." Since Sorkan Rena couldn't conjure anything, that meant it fell to Tasha to be her accomplice and conjure the fire and pretend the lizards were breathing it.

Angel tried to follow her down the stairs.

"No," Tasha said sternly. "You stay up here. I don't want you anywhere near Mom's pet shop. We barely got you out of there in the first place."

Angel whined and showed the image of the forest scene again.

"I *know*," Tasha said. "We'll look for it after I'm done helping Mom and I'm done doing my homework, okay?"

Angel howled and scratched at the carpet.

Tasha shut the door to her bedroom firmly. She hoped the puppy wouldn't be stupid enough to unlock it and go downstairs. Or smart enough, as the case may be.

She headed down to the kitchen, opened the door that led to the basement, and went down the second flight of stairs.

"Okay, here I am," Tasha said in a flat voice, pushing through the crowd to get to her mother, who was standing in front of the wall of exotic lizard cages. "We can get started now."

"What do you mean, 'get started'?" one of women demanded. "I thought you were getting feed for the dragons!"

Sorkan Rena gave her daughter an evil eye. "The fireflies, Tasha. From the back room."

Tasha nearly let out an audible groan. *You mean you want me to make it look like they're flying around catching those? You know I've barely started on my air conjuring lessons! I told you I wasn't ready to do that trick in public yet! In fact, I don't want to do it at all!*

But she could hardly make that objection when the audience was standing right there. The last time she had refused to help Mom in one of these demonstrations, she hadn't been given her allowance for a month. She needed her allowance.

Since she'd agreed that Angel could be her only birthday present, she hadn't been able to ask for the six music albums she actually wanted, which meant she was going to have to save up her own money to get them. Now was not a time to irritate Mom.

"Sorry," Tasha said. "I'll get the fireflies."

She squeezed back through the crowd and unlocked the doorknob to the storeroom behind the stairs with a wave of her hand. There was a soft "ooh" from one of the wannabes.

You really shouldn't be so impressed with a simple keylock spell, Tasha grumbled to herself. *It's not like I'm unlocking someone's car that they're trying to keep me out of. This lock was made for that spell. Even Mom can unlock it with an amulet.*

That was one of the ways Sorkan Rena pretended she was a real witch: she owned dozens of amulets. They were difficult to make and therefore expensive to buy, and could only be used for a single spell, though they could be used for that same spell over and over again. Tasha could understand why her mother wanted to use magic so badly, but couldn't she have a cheaper hobby and increase her daughter's allowance instead?

Or maybe even run a normal pet shop, instead of pretending she had magical animals and selling them at a premium.

But no. She knew the real reason her mother did it. Sorkan Rena wanted a familiar *herself,* so that she could use its magic to do whatever spells she wanted whenever she felt like it. And as long as that was the case, her mother was never going to stop this magical pet shop thing. Heck, she probably wouldn't stop even then. If she finally did succeed in breeding a familiar, that would only make her see dollar signs and keep on going. Real familiars would mean attracting better clientele, actual witches, who would pay a lot more than the gullible wannabes.

Inside the storeroom was the usual assortment of cans of dog and cat food, boxes of dead insects for the lizards, and stinky cages of rodents that were used as treats for the kitties.

She found the terrarium full of fireflies, fetched a net and a portable container, and then paused.

Well, I need more practice, anyway.

She shrugged and waved her finger to create a small whirlwind. Twirling her finger back and forth to keep it going, she opened the terrarium a crack with her other hand, and swooshed the whirlwind close enough to the top to catch five of the fireflies in it. She dropped the lid before any more could escape and tossed the net to the side, where it thumped against a tall, curtained thing. There was a slurping, sucking sound from behind the curtain, and then it fell still.

"I brought the fireflies," Tasha said, heading out of the storeroom with her hands cupped. "You can release the dragons."

As Tasha could have predicted, the trick did not go as planned. The lizards scrambled desperately through midair, seeming intensely uncomfortable, and didn't even try to catch the fireflies that zoomed across the room in panic as Tasha whooshed the petrified predators after them.

Seeing the restlessness of the women, Sorkan Rena put a stop to the trick in just under ten seconds. "Thanks, Tasha. That'll be it. Why don't you hand the fireflies to them?"

It's about time, Tasha thought, swatting a firefly and catching a lizard out of the sky. The frantic lizard wasn't wild about eating, but she managed to shove a bug into its mouth anyway.

"AAAAAAAAAAAH!" two women screamed as fire burst out of the lizard's mouth as soon as she removed her fingers.

Tasha smirked to herself. *Now, see, that trick I can do.*

Her mother sold two of the confused lizards to excited women, and three more bought fluffy kittens by the time the presentation ended. No dogs or birds sold this time, and the rodents didn't interest anybody, but still, five animals in one day was a pretty good number. And three more women bought overpriced magical equipment for animals they'd purchased weeks earlier, supposedly to help their familiar skills develop.

"I hope this one will be the key," one of the women said anxiously as Sorkan Rena wrapped a scratching post for her. "Fluffy doesn't seem to trust me enough to let me use his magic yet. He never even seems to notice me!"

"Familiars are notoriously difficult to get to trust you enough," Sorkan Rena said, smiling. "And even then, compatibility with their magic is never guaranteed. It's normal for it to take years for a bond to develop sometimes. But he comes from a good bloodline. It's worth keeping on trying."

"Thank you," the woman said, bobbing her head in relief. "I will."

It was all Tasha could do to keep from groaning. All that was true, which was part of the reason why familiar sales weren't regulated. Getting one that was both compatible and willing to let you use its magic if you weren't a witch was tricky. But still, her mother knew *perfectly well* that none of her animals had magical pedigrees. True, one of them could turn out to be magical, but it wasn't very likely.

Once the final customer left the store, Tasha summoned a broom from the corner and started to sweep up an avalanche of kitty litter that had spilled from a box. The constantly-escaping-tom's mischievous fault again, no doubt.

"That's enough, Tasha," her mother said, taking the broom from her hands. "You go do your homework. I will handle the rest."

Tasha looked at her queryingly. Her mother usually loved it when she helped in the store.

"I have a new amulet," her mother explained. "I want to practice with it."

Tasha barely restrained herself from asking how much it cost. *Please tell me you have enough left to pay my allowance this week.*

"What does it do?" she asked instead.

Her mother smiled mysteriously. "That's for me to know, and you to wonder about. Let's just say it's something you ought to be practicing yourself right now."

Which meant air summoning, astral projection, or silence chants, one of the things she was currently studying with her magic tutor. Probably air summoning, since it was the most exciting, and Tasha had done such a horrible job of performing with the lizards. Well, if it meant Sorkan Rena could make the lizards fly around the room by herself next time, she was welcome to it.

Tasha went upstairs, then up the next flight of stairs, and entered her bedroom to find the puppy worrying the bottom ruffle of her bedspread.

"Hey!" she complained.

Angel immediately scrambled under the bed and hid there.

Tasha sighed and flopped on top of her bed. *Homework . . . homework . . . have to do homework . . .*

Well, she'd more or less practiced enough air summoning today, and it was hard to get motivated to do normal homework, given that she'd been interrupted in the middle of math. She could do silence chants, but . . .

Tasha grinned sneakily. *Or I could use astral projection and watch Mom try out her new amulet downstairs.*

That was technically doing her homework, even though she'd already practiced astral projection today. Of course, there was one thing that she definitely had to make sure of before she did it again. Angel, the pest, had to behave.

Tasha slid off the bed and gave her sternest glare to the puppy under the bed. "No borrowing my body while I'm astral projecting this time. Got it?"

Angel wagged her tail and barked excitedly.

She wasn't sure if the puppy had actually understood her, since communication between them could be extremely fuzzy at best, but she hoped the dog had agreed.

Tasha lay down on her bed, facing upward, and put her hands on her stomach. She closed her eyes and lifted up out of her body.

It was a weird feeling, being separated from her body, but she was getting used to it. Astral travel was useful for many reasons, not the least of which being able to go through portals that were too small for your body to fit . . . or to sneak downstairs to spy on someone who thought you were doing your homework and didn't have astral sight because she wasn't a witch.

Tasha grinned.

She slipped through the floor, and then down through the floor again. Now she was back in the pet shop, but her mother was nowhere to be seen. Where . . . ?

Oh, probably in the storeroom. She couldn't do magic in this form, but that was all right, because she could just walk through the door anyway. She floated through it . . .

Tasha stared at the sight before her, not believing her eyes.

Sorkan Rena lay on the ground with her hands clasped over her stomach, in exactly the same position Tasha had just left her body. Off to the side, the curtain had been pulled away, uncovering a glowing swirl of light near the floor about half a foot wide, just big enough for a puppy to fit.

A portal! Tasha would have gasped if she'd currently had breath to gasp with. *Is that THE portal?*

Her mind raced. It would make perfect sense. She'd always assumed her mother had found Angel wandering around outside, but maybe she hadn't. Maybe she'd hired a witch to create a portal in their basement, in the hopes that something magical would sneak through. It wasn't exactly legal to create portals without filling out the appropriate paperwork, but her mother lived sort of on the edge of the law anyway. It would be just like her mother to think that a creature from another world would be a better shortcut to breeding familiars, even though most otherworld animals weren't magical.

Which means she lucked out with Angel. Tasha tried to swallow. *Which means she'll know if Angel goes through, because the portal will close. Which means she'll hire someone else to open another one. Probably paying a lot of money to do so.*

Sudden misgivings rose. Spying on her mother had seemed so funny before, but now it seemed dangerous. The new amulet Sorkan Rena had bought had to give her an astral projection power. If she was astral projecting right now, she was probably on the other side of that portal. And if she came back, she would see Tasha, because she'd have astral eyes.

Tasha turned to leave, but she was too late. Her mother was already coming through the portal.

Sorkan Rena caught sight of her, and immediately did a double take. Then she rolled her eyes heavenward and disappeared into her body.

"Spying on me was not what I meant when I said to do your homework, Tasha," she said, opening her eyes. "But all right, you can help me. Come downstairs."

Feeling sheepish, Tasha rose up through the ceiling, then up through the ceiling to the next floor. She went to her bedroom, and—

Oh, for crying out loud! Where was her body *now*?

This was not the best time to steal it, Angel! she fumed.

She hurried to the kitchen, and sure enough, there was her body, rummaging through a box of doggie biscuits and putting one in its mouth to bite on it. Tasha's body wagged its rear end excitedly.

Tasha put her astral hands on her hips and glared at the dog.

Tasha's body beamed and wagged its rear end further.

Tasha tried to shove the puppy's astral form out of her body, but the dog was being stubborn. She could have forced the issue, but she knew from astral lessons that shoving someone out of your body could hurt them, so it was better not to do it unless they were actually an invader, as opposed to a friend pulling a dumb prank.

Well, all right. Let's see how you like it!

Tasha whooshed upstairs and found Angel's empty body hiding under her bed. The disobedient puppy must have taken her body the instant she'd left it.

She dove in, and immediately everything looked huge around her. Crawling out from under the bed, Tasha jogged out the door and down the stairs with tiny puppy legs.

She found Angel now chewing on another doggie biscuit and tugging the loops on her sweater with great entertainment.

Tasha barked in annoyance.

"For crying out loud, what's taking so long?" Sorkan Rena called, coming up from the basement. The door opened. "Tasha, come on. You're going to help."

Angel stared at her enemy with wide, frozen eyes. In Tasha's body, she let out a small whimper.

"It's not going to be *that* much work," Sorkan Rena said, shaking her head in exasperation. "I just need you to help me find some animals on the other side that can see us in astral form. That will mean they have astral sight, which will mean they have magic, which will mean they'll be workable as familiars. If we give them a good scare, we can get them to go running toward the portal, and hopefully through it."

So that's what she's planning, Tasha thought. She had to admit, it was a good plan. Kind of mean to the animals, but it was no worse than, say, hunting, and that was legal. The only thing was, she had promised to get Angel back home. And if she did that, the illegal portal would close, and her mother would have to pay someone a bundle to open another one.

Putting her mother in a crabby mood was something Tasha was willing to do, for Angel's sake. But how was she going to pull it off in the first place? There was no way Sorkan Rena would cooperate, and if she dragged Angel-in-Tasha's-body downstairs, and the puppy saw the portal . . . there was no telling what Angel would do. She definitely wouldn't do anything as smart as waiting patiently till she and Tasha could sneak down there tonight.

"Come on," Sorkan Rena said, taking Tasha's body's arm.

The puppy yelped, and Tasha's body collapsed.

"Tasha?" her mother asked in alarm.

Finally! Tasha yanked out of the puppy's body and dove into her own. As she did, she caught sight of the puppy scurrying to hide behind the pantry door.

"I . . . I'm fine," Tasha said, scrambling up to her feet. "I just—slipped for a moment. Yeah. Let's go get started . . ."

"You didn't slip," Sorkan Rena said. "That was more like . . ."

She paused.

Tasha swallowed.

". . . more like an astral form leaving," she said slowly. "And the whimpering beforehand . . . and not talking . . ."

Darn it darn it darn it!

"Where's that dog?"

"Angel doesn't have magic," Tasha said desperately. "I was just, like . . . pretending to be Angel. Like, for a game. It's fine."

"Mm-hmm," her mother said, her eyes narrowed, not buying it for a second. "Have you been sheltering that dog this whole time?"

"Um, no?" Tasha said desperately. "She's just a stray. You found her outside somewhere, right?"

"Wrong," Sorkan Rena said. "She came through that portal. I had high hopes that meant she'd be magical, since magical beings are better at finding portals than non-magical ones. I see all my hopes were well-founded, and I was just being lied to this whole time."

Her voice was testy.

"Mom, she wants to go home," Tasha said desperately. "I promised her she could. We can bring other animals through first, so the portal will stay open in the future, but we have to send her back afterward. I promised."

"Go home?" Sorkan Rena said indignantly. "There's no question of that! You know how hard I've worked and how important this is. She can go back through the portal in astral form, but only once she'd been trained to find magical animals and drive them to us. As a dog, she'd be ideal to chase us cats or rabbits or rodents."

Tasha's heart plummeted. "But—but if you want to do that, the only way to keep her from jumping straight into the portal at the first opportunity—"

"—is a cage," Sorkan Rena said, nodding briskly. "Yes, she'll have to be in a cage. I'd say I'm sorry to take your pet away, but honestly, Tasha, you shouldn't have lied to me about this in the first place. I'm really very disappointed in you."

What am I going to do? Tasha thought frantically. *She'll make sure the cage is locked in some way that I can't unlock it—Angel will be in a cage for the rest of her life —she'll never get to go home to stay —*

An idea hit her.

Tasha flung the box of doggie biscuits that was still in her hand at the table, let out a howl to make it sound like she was sobbing, and wrenched away from her mother and ran to the living room. She ducked down into a crouched position, her face hidden in her knees.

Then she bolted out of her body and ran to where Angel was hiding in the pantry, trying desperately to climb the bottom shelf, which was too high up for her tiny body.

"Tasha?" her mother called, storming over to the living room. "Tasha! Throwing a fit does no good. I know you're disappointed, but—"

Tasha swiped her hand at Angel's face, trying to get her to take the hint. The puppy panted and wagged her tail, not getting the hint at all.

Oh, come on! You borrow my body whenever I DON'T want you to!

Tasha waved her hands and gestured at the box of doggie biscuits that was lying on top of the table. She waved her hand through the door to show that she was astral right now.

Angel stared at her, head cocked to the side.

Come ON, you dumb dog! Tasha thought, waving her hand through the door. *Get it!*

Her mother's voice continued lecturing, but it was not going to last much longer. She was going to notice Tasha wasn't moving.

Then Tasha realized what was wrong. Angel could *see* her. The puppy only borrowed her body when she thought she could get away with it—in other words, when she thought Tasha wasn't watching.

Tasha zoomed up through the ceiling, and then poked her head back down through it just in time to see the puppy's astral form race off toward the living room. Quick as a wink, Tasha leapt down and nabbed the puppy's body.

"Tasha," her mother was saying, "stop this sulking. Tasha, get up . . ."

Tasha raced down the open door to the basement, taking the stairs at a rapid pace. She got to the storeroom door, which was closed, but she could work magic in Angel's body because Angel was magical. She waved her paw, using the keylock spell, and the door opened. She darted through.

The portal was still uncovered, swirling light and awfully small. Tasha realized for the first time that Angel was a lot bigger than she had been a few weeks ago. Would she even still fit?

Tasha took a deep breath, and then she bolted forward. There was no use hesitating.

Squeeze squeeze squeeze—pop!

Her stomach was sore, enough that she suspected Angel's body was a little bit bruised, but she had just barely fit. Tasha lay just to the side of the portal, panting with her tongue hanging out, and waited.

"Now, stop sulking," Sorkan Rena was saying, and there was the sound of two sets of footsteps, one of them almost being dragged. "I realize you're disappointed, but it's not like she'll be ill-treated. You can even have one of the other animals for a pet later, as long as you're helpful and don't lie to me again. The tom, for instance."

The tom! Tasha wanted to laugh. *Even if that cat is magical, which we don't know for sure, he's a gigantic pest! No, thank you!*

The door to the storeroom closed, and her mother's voice kept lecturing from inside the room.

She snuck a peek at the edge of the portal. Had Angel noticed? Could Angel see what was near the floor? The dog seemed too agitated and worried to be noticing anything.

"Now, settle down," Sorkan Rena said. "Let me show you the first few steps inside the world. I think you'll see that's it's ideal for our needs, most of the animals being identical or similar to species on Earth . . ."

Angel suddenly went stiff. She had seen the portal. Tasha wanted to cheer.

". . . with luck, can interbreed them . . . Tasha?"

Tasha's body was wiggling its behind. Her voice barked loudly, the body went crashing backward, and the puppy's astral form exploded out of it, racing toward the portal.

"Oh, no!" Sorkan Rena shouted. "Tasha! What did you do?"

The puppy's astral form slid through the portal, and Tasha exited her body. Reuniting her astral form with her body, Angel paused to try to lick Tasha's face, found that it didn't work, and then barked happily and stood there, wagging her tail.

A hand reached through the portal and grabbed at her.

The puppy yelped and dodged just out of reach. She barked loudly, growled angrily, and sank her teeth into the offending hand. There was a terrible scream.

Barking loudly, Angel raced off through the forest.

Desolate, Tasha watched her go with a lump in her throat. She had known that Angel would go back home eventually . . . but she'd expected to at least be able to hug her farewell. This wasn't the ending she'd expected.

The hand drew back, and Sorkan Rena was glaring furiously through the portal. "Stay right there. Don't move. I need to put a firefly through or something."

Oh, to keep the portal open. Right, because I'm the only thing keeping it open now. Tasha sat obediently as she heard the faint sound of her mother opening the terrarium.

But then something occurred to her.

This was an illegal portal. If it were legal, her mother wouldn't have kept it a secret. If Sorkan Rena got away with doing things illegally now, she would keep taking bigger and bigger chances, and eventually end up in jail. Tasha didn't want that.

So she jumped through the portal as her mother turned around with a firefly in hand.

The portal sealed behind her and disappeared.

"*TASHA!*" her mother screamed, her face turning red. "Can you do one single thing I ask you to?!"

Tasha slipped into her body . . .

Ugh. She felt woozy, and she had a crashing headache. Angel hadn't been very careful at all about leaving it.

"If we're going to use a portal, we have to do it legally," she said, focusing cautiously around her headache. "We can't do it illegally, Mom. That's wrong, and it's dangerous."

"Do you know what that would entail?!" her mother exclaimed. "Do you know the licensing fees, and the taxes, and the quarantines? The quarantines alone are a nightmare! You're supposed to keep an animal from another world in quarantine for six weeks to make sure they aren't carrying any diseases that aren't in our world!"

Tasha paused. That sounded . . . like a really good idea, actually. She was more convinced than ever that this was right thing.

"It's bad enough that you keep conning those wannabes, Mom, and that's only a grey area," Tasha said carefully. "I'm willing to help, but only if you're doing things legally."

There was silence for a long moment.

"We don't have the money to do things legally," Sorkan Rena said tightly. "If we did, don't you think I would? If we had *one* provably magical animal, I could sell that to a witch, and maybe we could use that money, but you just got rid of the only one we've ever had."

Tasha looked away, uncomfortable. "Well, I'm sorry, but I had to keep my promise, and Angel was here illegally—"

She stopped. She stared at the shelf with her jaw dropping. She couldn't believe her eyes.

". . . because you cared more about some puppy than you did about me . . ." her mother was saying furiously.

"No, Mom!" Tasha cried. "Look! Look!"

She pointed at the locked rat cage, which was usually full of rats. Instead, there was a cat napping in there, with no rats in sight.

"That stupid tom!" Sorkan Rena exclaimed. "How in the world did he get in this room? Much less in there?!"

Tasha exploded in giggles. "Are you *sure* we don't have a provably magical animal? Because I think we do."

Sorkan Rena eyed the cat appraisingly. ". . . You know what? I'll call some witches in the morning."

A Knight's Tail

Sir Waylon Longhair Recalls the Battle of Hidden Sandbar

D. S. Coleman

I do not know how many summers it has been, nor do I remember all of them. There are some things I remember well, like the first time I met my prince, when old Chester dropped me at his feet. I remember that Prince Henry has always liked it when I brought him sticks, so much that if I bring him one, even now, he will throw it just so I can bring it to him again.

I remember well when old Chester told me about the people, about how they are different from us, and the story of the first knight. Before that, I always thought that people were just strange dogs, and tried my best to treat them, especially my prince, like part of my pack, even though they had patchy hair and couldn't really run very fast. Chester told me that they are different creatures from us, and that it is our responsibility to take care of them. He also told me that while they can't hear or smell as well as we dogs, they can remember things, many more things than we can.

That was when the old bulldog told me the story of the first knight, one thing I will never forget.

There was once a great king, a man called Artur, one destined to bring peace and prosperity to the land. He was so worthy, in fact, that one of us was chosen to be his companion, to watch over him, and to help him be a better king. That pup was called Lancelot. The music of the earth called to Lancelot and gave him great power and great responsibility.

Lancelot led Artur into the forest, where he dug and dug until Artur was able to see something glimmering underneath the dark soil, a great curved sword that glowed even under the dirt. He pulled the sword from the earth, and the powers of Grace revealed to Artur that it was a great gift—Calaburne, the Sword of the Worthy. It was not made of iron or bronze but of rock and bone and water and fire. Wherever Artur carried the sword, the land would flourish, and darkness and hatred would flee from its light.

Artur swore an oath to always strive to be worthy of this great gift, and Lancelot, at the same time, swore to always be loyal to his worthy king. The forces of the earth gave Lancelot majic, and he became the first knight of our kind, even though Artur would never know he was more than simply a brave and loyal companion. This is the way it has always been with us knights and the humans we serve.

Many summers passed as Artur fulfilled his destiny, and the land knew great peace and happiness. Lancelot did his best to protect and guide Artur, as he had sworn to do. It is said that Lancelot even once stood against Artur, defending his queen Gwenvere when others accused her of witchcraft and treason. Lancelot taught Artur to temper his might with wisdom, a lesson which was not forgotten for many summers and kings to come.

In time, however, the bright kingdom of Artur and Gwenvere faded, as lesser kings fell to greed and pettiness. The great sword Calaburne was lost, crumbled to dust. It is said that one day, a worthy king will rise and the great sword will return, and the land will know peace and happiness again. And so, the secret order of knights continue to serve the heirs of Artur, each chosen by the last, as I was chosen by old Chester.

"The majic is yours now, Waylon, the music of the earth is yours to hear," the old bulldog said to me. "Protect him, guide him, and serve him. He's a good boy. He will be a better king than his father."

I have been with my dear prince ever since that day, at his side through many summers. We grew from playing with sticks on the river bank to hunting geese and rabbits in the hills to floating the river in Henry's oar boat. It took quite some time for me to get used to floating on water. It made me so nervous, I wanted to just jump out and swim. Those days belonged to us alone, and while I can't remember how many summers there were, I cherish them all nonetheless. Then came the summer Henry's interests changed, the summer he started bringing girls on our adventures.

There were many girls, and most of them adored—or pretended to adore—my prince. There were some that I liked, but many I did not. Luckily, Henry seemed to trust my judgement, and before long, only sweet Louisa held his attention. I may have liked her even more than Henry did. She was always so kind to me and never felt false or untrue.

Yes, I remember that summer well, the summer of Louisa, and that fateful day in what they say was the thirteenth year of the Ogre war.

Henry rowed us, Louisa and I, to the big sandbar downriver from our home, a place where the currents were tricky, where no other boats ever went. It was a nice place, and a nice day for a picnic in the shade of the old oak that grew on the upriver side. He had promised Louisa a picnic to make up for the one that had been spoiled by rain a few days before.

We had fun playing in the sand, and I learned that Louisa liked sticks as much as Henry. She threw one stick so many times, I had to carry it off because I was sure her arm must be getting tired. Henry impressed Louisa by playing his flute and throwing his small axe at the remains of an old boat. He even taught her how to throw the axe as well, and they had fun hurling it and watching me run over and pull it from the wreck with my teeth and return it. I've always thought it would be nice to have paws like people have, to be able to hold things or throw them. But then, I wouldn't be able to run very fast with such odd paws.

Henry laid out a big old bear skin in the sand, and he and Louisa sat on it, enjoying the picnic while I chased shore birds.

Birds are not to be trusted. Squirrels neither. Devious plotting little . . . grrrrr . . . I'm sorry, where was I? Oh yes . . . the sandbar.

Henry and Louisa had finished their meal and were lying on the bear skin when I spotted the ogres. There were three of them, on a clumsy raft floating down the middle of the river. I fought my urge to bark at them, realizing that I should go and warn my prince instead.

As quickly as I could, I ran to Henry and Louisa. Henry knew right away that something must be wrong. Sweet Louisa held me in her lap and tried to calm me while Henry got to his feet, searching for the source of my panic. It was only a moment before he saw the ogres, drifting by in the current of the river. He crept carefully back toward Louisa and I. The serious look on his face must have frightened Louisa. She pulled me closer. I caught the slight scent of fear on the breeze.

"Stay here, Waylon," he said to me, "they likely haven't seen us. You're a good boy for not barking." He rubbed my head. He always liked to rub my head. I have to admit, I like it too, and not just because I would do anything to make my prince happy.

We three stayed low, as Henry dug through our bags for his pistol. The ogres passed us by, pushed away by the swirling currents near the sandbar's edge. It was a good thing Henry had pulled his boat into the brush when we got there or we would have been easy to spot.

"What are they doing here?" Louisa asked in a quiet voice. "Ogres don't come this far south. How did they get past the garrison?"

"They must be fleeing the war," Henry replied as he shook his head. "Don't know if I blame them."

It was the first time I ever heard Henry speak of the war that way. His father hated the ogres. So did most people. To this day, I don't know how the war started, but I remember that no one seemed to want it to end. The war was bitter. So much hate, I don't know how to even explain it. Many of our friends had gone off to fight, friends we would never see again. Henry's own older brother had been lost, the winter before I met my prince.

Henry and Louisa relaxed, and she fell back into his arms. Henry still kept his pistol close. I did not relax and decided to spend the rest of my day watching the water vigilantly for more ogres. I paced the sand, keeping my ears up, my nose to the wind, watching for the slightest movement, fighting my urge to chase the scheming shore birds.

No more boats came, and after a time, I wandered back to my prince and his lovely companion. I had only just neared them when I heard a sound from the tall grass on the downriver edge of the sandbar. Something was crawling our way. I let out a loud and angry bark, instinctively. Henry sat bolt upright as the three figures in the grass got to their feet and ran at us. It was the ogres.

One of them, a big one, had a musket and fired at me as I ran at them. Those fire-sticks always did scare me. Even today they make me jump. I thought I was shot, but it was just the noise and fire from the thing. Another blast sent me running toward Louisa. I realized quickly that the second thunder clap wasn't from the ogres but from Henry's pistol. The big ogre fell down and never got up again.

I felt a sharp pain as an ogre arrow grazed me. If not for my thick hair, I may have fallen right then. I reached my prince, scrambling over the remains of the now-ruined picnic, dodging bits of broken glass from a shattered jars and dishes. Quick-thinking Henry had snatched up the big bear skin and sheltered Louisa and himself behind it. Ogre arrows are crude, and there was no way one would make it through that bear's hide. Unfortunately, ogre arrows are also poisoned.

I was already feeling sick, as I reached the safety of the bear skin. The ogres charged toward us, growing ever closer. They would be on us quickly if we did not act. Henry's pistol had only one shot, and there was no time to reload now. I tried to ignore the sick feeling as I readied to attack, wondering if I could get one off its feet. I accidentally stepped in something sticky as I stumbled to the edge of the bear hide. Honey. Even though I felt sick and anxious, my tail wagged at the sight of it. Henry had commandeered a big jar of honey from the kitchen for our picnic.

My eyes caught Henry's as he glanced at the broken jar and then to the axe still stuck in the old boat hull. It was clear in an instant we were thinking the same thing. Without a thought, I dashed out from safety and retrieved Henry's axe. He took it with a nod of thanks and grabbed up the broken jar, smearing honey first on Louisa, then some on me, then himself, and finally, on his axe with his now-bloody paw.

You see, ogres are highly allergic to bees. To them, honey is poison. The beeswax and pork fat used as lubricant in Henry's pistol barrel is the reason the first ogre fell so quickly. Even cut badly by the broken glass, Henry's first thought was to protect Louisa and me with the honey.

Henry peered out from behind the skin and saw the bigger of the remaining beasts scrambling forward through the deep sand. It was huge, though not as big as the first one, with sharp yellow teeth to match its angry yellow eyes. My prince waited, the axe cocked in his paw as the creature neared. I could almost smell its breath when I saw the look in Henry's eye change. I jumped out from behind the hide and growled loudly at the thing, distracting it as Henry let his axe fly.

The axe sank deep into the chest of the ogre. Black streaks appeared on its skin. It fell, like the other, never to stir again. One last arrow flew at us, but it was from farther away this time as the smallest ogre was now fleeing frantically. The danger passed, I fell down onto the sand. The poison was getting to me.

Henry sat next to me as his eyes began to fill with tears. He knew that one of the poisonous arrows had grazed me and that I likely would not survive. His heart filled with rage. He left me there with sweet Louisa, retrieved his axe, and set out in pursuit. My eyes began to close, and the world became very far away. All became dark, warm, and calm.

All my worries and fears melted away, replaced by a quiet warmth, a feeling of peace, like lying by the fireside on a cold winter night. I could hear the gentle music of the earth, the music of everything. For a moment, I *was* everything, but I was also me, and time seemed to mean nothing. It was time to rest, for a moment, for eternity.

"Protect him, guide him, and serve him," a voice broke the still darkness. Music and the sound of a drum grew louder, and louder, and louder.

That day was the first and only time I ever used the majic. My eyes opened as my heart began to beat again.

I dashed from the arms of the incredulous Louisa and ran like the wind to my prince. I passed him and reached our quarry, knocking the ogre to the ground with one leap. There must have been some remaining honey on my forepaw because the creature fell down screaming and holding its face where I had struck it.

I had the beast at my mercy. I ran around it, barking furiously. Henry was fast approaching, axe in hand. We would finish off this last ogre together. His father would be so proud of such a great victory. These three ogres would likely have their heads mounted on the king's walls by the time of the next feast.

Then I smelled it. Fear. It was the same scent of fear I smelled on the breeze, before the battle even began.

I did not know that ogres could feel fear. I did not know that ogres could feel anything, but this one did. I could sense it, this profound fear. This child had felt little else in her life. This monster was really no more than a girl, running from the fear that ruled her life. It wasn't just a fear of us that I could sense, it was a fear of everything.

I felt a great sadness for her, though she had almost killed me. If my prince knew what I knew, he would have felt the same. I had to stop him from killing her. I had to make him understand.

Henry reached us and raised his axe high. I did the only thing I could do. I stood between my prince and the ogre girl. The poison still weakened me, but I stood strong, summoned all the majic that I had, and did something I had never done before and have never done again since that day. I spoke with the voice of a human.

"Mercy," I said. "Please, my prince. Please Henry. Mercy. She is just a girl."

I do not know if I actually spoke the words aloud or if it was just the majic, but Henry heard me. He knew what I knew. His anger turned to pity as he dropped his axe in the sand.

The ogre girl was spared. I did what I could to calm her and lick the honey from her wound, but her eye was injured badly. After some time, Henry and Louisa brought the remainder of the roast pheasant, which the girl eventually accepted as her fear of us began to wane. She spoke—in what little she knew of the common tongue —of her life and how she had arrived there.

An orphan, she had escaped the war by tagging along with two deserters from the ogre army, two who frightened and abused her as much as any of the horrors of war had. They had managed to slip past the garrison in the night and had been hiding in the tall reeds until they spotted Henry's oarboat. The deserters thought we would be easy prey. She wanted none of it, wanting only to keep moving, but feared them too much to protest. Thanks to them, she had almost died, alone and afraid in the sand.

She devoured the bones of the pheasant, picking them from the meat as she told her tale. Realizing that she liked bones, I dug up an ox bone I had buried near the big tree and gave it to her. She gratefully accepted and tore the big bone to shreds with her sharp teeth.

Louisa bandaged her wounded eye as best she could, and Henry drew her a map of a safe passage to the great southern marsh. There were no men living in the marsh, only bears and boars and turtles and deer and fowl and of course . . . devious wretched squirrels. Grrrrr . . .

Though the majic had mostly healed my wound, she gave us a root that helped lessen the effects of the poison. We parted, no longer enemies but not quite friends. Henry and Louisa told no one of the events of that day, though we are forever proud of our prince's triumph.

There was a great victory that day at the sandbar, a victory for mercy and honor, but not without some loss. The playful boy that I knew, my beloved prince, passed on, and the man Henry was born. In time, he and Princess Louisa were able to soften the king's heart of stone with mercy and wisdom and the long war came to an end.

The majic saved us all that day. While the venom of that arrow still pains me from time to time, I have lived long enough to see my prince become a great man, wise and just, the man who brought peace to our land.

And today, my pup, today is a great day for us all. I will be only a little sad to miss it. They will be looking for me, Henry and Princess Louisa, perhaps even Ciarra, the one-eyed ogre woman who is among the emissaries, but I hope they will not delay Henry's coronation on my account.

The shiny ceremony will have to go on without us. You and I must attend to something much more important, one last quest for an old knight. We must make our way to the big oak in the center of the great wood. There we will find what was lost long ago.

You see, the music of the earth calls to me from the forest, as it once called to Lancelot, as it will call to you some day. It proclaims that a worthy king has come again. We have some digging to do, pup, and one more thing to retrieve for my dear Henry.

Long may he reign.

BONDED

MAX FLORSCHUTZ

Queen Aneira Aren swept into the council chambers, head held high and arms folded in front of her as was the peaceable way. The hubbub of conversation, kept to a low rumble by the buffering fields, dropped away as the more attentive members of the court noticed her appearance, the effect creating ripples that spread across the entire expanse of the chamber.

Though she kept her expression serene, the sight of the chambers filled with so many representatives of her people still warmed her heart. Long gone were the days of her father's father's father, during which the chambers of old had been hidden deep beneath the soils of Earth and seen fit to host barely a tenth the number that they held today. Her father's father had seen the rise of the first great expansion, and the removal of their ancient halls from their place deep beneath the stones of Earth to the endless realms beyond mankind. Her father's time had seen the rebuilding of the famed ancient hall, modernizing and expanding it to fit the needs of their growing people. Her husband—the late king—had passed the edicts that had set in stone the fusion of old and new, assuring that the great chamber would always have a mark of its roots.

And now, in the twilight years of her reign, it was growing small once more. Perhaps one of her successors would widen it again. Or expand upon the smaller Chambers of Reckoning that were becoming popular across the Tylwyth Teg—though the great chamber would always be the beating heart of their kind.

The chamber stilled as she approached the low dais, the foremost part of the chamber, where her and her late husband's thrones sat. His was cold, empty Earth-stone, now, and the sight of it made her heart ache with grief, briefly washing away the warmth of her people. It was too soon, but it would always be too soon.

Still, she could bear it. She had to. Her people needed their queen. She swept out onto the dais, following the well-worn steps of queens past. Hundreds of her kin and kind waited at attention before her, standing respectfully with their hands crossed before them in the sign of peace, fingers relaxed—though a few instead held their palms together with their heads bowed, the sign of sympathy for the loss of the king, and her eyes caught sight of at least three others with both palms up and fingers laid across one another, the sign of sorrow. She came to a stop in front of her throne and bowed her head, returning the sign of sorrow before sitting.

The throne was ancient, carved from the stone of Earth long before, when mankind had first driven the fairies from the land above to the space below. As she sat, ancient lines of power inscribed into the stone lit up, symbols and patterns of ancient magics spreading out from her seat and lighting the entire grand chamber. Magic meant to both empower and remind the rulers of the folk of their duty to their people, and bound the Tylwyth Teg to their core, facilitating the favors, fealties, and laws that governed the folk.

Around her the assemblage began taking their seats, the sounds of their shuffling hidden by the baffle spells. Wings shimmered in iridescent colors across the chamber, some showing momentary discomfort or concern, others simply adjusting their positions. As she waited for the assemblage to settle, Queen Aren tapped at the modern adaptation made to her throne: a small touch display floating above the stone. A wonderful invention taken from the realm of man that, when mixed with the magic of the folk, was a truly useful tool. Some disdained the new advances that had been championed by her late husband, but . . . she thought they were marvelous tools.

The faint tapping of her slim fingers against the display was echoed by the clicking of claws on stone from her right, her bondmount moving up beside the throne. She felt the effort it took the ancient beast to make the trip—her hip was bothering her again and would need another visit from the palace physician—but her presence soothed the ache that had again reared its head with the sight of her late husband's throne.

"Faithful friend, Orwena," Aren said, ceasing her search of the display and reaching up to pet her bond's head. The war corgi was of ancient, royal stock, and a prime example of the breed even in her old age. "Rest beside me." Only by Aren's leave did Orwena lie on her belly beside the throne, panting slightly, her head resting just above the stone armrest.

Once there had been two such royal bondmounts occupying the throne room. But Niclas' bondmount was gone, having followed him faithfully to the grave shortly after the king's passing, the poor corgi's heart broken.

A wet nose touched her arm, Orwena sensing Aren's heartbreak through the bond and reacting. Aren reached out and stroked her faithful companion's head once more. "Thank you, Orwena." The ache faded slightly, and she turned her gaze back to the display along the throne's arm, a change in its report calling for her attention.

House Hier's lord was out of place. They'd taken a position closer to her throne, shoving one of the lower houses whose place they'd claimed further back and upward. Her wings twitched, one of the few tells she'd never been able to hide despite her best efforts.

They chose to move now, so soon after Niclas' death. Holding back a sigh, Aren tapped an ancient sigil in the left arm of the throne. The intertwining knots carved on the chamber's pillars glowed as ancient magic took hold, projecting her voice to every part of the hall.

"House Hier," she said, keeping her voice clear and steady. "It would seem that in your haste to be seated in our chambers today, you have taken a place in the wrong circle." A tap at some of the ancient sigils in the stone brought ancient magics to bear, the lord of House Hier—along with his seats and accompaniments—changing places with one of the poorer houses they'd pushed upward. Other high houses, Aren noted, sent glares of disapproval Hier's way as they appeared in their proper position. "It is understandable that in light of so much that has happened recently, and in your urge to please the royal house, that this error has been made." An out, one that would let Hier's ruler save face. "But I hope it will not happen again." And a warning.

She had hoped to give the chambers more time to compose themselves before opening the assembly, but House Hier's bold move had made that impossible. Holding back another sigh and ignoring the pain in her heart, Queen Aren stood.

She kept her hands still, slim fingers interwoven as a sign that she was intending to speak at length. "My fae," she said, holding back the faint urge of her voice to crack. It was "my fae" now. No longer "our". "I thank you for heeding the call to gather in our great chambers today. I know these last few weeks have been trying for each of us. The passing of a great king weighs on all our hearts, and not just mine." Her wings twitched once more, and behind her Orwena let out an almost inaudible whine.

"Life is not complete without sorrow," she continued, casting her eyes over those houses nearest to her. "But we have persevered through greater sorrows before, and we will continue to do so. Though we will miss our king, we will carry on, ensuring that the future of the folk is great indeed."

She paused, running her eyes over the middle levels of the great chamber and then at long last looking to the high levels. "The future of our folk is why we have gathered here today. Through the last generations of kings since we fled the Realm of Man, the folk have prospered. We have grown like never before. We have found refuge in new realms, realms untouched by man or others of their kind. We have reached out into the stars and found resources and supply beyond our wildest means. We have made contact with kin once lost. Our ships sail the void between worlds. Our people dance among the grasses under stars that are new. And our windows to the Realm of Man have given us great strides in our understanding of the world of science as well as magic." She flared her thumbs, a sign of pause, and many in the assemblage responded with polite applause, striking the backs of one hand with the fingers of the other.

"Such transition has not always been easy," she continued once the applause had died down. "We are a folk bound by tradition, and each change brings a new needle to the tapestry of our culture, our people, and our way of life." Again her wings twitched; the tapestry line had been Niclas' idea, before his passing, as he'd helped prepare her for the current assemblage. "Time and time again, we have gathered to discuss the greater laws and rules that bind the folk, at the behest of changes small or changes great."

Good, she thought as she saw knowing nods from the assemblage. The reminder of similar decisions weighed in the past would give weight to her words. "Many of you sit in these chambers today because of decisions that were made to increase the number of houses or to change the laws of tribute. To give equity to those who were able to earn it. To bring matters to the king—and in certain circumstances, force a decision to be made, but not in the fashion of the kings and queens of old."

She paused just long enough to let the assembly's minds linger on the punishments of old before continuing. "We have changed for the better of the folk," she said. "Adapted. But some traditions we have kept. Held firmly, even as we have moved forward. For symbol, or for cause. The lower dais of this great chamber, for one, we shall never remove, not until the folk have changed so much that they no longer need this rule. The thrones hewn of stone made from Earth. These things we have kept, as reminders of our past, our heritage, our order, and our roots."

More nods from the assemblage. Niclas had been right about her words. Just as he always had been. "Today we assemble by request of a number among you, a petition that was laid down before the untimely passing of my husband." A few in the assembly showed discomfort with referencing him as such rather than as king, but Niclas had been a joint ruler with her his entire life, and she was not about to let them forget it. "A question of whether or not it is time for one of the old ways to be set aside. Of whether we should continue to levy taxes for the support of bondmounts."

She gave Orwena a pointed glance. The corgi's tail gave a tiny wag, a spark of warmth coming across their bond.

"You have heard the debates," she said, bringing her eyes back. "Discussion has been given, and voices have been heard prior to this assembly. Today we will make a decision: whether to continue the bond program or end it entirely. Once, there would have been no question of such. The bond-levy was necessary. Our bondmounts were our loyal companions, dutifully serving us in times of war or desperation. We tell our children of the bravery of the great war mount Cian, who bore the king back from the battle lines after war with others of our kind, or the loyalty that saved Clan Teg."

Again she paused, and again members of the assembly nodded in concert. "Once requiring that each clan or home levy in support of our bondmounts, it has been said, made sense. But now, many of the houses have done away with the bonding. I quote: 'We have no need of stables when those who protect our people ride forth in cockpits of fighters or clad in walking armatures.' Their words do ring true . . . to a certain extent."

Again her wings twitched, but this time in anticipation of what was about to come. "Those who have lent their voices in support of ending the levy argue that we no longer need our bondmounts. That the breed that has supported us for so long is no longer needed. They have pointed back at our own recent history, noting that the corgi no longer serves us in battle, nor do they ride alongside us to such. The last three generations of rulers, they have argued, had no need of a bondmount save in ceremony only. That they no longer have a purpose when they cannot, as they have stated, 'be expected in any way to model the image of Cian in saving the lives of our great royal family.'"

The nods she saw this time were from those who supported ending the levy, though she noted that the one whose words she'd quoted looked skeptical, unsure of where her words led.

"I disagree," she said simply. "I fear that in not having a bondmount of their own, many have mistaken or misunderstood. For you see, my fae, my bondmount has indeed saved my life and aided our kingdom. On more than one occasion."

A rustle of surprise swept through the crowd, wings shifting as various houses turned to one another. "Do not worry," she said, shifting her hands momentarily to a gesture of peace before returning to the interwoven position. "I shall explain. My fae, I give you three moments in my life to consider. Please listen, and you will understand."

"Aneira! Aneira! Come back! Aneira!" Her father's voice echoed in her ears as she rode Orwena deeper into the woods, fleeing from the unwelcome news that had pulled her whole world out from under her. "Aneira!"

She didn't turn back. Instead she buried her head deeper in Orwena's neck, trusting her bondmount to carry her safely forward deeper into the forest as she exhausted every one of her tears.

Father is sending me away. Far away. Away from her home. Away from her clan. Away from the beautiful world they'd claimed deep in the void, with its wondrous stars and brilliant vistas. Away from running through fields of moss and grass barefoot, from hunting smallbeasts with her mother or helping her father establish the house.

No, not sent away. Sold.

Father had tried to make it sound kind. She'd known that he'd been laboring extra hard through the last season, accruing favor after favor with other clans and even high houses. She'd even helped him with some of them.

If only she'd realized that those favors were going to be used to secure her betrothal to the son of the king. Sending her away from her folk and everything she loved.

"I never would have helped him," she said, the words bitter with betrayal. Beneath her the smooth motions of Orwena slowed, and she felt her faithful companion's neck shift as her head tilted. When Aneira opened her own eyes she found one of the corgi's looking back at her, worried.

"It's okay, girl," she said, hiccupping slightly as she stroked the dog's cheek. "It's not your fault." She sat up, noticing that the formal—and expensive—dress she'd been asked to don had been mussed during her flight from the betrothal meeting, stained by brushes with blades of grass and the leafy ferns that dominated so much of her world. The subtle shading, once meant to look like a shifting array of leaves, was now smeared and the effect broken. "Now . . . where are we?"

Aneria peered up at the towering trunks, searching for familiar marks on the bark that would serve as clues to what part of the forest she'd run to in her mad dash. When she didn't find any, she patted Orwena on the side rather than panic, urging her bondmount to move forward to a new vantage point.

"I can't have gone too far." The words came out broken by hiccups. Just looking up at the vast forest growing around her, with stern, strong trunks and mushroom-like leaves, made her want to cry again. Father was sending her away. She'd never see any of it again. She'd be stuck in the king's palace, never able to leave, and then she'd be married when she and the prince came of age and she'd still never be able to leave, and she'd live her life trapped—

No.

"Maybe if I just don't go back home and hide out here, Father will give up. Mother will convince him it isn't worth it. And the king will leave, along with his dumb son." A glance upward showed a familiar pattern of forks in the branches matched by bark colors she knew. She'd raced almost halfway to the river.

"That's what I'll do." One of her shoes was home to a tracking spell though she wasn't supposed to know that—and she kicked it off, followed by the other. "I'll run and hide. Just you and me, Orwena." The corgi let out a quiet *yip* at the sound of her name. "We can cross the river. We know just the place, don't we, girl?" Another *yip*, and she felt Orwena's agreement through the bond.

"Then it's settled." She gave Orwena a soft squeeze with her heels, and the bond-mount raced forward, darting through the underbrush and heading for the river. Though it wasn't much of a river, not truly. The treefolk didn't call it a river, and neither did the fishers. It was a creek. But since she'd never seen a *true* river, she called it a river anyway.

She wasn't supposed to cross it. If she wanted to see the other side, she was to be careful and take a skimmer, or better yet a flyer. Using her own wings to fly across wasn't safe. Whyents, a many-winged bird that hunted smallbeasts in the area, would attack any of the folk they saw in the air, considering them prey. But she'd bribed one of the treefolk to show her a hidden crossing, a place where the waters were slow and deceptively shallow. She and Orwena could ford the river there.

She had almost reached the edge of the river, able to see the smooth stones that made up the shore through the thick brush, when Orwena suddenly slowed, her muscles tensing and ears standing straight up. Aneira froze, a spike of sudden *interest* and *worry* coming to her through the bond. She listened, her own ears straining as Orwena's twisted and turned, but she couldn't make anything suspicious out over the sound of the nearby creek.

Orwena clearly could however, and she trusted her bondmount. Aneira bent down, one hand reaching for the slinger she kept holstered along Orwena's side—and her fingers closed on empty air. A curse almost escaped from her lips as she recalled her mother's insistence that she leave the slinger at home for the "event."

Leave a slinger at home. Who does that? Dead fairies, that's who! So she was unarmed, but Orwena had zeroed in, her head pointing downstream, and Orwena was easily worth several slingers and ready to bolt at her command. All that was to be determined was whether to run toward danger or away from it.

It was not a hard decision to make. She crouched low, grasping the fur tightly around Orwena's neck, and whispered the command Orwena had been waiting to hear: "Go *get* it."

Orwena was off like a shot, bolting beneath the tall ferns. Aneira rode smoothly, rocking with each bounding undulation of the dog's body, her senses alert for any sign of the threat. They broke free of the brush with a single leap, Orwena landing atop a large stone by the edge of the river then bounding downstream. Further from the crossing that would take them to safety, but closer to—

She heard it now. The yips of another bondmount, mixed with lower growls. Then a keening cry from somewhere around the next bend, one that made her blood run cold: a whyent.

For a bondmount to be engaging with one of the large birds, someone had to be threatened. A child from one of the nearby outposts, maybe.

"Orwena, attack!" Their speed surged at her command, the corgi leaping from stone to stone along the river's edge. Ahead the waters narrowed, rushing fast as they swept around a bend . . . exactly the kind of place a fairy looking to fly from one side to the other would choose to cross, absent the danger of a whyent.

They rounded the bend, the other corgi's yips growing more frantic, and Aneira saw exactly what she'd feared: a wet bondmount standing astride a small island of rocks near the middle of the river, growling and barking as it tried to hold back a ferocious six-winged whyent. Someone had foolishly attempted to fly across the river, the whyent had struck, and their bondmount had swum to the island to save them.

But the bondmount's sides were already matted with blood, courtesy of the whyent's long, wicked beak, and Aneira threw one hand out, uttering a string of words her mother and father both were unaware that she knew. Water flowed upward from the stream as Orwena launched them both over it, crystalizing into a thin, razor-sharp blade of ice.

Orwena landed squarely on the whyent's back, the bird letting out a startled *squawk* as the sudden weight drove it down. Its belly hit the shallow water with a splash, and Aneira leapt, soaring over the creature's many-jointed shoulders, spreading her wings to land atop the long neck just behind its head.

With a shout, she shoved the ice blade deep into the back of its skull. The whyent let out a startled *screech*, the body jerking as her sword punctured its brain . . . and then collapsed as she yanked the blade to one side, breaking it against the side of the bird's skull.

She flared her wings as the beast slumped to the side, steadying herself with a quick wingbeat that she hid just as quickly once she was safely on the rocky island, scanning the sky for sign of any other whyents that might have seen the brief flash of membrane. Her heart felt as though it was pounding a thousand beats a minute, a faint buzz in her pointed ears as blood rushed through them. *I just killed a whyent.* It was not so uncommon an occurrence, but most who hunted the bird usually did so from the safety of a flyer or with weapons and spells far grander than a sword.

The bondmount she'd saved seemed as shocked as she felt, clearly taken aback by her sudden appearance. It didn't take it long to recover, however, and it growled, baring teeth.

Orwena responded, jumping off of the whyent's back to splash in the shallow waters next to Aneira and growl in kind. Aneira lowered her center of balance, ready to jump back if the bondmount was so untrained as to attack its savior in the heat of the moment. It was, she noted, a very well cared-for bondmount, its body muscled and its fur shining despite its injuries.

"Glyr! Hold! She is a friend!" The voice was unfamiliar but had an aura of command to it, and the bondmount immediately ceased its growls, though it stayed on guard.

From behind the bondmount, between some boulders, a fairy appeared, limping. A boy, near her own age given that he showed the signs of entering his second growth spurt, his wings almost too long for his height. He didn't look familiar, but then she hardly knew every boy—or young man, really—from the surrounding outposts, much less her own hometown. The cut of his clothing—and the appearance of his bondmount—suggested that he had influence. Which made his injuries all the more galling. One of his wings was bent, and there was a glowing magic seal on his forehead where he'd gotten a gash, either from the attack or what was likely a crash-landing on the rocky island.

He was carrying a slinger, she noted, and a nice one. Partially loaded, so he hadn't been completely helpless.

"My thanks," he said, leaning his slinger against his bondmount's side and then holding out a hand, palm up, in a show of peace. "I hadn't—"

She ignored the open palm and stalked toward him. "What were you *thinking*?" The words burst forth unbidden, and she had a vague sense that something in her had just given way, frustration and anger at her father's betrayal suddenly boiling over in a way that perhaps wasn't *quite* fair. But she *had* just slain a whyent in order to save the young man's life. A little thing like decorum wasn't going to be enough to hold her back. Or the sudden warning growl of his bondmount, which he stilled with a single motion of his hand. Still, he at least had the good sense to look shocked as she bore down on him.

"Is your head full of *tuft*?" she asked, coming to a stop an arm's length away. "Did your parents never teach you not to fly near a whyent's hunting grounds? That our wings strike them as the same as the smallbeasts they hunt? You're lucky to be alive!"

She stepped to one side, getting a better look at his injured wing. There were several broken veins, as well as a tear in the thin material that made up the fold. "You're lucky it didn't rip your wing off!"

"I saw it coming, luckily, in the reflection of the water." He turned, trying to keep his wings away from her, but her hands snapped out, grasping his injured wing before he could pull away. His bondmount let out a sharp bark of warning, but he raised a hand and it quieted again, sitting as she ran her fingers over the damaged limb.

"Lucky or not, you were foolish to fly at all," she said, eyeing the breaks in his wing. He wouldn't lose it, but it needed care or else it would simply continue to ooze blood. "This needs to be set. It will hurt."

"Wait, you—?" His question was cut off by a sharp gasp of pain as she tugged his wing between her hands, straightening the bend. His bondmount stiffened again, but didn't otherwise attack. Well-trained then, enough to know the difference between an attack and someone providing healing.

"There," she said without letting him finish his question. "That's straight now. I have some medical salve in my . . ." Her mind caught up with her current state, and the "formal" harness Orwena wore that lacked her usual bags with any of her supplies. "Or rather, I usually have some. Today is . . . It doesn't matter. There's a treefolk village nearby that will have some."

"Well, thank you," he said as she let go of his wing. "But—"

The buzzing in her ears hadn't quite faded. "What were you *doing* out here?" she asked, stepping close and putting on her best royal expression. It wasn't hard, since she and the boy were almost the same height. "If you aren't capable of avoiding whyents, do you know about any of the other dangers that the forest holds?"

"Probably not," he admitted with a somewhat sheepish look. "I'm realizing now that this might have been ill-advised."

"Ill-advised?" She changed her look to one she'd seen her mother give her siblings —and her—when they'd done something overly foolish. She'd used it once or twice before with some success. "There are much more dangerous largebeasts out there than whyents, once you pass the wards on the edges of the outposts. Things that would hunt us with no more effort than we would a baby smallbeast! And you only have a slinger?"

"You don't even have that," he pointed out.

"*I* just slew a whyent with a magical sword made of ice," she said, putting an emphasis on her ability to cast the spell.

"I'll admit that was spectacularly stellar," he said, using a term that sounded like a positive but wasn't familiar to her. "And I give you full credit in that regard, but . . ." He shook his head. "No, that was amazing. You were amazing."

The compliment came as a surprise. Maybe he wasn't *quite* so tuft-headed. "Well . . . thank you. But what are you doing out here if you don't even know to avoid a whyent? And who let you out?"

"I . . . uh . . ." He gave her an embarrassed grin, the kind her brothers gave her parents when they'd been caught with hands sticky from honey. "I wasn't so much let out as I snuck off."

"Oh." She'd heard of tuft-heads like him, butterflies whose parents didn't let them outside of the compound for their own safety. "You escaped? You're running away?"

"What? No. I just . . . I wanted to help fix something that I think was my fault."

"Well that's vague. Did you set the stable on fire or something?"

"No?" He gave her a curious look. "Do you mean to cover an escape, or to run from it? And why would you—?"

"No reason!" she interrupted, her ears flushing. "How does running away help fix something?"

"I'm not running away!" he said, throwing his hands up and spreading his wings, then wincing. "And . . ." He glanced at his bondmount, then muttered a spell of sealing and moved his hand over one of its injuries, glowing magic helping to close the shallow wound. "There was a misunderstanding, and I wanted to help. I thought if I could find her before anyone else could or before she got too far away, maybe I could explain things and, I don't know, help."

All of the sudden everything fit together like the motions of an exquisitely complicated dance, and Aneira's stomach did a flip, her whole body feeling like it had the time her siblings had dared her to jump from the tallest branch of the family manor and fall all the way to the ground. The unfamiliar face, the well cared-for bondmount, the rich clothing, and then what he'd just said . . .

He seemed to have realized it as well, his eyes going to the smudged and dirty dress that was still *clearly* meant to have been formal wear before its adventure, then back to her face.

They spoke at the same time, their words overlapping.

"Prince Aren?"

"Lady Coslott?"

"Oh. Oh no. I—" Her thoughts felt like a bundle of sticks dropped into the river and jumbled around one another in the white waters.

"Wait!" Prince Aren cut her off, his hands outspread in a sloppy but formal gesture of pleading. He looked almost afraid. Panicked. "Please, let me speak first. I'm sorry."

She almost staggered backward but settled for shaking her head as her wings twitched, extending halfway out. "What?"

"I'm sorry! I didn't . . . I hadn't . . ." He let out a sigh and shook his head, sagging as he looked at the ground. "I'm sorry." He looked back up at her, straightening once more and repeating himself with more firmness. "I'm sorry. I wasn't . . . made aware . . . that you had not been told what was happening. I thought maybe once I met and spoke with you we could both discuss it. I didn't know otherwise, until my father told me we were leaving last week to come to your realm. And I wanted to reassure you," he added quickly, "that we do not have to go through with it in the end. I cannot go against my father, but . . ." He shook his head. "I would like to get to know you, but I did not know you had no idea I was arriving, or that this was happening. And if you truly, truly do not wish this to happen, I will make certain that it does not. You may have to come to the palace for a few years, but there is nothing that says we must marry. If you do not wish it, as soon as I am king, I will release you. And I'm truly sorry your father deceived you concerning my—our—arrival. I . . . was led to believe that you were aware of the purpose of our visit."

And then, to her surprise, he bowed. Low. "You have my humblest apology."

The buzzing was back in her ears, but she hesitated, unsure. His confession was a bit of a surprise, as was his manner, but . . . She'd met others before who had acted in a similar manner just to get close to her father. But . . .

She glanced back at Orwena, the prince still deep in his bow, and felt for the bond. Orwena had always been a good judge of character.

And her boundmount just seemed content, unalarmed by the prince or his bondmount. Seeing the glance, the corgi moved forward and stuck her nose against Aneira's arm, nudging her forward as if to make her thoughts on the matter clear.

"I . . . apology accepted, Prince Aren?" He peered up from his bow as she offered him one of her own. "And . . . I owe you an apology. For being a tuft-head and running off to—"

The rest of her formal apology died on her tongue as he cut her off. "No," he said with a shake of his head. "It must have been a great shock. I was unsure when my father told me, and that was months ago. To find out on the day of—"

"Wait." Now it was her turn to interrupt again. "You knew months ago? And you didn't send a message?" But she knew the answer before Prince Aren even spoke.

"My father said not to, that a first impression meeting face to face would be better for making an unforgettable impression. I . . ." His words trailed off as she began to laugh.

She couldn't help it. After everything that had just happened, the laughter just began to boil out of her. "You know what?" she asked between titters. "He was *right!*"

The prince's eyes widened for a moment, and then he too smiled, shoulders shaking. "All the wrong reasons entirely," he said, his laughs merging with hers and rolling out over the river. "But he was right!"

The laughing continued for minutes, slowing once but resuming as soon as they looked at one another and broke out laughing all over again. Finally they slowed, speaking through their laughs.

"He was right," Prince Aren said. "I won't forget the sight of Lady Coslott, barefoot, leaping from the back of her bondmount over a river to slay the beast attacking me with a blade of ice."

"And I won't forget that you charged blindly into an unknown forest to make up for my father's mistake," Aneira said. "It was tuft-headed . . . but in a noble way. And . . . less tuft-headed than my trying to run away. I apologize for ruining our introduction."

Prince Aren let out another laugh. "Lady Coslott, I believe this is a far better introduction than anything my or your father might have planned. Peril and danger aside, it was, I believe, worth it. I just hope . . ." He paused for a moment, and then extended a hand. Formally, the way one would for an equal. "You'll forgive my empty head in my haste to fix things, accept my thanks for your aid, and perhaps call me Niclas?"

Orwena nudged her from behind before she'd even fully digested his question. She reached out, catching up and forming an answer as she took his hand in hers. "I will if you forgive mine. My empty head, I mean. In running. And I will accept your apology. And, if I'm to call you Niclas . . ." She looked into his eyes, then smiled. "Call me Aneira."

THE CHAMBER FELL silent as Queen Aneira Aren finished recounting the events of her and her husband's first meeting. She stayed standing, letting the tale sink in.

One of the high houses spoke out. "An . . . enlightening tale, our queen. But surely you don't mean to suggest that you never would have been queen if not for your bondmounts? That King Aren would have been slain in a moment of fool-headed whimsy if not for his bondmount being there to save him?"

"Not quite," she replied. "As I stated, I will give you three moments. Listen now to the second."

LADY ANEIRA COSLOTT, soon to be Princess Aneira Aren, strode back and forth across the waiting room, ears buzzing and wings twitching with each errant step. *Am I doing this? Is this happening?* Her mouth felt dry, her toes tingled, and her hands had gone so cold she'd stuffed them into her armpits to keep warm. *Can I do this?*

She'd dismissed the servants, not wanting to be reminded by their fussing over her gown—which was thankfully tasteful in its simplicity—or her anxiety over what was to come. They'd left, her only companion in the waiting room now the large clock on one wall, unhelpfully timed to count down to the exact instant she was expected to leave the room through the door on the far wall, to walk out into the short hall that would then lead to a grand arch, which would lead to the palace grounds, which would lead to the path to the ancient temple, which is where she and Niclas would be—

She spun on her heel, buzzing in her ears increasing and wings twitching further away from her sides, threatening to ruffle the fabric of her dress.

Eleven minutes. She could feel her body shaking like a blade of grass in a light wind. *Can I do this?*

It wasn't that she didn't want to marry her Niclas—she did. Desperately.

It was everything that came with it that filled her with a pure terror, deeper than anything she could ever recall. Once she was married, she would no longer be Lady Aneira Coslott. She'd be *Princess* Aneira Aren. And once the current king and queen passed on or stepped down . . . *Queen* Aneira Aren.

Responsible for the entirety of the Tylwyth Teg. More than fourscore realms her and Niclas' responsibility.

Which was enough on its own, but then there were the other aspects of, well, *marriage.* She'd never lain with anyone, nor had Niclas—though they'd both discussed it, as couples were wont to do before officially becoming one in the eyes of the Great One. But as much as she yearned for that closeness, a part of her couldn't deny that she was terrified of actually engaging in the act.

Think of other things. Think of other things. She could feel her ears burning, growing hot beneath her woven wreath of petals, while her wings refused to stop twitching. *Millions of fae watching our wedding across the realm—No! Not helping!*

Her pacing increased in speed, the simple back and forth becoming more of a circuit. *Can I do this? What if I can't? What if I forget what I'm saying? What if I say the wrong thing and embarrass the royal family?* It was a small fear, but a fear nonetheless, piled atop the others like a garnish atop an extravagant dinner.

I don't know if I can do this. The doubt wormed across her mind like an insidious ribbon. *I love Niclas, but . . .* She swallowed, unwilling to finish the thought. *I know he loves me, but can I really be a princess? A queen? Responsible for the entirety of the Tylwyth Teg?*

Six minutes to go.

What else am I to do? Run away? She already knew from experience that it was a terrible idea, and would solve nothing. *Back out?*

But she didn't want to do that either. *Pass out?*

That felt strangely feasible. But no less embarrassing, depending on where it happened. And she'd never passed out before. But right now with her ears buzzing and her wings twitching and her breath coming in short, hiccupping gasps and her hands being all tingly and—

There was a *thump* from the door leading out, and her pacing stopped, thoughts piling to a stop and tripping over one another. *What?*

She'd left specific instruction that she wished to *not* be disturbed, but the *thump* had come from the outer door of the chamber, not the inner. The door that would take her to the path that she and Niclas would walk.

By tradition, *no one* was to come to that door before she stepped out of it. The buzzing in her ears, already a mark of her elevated heart, increased, icy tendrils of fear moving through her as she began to wonder who would dare—

A familiar presence brushed her mind, and the panic evaporated, breaking like ice across the surface of a pond before a spring thaw. She rushed to the door and threw it open, Orwena's concerned muzzle poking through.

"Orwena!" Aneira threw her arms around her bondmount's head, pressing her face into the dog's golden fur. No doubt the palace staff were quite confused and concerned at the sudden disappearance of the bondmount from her ordained place along the path, but . . .

"Oh Orwena." She draped herself over her bondmount's head, doubtlessly marring her dress with golden hairs. At the moment she didn't care. "Thank you." Just holding onto her faithful companion was already helping.

"I just worry I won't be able to do it," she said at last, pulling back to look into Orwena's big, soulful eyes. "I know it's foolish, but a princess? Married to Niclas? I . . . I'm just worried." Orwena, still panting, leaned forward and gently licked one ear with the tip of her tongue. It tickled, but it helped take her mind off things. "Thanks, girl." Her wings began to settle as she stood there, holding tufts of Orwena's fur in her hands, the panic and worry fading like steam.

Her fears weren't simply gone. Millions of fae would still be watching as she and Niclas walked the path together. She'd still become Princess Aneira Aren.

But her fears felt more *distant* as she held to Orwena, her sense of calm returning. Her fears were just that: Fears.

No one would call for her to be publically cursed if she forgot her lines, or stumbled as she walked the path hand in hand with Niclas to the temple.

She still felt like she was walking on a thin pane of glass, but holding onto Orwena gave her something to focus on, something her spinning thoughts could coalesce around. Slowly her emotions calmed, the buzzing in her ears fading.

Still she stayed, leaning on Orwena's muzzle and feeling her bondmount's heartbeat until the countdown on the side of the room neared zero. Only then did she thank Orwena and order her to return to her place on the path, the corgi obliging with another lick of her ear.

She was still pulling large golden hairs from the fabric of her dress when the timer reached zero, but it gave her something else to think about. She steeled herself, making a last-minute check of her apparel in the mirror and giving herself a nervous smile as she prepared to leave through the door, and begin the path with Niclas.

She'd missed a hair or two on her dress, but it didn't matter. The first thing she noticed after seeing Niclas' relieved face coming in the other direction wasn't the cut of his suit or the stretch of his broad shoulders, but a familiar reddish hair clinging to the sash of his own robe. It could only have belonged to Glyr, Niclas' own bondmount, and the realization made her smile.

She still felt the storm of her fears, the millions of eyes resting on her as she reached out and took Niclas' hand in hers, but the electric jolt that moved up her arm helped reinforce the calm that Orwena's presence had brought. Niclas' hand gave her own a gentle squeeze.

She smiled as she returned it.

AGAIN THE CHAMBER FELL SILENT. Queen Aren watched, waiting to see if anyone would speak. But no one did.

"I don't doubt that many of you felt the same way on the day of your marriage," she said quietly, her words conveyed in that same quiet to the far reaches of the chamber by its ancient magic. "Nervous. Afraid. Elated, but alarmed." She set one hand on the railing of the lower dais, looking up at the eyes of the lower houses. "I do not share this story to make you feel as though my fears were greater or my overcoming them any more brave than your own walks along that long path."

She paused once more, eyeing the expressions of the court. A few still looked unsure, as if they hadn't yet grasped the meaning she endeavored to guide them toward.

"And I cannot say that had my bondmount not been there, I would have become a coward, and stepped away. At least, I do not *believe* I would have done such. But in that moment, when my fears and anticipation were great . . ." She let the final word hang in the air for a few seconds, not finishing her thought. *Let them work it out for themselves.* Her wings twitched.

"I have one last moment to share with you," she said, pausing to take a deep breath before she began. "And then we will decide."

Lowering her hands behind the wall of the dais and closing them into fists, she began to speak.

GONE.

Niclas, her love of seventy-eight seasons of the realm, was gone. Her companion. Her husband. Her king . . . was dead.

The world felt empty. Cold. His death had been sudden and unexpected, a failing of his heart that the best medical powers of the Tylwyth Teg could not heal. There had been time for him to hold her hand one last time, wish her well and bid her to take care of their children and the kingdom . . . and then he'd slipped into eternity.

Gone.

She'd stayed by his side as his grip had grown weak, the hand cooling as his spirit fled, weeping tears of grief as slowly but surely the fingers that had held her own for so many seasons had fallen away to the bedside. The world itself had grown cold and grey as his life had left him, losing color and time.

He was gone.

She'd been guided from his bedside by one of her daughters. She couldn't even remember which one. The world had passed her by in a daze. They'd both known that the specter of death had loomed on the horizon, but the suddenness with which it had arrived—

She'd seen to the rites, seen to the proper protocols for a king who had been one half of the magical focus of their people. Seen to the proper steps, authorizations, and preparations. She'd washed his body one final time, prepared him in the funeral clothing, and bracketed his body with sweet-smelling herbs and finally a spell of stasis. She'd been present at the wake in body, vaguely aware that one of her own sons had taken the role of chief mourner for the Day of Gwylnos, but it had been like she was watching herself from afar, her own mind hijacked by a teleoperator giving her commands on autopilot. She'd used her magic to carry and lead the procession along the final path, feeling the weight of the slab of marble that was to be her husband's final tomb, until the day that the kings of old arrived and restored that which was.

All had been carried out by the strongest traditions. The seal on her husband's final casket had been formed by the magic of her and their children, only to be broken when it was her turn to join him. Tears had been shed. Sorrows had been bared.

But the abyss in her core had remained. The next day had passed like a dream, waking to a bed that was no longer shared, a room that felt cold and empty. It was like a part of her soul had faded with his. She'd attempted to tend to her work, but the numbers were meaningless, the reports empty and without logic.

The next day hadn't fared any different. She still felt hollow on the inside. Stretched, as if Niclas' departing spirit had somehow taken part of hers with it. She heard the staff whisper, her own children expressing concern at her state. It was as if her body was not her own, her own face a stranger in the mirror, haunted and empty.

Part of her knew it was grief, that she was drowning in it. But she couldn't force the words to come, nor force the sense of loss away. She found herself wandering the halls, lost in memory as she moved aimlessly through the palace, faintly aware that outside its walls the entire people of the Tylwyth Teg relied on her rule. But trying to force herself to act was like pushing against a river, one that was completely immune to her magic or her will. It sucked her back, carrying her along its eddies and currents with no care for her own desires or wants. Instead it washed them over with its own.

Sometimes the tears came, unbidden, erupting like a breaking dam as something deep inside her soul gave way . . . but leaving her feeling no better or worse afterward. Other times she felt nothing at all, her emotions and feelings as much a void as the empty space beside her each morning in her bed. She carried out the motions of her office as best she could, taking care of the final obligations left by her husband's passing, but found it difficult to focus on anything else. Their eldest son—Aneurin— took some of the responsibilities from her as she struggled, but deep inside she knew it couldn't last.

The Tylwyth Teg needed their queen. Aneurin was only a prince, and without the very real powers derived by kingship, the houses would soon move amongst themselves.

She ate mechanically when food was placed before her. Turned down requests to speak with her on all matters, not just those concerned with Niclas' passing. Whispers passed between her staff, between her children. Both tried to console her. Though her heart felt elated when they tried, the feeling did not stick. The days passed. Her children needed to return to their own realms, their own duties, responsibilities, and kin calling.

Niclas remained gone. The hole at the center of her being yawned like an abyss.

One week from the day he had departed, Aneira awoke in the early hours of the night, once again reaching for the other side of her bed only to find that same abyss when she found it empty. She could feel herself teetering, fighting against falling through the hole in her heart.

Through the dark, a faint glimmer sparked deep inside, breaking through the barriers around her mind.

Aneira rose, throwing a silken robe over her nightgown before slipping from her room without alerting the night staff. A simple glamour concealed her passing from their eyes, hid her movements from even the wondrous security cameras and systems and magic-sniffers concealed around the vast structure. As queen, no door was barred to her and no wing of the palace off-limits. She and Niclas had more than once made use of that fact for late-night rendezvous unknown to any of the staff.

The abyss widened.

She stepped outside for the first time in days, the pavement still warm beneath her bare feet. She passed by palace guards without so much as a whisper, moved through the grounds, through plants from the old realm of Earth as well as those from their new homes, without bending so much as a blade.

She reached the front door of the Royal Stables, pausing only for a moment before opening it with a wave of her hand.

They looked much as they had the last time she had seen them, the night before Niclas had passed. The two largest and grandest corrals were at the front, reserved for her and Niclas' bondmounts. Spells glowed from the edges of the wood, spells of containment and sealing.

Aneira gasped.

Beyond the spell, she saw a pair of ears lift up, matched by a sudden flare from inside her own heart that she knew came from the bond. Orwena rose into view, and Aneira broke through the spells with a single wave of her hand. Orwena almost bowled her over, followed by Glyr, both of them licking her and pressing their bodies against hers.

Though she had no bond with Glyr she could see the bondmount's distress. He'd lost weight, and what little luster that had remained in his coat was gone. She could see pain in his eyes as he searched the rest of the stable for Niclas. She shut the doors with another wave of her hand. Orwena, meanwhile, licked her ears, circling around her, tail wagging with a clear sense of *worry* that poured through the bond now that they were so close.

"Orwena. Glyr. I . . ." She knew why the doors had been sealed by magic. To keep both animals from escaping their corrals and rushing through the palace. She'd been so lost in her grief . . .

"I . . ." She threw her arms over the necks of both faithful bondmounts, fully aware that they'd *been* there during the walk to Niclas' final resting place, that her grief had been so full she'd not even realized it.

Her legs gave out beneath her, the yawning abyss she'd kept at bay for so long swallowing her at last, and she cried. Raw, unfiltered loss poured out of her like a river, and she buried her face in Orwena's side in a way she hadn't done since she was a little girl. She held them both as close as she could, her bondmount and her husband's both, sobbing as the very emptiness leaked out. At long last, she fell asleep, draped against Orwena's side like a child who had yet to reach her second growth spurt, exhausted in mind, spirit, and body.

When she woke the next morning, Glyr's body was still, his spirit gone to follow his departed master, the body cool beneath Aneira's hand. But Orwena's was warm and full of life.

For the first time since that moment Niclas' hand had slipped away, Aneira felt awake. Not complete. The hole was still there, ragged and raw. But it was no longer an abyss.

She rose from the ground and gave Glyr one last kiss on the forehead, bidding the faithful creature farewell. She would see to it that he was interred in his proper place.

But first she needed to return to her quarters. The faint horizon bore the marks of the soon-to-rise sun, and she needed to prepare for the day.

Her heart still ached. Niclas was still gone. But the Tylwyth Teg needed their queen. She left the stables, Orwena padding behind her, faithful to the end, and walked into the rising sun.

QUEEN AREN FINISHED the final part of her tale and paused, glancing back at Orwena, who lifted her head and wagged her tail.

"My fae," she said, placing her interwoven fingers atop the railing of the dais. "I did not share these moments from my life with you to ask for your sorrow at the loss of my husband, or to suggest that without my or Niclas' bondmount we would have met our end by my family's home, slain by a whyent. I could explain to you *why* that would be so, but that is not the point."

She paused, sliding her gaze over the many watching with rapt attention. Her wings twitched. "I did not tell you of my wedding day to suggest that without Orwena, I would have fled and never served as queen. And nothing about either my or my late husband's bondmounts could have prevented his death. But . . ."

She swallowed, clearing her throat. "Without them, our lives would not have been what they are. Panic would have lengthened. Fear would have risen. Sorrow would have consumed. We are Tylwyth Teg, and as long as our kingdom has been, our bondmounts have stood by our side. My Orwena, my husband's Glyr . . . they saved this kingdom and helped it prosper just as much as the warrior mounts of old, by helping *us*. Our bondmounts may no longer face the battlefields of war, but they are still there when we face the pain of loss or the stress of rule. They are confidants, trusted friends unlike any we may ever have save our spouse. Those who now seek to put an end to the bond levy sell our faithful friends short. If not for my bond, I might still be lost to grief."

Her voice cracked, and she paused, composing herself before continuing. "Whether or not I would be lost is not the question. Because of my Orwena, I am *not*. I am here, leading the Tylwyth Teg forward as is my duty. I was there, on the path with my Niclas. I was there, at the river, because she heard the whyent's hunting cry and the brave barks of another bondmount."

"A bondmount's place was never just a battlefield. It was in our homes. At our hearth. In our hearts. And without mine . . ." She glanced back at Orwena once more, the corgi giving another small wag. "I would not wish to think of what that world would be like. She has never saved me from an enemy's blade . . . but she has saved me many times nonetheless."

She paused, giving the chamber one last commanding gaze. "As queen, I agree that some things must change. Spells come and go, as do habits, popular songs, and other elements. But they never truly leave us. And nor, I believe, should the bondmounts."

With that, she unclasped her hands and offered the sign of peace before turning and striding back to the throne to sit once more. Orwena put her chin on the arm of the throne, and she gave the corgi a quick scratch between the ears. "Good girl," she whispered as the houses began to debate. She could already see that she'd swayed some of those that had stood against the continuation of the program. "Good girl."

Orwena didn't understand what she'd done, but Aneira felt the dog's satisfaction flow through the bond. Again she scratched between Orwena's ears, glancing over at her husband's empty throne before looking into Orwena's eyes. "And thank you."

Iwiw

Joe Ficklin

I t's hardly dignified." Bast'et lazily batted at a floating dust mote. Down on the mortal plane, a stone carver lost his footing to fall half a dozen cubits, thudding heavily at the base of the monument to Thoth, the breath knocked out of him temporarily. Other dust motes swarmed into the goddess's view. "Oh, don't give me that look!" She studiously ignored the jackal-headed figure crouched on the marbled bench amidst the billowing linen drapes.

Anubis finished licking the marrow from the satisfyingly thick auroch femur he'd been chewing on since Ra had tossed it his way while heading out to the garage where the sun had been parked all night. "It's m'job," he semi-growled around the glistening bone. "It's the parau'ah, the 'great house.'"

"Still, only a human, however much they might pretend to immortality." The cat-headed goddess gave a disdainful sniff. "They either die young, or they grow too old too quickly, and go frail and weak, stinking and leaking, covered in lice." She shimmied over to the cedar table on which rested a bronze goblet filled with ever-flowing water. Not that she ever needed the drink, but it provided a momentary cooling refreshment. "Like this parau'ah."

She lapped from the goblet.

"He's not going to live past the passing of Ra's chariot." She still refused to look directly at the demigod, worrying his bone. "Send an aspect. It's not as though you personally need to be the guide dog for the recently dead."

"It's expected." His voice was clear and cold as the water in the goblet, all traces of the auroch bone consumed. "My aspects are fine for the peasant and the priest, the babe and the crone. This is parau'ah. The king. I must attend."

"It's a small kingdom." Bast'et replied.

"It's ancient. Filled with traditions."

"You mean it's old. Feeble and weak, stinking and leaking. Covered with humans."

When there was no response, Bast'et finally looked over to where the jackal-headed god had been crouching. Anubis was gone and she was alone. Annoyed, she headed for the eternal gardens where a few sacred heron could be found. And slaughtered.

A lone voice chanted, mumbled harsh syllables that bounced and tumbled in the murky stillness of the king's chamber.

For Kunijekt, eighth of his line of parau'ah, awareness swam up slowly. He heard first the priest's chanting. He felt the slight yielding of the linen-wrapped reed mattress on which he lay. There was a red-tinged darkness and the slow pounding of a muffled drum, as though coming from a great distance, which he realized was the blood pulsing through his body. He heard the dry rasp of each in-drawn ragged breath. Dry linens wrapped his head and covered his brow. He felt both chilled by the bed and yet warmed by the musty air within the chamber—it must be a chamber, right? Thought returned. With thought came understanding, or a little measure of understanding, at least. With the return of thought came questions. The most important question being, of course, "What is happening?"

With an effort that left him softly gasping, he managed to partially open one eye. Most of the room slept in shadow except for where a brilliant halo of light peeked through the edges of the drapery-covered window opening. A single priest leaned against the paneled far wall, chanting in the mystic tongue, not quite looking at the dying monarch, not completely ignoring him. At best, he appeared . . . disinterested.

A flower of pain took root, grew, and blossomed in Kunijekt's chest. He gasped again as a great weight settled into the pain, his breath hissing out in a final cessation. The weight and the pain lifted, suddenly, like a bird taking flight, and he felt himself pulled along with it out of the old, dried husk stretched out on the bed.

His vision cleared and the room seemed suddenly lightened. Not a shadow was visible. The priest continued his lackluster chanting and Kunijekt could see there was one other in the chamber, a tall man with jet hair, wearing ceremonial robes and a gold diadem.

No, not a man—a dog, thin and black with alert eyes. Kunijekt was confused for a moment, but then the man was back and looking at him. In the perfect brightness of the darkened death chamber, Kunijekt could see the man's eyes were blacker than water at the bottom of a deep well. For a moment, those eyes were the spiraling center of the universe and the rest of the world faded to insubstantial ash and cobweb. The face was almost familiar, like a memory from a long-ago life, like the lingering aftermath of a pleasant dream.

"Is this a dream?" he wondered, not trusting to say the words aloud, yet somehow the familiar stranger heard.

"A dream?" The man's voice was deep and mellow. "Oh. No." He stretched out his right hand and gestured at the chamber and the priest starting to move toward the sleeping platform holding the discarded husk. "The dream is over. Come." He beckoned.

There was no sensation of movement. In one instant, Kunijekt was standing next to the deathbed, and in the next non-breath, he was standing in front of the black-eyed, golden crowned man. As parau'ah, he liked to believe he'd been able to sense a man's character at first meeting, but there was something—almost a veil—between this person and himself.

One moment, it seemed as though he was addressing a man, like any other man, with dark hair and an open expression. In the next moment, Kunijekt was as an ant between the man's feet, staring at a figure towering up into the highest heavens. Another heartbeat and he was standing next to a black dog with a wild mane and a twisted, bushy tail. There were a thousand thousand images all infused in the essence of the personage before him, each one separate and distinct, as though a huge crowd had been pulled down into the space occupied by a single body.

"I have questions," he began.

"You are dead, parau'ah. I am your guide. I am Anubis." The "man" spoke, and Kunijekt recognized the voice as the wind that whispered over the dunes and through the trees. "Take this gift. Do not lose it." He stretched out his hand and Kunijekt took the white ostrich feather Anubis offered.

"A gift. From Ma'at. The ever-gracious Ma'at," said the god, with no trace of irony. Truthfully, Ma'at *was* ever-gracious.

"You look different, Lord Anubis, than how I imagined you'd be. How the priests said you would be." Words of a dead man to a god of the dead.

An emaciated man with priest's garments replied. "You only see what you are limited to see. You do not see me at all. Or rather, as I should say to you in your speech, you do not see all of me. Not yet. Come. They await." The command could not be denied, even if Kunijekt had felt so inclined.

This time, there was the sensation of great movement and an immeasurable distance travelled, and the two stood together on dark sand under a sky blazoned with stars and ribbons of color.

"Forty-two judgments await," the wolfish demigod said, his voice whispering like a breeze through endless fields of wheat. "I will attend you, as did I previously."

Previously? Kunijekt wondered at when that possibly could have been, but in this *place-that-was-not* and *time-that-was-not*, he knew an answer would not be forthcoming. Still, he had questions.

"Lord Anubis," he said, and the figure turned eyes on him that were both hard and cold, yet also gentle and loving. Merciless, yet merciful. It was an odd attribute of the gods that several of their aspects could be viewed simultaneously. "Where is this place?"

"Ah, parau'ah. You know this place. It is as it ever was, since man first called us into being. Or since we first walked with you across the grasslands." The jackal-head gestured at the scene stretched before them. "Man feels a need to be justified for having lived. This is the place of justification. A place of purification and sanctification. Or a place where a sick and polluted soul shall be consumed. Do you understand?"

Kunijekt nodded in affirmation. "I have heard of this place."

"You must confirm aloud," his guide admonished him.

"I understand, Lord Anubis. This is judgment."

Before them stood a chest-high altar of black, glass-edged stone on which lay a furled papyrus scroll. Beyond the altar spread ranked tiers of limestone seats upon which sat an assemblage of creatures, vaguely human shaped, in robes as dark as the skies were brilliant. Eyes glowed like embers, piercing the parau'ah's breast. Their names and essences welled up within his awareness, like a primordial memory surfacing. These were the assessors. His judges.

Other figures faded into and out of the background. The judge's attendants, he thought. Or their aspects, called away in response to prayers or curses, or both.

A crocodile-headed creature, a pitiless void, waited impatiently at the side of the obsidian alter. Amemait. Eater-of-hearts, Destroyer-of-souls, waiting for the judgment to conclude. Yearning for Kunijekt's heart. Kunijekt found himself wiping his palms on his thighs as if to dry them. Anubis, at his side, touched him on his forearm and the fear that had welled up in him faded.

The voice of majestic Atun was that of a mountain being caught up in an earthquake, encased in thunder and echoed in crashing ocean waves. It was the sound of creation, the universe emerging from an infinite spark.

"SPEAK!"

The papyrus scroll on the altar unrolled itself displaying characters written in fire and gold and lapis lazuli with vignettes that flowed like wine. Commanded by the god, Kunijekt's mouth opened, and the phrases written on the papyrus moved his tongue.

"Hail, far-strider, Usekh-nammt, who comest forth from Annu, I have not committed sin." Knowing his assessor, but not knowing how he knew, Kunijekt faced the dark-robed Usekh-nammt and let the flood of memories of his earthly life wash up and carry him into an endless, patient, eternal sea.

The dog's bark startled him. The child Kunijekt hefted the rock in his hand, preparatory to throwing it. A hand on his shoulder from Mehkt-anun, the lame soldier-turned-teacher who seldom left his side, stopped him.

"It's just a dog," the veteran said. "Dogs bark. It's their nature." He went down on one knee before the son of parau'ah. "The bark is like a shout. It can be a warning or a greeting. Or nothing at all, just noise." He clapped his hands twice and held his palms down and out. The dog kept barking, but Kunijekt could see it wasn't coming any closer.

"You see? He's all noise. No real teeth." The soldier dug a piece of dried meat from the bag at his hip, tore off a piece and tossed it to the dog, which sniffed at it suspiciously before wolfing it down.

"Well, he does have teeth, after all. But not for us." The two, man and boy, continued down the dusty path, the dog following a dozen paces behind, occasionally letting out a single bark or two.

"I shouldn't have fed it." Mehkt-anun sighed. "Just like some people, all noise and no action, but if you feed them, they'll follow you to where the river waits." A line of date palms in the distance showed the border where water met earth. The dog followed the boy and the man to where the barge waited. It barked several times, as if in displeasure, then lay down in the dust of the road and watched them board, its eyes black as a mist-filled night.

When the barge returned several weeks later, the dog was nowhere to be found, as was expected. Still, the child Kunijekt remembered and was disappointed. Until, passing back the way they had first come, he heard a distant bark and turned around to see a dog, possibly the same as before, come loping up. No, not possible. Yet it *was* the same as before.

Mehkt-anun signed heavily and pulled a piece of dried meat from his pouch. "Dogs and old guards," he said. "Be careful what you feed us. We have long memories."

The dog continued to follow them all back to the city wall, and within. By the time they reached the palace gate, the dog was pacing at the guardsman's side, tongue lolling out as it panted.

A lesson taught. A lesson learned. Each creature is true to its nature. A pattern employed through life. Dust swirled up in a cloud as the memory was replaced by another.

"Hail, Hept-khet, the fire embracer, who comes from Kher-haa. I have not committed robbery with violence." Kunijekt faced the assessor and nearly smiled. What need has parau'ah of robbery? And yet, sand swirled up and a long-forgotten memory returned, unbidden and unwelcomed.

The child Kunijekt and the old soldier-turned-teacher sat on a stone bench in the east gardens, the boy holding back tears.

"It is in our nature," Mehkt-anun said. "All things that live must die." He stretched out his legs and rubbed at the old scar on his shin, wincing slightly.

"It was just a dog," the boy mumbled, defiantly, as if by denying reality Dog would return and be waiting for him in the palace.

"Yes," his teacher confirmed. "He was a just a dog. And also a loyal friend. It is a dog's nature to be loyal to his friends." He stared out into the empty sky past the high garden walls. "Loyalty given must be returned." He looked at the boy sitting beside him and his eyes softened. "Loyalty is a gift."

There came a sudden bark from the other side of the garden wall and the boy Kunijekt jumped to his feet. "It's Dog! He's returned!" He called over his shoulder as he sprinted back into the palace, heading for the nearest exit.

"Prince Kunijekt! Wait!" Mehkt-anun shouted, but he was too late, and the boy had disappeared back inside. Rising to his feet with a grunt of effort, the old man limped as quickly as he could after his charge.

Out in the bright sunlit street, Kunijekt, trailed by one of the palace guards, hurried toward a handful of children throwing a barley-filled, sewn-shut sack around, while a brown dog with black stripes ran around their feet and barked at the sack flying overhead. It was a dog, but it wasn't his Dog. His chest hurt from running, and another feeling that twisted black cords around his pounding heart.

The children paused in their play, glancing curiously at him as he stopped at the edge of the small plaza, the guard stopping a few paces behind. They seemed about his age, perhaps a little older than the parau'ah princeling. The dog sat in the dust, panting, wet tongue lolling. This dog's eyes were brown, not black like Dog's eyes. The few adults conducting business in the plaza—or passing through—studiously avoided the visitors from the palace. Their only obvious spectator was an old man sitting on the stoop in the cool of a doorway, sipping from a clay jug half-empty with tepid beer, his eyes alert for any entertainment that might be forthcoming.

"Does he have a name?" Kunijekt asked, pointing at the dog.

The children chattered amongst themselves for a moment before a boy, presumably the eldest said, "We call her Iwiw." Dog. The same name he used for his dog. Iwiw. Dog.

"Give me your Iwiw," He commanded. He placed his hands on his hips as he'd seen his father, parau'ah, do many times before when giving orders to others.

The boy looked shocked. The other children started protesting. The guard took a single step toward the children before a hand on his shoulder stopped him.

"No." Mehkt-anun's voice carried only to Kunijekt's ears. "This dog is not yours. If you take her, you break her loyalty to her master." Kunijekt looked back over at the children now clustered around the confused dog as the boy who spoke knelt on the brickwork and hugged it tightly. She licked his face.

The princeling's eyes flickered with irritation and he opened his mouth to complain, but the look of disappointment in his teacher's face caused his own cheeks to flush red and burn with embarrassment. "I could take it, if I wanted to," he murmured. "And have them beaten for their defiance!"

Mehkt-anun nodded. "You could order it, yes. But do you not already have enough? Why take from those who have so little?" He put his hand on Kunijekt's shoulder, but gentler than he'd gripped the guard. "Come, let us go back to the garden and discuss this," he said as he guided his pupil back toward the palace door.

That night, alone in his chamber where no one could see, the child Kunijekt cried himself to sleep.

Crouching next to the altar, Amemait gnashed his crocodile teeth in frustration.

"Hail, Fent'i, the Nosey One, I have not stolen . . ."

"Hail, Amk'hal'bit, Swaller-of-Shades, I have not murdered men and women . . ."

"Hail, Neha-her, . . ."

"Hail, Ru'ru'ti, . . ."

One's life does not simply flash before one's eyes while confessing to the gods in the Hall of Judgment. Each action is retrieved, reviewed, relived; often from several vantage points simultaneously. Each decision debated as the consequences were examined and the overall good weighed against the inadvertent evil. As parau'ah, an almost inexhaustible throng of teachers, soldiers, priests, wives, children, and the countless merchants, farmers, cripples, beggars, travelers, whores, and more that his decisions touched paraded across the altar. Amemait waited nearby, impatient as each vignette danced in the pristine air.

More often than not, in the periphery of his deeds, a dog waited. A dog sleeping in the dust of the road. A dog picking through horse bones. A dog running alongside him on the hunting grounds. Dogs that warmed him in the cool of the night. Dogs that warned him when the wild pigs were near. Dogs that barked or silently watched with tongues lolling out of their muzzles.

Kunijekt watched his life play out on the altar of the gods. "I have not murdered. I have not defiled myself. I have not stolen the altar cakes meant for the gods. I have not raised my voice in anger." With the clarity that comes with a soul unburdened by guilt, he saw each choice in the open light of Ra. Each choice being true to his own nature, as all creatures must be subject to their own nature.

In time that could not be measured in heartbeats, or days, or centuries, the confessions concluded. The sky lightened as Usir, Lord of the Underworld and Judge of the Dead, appeared. Gleaming bronze scales were visible where they had always been on the altar.

Atun spoke. The ground trembled at the softness of his voice and stars danced in the echoing rumble.

"THE FEATHER!"

Kunijekt looked at the ostrich feather still clutched in his hand, then looked to his guide and companion at his side.

Anubis stood, as he always would, faithful and true at the parau'ah's side. For an instant, Kunijekt thought he saw a long, rough tongue lolling out of the god's mouth below twinkling eyes.

"The feather, Kunijekt." He held out his hand. Kunijekt handed it over.

"Your heart, Kunijekt," the dark god said. Kunijekt looked down at his hand to see his beating heart. He handed it over.

Kneeling, Anubis, God and Guide to the Underworld, Protector of Man and Companion to Parau'ah, offered up the heart of Kunijekt of Akkumeht, Parau'ah, along with the feather of Ma'at, Goddess of Balance.

Usir took the feather and placed it on the scale. The bronze plate settled.

Usir took the heart and placed it on the other plate. And smiled in radiance that banished all darkness.

Amemait clashed his crocodile teeth in frustration as hot tears of relief welled up and filled Khamjekt's eyes, spilling over in wet streaks.

Parau'ah embraced Anubis, the god's aloofness disappearing as he hugged his charge in return.

"Thank you, Lord Anubis!" Kunijekt cried, his face wet as the weight of judgment lifted. "I truly see you now, as you've always been, as you always will be. I know your nature now!" Gone from the Halls of Judgment, the golden light of Ra illuminated Sikhet-A'Aru, the paradise known as the Field of Reeds in which they now stood.

The jackal-headed god licked the man's cheek, eyes twinkling, tail wagging furiously. One last visage appeared, that of old Mehkt-anun, the lame soldier-turned-teacher, the *friend* who had guided him to proper manhood, who now turned a weathered face to the man who had been parau'ah. "Rarf!"

"So undignified," Bast'et sniffed from her palace perch.

Princess Lusandra
and the Dreaming Village
Jennifer Lesh Fleck

The Crown Prince of Zanathasia winks again. He's sitting on that black wrought iron park bench, same as ever. He leans his long, stringy body forward and twists his torso, coming in for yet another lip lock with me. His dreamily glazed eyes flutter closed—as they always do—and I catch a whiff of the strong black coffee he guzzled throughout our date. He reaches for my phantom hand and squeezes thin air. From a few feet away, I stand, observing it all, stomach clenching with a mix of pity and despair.

The two of us are imprisoned together in a kind of living natural history display. I'm conscious of this fact, but the prince is not. He and I share a single glass cloche, our giant bell jar one among twenty-five others just like it—a dreaming village of animate snow globes.

The glass walls are curved, so smooth and sleek, my fingernails can find no imperfections. These walls curve to become the dome above our heads. Below us is a floor made of some kind of molded hot pink plastic. We have this one park bench, and that's it for furnishings. The same bench we'd sat upon after our dinner date, ostensibly "to talk," once upon a time.

The prince is stuck, a living automaton. After some unknown number of minutes, his loop resets and begins anew. Feels like a minute to me sometimes. Other times, twenty minutes. When you have no day, no night, and no timepiece of any kind, the notion of time becomes a meaningless taffy.

The scene he reenacts is drawn from his never-ending bad dinner date with Lusandra, Her Royal Highness, the Crown Princess of Delanico. That's me.

I'm never hungry here. Yet I miss savoring a good meal. I miss *everything* that exists outside this cloche, including all the aspects of my former life that sucked. I miss stepping off a curb crookedly into a mud puddle and breaking the heel of a new boot. I recollect and I mourn the lost smell of the dirty city where my ancestral castle looms in craggy limestone. I grieve the gloomy, foul tempers of our region, its dark clouds and its rainstorms blowing in and blowing out. I'd give anything to be back on those streets that crawl with rats and pigeons, crowded with street peddlers and grifters and the tourists who come to gawk, hoping for a glimpse of royalty.

Sometimes out of boredom I stretch out at the foot of the picnic bench and nap. And when I wake up, he's still at it, still in his groove, recycling those same few motions. Lean, twist, grab, kiss. The prince, like a clockwork doll stuck in the "on" position eternally. Tall and gristly-looking and annoying, like something a bad steak would leave behind in your teeth. Clad in an ill-fitting but costly sport coat. And the most improbable and ridiculous hat ever, a wool tweed fedora adorned with a drooping purple plume. A lavish, ostentatious, look-at-me-and-not-her feather!

I watch that feather shiver as he—once again—offers a saucy wink to no one, thrusts his open hand where my hand should be, leans forward and twists with a surprising vigor, squinches those beady peepers of his closed, then puckers up, swooping in to deliver a fat, unwelcome smooch. A kiss that took my breath away the first time it happened, but not in a good way. I'd been mid-sentence, rattling on about my prized poodle, Humberto, and the seventeen individual tricks I'd taught him. I'd been thinking about how I'd escape our date politely but firmly. The prince's greedy kiss was a surprise, a big shut-your-mouth move!

If could go back to that evening, I would excuse myself long before this whole unnecessary park bench interlude. After our dessert concluded, I'd trust the silent assessment I'd made: this prince was a pompous blowhard, harmless enough, but not the one for me. I'd pay my half of the check, slip on my gloves, and offer a curt hand-shake goodbye. Then I'd text my coachman, Ferris, to come fetch me from the silly faux-fancy restaurant with its gilt and velvet trappings and its overly complicated recipes. (So many oozing gravies and greasy pastry layers! How devastating that these might be the last things I'll ever taste in this life.)

In a way, I envy the prince. He gets to dreamily live out his little time loop conquest, kissing nothing but air. Blissfully unaware of being trapped. A whole tiny village of bell jars around us, their occupants busy reenacting the same few motions, over and over, tirelessly. A little gymnast practices her flips. A grinning baker licks his finger of frosting and then pipes the last flourish on a wedding cake. A mother reads to her little boy in bed until he falls asleep. All these homey scenes, on repeat, in perpetuity.

I'm the only one here who has woken up.

I know who our captors are. The giants our history books claimed our old heroes had vanquished many eons ago. They weren't really conquered at all. They'd simply retreated to lick their wounds. Down to the hidden center of the world where it's said all the old monsters await, plotting their return and their vengeance. Well, now the giants are back, as big and ugly as ever, come to collect specimens and samples to take home to their castles. Whether we are meant for amusement or for study, I couldn't say.

It's something like a pollywog might feel. One moment shimmying along in its lovely warm mud puddle, the next moment scooped by a captor, a shadow that came from the sky.

It's His Royal Highness's fault we're trapped here. He'd gotten me going by asking me to tell him about my clever dog, a smooth move on his part. If I'd have simply ended the date after dinner concluded, none of this would have happened and I'd be free.

When he'd kissed me that evening, I'd immediately protested with a muffled "Hey, what in the—"

And at that very moment, out of nowhere, our cloche came down with a "whomp!" sound, trapping both us and this shared moment in our life.

After that, I don't remember anything. It was something like anesthesia, coming awake from my time loop—little sense of time passing, a cotton ball fog between my ears. Then I simply stood up and extricated myself from the prince's hapless embrace. And his loop has continued on without me ever after.

It's lonely in here. I miss my mom and dad. The court at large and my close friends, too. I've examined the prince from every angle, wishing he'd wake up, if only for the company and the extra help strategizing my escape. I know each crease of his face, each pit and each pore. I could probably tell you the exact number of whiskers he missed while shaving for our date. I've prodded him, pinched him, and hauled off and slapped him. I've even, out of desperation, kissed him! He doesn't wake up.

And no matter if I scream, yell, pound my fists on the glass, or cry, the other snow globe people don't wake up, either.

Every inch of this stupid globe within reach of me has been smudged by my frantic fingers. There are no cracks, fissures, or weaknesses in the glass. None that I've found, at least.

An exciting new idea came to me today, though. Thank goodness I'd dressed down for the date, wearing a cotton top and jeans cinched with leather belt with a big metal buckle. That buckle makes a handy digging device if you use one of its four points. I scratch at the pink plastic floor, and I'm making some progress, but it's slow. I have to work on my "project" in little fits and starts so I don't get caught, like an old timey jailbird digging out of her prison with a bent chow hall spoon. The rest of the time, I keep the belt on as usual.

You see, we now have a new and frequent visitor.

The Boy and his dog showed up—I don't know, several thousands of rotations ago? And by Boy, I mean a giant child. Red raggedy hair and eyebrows, blue eyes set deep, and big cheeks the color of a hunk of bloomy brie. He carries around a young Jack Russell terrier mix in his arm, wriggling, its nub of a tail wagging, body the size of an omnibus and fringed in shaggy fur, its spots the size and color of pancakes. That loyal pup is with this kid always.

Today when I see the Boy, I drop the belt and freeze in place. Then instinctively, as a distraction, I launch into a little tap-dance-y jig. For a split second, it seems we lock eyes, and he knows I'm awake. The Boy frowns. He stoops, leans close, nostrils fogging up the glass, his breathing loud as a dragon's.

The prince kisses air, and kisses air again. I dance and dance in place. The Boy considers the scene. I worry he'll notice things have changed and believe his toy is malfunctioning.

His giant hand encloses the globe, blocking out the light like a meaty curtain thrown over a canary's cage. I fall to my side as he hefts our jar roughly, and hear the pounding of his feet crossing the room. I fear the worst. The prince winks, twists, closes his eyes, clutches my phantom hand, and kisses the air.

We come to a lurching stop, and there's a clunk as our jar's base hits a solid surface. I hop to my feet and begin my absurd dance again—a variation, I realize, of one of the tricks my poodle Humberto knows.

The Boy's moved us to a different display shelf. In the bell jar opposite me, a grim-faced mime wearing braids climbs her imaginary ladder endlessly. The other side features, ironically enough, a child and a puppy ceaselessly romping. The Boy steps back and considers this new arrangement. Then those bushy eyebrows slam down in a frown, and he lifts the glass cloche from us. The cool air of the room hits me, and I want to cower. I keep dancing in place, tapping gracelessly, my heart about to explode from fear and exertion.

"*That* don't belong there," the Boy says, his voice a thunder of halitosis. His massive index finger intrudes into our space, scrapes at the pink floor. I smell the dirt under his nails.

My belt! My belt with its precious metal buckle! He pincers it up like a stray bit of dental floss, then tosses it to the floor. The lid comes down over us once more, and he gives a twist till it locks again to its base.

The dog yaps twice, leaps up and pushes her forepaws against the Boy's leg insistently, her belled collar ringing.

"Fine, Ladybug. Walkies it is."

The door slams in the distance like a keg of gun powder exploding. I collapse to the pink plastic, wrap my arms around my knees, and weep.

THE BOY'S visits to his collection are frequent yet unpredictable. He's always got that overactive terrier, Ladybug, with him—jingling her collar, begging for her walkies with her harsh little bark. Sometimes her insistent hops and leaps bring her snout level with my bell jar, and I hold my breath, afraid she'll somehow rat me out.

When he and Ladybug come, I dance my heart out for them. When they're gone, I slump and scheme and miss my lost life.

Days or weeks pass in this fashion.

The tiny boy and his golden retriever leap and feint in the jar to one side of me, witless witnesses to my misery and my machinations. The mime climbs the air. The prince, well, you know what *he's* up to. Meanwhile, as of today, I've successfully loosened the second-to-the-last screw holding the bench's right arm to its base. You probably don't want to know how I did it—the levels of desperation I've reached—but several of my molar teeth must be cracked, by the way my mouth feels. My jaw aches with a relentless second heartbeat, and I wipe sticky blood from my lips using the inside of my black blouse.

I'm going to break this glass. Improbable and unlikely as the idea might be, it's the hope that keeps me going. The two middle bolts and screws of this old bench were missing altogether, a bit of luck. So now I've got one to go. I twist and turn its wrought iron arm in every direction, hoping to loosen that stubbornly remaining screw. Jiggle it, turn it on its base like a busted record player's arm.

I am so fixated on my task that today I don't notice the Boy as he approaches to inspect our row of jars, Ladybug cradled in his arms like a spotted loaf of white bread. Her attention is laser sharp. She sees I'm not in my ordinary place on the pink platform and gives a low warning growl, the infamous high predator drive of her terrier blood kicking in.

I leap and scramble to the center of the pink platform and start dancing.

But it's too late. I've attracted the Boy's attention again, his cocked-head, bushy-browed scrutiny. I try to keep my face calm and impassive as he thinks. He scratches his head slowly, luxuriantly, dandruff drifting like a snowstorm just beyond the glassy walls.

You done messed up, as my wise father, the king of Delanico, would have said.

Got yourself in a real pickle . . . jar, says my mother, the queen, in my head.

"I always *thought* this one was a dud," the Boy says. "It's broken, anyhow. Father will have to fetch me a better one. The prince is supposed to be smooching his princess. Welp, Ladybug, we gonna have to scrap it."

And with that, we are lifted again, clamped under the Boy's arm (so dark, so humid and foul), and carried out of the room. Everything in our bell jar slides to one side and clangs and clatters and bumps against the glass, including me. I'm trapped under the prince, his body still spasming mechanically.

From this awkward position I view the world of the giants' castle and all its outsized contents as it passes us by. The Boy carries us outside, a rush of sunlight and color.

THE BOY CHUCKLES.

"Good thing it's trash day. Y'all gonna ignite in about, oh, ten minutes. Can't wait to see how a fire like this'un burns." He claps his hands and hoots. Then the shadow of his bulk retreats, presumably as he heads off to fetch incendiary tools. I cower under the tipped-over bench. The prince lies on his side, barely wiggling now, his wink stuck at the halfway mark. I don't know if the throw onto this junk pile has damaged him irreparably. I don't have the time to sit and worry about him.

Our bell jar is tipped on its side on top of a pile of kitchen garbage and ruined toys. A family of grinning marionettes with broken limbs and busted strings, a board game somebody broke over their knee, a stuffed bone-shaped dog toy, its white fluff extruding from a hole ripped in its middle. All this, and our bell jar prison hasn't so much as cracked.

Except for that short, enticing seam where the seal between glass and plastic base now appears to be loosened.

The Boy's feet thunder through the foliage in the distance as he makes his way back to his castle. Then silence. I run my hands along the jar's seam. And then I hear sniffing and snuffling and crashing all around me, the trash heap under me now unstable, full of tremors.

LADYBUG DIGS through the junk pile, growling, on the hunt—she's the size of our ceremonial royal carriage back home, but every bit as determined as any terrier going after a rat. Her frantic energy reminds me of my coachman, Ferris, when he searches for his perpetually misplaced keys in his many pockets.

How I miss Ferris, and Humberto my poodle, and my parents, and our over-worked cooks, and our gruff guards—I've saved a golden spot in my racing heart for even the snarkiest and most conniving of our courtiers. All of these people made up my life and have supported me in immeasurable ways. I will show them my gratitude, if I can only break free of this nightmare.

I throw my weight against the base to try to knock it loose. I claw at the opening seam, try to slide an arm through it to wiggle it open. No luck. I'm sweating, cursing in the three languages I know. No dice.

"Ladybug!" I shout. "Lay-deeeee-bug!" Maybe I can attract her attention, get this pup and her one-track mind involved. Maybe she can help me bust out of this death-trap? What's the very worst that can happen, other than a massive terrier pouncing and tidily disemboweling me like a plush toy? I pound the glass, wave my arms, jump up and down, even turn a lopsided cartwheel. She's moved closer to the jar in her digging, but she pays my efforts no mind. The ground beneath us vibrates from her excavation efforts.

Then I remember Humberto, his early days, his puppyhood. He had a shaky attention span but a bright mind, like most puppies. A baby, still, he could be distracted easily. Instead of fighting this trait or punishing him for his natural instincts, I used them as part of his training sessions. I had this tool called a "flirt pole." Basically it's a toy fishing pole with a long braided nylon line, a scrap of faux fur tied to its end. If I wanted Humberto to drop a tennis shoe he was busy mauling in my closet, I'd fetch the flirt pole and make that scrap of fur hop and dance for him.

Worked every time.

I run to the prince. He's awake and sitting up!

"Where am I? Man, I just had the strangest dream . . ." He clutches his head and shakes it. "What *is* this place?!"

"No time for small talk—where is it?!"

"Huh?"

"Your hat! The stupid fedora you wore on our date. The feather, I need that big purple feather!"

He blinks at me wordlessly, then yanks his crushed wool tweed hat from under his rump. The feather on the hat, though—that ridiculous purple plume pops up, undamaged and as vibrant as ever, like something with its own life. I want to kiss it!

Instead, I cry "flirt pole!" and pluck the feather loose.

The prince shrugs woozily at my non sequitur, mild intrigue in his eyes.

I begin waving that long purple feather from side to side above my head like a semaphore, screaming Ladybug's name. The prince catches on, too, and struggles to his feet and launches into a set of awkward jumping jacks. Without stopping to ask where we are or why we're doing this, the prince joins me in frantically crying:

"Ladybug! Ladybug! Down here! Here girl! Ladybug! Good girl!"

In the near distance, branches snap as trees are crushed flat. The boy giant in his boat-sized sandals tromps our way, humming and singing to himself. "Burn, baby, burn . . ."

That's when Ladybug's nose bumps the side of the cloche. The whole glistening black beanbag-sized nose wriggles as she sniffs. She finds the seam on the jar and her snuffling grows louder still. An exploratory paw smacks the glass. Then she commences to claw at it with vigor and ferocity.

"Good girl, good girl! Go Ladybug, go!"

The Boy crouches, and I feel the heat of his lit torch. Its flame looks small held in his fingers but huge reflected in his excited eyes.

"Outta the way, Lady," he grumbles. "You don't wanna git yourself burnt."

Implacable as ever, Ladybug keeps going. Her claws skitter and scrabble against our glass jar. And finally it splits open, the pink base falling away.

"C'mon." I motion to the prince as I scurry out. "We're catching a ride out of here!" And with that, I duck under Ladybug's belly, jump, and grab at the long tendrils of fur curling behind her front legs, pulling myself up.

As the flames crackle, licking along the poor marionette family and devouring their painted grins of perpetual delight, the prince leaps once, twice, then finally manages to haul his long frame up beside me. We tuck ourselves tick-tight to Ladybug's warm undercarriage as she yelps and runs, her nose nipped by the heat of the glass.

IT WAS a perilous journey we took, clinging to the belly fur of a scampering terrier as she skedaddled past the castle gates, whimpering lightly while pursued by nobody, the bells on her collar a deafening clamor. Then began many months of journeying, alone and on foot, as the prince and I made our way home. Finally we bribed and befriended a golden dragon. She carried us out of the center of the earth, up through the mouth of an icy, extinct volcano, and finally deposited us safely back at my castle in Delanico. The dragon was amenable to lending us an ear during our flight home, and we've secured a promise of peace talks ahead.

But those are other stories for other times.

No, today we're out taking our walkies, the prince and me. Humberto, my beloved white poodle, trots down the park path, head up and showing us the way. As we amble along, we plot and plan, getting our strategies straight. Because we're going back to rescue them soon, those unlucky souls still trapped in the Dreaming Village: the mime, the gymnast, the baker, and the others. And we have a powerful ally who's sworn to help. Turns out, dragons aren't fans of secret stockpiles of living playthings either. It deeply offends their ancestral code of ethics.

The Crown Prince of Zanathasia isn't destined to be my future husband—there's no wedding in this story, no romantic conclusion. Gerald's not my type, not that way. But turns out Gerry makes a great adventure partner and an even better friend.

"You're a fine pal, Lu," he always jokes when we part at my castle's back gate. "But this hug's all you get from me—I've had quite enough kisses for now!"

A Drop of Endur

Jess Smart Smiley

H ear that?" Wiccom asked, placing a hand on his sister's wrist.

Aera stiffened. "Is it bad?"

The dry branches rattled and a smile spread across Wiccom's face.

"No, Aera—it's not bad. It's good. Listen."

A flickering confusion of question and surprise colored the swirling endur-clouds of Aera's eyes before she closed her them to concentrate, lowering the snow flowers in her hands to the rough folds of her skirt.

Through the hushed sounds of the wind licking at the fallen snow, Aera heard what at first seemed to be someone calling for help—but, as her ears adjusted, it became clear that the sound was unlike any other sound Aera had known.

A melodious warble pulsed through the air and Aera waited for a rest in the song before turning to her brother. "Wiccom, what is it?"

He seemed caught up in a trance by the shape the tones put into the world.

"It's such a lovely sound, Wiccom. Don't you think? It sounds *warm*, like Mother's tea. And it seems to go in and out of itself somehow—like one of Mother's tapestries!"

Wiccom smiled, pleased by his sister's enthusiasm. "That's a moonwing." Then, answering his sister's expression, added, "A special kind of bird."

The song appeared again but only briefly, as a wink of warmth in frosttime.

"Where is it? And won't it freeze out here in the cold?"

Wiccom laughed. "You ask too many questions."

He pulled some dried citricots from the square of fabric tucked into his coat pocket and handed several orange-red pieces to his sister.

"Moonwings are frostbirds. They're made for the cold."

"No," Aera laughed. "You're joking."

"I'm not!" Wiccom laughed back, wiping the sudden appearance of juice dribbling down his chin. "Their bodies are covered in white fur and they only come out
in the frosttime."

"Like the nursery verse?"

"It's not *just* a nursery verse," Wiccom replied. "It's writ down because it's true.
The song is a reminder. Though endur doesn't keep, which seems a bit odd."

"How's it go, again?"

Wiccom swallowed the last of his fruit and quietly sang,

That all the world could be as Accord,
 When the land is white from the frost taking o'er;
and that we were moonwings
 in need of few things,
resting atop sweet endur's reward.

 Halloo and hail thee, halloo and hail,
 Drops from the endur will surely make well.

As beloved and dear Empress Lilith is pure,
 The drops of the endur are medicine's cure,
Afflicted however
 find remedy's treasure,
May the call of the moonwing lead you to endur.

 Halloo and hail thee, halloo and hail,
 Drops from the endur will surely make well.

Well, well—the trunk is a well,
 Should a taste of her nectar compel
The ill and diseased,
 they'll be put at ease,
Just as moonwings in Accord will foretell.

 Halloo and hail thee, halloo and hail,
 Drops from the endur will surely make well.

Aera's face brightened with familiarity and she joined in,

 Halloo and hail thee, halloo and hail,
 Drops from the endur will surely make well.

Wiccom's voice cut out suddenly with a swell of admiration for his sister, so he
simply watched and listened.

Aera suddenly stopped. "What?"

"*What?*" Wiccom replied. "Why'd you stop?"

"You were *looking* at me."

Wiccom grinned, causing Aera to leap at her brother, and the two fell into the soft snow, tumbling and laughing, until Aera claimed the last of the fruit and the bleary sun tipped behind the hills.

"I WONDER what Mother's been cooking," Wiccom said, eyeing the rising chimney smoke in the nearing distance. "Oh, I hope it's porridge!"

"Well, I hope it's stew," Aera added, hopping into the impressions of her brother's boots in the snow. "And cheese!"

"Stew *and* cheese?" Wiccom asked with an edge of disbelief. "You must think yourself the empress."

Aera's eyes lit up. "Yes—I *am* the empress. And I require stew and cheese at once." Immediately, she began running all around and throwing an arm out to her side.

"What are you doing?"

"You mean," Aera said, between clouded breaths, "What are you doing, *Your Highness?*"

Wiccom rolled his eyes.

"I'm riding in my carriage, of course." Aera's voice rose and fell with inflections of pretended elegance. She turned and ran past her brother, calling out, "My carriage is as quick as a comet!"

Aera flung an arm outward in a grand gesture and attempted the sound of a horse, snorting at her shortcoming.

"But what of your health, Empress? Haven't you got the condition?"

The carriage stopped long enough for Aera to sneer at her brother before returning to the empress and continuing her travels. She appeared to toss something into the snow, alternating sides as she ran.

"I'm the empress and I'm well and I'm sharing my riches with the people of my kingdom. A coin for each. A coin for all!"

Noting their striking color in the snow, Wiccom bent to examine the empress's castings.

"Citricots?" Wiccom shook his head. "Some riches."

Their hand-hewn home of wood and stone came into full view.

As Mother opened the door to greet them, the siblings took in the unmistakable scent of porridge, to which Aera joked, "Did I not call for cheese and stew?"

The world suddenly seemed to fall away when they saw Mother freeze in the doorway; her eyes fixed gravely on something behind them.

Aera searched Mother's expression and found nothing but dread concern.

Wiccom slowly turned to look, then placed a hand on his sister's wrist. "See that?"

The color drained from Aera's face. "Is it bad?"

"Yes, Aera—it's bad."

"Aera, you go in and fetch me Father's musket. Quick."

"But I can't—I'm scared!"

"You *must*, child," said Mother, pulling at her quailing daughter.

Though she resisted, Aera recognized the singular tone of finality in Mother's voice, and cried quietly through closed eyes as she stepped into the warmth of her home, safe from the threat outside her door.

Aera placed one foot in front of the other, cautiously approaching the mantle and taking the weight of her father's musket into her anxious hands. She winced at the weapon's lethal design as she tipped Father's powder horn into the barrel, then placed a lead ball in the muzzle, tamping down the ball into the power and returning to the open door.

"Tillie?" asked Wiccom.

"Sleeping," Mother whispered back, grabbing the long firearm from her daughter's trembling hands. "Did you load it?"

Aera nodded and showed the ramrod.

"Stay with the baby," Mother whispered, reaching with her free hand for the door handle. The muffled sound of Tillie crying could be heard through the two inches of shut door.

"Mother, you go inside, too—I've got this." Wiccom held out his hands to receive the weapon, but Mother jerked her head to the side, telling her son to move, which he did.

Two flecks of radiant green watched from the gnarled cover of thorny gumweed in the dimming light.

"They've never come so close to the house," Mother whispered, taking the barrel and stock into both hands.

"Oh no," Wiccom gasped.

"Wiccom? What is it? Is there another?"

"It's our fault—we didn't mean to, but it was us who did it. It's the citricots, Mother." Wiccom scolded himself silently. "Aera made a trail. It must have drawn it out and it followed us home—"

The hovering green flecks advanced from their cover and, for the first time, the entirety of the fox could be seen.

Mother raised the gun into position and half-whispered, "'Least Aera'll get that stew she wanted."

Aera shivered, hiding between her family and the door.

Wiccom watched the fox closely, its vibrant coat in stark contrast against the fading white of the snow.

Mother lined up the sight and felt for the trigger.

"Mother, wait!" Came a voice. "Don't shoot it!"

Though Mother held her position, she released her finger from the trigger.

"Aera, I told you—"

"But look," Aera instructed, no longer crying, but pointing at the fox before the group. "It's just a baby."

"Baby means mama's nearby," Wiccom cautioned. Then, noticing the lowering gun, asked, "Mother?"

Mother watched intently as the fox hungrily snatched up the bits of fruit on the frozen ground.

"The poor dear is starved." She handed the rifle to her son. "Aera, bring out more fruit—and a dish of water."

"But what if there are more? We always keep foxes away," Aera sniffled.

"We keep *death* away," Mother rasped. "Lost life—human or otherwise—begets loss of life. Go, child."

Wiccom trained the rifle on the fox as Mother gathered the few citricots from around her and placed them in a small pile between her and the fox. Immediately, the fox moved toward the pile and Mother held out a hand when Wiccom followed the movement with the rifle's barrel.

"There's no need, son. Let her down."

"But what of its mama?" Wiccom asked worriedly, scanning the darkness for another pair of green shine.

Just then the door opened, spilling firelight from inside the home onto the dark of snow outside, creating a warm, glittering carpet leading to the doorway where Aera stood.

"Here," Aera said, extending the water dish toward Mother. Then, "Oh, dear!" when she accidentally dropped the citricots. The thumb-size fruits fell to the packed-earth floor in a dull volley. The fox stumbled forward, snapping eagerly at the fruit.

Again, Mother motioned for Wiccom to lower the gun.

Aera screamed at the rush of the wild animal, dropping the water and backing into the bedroom, as the fox snatched up and chewed several of the fruits, then lapped up all the water that hadn't been drunk by the hard dirt floor. It was from their vantage point in the dark of the cold outside that Mother and Wiccom could see the fox more clearly.

A vibrant coat of oranges and reds showed every rib as the fox crept toward the burning hearth.

A breeze lifted at Mother's soft hair, so that she ushered her son inside, closing the door behind her. The fox panted loudly, so Mother motioned for her son to get new water while she replaced the musket above the fireplace.

The animal lapped up the new water, its skinny legs shaking and buckling as it bent its scrawny neck toward the dish. Mother kept a cautious eye on the canine, while scooping a helping of porridge into a bowl for her son. A second bowl was prepared and Mother walked with guarded steps into the bedroom, where she found Aera weeping beside the sleeping toddler.

Watching from across the room, Wiccom was mesmerized by the fox's breathing and the soft, chattery mewlings it made as the spark of fire reflecting in its eyes closed behind tired lids.

"Huaghh!"

Wiccom sat up at the sudden presence of something wet and textured sliding against his cheek.

Stumbling backward on his heels and palms, he was stopped by the wall of the home. The window allowed dawn's glow to warm the mulberry-tinted shade within, illuminating a confused-looking fox in a wash of reds, oranges, and endur.

As Wiccom wiped his cheek, the fox turned its attention toward Aera, curled and slumbering in front of the glowing fireplace, rather than in the bedroom, where they two—along with Mother and baby–should have been.

The fox licked Aera's cheeks, startling Wiccom.

"Good morrow, dear Wiccom," said Mother, in her strong-and-tender voice. "Still making pleasant company with our foxy friend, I see. He seems to have taken a liking to you two." She ran colored threads in and out of each other on the wooden loom that occupied the back corner of the room.

"Mother," Wiccom asked, cautiously leaning for a better view of the fox licking Aera's cheeks, "didn't you sleep?"

"Oh, here and there, I suppose," she answered. Mother lifted a vertical warp and pulled a horizontal weft over then behind. "But I spent my waking hours with good company." Another knowing smile reminded Wiccom that his mother somehow lived in an unseen place within his same world.

Wiccom caught a hesitation in his mother's eyes and asked, "Then what troubles you?"

A moment passed as Mother thoughtfully worked a weft to the center of the tapestry, where she came to a stop.

"What do you think, Wiccom?" she asked, tipping her head.

Wiccom stood and took in the tapestry for the first time, noting the intersections of colored threads. An excitement danced in Wiccom's eyes. "That boy looks like me! And those girls—they look like Aera and Tillie! Oh, Mother—is it us?"

Mother's smile was all the answer Wiccom needed.

"And that's you," came Aera's voice. "You and Da."

Aera lay in front of the fireplace, stroking the fox, who seemed equally at ease laying beside her.

"There's no fooling your bright minds," Mother smiled. She put out her hands and both children ran to be gathered into Mother's arms. "It's a surprise for his return. Think he'll like it?"

Wiccom's excitement continued. "Oh, Mother—it's your finest yet. The likenesses are brilliant and it'll hang perfectly beside the fire. Da will think it a true treasure!"

Mother laughed. "No need to fabricate."

"But Ma," Wiccom asked, "what of that bit there, beside Tillie?" Knowing not to touch the tapestries, Wiccom pointed to the open space that evaded Mother's threads.

"Ah. Sharp as a needle," Mother replied. "You may well be a weaver." And, after drawing in a breath through her nose, Mother answered, "Yes, something's missing— I just don't know what."

"Can't you add more flowers?" Wiccom asked. "Or a moonwing?"

A series of expressions tried for footing in the features of her face, before Mother concluded, "Perhaps."

Aera sniffled and drew the attention of the others.

She wept, with the fox as weft to the warp of her legs.

"Why does frosttime have to be so long?"

"Oh, Aera," Mother soothed, stepping toward her daughter and running her hands through Aera's ember hair. "He'll be back before long." Mother's eyes glanced at the depiction of her husband in the developing tapestry, then closed with concern. "You should be very proud of your da. Very few stablemen are qualified for enlistment to the empress for a season. Besides," Mother added, "he's to return with a fortune. Just imagine all the stew and cheese we'll eat then!"

Though Mother laughed, Aera stayed silent, wrapped in Mother's embrace.

Wiccom looked longingly at the rifle held above the mantle. The initials "N.E.G." glimmered a radiant gold in the increasing brightness of the morning and Mother couldn't help softly repeating, "He'll be back before long."

The ensuing quiet was broken by a volley of babbles from the bedroom.

"Wiccom?" Mother asked, and her son went at once to fetch his sister, who shortly ran out to the parlor in her nightclothes.

"Tillie!" Aera called, dropping to her knees and holding out her hands.

But the toddler stopped at the sight of the fox and her eyes went big.

The older group laughed.

"She's never seen a fox before!" Wiccom grinned.

"She has in Ma's pictures!" Said Aera.

Mother laughed and joined Aera in lowering to her knees. She spoke in clear, warm tones to her youngest. "Want to say hello? He's a fox." She stroked the animal's coat, running her fingers down the length of his back in a welcoming display. "Soft."

The toddler stared for a moment more with her eyes wide before cautiously approaching the new creature.

Another small moment passed with a playful tension, ending with the fox stepping out from Aera's legs and circling the curious child. The fox made a cheerful squealing sound and reared back, lightly patting Tillie's chest with the black, clawed toes of her forepaws.

"Oh, Mother," Aera pleaded. "Can we keep him?"

"Yes, Mother—please?" Wiccom added enthusiastically.

Tillie buried her head in the fox's fur, giggling from the ticklish brush of silky bristles.

"Well," Mother reflected. "He'd need to earn his keep."

The older children's eyes ballooned with excitement.

"Really, Mother? We can keep him for our own?" Wiccom asked.

"And," Mother added, with a tone of instruction, "We can't very well keep him without possession of a proper name."

The momentum of the accord seemed to pinch sharply, peaking just when Tillie dropped to the floor with the fox and rolled, howling with laughter, and loudly proclaiming, "Ga-wa!"

All but the toddler and fox fell silent, then the household burst into peals of laughter at the nonsensical word.

"Gawa!" the children repeated.

"So," Mother declared, "I suppose Gawa can stay."

The rest of the day—save for the cooking and cleaning—was given over to playing with the newest member of the Grandahl family.

"Gawa!" Wiccom called, tossing a stick into the whiteness outside and delighting in its quick and jubilant return.

"Gawa!" shouted Aera, challenging the fox to tireless foot races in the falling snow.

"Gawa!" Tillie cheered, tackling and wrestling the mass of claws and fur. "Gawa! Gawa! Gawa!"

Even Mother took moments away from the keeping of the house to chase the chattering fox, feeding him nuts and scraps whenever he wandered back inside.

THE NEXT DAY and weeks that followed were spent much the same, though Wiccom was away during daylight tending Ott Brewer's hogs and all-season beans. Aera helped Mother at home with keeping Tillie happy, fetching wood and water, and cutting vegetables for cooking. All the while, of course, with the adopted red fox underfoot.

Gawa seemed entranced by Mother's weaving, sometimes watching for hours as Mother's nimble fingers worked before the fox would drift off to sleep, chattering and flicking its tongue in the air.

Each day was a new adventure, with Wiccom training the eager fox to hunt small game, which could be added to Mother's pot, or tanned and made into pelts and then traded for wool that could be dyed and used in Mother's tapestries. But the fox's attention seemed fleeting and drawn toward something in the unseen distance, which frustrated the lessons of his teacher.

Ott Brewer told Wiccom that foxes have an excellent sense of smell—which Wiccom surmised was the reason for Gawa bounding up the path to him one hundred paces away from home on his returning from "hog-work", odorous from the day spent with Brewer's swine. It was a pleasant discovery, then, when Wiccom learned of Gawa's exceptional hearing.

Several times, Wiccom had trained his Father's gun on a groundling, attempting to educate the fox on the potential food source, but it seemed lost in distraction. It was on one such occasion that Wiccom surrendered the hunt and gave his senses completely to his surroundings. Immediately after noticing the quick and sudden rotation of Gawa's ears, Wiccom heard the distant but unmistakable call of a moonwing. Cloaked by the snow and concealed by constant whispers of the wind, Wiccom vowed to listen more closely and to open himself up to further teachings from his fox.

Aera, too, spent many meaningful hours with the fox—usually running through snow powder pretending to be the empress or singing.

As beloved and dear Empress Lilith is pure,
    The drops of the endur are medicine's cure,
Afflicted however
    find remedy's treasure,
May the call of the moonwing lead you to endur.

Each night and most mornings, Aera would call to the fox, who she had taken to calling "my Gawa":

Halloo and hail thee, halloo and hail.

So often were the lines sung, that Mother took to calling her daughter and fox collectively *Halloo* and *Hail*, though Aera was never sure who was who.

During their weeks of frosttime together, Gawa made as much merriment and mischief as Wiccom, Aera, and Tillie, so Mother also took to calling Gawa "child".

On a day during midweek, Wiccom ventured to take Gawa with him to Ott Brewer's, but the fox ended up scaring one of the hogs into the bean field, and Wiccom spent the rest of the day chasing down the hog, then trying to direct it back into the pen.

The same night, Gawa tunneled after a mouse in the parlor's dirt floor and Mother scolded him for days, getting after Wiccom to fill the hole and tamp down the new dirt.

Another night became known as *The Night of Noise* in the Grandahl family.

After pretending the role of empress and playfully enlisting Wiccom as her Imperial Hound, Aera noticed Gawa behaving in a strange manner. His ears perked this way and that. He yipped incessantly, bounding throughout the house, leaping at the door and window. With the night coming on and the day being bitter cold, Mother kept everyone inside, seated in her rocking chair with her husband's rifle in her lap. At one point, Gawa's behavior became so erratic that Mother decided to let him out of doors for the safety of her children, though they protested terribly.

Not thirty minutes later, Wiccom heard a low, haunting, mysterious sound outside that chilled him to the bone. He begged Mother to let him call out for Gawa, which she let him do. The fox quickly returned, shivering with his fur standing on end. Wiccom was awakened in the middle of that night by the sound. He rushed to unshutter the window, where he clearly saw an enormous cack-owl perched on the empty branch of a nearby tree, staring with endur eyes, before lifting its broad wings and vanishing into the endless abandon that was the night sky.

THOUGH NO MORE MOONWINGS WERE SPOTTED OVER the next few weeks, Aera kept every feather she found, then fashioned a feathered necklace for Mother's name day. Wiccom made a bean cake, and put in two nights' work to help Mother with her woven family portrait.

Wiccom and Aera took infinite pleasure in watching Gawa pounce in graceful arcs over groundling holes. A similar joy was had by exploring tunnels the children had dug into the snow, decorating the entryways with the prints from the fox's paws.

The Grandahl family learned the hard way that fox urine smells worse than a skunk's fog.

All this, while singing:

> That all the world could be as Accord,
>   When the land is white from the frost taking o'er;
> and that we were moonwings
>   in need of few things,
> resting atop sweet endur's reward.

>   Halloo and hail thee, halloo and hail,
>   Drops from the endur will surely make well.

Above all else, the family reveled in the warmth of their togetherness, their hearts entwined like the tight, delicate strands of Mother's tapestry.

Mother declared on what became known as *That Night* that she knew at last how to finish her family tapestry, what would fill the empty space beside the children on her otherwise complete portrait.

"Well, isn't it obvious?" Mother asked, addressing the children.

Gawa turned his feathery ears and tilted his head. Tillie bounced on Wiccom's knee.

"The sky is a cool blue. The grass and trees, cool greens. They make up the background so that the warm colors of our skin stand out."

"So you'll fill it with something cool?" asked Aera.

Gawa yipped, his way of imitating Aera's speech.

"Something *warm*," Mother explained. "And what warm color stands out against blue and green?"

Only the crackling of the fire sounded during the children's hesitation.

"Orange!" Mother exclaimed. Then, picking up Gawa, who licked at her face, Mother clarified: "Gawa Orange!"

What would have been a moment of celebration was broken by the sudden opening of the door with an accompanying flurry of wind and snow.

The fire flickered wildly as Gawa barked and growled at the intruder.

Both Wiccom and Mother made for the rifle, but it was Mother who grabbed it first, immediately withdrawing a paper cartridge and adding powder from the hearth, shouting, "Get out! Get out!"

But the figure advanced and, through the fox's wet snapping and Aera's sobbing, a familiar voice said, "Hettie."

All fell silent and still.

A rapture of grateful surprise ignited the room as the children rushed to greet their father, Gawa watching cautiously from near the fire.

Mother fell into her husband's eager arms.

"Nort'," Mother wept through the tears that ran into her open smile. "Oh, Nort'!"

Father's face hardened and was overtaken by a grim expression. As he looked into the faces of his dear ones, his voice was heavy and laden with sorrow.

"I have returned ahead of schedule, for the Empress Lilith is perilously ill and near her end."

An air of concern and apprehension filled the room as Father left and returned with an ailing woman in her twentieth year, gaunt and pallid. An older woman, heavyset and strong, followed the pair inside.

Mother nearly jumped at the sight, stating, "I'll fetch some water and bread."

Wiccom, still with Tillie in his arms, stepped back with Aera at the sight of the very empress he had seen his sister imitate with so much elegance and distinction but who now appeared weak and frail. Nothing like the ruler he or Aera had imagined.

"Wiccom," Father commanded, "You and Feddrah bring the bed out by the fire. Aera, move aside the table and chairs. This is Ethe empress's room now."

Tillie began to cry amidst the commotion and ran to hold Mother's leg. Gawa let himself outside, unsure of his place.

Mother shut the door on the cold then brought a cup of warm water to the ailing empress cradled feebly in her husband's arms.

With much distress, the empress cracked her lips and accepted a small sip of water. Then, struggling to swallow, the empress made a pained expression and turned from the drink.

Once the bed was situated by the fire, Father gently lowered the empress to the mattress, covering her with Mother's handmade patchwork comforter and carefully placing pillows beneath her head.

"Empress, Feddrah," Father introduced, looking to each as he spoke their name, "this is my family. My dear Hettie, Wiccom, and Aera. The little one is Tillie."

"An honor to meet you all," Feddrah said in a gravely voice that seemed textured with lifetimes of triumph and loss. "Hello, Tillie," she said, with a brightness in her eyes.

Tillie stepped behind Mother and peered out through her legs.

"You know of the empress's ailment—same as what took her parents, rest them—but the illness has fast overcome her and we fear the worst. Feddrah is Lilith's Imperial Medic. She is committed to the health of the empress but has yet to find any remedy or treatment with any effect."

Feddrah turned to Mother. "Thank you, Madam Harriet, for lending us the use of your home. I assure you that you will be well-compensated for your sacrifice."

Mother shook her head, "It is offered respectfully, Madam Feddrah. May I ask what brought the empress here?"

Father forced a smile through his otherwise grave expression.

Still intimidated by the presence of the empress, Aera and Wiccom called over Tillie, then stepped into the bedroom.

"Of course," Feddrah said. "I'll speak plainly. Time is in short supply."

"Of course," Mother returned.

The medic drew in a sharp breath and looked to Nort', who adjusted the empress's covering. "We have tried everything. All that I know, all that the kingdom offers. *All*—save for one potential cure."

"Oh?" Mother asked, handing a piece of bread each to the empress, Feddrah, and her husband.

"She won't eat," Feddrah said flatly. "Believe me, we've tried. Here," she offered, taking the slice from Mother's hand and putting it into Nort's. "He needs it. Anyway. Nort' sings of the endur of Accord. All the day singing, singing in the stables. So. We've come to Accord for drops of endur. Fable or otherwise, it is our last hope."

Mother caught her breath as a realization came to her.

"Hettie?" Nort' asked.

"I'm sorry," Mother confessed, nearly in tears, "but you've come too late!"

She wept openly as she told how the moonwings had been silent ever since *The Night of Noise*.

"I don't understand," Father said. "What are you saying?"

"The owl—it either scared them into hiding or chased the moonwings away altogether. The trees all look the same and without the moonwing's call, we'll never find one with endur. Oh, Empress!" Mother's face was wet with streaming tears as she leaned toward the empress who was jerking sporadically.

"Please," Feddrah demanded, pulling Mother by her shoulders. "The empress can't tolerate the noise of crying or the punishment of unwanted touch."

Nort' drew his wife to his chest and considered the circumstances before kissing her and pulling his coat's heavy leather-and-wool hood over his head.

"I'll be back with endur," he said to the group. "Keep her warm and tend to her every need."

"Father?" Wiccom called as Father opened the door. "Can I help?"

But the door closed with the two on either side, and Father could be heard shouting to the horses over the swells of wind, with Gawa barking, barking, barking.

THE FIRE POPPED, spitting ash onto the floor, and casting new shadows on old walls.

Mother's shadow rocked and rocked in her shadow chair, Feddrah's shadow stood and sat and paced and watched the window. The shadow of the empress looked less like a figure and more like so much cloth bunched atop the bed.

Tillie had long since fallen asleep on a blanket draped across the bedroom floor and Aera caught herself dozing a few times, still unable to believe the empress herself was in her home. Wiccom sat in the frame of the bedroom doorway, drawing nothing in particular with a stick into the dirt, the fox nestled at his feet.

Hours passed, and still the empress refused food and drink of any kind. Her convulsions had become much more pronounced and closer together.

"She won't last long," Feddrah finally said, looking longingly upon her patient.

Wiccom raised his head and Mother turned in her chair.

"How can you be sure?" Mother asked, reaching for the water glass.

But no answer came.

The door opened and Father stepped in, his shirt and pants torn, snow dripping in the heat of the room.

"Oh, Nort'," Mother exclaimed, rushing from the chair to meet him. "You're just in time! Feddrah said—"

"I didn't find any," Father said. His voice was quiet and ragged, run through the rigors of exhaustion.

Feddrah closed her eyes.

"But we simply have to listen," Aera said, walking with full innocence into the parlor. She continued,

> *"The drops of the endurr are medicine's cure,*
> *May the call of the moonwing lead you to endur."*

"The moonwings are gone," Father said. "I've looked."

"But you *won't* see them. Wiccom told me—they're covered in white fur so they blend in with the frost."

"I saw the frost," Father stated coldly.

"You have to *listen*," Aera explained. "You have to listen for the moonwing."

> *"May the call of the moonwing lead you to endur."*

"Aera," Father started, his head bent forward and his eyes closed. "Aera, I've been looking and listening all night. The empress's best horse is run weary. The owl must have scared them off."

"Halloo and hail thee, halloo and hail,
  Drops from the endur will surely make well."

Gawa's ears perked up as Mother sighed heavily and turned to her daughter. "Aera, I know you're trying to help—"

"But Ma, Da's done all the looking and listening he can, but he can't find the moonwings."

Mother massaged her forehead as the empress kicked uncontrollably.

"But maybe we just need different lookers and listeners—Halloo and Hail."

Gawa barked cheerily at the mention of his moniker and moved to Aera's side.

"Here," Aera said, reaching behind Mother's neck and unclasping her name day gift. "Gawa has a great sense of smell—we just have to show him what we're looking for." Aera dangled the feathers over the fox, who inhaled the scent and ran in circles with excitement.

As Mother and Father exchanged worried glances, Wiccom stood and joined his sister's side. "Gawa and I will go—he's a great hunter and can hear, even through the wind."

Father took in a deep breath and stood reluctantly. "Very well."

"No," Feddrah countered, noticing the gashes cut into Father's clothing, where blood had dried on his exposed skin. "You've had enough gumweed for the night. I'll go."

Father stood silently, gathering his thoughts through the heavy confusion of fatigue.

"So," Feddrah concluded.

The medic, along with Wiccom, Aera, and Gawa, moved toward the door, with Mother and Father surprised.

As the door opened, the empress strained to turn. Her body kicked and jerked and convulsed in painful spasms.

"Empress?" Father asked, leaning toward his ruler.

Her dry lips parted and the faintest of whispers emerged.

Father looked at Mother, who blinked, then said, "She says she wants to go."

The empress wheezed once more through the smallest crack in her lips.

"She says she wants a final ride through the country."

Father's face flashed shades of dread, before he finally nodded and gathered the delicate skeleton of the dying empress. "Ready the carriage," he said to Feddrah, who left at once with the children and fox.

In the final movement of lifting the empress, Father's eyes caught the picture in the shadowed corner and blinked. "Is that *us?*"

"GOT IT, Gawa? You got it, boy?" Wiccom teased the fox with the moonwings' feathers, working the hunter into a hungry excitement. "Go get it!"

Gawa took off running at lightning speed, racing effortlessly through the snow.

Wiccom followed closely behind on his father's horse, and behind him Feddrah drove the Imperial Carriage, rushing Aera with the empress as quick as a comet.

That all the world could be as Accord,
  When the land is white from the frost taking o'er;
and that we were moonwings
  in need of few things,
resting atop sweet endur's reward.

The brisk frosttime air bit at Wiccom's cheeks as he studied Gawa's quick movements through the powder and crust, turning when the fox turned, dipping when he dipped. Inside the carriage, Aera braved the necessary task of holding the empress as closely in place as possible, while the transport fought with the empress's jerking, shaking body.

As beloved and dear Empress Lilith is pure,
  The drops of the endurr are medicine's cure,
Afflicted however
  find remedy's treasure,
May the call of the moonwing lead you to endur.

Suddenly, the fox stopped and turned its ears this way, then that. Wiccom expertly stopped his horse and motioned for Feddrah to do the same behind him. Then, as quickly as the momentum had ceased, Gawa bounded directly into a wooded area, which Wiccom combed with his eyes, assisted by the moonlight, finding a path that both he and the carriage could fit through, while also keeping an eye on the bounding fox.

Well, well—the trunk is a well,
  Should a taste of her nectar compel
The ill and diseased,
  they'll be put at ease,
Just as moonwings in Accord will foretell.

Wiccom lost sight of the fox and panicked, before spotting the beloved red coat of his pet dart directly in front of him and stop at the base of the tree, where Wiccom and the carriage halted. A familiar melody filled Wiccom's ears and he knelt into the snow to thank the fox.

Halloo and hail thee, halloo and hail,
Drops from the endur will surely make well.

In a quick succession of movements, Feddrah dismounted from the driver's seat, reined in the horses, and entered the carriage, where the empress moaned in agony, her body thrashing in Aera's hold.

"Hear that?" Feddrah asked, placing a hand on the wrist of the empress.

The empress labored to speak. "Is it bad?"

Feddrah caught Aera smiling beside her, her cheeks wet with grateful tears, and took her hand into her own.

"No, Empress—it's not bad," he said, trying not to laugh. "It's good. Listen."

THE ENDUR ACTED QUICKLY in a warm mixture of Mother's citricot-and-gumweed tea. The Grandahl family fire warmed the empress's sleeping body, while the endur healed the Empress Lilith, coaxing health into her cells and mending the paths of her illness. Heavy snow fell and the night hours passed for the slumbering household.

In the morning, Ott Brewer's face flushed at the sight of the empress standing at his door.

"Lilith! I mean, Empress! I mean—" Ott drew in a breath, wiping his forehead as he noted Feddrah, Wiccom, and the Grandahl family surrounding the ruler. "I mean, what an honor to meet you!"

Ott knelt. Then, turning to Wiccom, as though no one else could hear, he added, "She's even more fetching than they say!"

The empress blushed and pretended to not hear.

"Please stand, Mr. Brewer. I'm told you have some horses," the empress stated, her voice a lacework of honey.

"Horses, yes!" Ott exclaimed happily, shifting his weight to a standing position. "Yes—horses, hogs, beans. Whatever Your Majesty needs."

Feddrah stepped forward. "We need to return to Affa. Her Majesty's carriage is frozen beneath the snowfall. We need a team of horses to carry us. Are you willing?"

Ott Brewer's expression shifted from embarrassed to dutiful.

"Yes, Empress," Ott said, bending one knee.

AND SO IT came to be that the hog farmer escorted the empress, along with her Imperial Medic, back to the Imperial City, causing the villagers to solemnly bow their heads in respect to the passing Empress, until Feddrah cheerfully shouted to the people, "The empress lives! The empress is well!" To which the villagers clapped and cried tears of grateful joy.

In Accord, Nort' and Wicom honorably tended to Ott Brewer's beans and livestock, and Ma Harriet Grandahl worked new fibers into a new tapestry with the help of Aera, while Gawa played with young Tillie by the hearth.

YEARS PASSED PEACEFULLY, with each new shifting season offering new joys and surprises.

No longer employed by the empress, but granted a generous wage, Nort' extended the walls of the Grandahl home to more comfortable dimensions, though the family found themselves gathering closely together most days in the parlor, as they had done before, effectively leaving a room's worth of unoccupied space in the home, which they kept in remembrance of the empress and her visit.

A healthy grove of citricot trees slowly took the place of a field on the east end of the Grandahl farm, which Aera tended lovingly. She instructed Tillie on how to properly cultivate the ground at the base of each trunk, how to prune at the proper time, and how to join Mother in drying the fruits, preparing jams, and combining with nuts, creams, and other foods to create desserts and dishes. Their favorite was a new recipe that combined a savory mash of beans from Ott Brewer's farm topped with a sweet citricot glaze that sent Tillie's taste buds into a frenzy, which prompted Aera to call the dish "Juice from the Tail of a Comet".

Time wove strands of gray hairs onto Mother's head, Father's beard, and Gawa's coat, which shimmered like silver in the sun, splitting the light into thousands of dancing illuminated splinters.

Aera took up Ma's tapestry work and began to travel, weaving the tales of each population she visited into colorful banners that were proudly displayed in city centers and along popular trade routes. Tillie followed in her sister's footsteps, caring for the grove of citricots, which she saw as a living, thriving population of gentle, benevolent beings whose trees produced subtleties of size, texture, and flavor, similar to—but unique from—their neighbors'. She admired her parents and delighted in the coming of each frosttime, when she and Gawa would listen carefully for moonwings, then offer them gifts of "Juice from the Tail of a Comet" in gratitude for their presence and for their singular role in restoring vitality to the empress and her homeland.

IT WAS in the warm season, just after the refreshment of a sweet rainfall, that Wiccom strode home on Ott Brewer's swiftest courser, with a quickness and excitement that toppled a working Tillie, whose upper half was buried in the green leaves of a fruiting citricot tree.

As the ladder fell from under his sister, Wiccom leaped from the horse and caught Tillie in a cluster of tall, soft grass.

"Wiccom!" Tillie exclaimed. "You startled me!"

"I'm sorry, sister. I didn't see you up there."

"But I'm always up in the trees." Tillie laughed as Wiccom took her hands in his and helped her stand. "It's harvest season. Have you come to help?"

"Oh, sure," Wiccom laughed. "You think Brewer doesn't keep me busy enough?"

Harriet and Nort' rushed out of the home, Ma racing to Tillie's side.

"Did you fall?" asked Ma. "Are you hurt? I looked out and saw the ladder on its side. I thought—"

"Ma, I'm fine. Look who's here!"

Ma clapped and Father took Wiccom's face into his hands, heartily patting the son's cheeks in his hands until Wiccom jerked away in laughter.

"Supper's not on for an hour," Ma stated. "What brings you home at such a time?"

Father stepped back, registering the presence of Ott Brewer's dark bay horse—the one Wiccom reserved for chasing down runaway hogs or racing into town for a quick supply run.

Father's face turned serious.

"I bring news!" Wiccom shouted, pulling a letter from the horse's satchel.

Tillie's eyes sparkled as she whispered, "The empress's seal."

"Well," Nort' cut in. "What's it say?"

Wiccom drew in a deep breath and shook his head. "I don't know. Here," he said, handing the letter to Mother, "you read it."

Tillie fed a citricot to the horse while the family gathered around Mother.

Dearest Grandahls: Father Nort', Ma Hettie, Master Wiccom, Lady Aera, and Miss Tillie,

It's me—Ott Brewer!

To begin with, I hear Master Wiccom has done well with the farm. Good on you, boy. The work is not easy and it takes a disciplined mind and body to do it right.

My whole livelihood up until now has been that farm. Since I was a boy, every coin I made from beans was invested into more beans, which eventually became enough to raise and sell hogs. In many ways, that way of life seems so distant from me as to belong to someone else entirely. Still, I often wake out of habit before the cockeral, only to realize there are no hogs for me to tend to. All of this to say that the farm is yours now.

Next point: you may be wondering if I've spent my years in Affa learning to write. Wrong! The empress has appointed me a scribe. Each word I dictate must be written word-for-word by the scribe with

Imperial Ink on Imperial Paper—even if I say something like 'drivel' or 'claptrap' or goolygumstrumpling. Ha ha ha!

Oh, fie. The scribe says he's annoyed.

Well, I'm annoyed that you're annoyed. Write that!

Anyway.

My third and final reason for this letter is to invite you to Her Majesty's wedding. TO ME!

That's right—it turns out the empress has a taste for hogs, beans, and Brewers! Ha ha!

The load of you are expected on the morning of this year's half—"Night of Noise" (I believe that's what you called it). We'll feast for days, and I'll show you how I've trained Her Majesty's horses. I think Aera especially will take to an endur-colored filly I've named Citricot. Oh! And the tapestry Hettie sent for Lily—I mean, for Her Majesty—will be the backdrop for the ceremony. It really is the loveliest moon-wing I've seen.

I'll watch for you in four weeks' time.

The family took turns laughing and crying, joyously surprised by their friend's good news, which was signed at the bottom with Ott's smudge of a thumbprint.

AERA WAS IMMEDIATELY CALLED home from a village two days away, while Mother and Tillie purchased fabric and started the tedious work of measuring, cutting, and stitching family dresses and suits. Wiccom enlisted Father's help in the long days on his farm, training a team of farmhands to oversee the work during their absence.

At last came the Grandahl's journey to Affa to see their friend, the hog-and-bean farmer Ott Brewer, wed to the once-ailing Empress Lilith.

Wiccom and Father took turns driving the carriage given them by the empress herself those many years ago, while Ma Grandahl led Aera and Tillie in weaving a new tapestry, depicting a hog wearing the Imperial Emblem, flanked by fields of beans and an arc of delicate moonwings. Gawa, dressed in the noble silver threads of age, smiled out the carriage window, enjoying the shifting movements of the wind against his fur and occasionally snapping at a passing swarm of insects and licking his satisfied snout.

Conversation switched between subjects related to traveling and tapestry work, to farming, harvesting citricots, Gawa, and Ott Brewer and his empress bride. At each appearance of the last subject, the family would laugh for minutes in delighted disbelief.

When conversation fell quiet and the only sounds heard were the trodding of horse hooves and the turning of carriage wheels, Aera would hum. Regardless of the song she started, each melody inevitably turned to that of the nursery verse she had learned young from Wiccom. All would join in singing, though Tillie found herself asking questions of the song that somehow didn't seem to trouble her family.

> *That all the world could be as Accord,*
>   *When the land is white from the frost taking o'er;*
> *and that we were moonwings*
>   *in need of few things,*
> *resting atop sweet endur's reward.*
>
>   *Halloo and hail thee, halloo and hail,*
>   *Drops from the endur will surely make well.*
>
> *As beloved and dear Empress Lilith is pure,*
>   *The drops of the endur are medicine's cure,*
> *Afflicted however*
>   *find remedy's treasure,*
> *May the call of the moonwing lead you to endur.*
>
>   *Halloo and hail thee, halloo and hail,*
>   *Drops from the endur will surely make well.*
>
> *Well, well—the trunk is a well,*
>   *Should a taste of her nectar compel*
> *The ill and diseased,*
>   *they'll be put at ease,*
> *Just as moonwings in Accord will foretell.*
>
>   *Halloo and hail thee, halloo and hail,*
>   *Drops from the endur will surely make well.*

As she pondered the words, Tillie began to form a new verse—first in her mind, then through a nervous voice, as her family listened with surprise.

Formed a new verse, over which her family was elated, and heartily joined in singing:

Away we to Affa, to see dear Empress wed,
  made well from the drops that sweet endur did shed.
We'll travel by moonwing
    To this song's sweet tuning,
As quick as a comet, to Affa we tread.

Though the horses kept traveling, the Grandahl family seemed to stop altogether to stare as Tillie sang the last phrase.

"Oh no," Tillie worried, her voice falling and her face tensed. "Is it bad?"

"No," Wiccom smiled. "It's perfect."

And so the family journeyed onward, everyone singing

Halloo and hail thee, halloo and hail,
Drops from the endur will surely make well.

Talketh and the Grasilisk

Robert F. Lowell

Princess Talketh squared her broad shoulders and placed her hands on her substantial hips. Her carrot-colored braid fell almost to the hem of her elegant blue kirtle. "Mother, you *can't* do this! I've taken the Sentinel training and passed every stage with top marks! You've *got* to let me test for the Red Hat!"

The Royal Burrow's circular presence chamber was the arena for many arguments between mother and daughter. The queen let its domed ceiling fall silent for a few heartbeats before she responded. "My darling child, the training hall has not prepared you for the dangers that live above the roots."

"I'm not a child, and Father would have let me take the test," Talketh snapped. "He knew I could take the teeth from a gnawgart as well as any of the men in my cohort."

The queen rose from the ornately carved throne and advanced on her daughter. "The gnawgarts are nothing. A razorclaw can tear you to ribbons before you can blink. A bloodfang, even a tame one, can chomp you in two and swallow both halves in one gulp. And the worst by far is the grasilisk. First its eyes paralyze you, then it bites fire into your veins, and finally it crushes you in its coils so you'll slide smoothly down its gullet. As for the giants," she continued, "they do their part to tend the lands from their side of the roots. But they can also pick up Sentinels on a whim and hurl them like pebbles."

"That's what the Red Hats are for," Talketh countered. Every Sentinel's tall, conical Red Hat was felted with deep, ancient magic, giving those who wore them the power to become living stone, hard and unmoving to most eyes, yet still awake and alert. A Sentinel in that state was not invulnerable but could stand watch above ground indefinitely, immune to tooth and claw, while a thousand unknowing giants walked by.

"The Red Hat is not for your red head," the Queen proclaimed. "That's an end to it."

"Fine," Talketh grumbled. "I'll just go to my bedchamber and knit a pair of mittens." She wheeled around and stormed off, knocking Milketh the kitchen maid head over heels with the presence chamber door. Their collision sent a tray of sweet mushroom cakes flying. The princess barked an apology over her shoulder as she stomped through the stone-lined subterranean corridors. Everyone else she met was careful to stay out of her way.

When she reached her apartments, Talketh did not reach for her knitting needles. She took her sword down from its place of honor beneath her father's portrait. Short and broad but honed to a fine edge, the blade was sized to conceal under a Red Hat. Eyes fixed on the king's fork-bearded image, she grabbed her long braid and cut it off with a single stroke. Her remaining hair fell loose to her shoulders as she kicked away her fur slippers, threw off her kirtle and bodice, and put on a heavy woolen tunic and trousers. She buckled her wide leather belt, pulled on a pair of hard-soled boots, and donned a cap she knitted herself. Taking up her blade again, the princess raised it in salute to her father and tucked it into her belt. She left her braid on the floor behind her and marched off to face the world above.

Sentinels guarded the exits well and would never let Talketh pass, but her father had taught her another way out, a secret way. Hurrying along, making sure she was not observed, she left the well-kept tunnels that housed her people for a dank passage that looked as if it had seen no traffic for years. She pulled off the loose stones that marked her goal, squeezed through a slime-coated fissure, and crawled into a half-collapsed cavern filled with the stench of decay. Wading through writhing worms, the princess slipped past rot and ruin until she found a gnarled taproot through which life and power still flowed. Talketh placed both hands on the root and quietly chanted words passed down to her through countless generations.

As she spoke the last syllable, the earth above her began to swirl as if she had pulled the plug from a sink that drained upward. The spinning soil opened a straight round shaft many times longer than Talketh's height. A tendril sprouted from the taproot and spiraled up the side of the shaft, providing holds for hands and feet. Through the top of the shaft, the princess could see stars. She climbed.

When she emerged, she thanked the Deep Gods that it was dark. Her people's eyes were unused to strong light. She felt the air move faster and freer than it did beneath the roots. A broad green plain spread out in front of her, broken a few hundred paces away by a towering gray block, perfectly rectangular, that hid some of the stars. That, Talketh knew, was the giants' castle.

Talketh heard a grinding sound behind her. She whirled around to see a tall striped stone sliding to cover the shaft through which she had come. That was the portal stone, marking the spot to which she must return in order to go back underground. Beside it stood a black-bearded Sentinel, still and hard as the stone itself. His eyes glanced at Talketh and widened more than she thought possible. Only her people and a few other creatures would notice his glance. In the giants' eyes, he would continue to stare out at the grassy expanse surrounding their castle, unmoving under his Red Hat.

The Sentinel's eyes followed Talketh as she turned and ran toward the castle, but he did not. She knew he could leave his post only for the direst of emergencies, and a disobedient princess would not rise to that level no matter how hard her royal mother might rage. He said nothing as Talketh charged around the side of the castle out of his sight, into part of the field unobserved by any of the Sentinels. Talketh knew their ranks were too thin to cover every part of her family's lands all the time. She risked coming above the roots to add herself to their numbers.

To accomplish that, she would have to find a gnawgart's lair, venture into it, kill one of the foul-smelling beasts, and bring back its huge incisors. Finding one of the holes gnawgarts dug shouldn't be difficult, as they were entirely too plentiful on these plains. Loremaster Morgrae once told her that in their language, the giants called this place *Phrawgmaoth*, meaning "place where the river Phrawg meets the sea." He didn't know who or what the river itself was named after. He did know the giants called her people *noems*, but most of them refused to believe her kind really existed. They thought the Sentinels were only stony decorations for their gardens.

Talketh's goal was not ornamental, and it didn't take her long to find what she sought. She saw the spoil from a gnawgart lair piled waist-high around its entrance. The opening was about half as wide as she was tall, and the sausage-shaped monster would fill all of it. She would have to crouch or crawl into its burrow, putting herself at a disadvantage against the beast's ferocious incisors.

The princess crept as close to the hole as she dared and stood in the tall grass, formulating her next move. Her plan to prove herself worthy of the Sentinels lacked detail. Her instructors made the task sound straightforward, but she found it more complex in practice than it was in the classroom. Struggling to devise a better alternative than simply walking into the gaping pit, she stared at it, tightly focused, barely aware of her surroundings.

Breath heavier than a blacksmith's bellows, stinking of rotten meat, blasted the princess from behind. In a single smooth motion, she drew her blade and spun around to meet the threat.

Two legs like black-furred tree trunks rose twice Talketh's height from sharp-nailed paws larger than the princess' head. Those limbs supported a long mass of muscle ending in another pair of legs and a tail that whipped hard enough to topple a stony Sentinel. The body bore a neck as wide as her chamber door and, above a circle of thick chain, an elongated head the size of her canopied bed. At the back of the head, pointed ears, pink on one side and black on the other, flapped like banners on a tower. A cavernous maw held a thick red blanket of tongue lolling between more teeth than she cared to count. Slits set deep in a snout darker than midnight flared as eyes as blue as the dawn peered straight into her soul. Talketh faced a bloodfang.

The princess froze. Her blade could hack at the monster's feet and legs, but she could never leap high enough to reach its heart. She could stab at its eyes or nose if, or rather when, it tried to bite her in half, but that would be the last blow she would ever strike. Her only hope was to keep stock-still and hope the behemoth would take her for a stony Sentinel, hard enough to break some of its many, many teeth.

Panting, the bloodfang lowered its head and sniffed Talketh from cap to boots. It curled its tail forward and crouched onto its forepaws, keeping its hindquarters high, ready to leap onto its prey.

Talketh fought the urge to tremble, fearing that the tiniest motion would prompt the creature to pounce. *Get it over with, curse you,* she thought. The beast kept panting, but its teeth were no longer bared and its short, staccato yips almost sounded like laughter. If the princess didn't know better, she would say it appeared playful. Why didn't it attack? Was it toying with her? Was it waiting for a signal?

A shaft of light leapt out from the giants' castle and a postern gate opened. A voice boomed out over the field. "*Toebee, kaam!*"

The bloodfang stood and jerked its head around to face the castle. With thunderous yaps, it turned and ran toward the light source. Talketh could see a giant's shadow as the drooling monster approached the postern gate. The gate closed, but with a sound like leather slapping on wood the bloodfang walked through an aperture at its base. The light blinked out.

Talketh exhaled. Her knees knocked for a moment as terror relaxed its grip, taking bravado with it. The towering beast was tame. It answered the call of its master. She thought it strange that the incantation of recall was so short, but perhaps the giants were people of few words.

She had survived her encounter with the bloodfang, but her mother was right. Talketh knew nothing about the dangers that lurked above the roots. It wasn't too late to return to the safety of her burrow. But she also knew that if she took a single step toward the portal stone, she would leave all hope of becoming a Sentinel behind her. And she would have to *admit* that her mother was right. She turned back toward the gnawgart's lair, climbed over the mound of spoil. Blade still in hand, she dropped to all fours and crawled inside.

It was pitch black in the gnawgart's hole, but Talketh's eyes could see well enough in the dark. Still, she smelled the creature before she could see it. Rounding a bend in the constricting tunnel, she caught sight of a long, naked, pinkish white tail. The princess held back a sigh of relief. She could strike at the beast from behind. Not the most honorable way to start a fight, but the most effective way to dispatch an enemy, as Swordmaster Vambrae would have said.

Thanking the Deep Gods for blessing her people with stealth, Talketh inched toward the gnawgart's hindquarters. She didn't see it move, or even breathe. *Even better luck*, she thought. *It must be asleep.* Taking care not to touch its tail, the princess drew back her blade as far as she could and stabbed it straight into the beast's underbelly.

The gnawgart still didn't move.

That blow wouldn't kill it outright, thought Talketh. Even if it had, it should at least have twitched in its death throes. Her blade bit deep into the creature again, then a third time. Blood and worse flowed out and deeper into the hole, fortunately away from the princess. *It's dead. It must have died earlier here in its own hole.*

Talketh's heart fell down a deep shaft. The rules of Red Hat test were clear: the candidate must kill the gnawgart before cutting the four incisors from its mouth. *I can't claim a kill on this creature. Did it smell this bad when it was alive? Anyway, I've got to find—*

The gnawgart's bloody hindquarters rushed at Talketh and knocked her backward. The princess lost her footing and dropped her sword. The beast's dead body kept on coming, shoving the princess toward the surface. It pushed her out of the hole and she tumbled over the mound of spoil, with the gnawgart's tubular carcass sliding out close behind. Talketh rolled to her feet and half-crouched, ready to fight hand-to-hand with whatever came out next.

She never got the chance. Black-slit yellow eyes peered at her from the dust-swirled darkness of the tunnel. Their gazes locked and the princess could not look away. A thin forked tongue sprung out and snapped back in. A pointed black head, half the width of the tunnel and armored in scales, gradually emerged, tasting the air with its tongue but never taking its unblinking eyes off Talketh. A sinuous body banded in yellow, black, and red trailed along behind it, gliding onto the grass without legs.

Talketh's limbs would not obey her. The sorcery in the slithering fiend's eyes rooted her where she stood as it encircled her with its coils. A chill crept out of the pit of her stomach and crawled throughout her body. This was her end. This was a grasilisk.

I'm sorry, father, Talketh thought. Tears filled her captive eyes. The grasilisk raised its head and opened its jaws, displaying needle-like fangs with a tiny drop of liquid at each tip. She began to pray silently, but found she could mouth the words, and even speak them aloud. The sound quickened a last, desperate hope.

"*Toebee, kaam!*" she screamed, mimicking the giant's call to the bloodfang.

The field stayed silent. The grasilisk, unhurried, raised its head higher and curled up its tail. The princess heard leather smack onto wood, but after that, nothing was louder than the pounding of her heart.

Talketh saw a blackness blot out some of the stars near the horizon. The blackness grew and resolved into a tower with dawn-blue eyes. Thunder clapped behind the grasilisk, and it whipped its head around to strike at the dark shape. Talketh fell in a heap, but when she tried to stand her legs complied.

The bloodfang leapt away from the grasilisk just in time to avoid its lethal bite. The blue-eyed beast snapped its own fangs at its serpentine enemy, but the grasilisk whipped its head out of reach, then shot it forward again, wide open. The two monsters whirled in their deadly dance while Talketh sprinted back into the gnawgart's hole to retrieve her blade.

The princess crawled out of the pit just in time to see the bloodfang's jaws crunch into the grasilisk's neck. The scaly coils went limp, but the towering monster shook its huge head furiously until it satisfied itself that the serpent was truly dead. As the bloodfang lowered its head to spit the kill from its maw, the grasilisk's banded black head reared up for a final strike.

Talketh leapt. Wielding her blade two-handed, she sliced through the grasilisk's red-banded neck. Its head fell to the grass, venom dripping from its fangs.

The princess landed on her feet. She held her sword at low guard as the bloodfang turned to face her. If it was hungry after its struggle with the grasilisk, would the enemy of her enemy still be her friend?

The towering black beast flashed out its immense tongue and licked Talketh from head to toe, slathering her with a warm torrent of slobber. Talketh laughed and tucked her sword back into her belt.

The light shone again from the giant's castle. "*Toebee!*" came the cry from the postern. In the distance, Talketh could see several forms moving through the tall grass.

"Looks like we should both get back home," Talketh said to the bloodfang. "But I've got a little work to do first. I hope we meet again when we don't have to kill anything."

With booming yaps echoing off the castle walls, the bloodfang ran off toward the light. Talketh walked over to the gnawgart's remains. *The gnawgart must have looked into the grasilisk's eyes too, just before I entered its lair,* she thought. *It was paralyzed, but not dead, so I can claim the kill.* She bent down to cut out her prizes. When she finished, she turned to see Swordmaster Vambrae and three other long-bearded, Red-Hatted Sentinels approaching.

"Your Highness!" the swordmaster shouted. "Deep Gods, that was a bloodfang! Are you all right?"

Talketh grinned. Covered in blood, dirt, sweat, and slobber, she slid her sword back into her belt and picked up two pairs of orange incisors, each the size of one of Milketh's cake pans.

"Never better," the princess said. "Blessed to be alive. Let's go talk to Mother."

BANGERS THE MASH

RHYS HUGHES

Bangers the Mash was a sausage dog. He was a very long dog at the start of this story and he will grow much longer as it proceeds, but this isn't a tall tale because he never learned to stand just on his back legs.

So we have now established that there was once a dog called Bangers the Mash and that he was a sausage dog. You might be asking yourself why he is wearing a crown on his head?

The answer is because he is a king.

Dogs have kings too, unless they prefer to have presidents, and in this manner they really aren't so different from cats, who also have kings. In fact, all cats regard themselves as kings or queens. But that's not important.

Bangers the Mash was a sausage dog.

Let's not forget that fact.

He ended up the longest sausage dog that ever was. He was about as long as a human arm when his owner acquired him and within a year he grew to be as long as a leg, which is long but not too long. His owner was named Sally and she devoted much of her spare time to her allotment. She took her dog with her whenever she went to work on it.

He was known just as Bangers at first. His surname was earned in a most amusing and peculiar manner.

One day while they were on her plot of land there was an unexpected and ferocious storm and Sally and Bangers took refuge in her shed and waited for everything to calm down. It rained and rained and rained and there was thunder and lightning.

Then a bolt of bright blue electricity struck the earth where she was growing potatoes and the ground trembled and steamed.

The blast had stripped away the soil and exposed the potatoes and they were baked, all of them, as if they had been in a fire for a couple of hours.

Something happened to Bangers—some primal urge overcame him—and he ran into the rain with his tongue hanging out and began trampling the potatoes. The crispy skins split, the white floury interiors revealed themselves and the dog turned them into mash, into an entire plot of sky-baked spuds.

Thereafter, he became "The Mash" as well as Bangers.

In a not dissimilar way, Sally's previous dog, Vlad the Impala, earned his surname when it turned out he was actually an African antelope. But we are not here today to discuss such exotic creatures.

Bangers the Mash was a sausage dog.

I know I keep repeating myself but it's an important point.

"You've grown longer overnight!"

That was Sally exclaiming with surprise one morning when Bangers came up the stairs and into her bedroom to greet her.

He rarely or never brought her breakfast in bed but that's hardly surprising because he was a dog and dogs don't do that, certainly not dogs who also happen to be royal.

And Bangers the Mash was a king.

"In fact you seem almost to have doubled in length!" she added in amazement.

True. But how was this possible?

The fact is that Bangers the Mash had accomplished the amazing feat by a supreme act of determination. He had mentally willed himself to stretch longer and longer overnight and so he had.

This was an example of royal privilege.

Common or garden dogs wouldn't be able to do that.

Not very convincingly, anyway.

Sally shook her head, jumped out of bed and dressed quickly. She found a tape measure and used it to determine the exact length of Bangers the Mash. He was two metres long. She whistled a low note. "Remarkable!"

Then she went down for breakfast. She never ate sausages in front of him. It seemed cruel. She munched muesli instead.

"I wonder what's on the radio today?" she asked.

She pushed her bowl aside.

Then she walked over to the radio on the mantelpiece.

"Just an old sock," she said.

There was always an old sock on the radio. It had been flung there years before by Vlad. Sally sighed and asked, "What shall we do today?"

But Bangers had already decided what he was going to do. Grow longer. When she turned to look at him, he was four metres long. Sally frowned. Did this mean he was a bad dog or not?

"Well, I'm keeping my length the exact length it already is," said Sally. "But you can do whatever you like," she added.

Bangers promptly doubled his length again.

He found the trick easy now.

"You are longer than the kitchen," Sally pointed out.

And he was. His rear half was in another room entirely.

Sally went out to buy a newspaper. She assumed that when she got back home Bangers would have reverted to his previous size, but that isn't what he'd done.

On the contrary, he had doubled his length and doubled it again and now he was thirty-two metres long. His back end up was up the stairs with a twist on the landing and into the spare room. His front end was in the garden. She sighed as she tripped over his brown body.

"Maybe you find this new game amusing, but it's rather inconvenient for me. I suggest you stop growing physically and grow up emotionally instead. A mature and responsible sausage dog wouldn't annoy me in this fashion. 'Bad Manners Bangers' will be your next name!"

But a process had been set in motion that couldn't be halted. Even if he had wanted to stop growing, Bangers the Mash wasn't sure he'd be able to. The inexorable elongation of his body seemed to accelerate rather than slow as if it were being compelled by a cosmic force.

He concentrated on stretching longer and longer.

Sally left the house again later, this time in order to visit a friend. You might be wondering why she doesn't go to work and how if she doesn't work she earns enough money to pay the mortgage on such a nice house, but this is a short story and you ought to know that characters in fiction have an easier time of things than you do out there in reality.

In her absence, Bangers doubled his length and doubled it again, again, again, again and yet again. Then he tripled it and quadrupled it. He tripled it no less than three times and quadrupled it no less than four. Then he doubled it a few more times. For good measure he doubled it. Sally didn't have to leave the house of her friend in order to see him.

She watched his head move past the window. This house was on the far side of town from Sally's own home.

She jumped up and rushed out. "What are you doing here?" But then she realised he wasn't here, or rather that only part of him was and that some of him was still in her house.

So she couldn't tell him off for wandering. She decided to follow him on her bicycle, the same bicycle that she had used to visit her friend, even though I didn't mention it earlier.

I could go back a few paragraphs and do a rewrite, specifying that Sally went on a bicycle to visit her friend, it's still not too late for me to do that, but I won't. It's better to leave things as they are. The important point, the only thing that really matters here, is that Bangers the Mash was getting longer.

His body threaded itself down every single street in the town and he was already halfway to the next town. Sally pedalled furiously.

"What are you up to?" she panted when she finally caught up with him, but he promptly doubled himself and was suddenly gone. She stood no chance of matching his velocity and talking just to a body was pointless, so she went home and ate one hundred jam tarts instead.

Why not? It's what I would do.

The days passed, the weeks passed, the months passed and even a year or two passed. Bangers the Mash had now lengthened himself to such an extent he occupied every road and street in the land. There wasn't a single thoroughfare where his body couldn't be found. He was the longest sausage dog ever to exist in the entire history of sausage dogs!

I promised you earlier that this would happen, didn't I, and now I have delivered. Bangers the Mash resembled an elevated walkway that matched the streets below, so that every street seemed to be double stacked, and the reason he had done this to himself? Let me tell you.

It was for the sake of cats.

Yes. Believe it or not, Bangers loved cats.

No, he hadn't turned himself into a hairy catwalk for cats, though a few utilised him for this purpose. He had constructed a roof so that cats might walk the streets in the rain without getting wet. The cats were supposed to walk under him. Theoretically they could go anywhere they liked because his body covered all the available geographical options.

Unfortunately his legs were very short.

So the arcade he had turned himself into wasn't very high.

Only kittens and mice used it.

It was a supreme act of misguided altruism by a sausage dog who had probably had his brains scrambled on the night of the storm in the allotment. Still, it's the thought that counts and—

Someone is tugging at my sleeve. It is Sally.

She has approached on her bicycle and I didn't hear her coming. I think she wants me to stop writing this story now. It turns her dog into a figure of fun and he's not really that. She is enticing me away with freshly baked jam tarts. I can't resist. I am going . . . going . . . gone . . .

But Bangers the Mash is still a sausage dog.

And his crown?

It's invisible, of course!

Whoever heard of a dog wearing a *visible* crown?

THE PROFESSIONALS

STEVE DUBOIS

The Techbros came rolling up the road with rage in their eyes, fleece vests zipped tight and keyboards raised for combat, the wheels of their electric scooters bouncing over the cracked and rutted pavement. One of them hurled a slide rule, and Hektor brought his badge up just in time. The badge was cracked and pitted from hard use by twelve generations of cops, its paint flaking, but even now, its magic held firm. It pulsed, and a blue disc of translucent force intercepted his assailant's weapon and jolted it aside.

As the mounted tribesman went skittering past, Hektor brought his baton in beneath in a sweeping arc; it caught the Techbro in the ribs with a sickening crunch. Hektor lurched aside just in time for Maxx's axe to cleave their enemy's skull in two. The firefighter yanked the axe free with a grunt, a patter of blood droplets cascading in an arc up across the chest of his yellow rubber coat and spattering the ruggedly handsome features of his half-shaven face. Beside him, Smoky—his dalmatian—was tearing out the throat of a second adversary.

In his peripheral vision, Hektor could see Kile, dressed in motley, capering artfully between two of their attackers. The clown's orange hairpiece had come askew and his greasepaint ran down his face and into his ruffled collar. Behind him, one of the tribesmen swung a laptop two-handed, but Kile assayed a pratfall; the laptop narrowly missed braining him and instead caught the tribesman's comrade in the noggin, knocking her senseless. Kile brought up his slapstick into the groin of the laptop bearer, sending him tumbling, his breath rushing out in a WHUFF.

"OHOHOHO!" Kile cackled, his legs splayed in a perfect split, his voice mad with mirth. He popped to his feet and began hammering his assailant's cranium into jelly. "OH, YES!" Kile cried. "AND AGAIN YES! AND YES! AND YES INDEED!" He punctuated each sentence with a stroke from his weapon.

Two of the Techbros had gotten around their flanks and were closing in on their rear. Haruld cringed in front of the wheeled bassinet, bug-eyed and pallid, fists raised shakily in what, from a more formidable man, might have been a fighting stance. In front of him stood the librarian's cart and Beccah behind it in her black, shapeless frock, her dark hair pinned in an immaculate bun and her pince-nez reading glasses perched perkily atop her nose. As the Techbros closed in, Beccah opened up the immense leather-bound volume on the varnished surface before her, and began to read. "The female tarantula hawk wasp," she whispered, "uses its stinger to para—"

Hektor and Maxx plugged their ears with their fingers. The Techbros were not as prepared. Upon hearing the librarian's voice speak a Brutal Truth, their eyes went wide for an instant, the forbidden knowledge flooding their brains. Then their heads exploded, showering the cart, the bassinet, and their defenders with grey matter and skull shards.

Silence descended upon the prairie. Beccah exhaled noisily and gave Haruld a silent signal, and the man in the white lab coat raised his hands to his ears, removing a pair of earplugs. The sun was low and bloody in the west, and the shadows of the cottonwoods on the horizon reached for them like fingers. A light breeze whispered in the tall grass—bluestem, switchgrass, and wild, mutant maize, taller than a man's head, stretching to the horizon. Corpses cooled on the crumbling asphalt of the Ozroad. Hektor wiped his baton clean on the chinos of one of their luckless rivals, then tucked it into his belt. "Not as bad, this time," he remarked. "Not as many of them, anyway. A foraging party, probably. Out looking for snacks. Had it been a full tribe, bearing a mainframe . . ." He shuddered at the thought.

Beccah glanced up, her dainty features full of concern. "There shouldn't be *any*," she said, her voice timid. "Techbros are native to the Silicon Valley of the Golden Coast. What are they after in Klahoma?"

"Why, the same thing that the Brokers were after two weeks ago, and the Accountants the week before that," Kile cooed. His eyes glittered, and his snaggle-toothed smile was yellow against the stark white of his facepaint. "Ourselves! They come for us and for . . . ," he nodded at the bassinet, "our cargo."

The four of them approached the bassinet, which was spattered with the residue of Becca's victims. Haruld lowered his gaze and simpered aside. Within, wrapped in swaddling clothes, was a tiny, bright-eyed infant. He smiled and giggled at them. His tiny fist was closed around a clot of brain matter, which he waved merrily in the air. Smoky watched the scene carefully, hackles raised, muscles tensed to spring at the slightest hint of danger to the child.

They stared down at the baby. Maxx shook his head. "Crazy bastards in Dall-Oz," he muttered.

"Transmigration of the soul, they claim," Beccah said. "When their old Kennedy dies, they believe that his soul migrates elsewhere, to a newborn member of the ancient bloodline. And so he must be brought to the Holy City to take up the ancient mantle and to lead the faithful to glory."

"Whatever," Maxx said. "So long as they're paying. Professionals get paid."

"Oh, and how *very much* they pay!" Kile was practically cavorting in his enormous floppy shoes. "Steeped in superstition, the people of Tejas . . . but steeped in petroleum as well! The very stuff of wealth itself! Ten thousand in gold! Why, a clown could start his own carnival!"

"Got some Kennedy blood in me, as it happens," Maxx said. "Could save 'em some trouble if I just accepted the pay in exchange for the job."

"No good," Hektor responded. "You might pass the blood test, but you're about thirty years too old to impersonate a newborn." He reached into the cradle and plucked the piece of brain away from the baby, who had been about to put it into his mouth. "It's gotta be the kid."

And that was the pure dumb hell of it, of course. They'd started out down the Ozroad with a contract, a dozen of them under the Judge Perspicusius, massive and ebony-skinned in his black robes, insistent on being addressed as "Your Honor" at all times. He'd never even made it out of the Sunflower Confederacy; they'd found him on the streets of Fort Scott one morning, brained with his own gavel. From there, it had only gotten worse. Their carpenter had died of a bad belly, poisoned by the leaded streams of Picher. Rudrig the landscraper, merry upon his cutting machine, had died screaming, paper-cut to ribbons by the injunctions of a clan of wild Attorneys. They'd been picked off one at a time by marauding bands, coming by day and night or lying in ambush. Now, as they approached the Red River, only five of them remained. *Six, if you count Smoky*, Hektor thought. *But if you count the dog, we started with thirteen. A bad number. Maybe it doomed us.*

There was, of course, a more likely explanation, but only the garrulous clown was willing to give voice to it. "Oh, we are sold out, comrades!" he chortled. "The tribes have learned of our mission. One among us has struck a deal with our assailants, for a reward split evenly with them is much greater than an award split five ways. But who is the betrayer, my fellow travelers? Who?" He raised an eyebrow, grinning wickedly.

"Might be the guy who's having the most fun fighting," Maxx said, staring levelly at the clown.

Kile threw back his head in a wild laugh. "And that is I, no question! But . . ." Against mathematical probability, his grin grew even more wicked. "Who among us has the largest expenses, eh? Who must care for a canine companion, and refill his extinguisher in every port?" He waggled his eyebrows, then leveled his gaze at Beccah. "And who is it that seems to know, somehow, everything about the tribes we face?"

Maxx's expression grew stern; he reached for his axe, but Becca stilled him with a gesture. "It's my job to know things," she said, a bit of an edge in her usually mild voice. She turned to Hektor. "For instance: I know this cop spends a lot more time around the bassinet than I'm comfortable with, especially at night. And I know that he's bleeding right now."

Hektor blinked, then glanced down. Sure enough, there was a rivulet of blood running down his right bicep. Pulling back the sleeve of his stained and battered blue uniform, he uncovered an impressive gash. *Sonofabitch*, he thought. *One of the bastards got through my guard after all*. He'd been so hopped up on adrenaline and righteous fury that he'd never even noticed.

Maxx grunted. "Best get that taken care of." He raised his voice in a shout. "PHARMA!"

Haruld came scuttling forward, pockets rattling at every step. "A pill! A pill!" he chanted. "A pill for every ill!" He opened up his white lab coat, revealing a chest criss-crossed with at least a dozen bandoliers, each containing multiple vials of medication. He sorted through them hurriedly, then withdrew one. "I have just the thing!" He unscrewed the top of the vial with a practiced and precise flick of his wrist, and with-drew a single green capsule. "If you'll just place this on your tongue, officer . . ."

Hektor did so. Haruld watched him carefully. "For best results," he said, "imagine soothing images. A golden retriever running in a field of wheat. An elderly couple sitting in twinned outdoor bathtubs. Things of that nature." He licked his lips, then began the ritual intonation. "Ask your doctor about PLACEBO," he said, solemnly, giving the pill its name. "PLACEBO may not be right for all patients, including those with heart conditions, asthma, kidney stones, pancreatitis, or low liver function. Do not take PLACEBO while pregnant or while operating heavy machinery." He inhaled. "It's time to live your best life again. Find out whether PLACEBO is right for you!" When Hektor glanced down at his arm, the wound was gone, leaving only a smooth, unblemished patch of hairless skin behind.

From behind him, Beccah spoke. "An impressive trick, pharma," she said. "What other tricks are you up to? I can't help but notice that you never seem to come under attack when the raiders arrive."

The pharma raised his hands, all affronted innocence, but surprisingly, it was Maxx who spoke first. "Ain't him sold us out, lover. He ain't got the balls."

Haruld smiled nervously. "For a certainty, madam," he replied. "Where physical courage is concerned, I am an entire eunuch."

"In any case," Kile interjected, "it is long past time we left this accursed road, do you not think? While following it, we are an obvious target. A jaunt overland would both shorten our journey and . . ."

Maxx guffawed. "Oh! Sure! Right, clown! Lead us off into the wilderness, and straight into a raid! At least from the road, we can see what's comin'!"

Beccah crossed her arms and shook her head. "The library cart won't go off-road. And I mustn't leave it behind. If the books go overdue . . ." She shuddered at the thought.

"We're close to the Tejas border at this point," Hektor replied. "Only two or three days out of Dall-Oz, a week at most, provided we stick to the Ozroad. If we take the bassinet or cart into the deep grass, it'll slow us to a crawl. And at this time of year, there's no navigable river crossing except the bridges, so leaving the road won't save us from ambush." Hektor gritted his teeth. "You're not wrong about us being an obvious target, though. At minimum, we need to set up camp off-road from this point forward. And no fire tonight; we've been advertising our presence to everyone within fifty miles." He glanced at their surroundings. "Off there in the creek bed's the best spot. We won't be visible from the road. Who's got the first watch?" He glared at the librarian and firefighter. "And it's a *watch* I need from you two. Not . . . other activities."

A grin crossed Maxx's action-hero mug, and he wrapped a brawny arm around Beccah and drew her to his side. "Not to worry, bud," he rumbled. "Got an extra pair of eyes available for the purpose." He nodded at Smoky, who sat on his haunches and offered up a single loud bark. He winked at Hektor. "You wouldn't *believe* what she's got under that baggy dress, copper."

Beccah smiled shyly, her eyes downcast. "We'll be quiet, I promise. It's a librarian's specialty."

Hektor sighed. "Not like I can stop you, I guess." He paused, feeling a cramp in his stomach, followed by a low, rumbling gurgle that the entire party could hear. "What the hell?"

Four sets of eyes went to Haruld, who gulped. "Side effects of PLACEBO," he recited, "may include mild nausea, stuttering, redness of the skin, uncontrollable anal leakage, perspiration . . ."

Hektor scowled. "First watch is yours, pharma," he growled. "I got business to take care of." He unbuckled his belt and went sprinting toward a nearby ditch, the laughter of his companions echoing behind him.

WELL PAST MIDNIGHT, in the midst of his own watch, Hektor stood beside the bassinet, rocking the infant and watching him guzzle the last of the pharma's infant formula through a rubber nipple.

The kid's own mom sold him, he thought. *Back in the slums of Kansa See. When we came to take her child, she didn't even put up a fight. All she did was haggle out the cost.*

But how am I any better? I'm dragging him down this broken road in order to sell him again. This time to religious fanatics, who'll . . . well, make him a king, I suppose.

And I took the job. The job of selling a child. Willingly. Because I'm a professional.

He glanced down at the badge he'd inherited from his father, who'd inherited it from his own father before him. It glowed faintly blue under the starlight. *They say that in the Beforetime, before the world twisted and the professions gained their powers, there was something more to being a cop than a badge, a gun, and a baton. Something more than getting paid. They had a code, and a motto: "To Protect and Serve".*

Hektor glanced down at his chubby-cheeked charge. His eyes were half-lidded; late feedings always left him sleepy. *He'll have a wet-nurse in Dall-Oz, of course. Wealth, prestige . . . the best of everything. Far better than he'd have managed with that junkie mom in Kansa See. But . . . to just leave him there, unprotected . . .*

Better not let myself care too much. Better that we never named him.

He stared down at the child's moonlit face. *Yes. Certainly.* He reached into his belt, withdrew a small black plastic square, and tucked it away in the baby's blanket, then swaddled him securely and replaced him in the bassinet. *A job well done, officer. You are surely the most moral and honorable of all child traffickers.*

He sought sleep, and did not find it.

"WELL," Hektor said, "I'm guessing he wasn't the traitor."

"Reckon not," Maxx replied.

The two of them stared down at Haruld, who stared sightlessly up at them in the morning sun. His face bore a strange smile, and his throat bore a wider, redder one, stretching from ear to ear. Off to their left, Beccah was retching into the drainage ditch. *Poor girl*, Hektor ruminated. *She's been nauseous for half the trip, and it seems like she's more exhausted every day. Perhaps our accumulating misfortunes have become a bit too much for her.*

"No healer for us, then," Hektor said. "Whatever wounds we take, we'll bear with us to Dall-Oz".

"Or to our graves, comrades," interjected Kile. He seemed nonplussed by the whole business; he was chewing on a stick of jerky, and his eyes were on the tall grass nearby. "To our very graves." And there was that hideous grin again. "Behold! It begins anew!"

Faces slowly emerged in the field, as if rising from deep, murky water—one, then two, then more. They were painted as pale as Kile's own, but the eyes were shadowed within black diamonds, and their threadbare garments bore black and white horizontal stripes. They returned Kile's cruel smile, their features caricatures of hideous expression—and as they emerged on stockinged feet, not one of them made a single sound.

"*Mimesssssss.*" Kile hissed. "The ancient enemies of my people. Negotiation is pointless! To the trenches, comrades!"

"Hold off, Kile!" Hektor shouted. "We need to protect th-" It was no use. Kile had already hurled himself forward into a tumbling run, cartwheels and handsprings forcing the Mimes to drop to their knees, temporarily helpless, shaking with uncontrollable paroxysms of silent laughter. Then he was in among them, slapstick a-whirl. "Aw, hell!" Hektor groused. "Maxx, with me! Beccah, back to the cart! Protect the kid!" Then his service pistol was in his hand, and he was moving forward, firing.

As Hektor charged toward the melee, the sound of his gunshots diminished, then faded entirely, though fire still erupted from the weapon's muzzle. Smoky's barking likewise dissipated, and as Hektor switched to the baton, he found himself shrouded in the utter silence that was the Mimes' constant companion. Vision became an issue as well as the troupe retreated into the tall grass, drawing their pursuers after them. They were defensive fighters, essaying flamboyant, sweeping hooks and thrusting jabs, then retreating into their invisible boxes on the counter-stroke. Maxx hacked away beside him, and every now and then Hektor caught a glimpse of Smoky darting around at his ankles. Of the clown there was no sign.

Deeper and deeper they went, accomplishing little; they left a whitefaced corpse or two in their wake, but the Mimes pulled back and back, denying them a decisive engagement. Over the entire engagement hung the eerie hush of mimesis. Eventually,

Hektor felt himself grabbed by the shoulder; turning with baton raised, he found himself staring at Maxx. The fireman's face was as red as his helmet, and he shouted wordlessly, pointing back the way they'd come.

Not to worry, Hektor thought. *Beccah's more than capable of holding down the fort. A single Brutal Truth from her lips should be enough to bring down a whole phalanx of them. A single word spoken aloud . . .*

The realization descended upon him. *Spoken aloud. Oh, goddamn.*

He turned on his heels and went racing back toward camp, Maxx ahead of him and Smoky trailing behind, his frantic barks rising into audibility as they cleared the mimes' area of influence.

They burst onto the road to find the bassinet gone and the library cart overturned. Sound had returned, but there was naught to be heard but the wind and Smoky's desperate yips. "BECCAH!" Maxx cried. "I SWEAR, IF THEY'VE . . ."

As if summoned, she came crawling out of the grass on the opposite side of the road, eyes glassy and face wan, her hair unpinned and lank at the sides of her face. Maxx raced to her side, fell to his knees, and embraced her; she sobbed in response. "I couldn't . . . I couldn't say anything . . . I had the books open, but . . . I couldn't speak . . ."

Maxx attempted to shush her—an irony, given her profession—but she stared over his shoulder and up at Hektor. "They . . . they took the baby," she babbled. "I ran and hid, and they took the baby. Off into the grass. South, I think." A single dot of scarlet appeared on each of her cheeks; Hektor knew, from prior experience, that that meant rage. "Kile!" she cried. "Hektor, *Kile was with them*! He was *leading* them!"

Hektor's mouth twisted. Maxx still had his arms wrapped around her, and the words rushed out of him in an uncontrollable torrent. "Baby . . . baby, it's all right. The kid's not important . . . the kid doesn't matter . . . we're fine . . . we've still got . . ."

"*Like hell*." Hektor's voice was a whipcrack, and even Smoky's eyes swung to him in response. "I did *not* spend months carrying a helpless child across two territories in order to get my bounty yanked out from under me by a goddamn *rubbernose*." His eyes blazed as he raised his badge. "I am of the Thin Blue Line, that which stretches back to the Beforetime, and into the infinite future, and I *will not disgrace it*."

The three of them stared at each other—the cop standing, arms akimbo, the firefighter and the librarian on their knees. "Hektor," Beccah finally said, "I'm sorry. But there's nothing to be done. I mean . . . you and Maxx could take them in a straight fight, I'm sure . . ."

"Damned right," muttered Maxx, through gritted teeth.

". . . but there's just no way of finding them. They're out there, in the high grass, and they could be *anywhere* . . ."

Slowly, a wry grin crossed Hektor's face, and he reached down toward his belt. "The Thin Blue line stretches back to the Beforetime," he repeated. "And sometimes, we bring a little of the Beforetime along with us."

Hektor withdrew from his belt a small rectangle of black plastic, bearing a grey window in which a single light blinked. "We've known for a while that there was a double agent amongst us, and that the kid was their ultimate objective. What we have here is a piece of Beforetime technology. My ancestors called it a LoJack. Every night, after feeding him, I've been tucking one of these into the kid's diaper. This'll enable us to track him."

Maxx and Beccah exchanged a momentary glance, then Maxx scrambled to his feet and moved to stand beside Hektor. He stared at the winking dot. "South by southwest, looks like," he said. "Moving in the direction . . ."

". . . of the railroad bridge. And having moved off-road, they'll be moving at a snail's pace."

Beccah rose, clutching at her stomach. "I'm not well. I'm not sure how fast I can travel . . . and the cart . . ."

Hektor raised a palm. "The cart won't help us in this fight," he said. "We'll come back for it later. And I'm sure you'll be fast enough that the three of us will be able to set up shop by the time they arrive. We should start now; we'll talk as we walk." The three of them turned, Smoky at their heels, and began moving south down the Ozroad. As they did, Hektor reached into his holster, withdrew his pistol, and displayed it to Beccah. "I'll be using my baton. You'll be making heads explode, as usual, but by a new method. This marvelous device, still in working order after centuries, is known as a Sig Sauer P226. Its ammunition loads via the barrel, like so . . ."

THE OZROAD WAS black and white and red all over. Mime corpses, intact and otherwise, littered the pavement. Some had their jugulars torn; others bore skull fractures or missing limbs; a solid half-dozen were frozen solid, reduced to mimesickles by the freezing mist of Maxx's extinguisher. A few bore bullet holes.

The pitted, rusting frame of the railroad bridge stretched out over the rushing torrent of the Red River. Leaning out precariously with his feet anchored in the concrete at the bridge's edge, stood Kile. His right hand gripped the ancient, decaying railing. His left hand held the top of the baby's blanket. Cradled within it, the child dangled, gurgling happily, over twenty feet of empty space.

"What a pickle, comrades!" Kile cackled. "What a terrible pickle we find ourselves in! Oh, what a conundrum we face!"

Smoky's fangs were bared in a fierce snarl, a growl rumbling deep in his throat as he sought to launch himself at the figure in motley; it was all Maxx could do to restrain him. Beccah had the pistol locked in a secure, two-handed grip and trained on the clown.

"Give it up, Kile," Maxx grunted. "We know you're not throwing our meal ticket away."

Meal ticket. Hektor turned over the phrase in his head. Hating it. Hating himself for ever having endorsed it.

Kile dangled the child still further out over the edge. "Oh, mightn't I?" he cooed. "What have I to lose? What alternative have I? What security? Shall we resume our fellowship, do you think?" He did that idiot eyebrow waggle of his, making Hektor half wish Beccah would blast them off his skull.

"No chance of that," Hektor acknowledged. "Nobody's going to go to sleep and leave you on watch to slit another throat, like you did Haruld's."

A momentary look of astonishment crossed Kile's face. Then he threw back his head and howled with laughter. "*I?*" he hooted. "You think me a simple *murderer?* A traitor, yes, that's certain. I brought our enemies down on us, one after another, all the way from Kansa See. My silent comrades stalked us for days, awaiting my signal. But what point in killing the pharma?" He shook his head. "My scheme was to wait until we reached Plano, then have my mimetic army swoop down from the hovels flanking the road, swift, silent, and certain! But the pharma's death put paid to that plan. Why, I might have been next! I called in the cavalry, and now, here we are. You, desperate for the child. I, desperate for my life, and my rightful share of the proceeds. So we must needs negotiate a—"

There came the short, sharp report of a pistol, and a hole appeared in the center of the Clown's forehead. His face went slack, and he toppled backward off the railing. As he did, he released the blanket, and the baby tumbled after him. Smoky gave a sudden, panicked howl and burst free of Maxx's grip; he raced to the edge of the bridge and leapt straight over it and into space. From below came the faint echo of two splashes, then a third.

"Oh, goddamnit!" Maxx swore. "I loved that dog."

Something inside Hektor which had been straining for weeks—perhaps for years —finally broke completely. He rounded on Maxx in a fury. "The DOG?" he roared. "The DOG?"

Maxx raised two placating palms. "Yeah, yeah, I know," he said. "The money, too. Damn shame."

Hektor gritted his teeth, then averted his eyes in contempt. He turned his scorn on Beccah. "What were you THINKING?" he shouted.

She stared him down coolly. And then, as if a switch had been thrown, she changed. All the fragility she'd shown over the last desperate weeks—her caution, all her panic, her desperation—simply vanished, as if it had never been. And in its place —stony calm, and Hektor's service pistol, held firmly in a two-handed grip, without the slightest sign of a tremor.

"I was thinking," she replied, "about the firearms training that every Librarian undergoes prior to entering into field work. I was thinking about the fact that I'd been keeping it under wraps for quite a while, and about how *patronizing* your little gun lecture was, and how hard it was to keep silent amidst your babble, all that way up the road, and for the weeks preceding." She glanced down at the weapon, appraising it idly. "I was thinking that I'd replaced the magazine twice back there, and fired six shots from the final one, leaving me four shots for our remaining business. I was thinking that the clown had been useful, to 'thin the ranks,' as he put it—but that now, he was just in the way. As was that goddamn screaming brat. As is a certain other party, who's much too trusting with his sidearm." There might have been a hint of a smile on her face. "I was *thinking*. You should try it sometime."

"Cops ain't too bright on the uptake, honey," Maxx inserted. "He doesn't quite get it. You're gonna have to show him."

Beccah echoed his grin, and slowly raised the hem of her dress, revealing her shapely legs, her undergarments . . . and the broad curve of her swollen belly.

Hektor stared. *Nauseous every morning*, he thought. *More exhausted every day*.

"What was it I told you last night?" Maxx asked. "You have NO IDEA what she's got under that dress, copper."

"They're expecting a baby in Dall-Oz," Hektor said, putting it together. "But they've got no clear idea about its precise age, or gender. All they have is the blood test."

"The test to ensure," Beccah said, "that it has *Kennedy* blood." She kept the pistol trained on Hektor with her right hand, but moved her left to the broad shoulder of the maniacally grinning Maxx.

"She's about ready to pop," Maxx said. "You've no idea what it's been like for her. Miles every day, big as a house, like she's been. Ain't been intimate with her for weeks. But she's took it like a champ."

"And that's the plan," Hektor growled through gritted teeth. "You never had any intention of selling the kid in the bassinet. You're going to replace him." He almost spat the final sentence. "You're going to make your fortune by selling *your own child*."

Beccah shrugged one shoulder; the hand holding the pistol never budged. "We all make sacrifices. It won't be the hardest part. Do you know what has been?" All trace of a smile was gone now. "Pretending to be a *stupid little girl*. Listening to the judge, and that clown, and you, and all the others, run your mouths. And having to act, all the time, like some *frail* goddamn *flower*. When what I am, in fact, is the sort of woman who *explodes heads*." She paused, considering. "I don't have my books with me." She raised the gun. "Lacking my own tools, yours will have to do."

Hektor raised his badge and, as he did, made a break for the edge of the bridge. There were two sharp reports, a shower of sparks, a flare of blue light, and a splash of blood. Then he was over the railing, tumbling, flailing in space.

Maxx and Beccah stared over the railing at the blank surface of the rushing river. "The second shot hit him," she said. "I'm sure of it."

"Great shooting, babe," Maxx muttered. "One bullet left, even."

"Yes," Beccah replied. "About that." She smiled up at him. "Do you figure he was right about me? That I'm the sort of woman who'd trade her own newborn child for twenty-five thousand in gold?"

Maxx wrapped his arms around her, smiling down from beneath his fireman's hat. "Damned right, babe. And you know I love you for it."

She gave him a quick peck on the lips by way of reward. "How, then," she asked sweetly, "would I not, by the same token, trade a lover for an additional twenty-five thousand?"

The smile left her face. "Thinking. Try it sometime."

And another shot rang out across the prairie.

BECCAH strode down Elm Street and into the glittering environs of Dealey Plaza, amidst bustling hordes of native Tejans, each of them wearing chaps, a gunbelt, and a ten-gallon hat. Her hair was pinned, her face powdered, her frock immaculate and trimmed with new-bought lace at the neck and sleeves. Before her she pushed her library cart, and slung before her at her breast was a robust dark-haired babe.

At the intersection of Elm and Houston, in a crumbling concrete bowl that might once have held a fountain, a wizened man sat atop a tall chair of immaculate white marble. His three piece suit and Stetson matched the throne in color and were accented by a black bolo tie. She rolled her cart up before him, then stepped out from behind it and essayed a perfect curtsy.

"Have I the honor," she asked, "of addressing the mayor?"

The elderly figure stepped gingerly down from his seat and swept off his white cowboy hat in a formal bow. "Might ought be y'do, ma'am. How might I be o' service to ya?"

"It is I who shall serve you," Beccah replied, primly. She raised the child from her breast and held him aloft. "I have the honor of presenting to you, sir, your new prince—young Maxx, of the royal bloodline Kennedy! You will find his pedigree immaculate, I assure you." She raised her voice. "All hail the new prince of Dall-Oz!"

"New Rome, act'lly," the old man replied.

Beccah stared at him, surprised. "New . . . new *what?*"

"New Rome," the old man replied, his bearing impeccable. "New times, ma'am. And a new ruler to go along with 'em." He raised his own voice. "Let's hear it for Romulus o' the Kennedy line, ruler o' New Rome, prince of the lands o' th' Trinity an' Brazos!" Instantly, the plaza filled with whoops and hollering. Stetsons were flung into the air, sixguns raised from every hip and fired skywards in celebration. Scarcely a hat survived unscathed.

"But . . ." Beccah stammered. "How can this be? I have traveled far to bring you your trueborn prince, from remote lands . . ."

"Be that as it may, ma'am," the mayor replied, "th' position's been filled. Right sorry about yer long walk. Might I offer ya a beverage?"

"Filled by whom?"

"Why, by young Romulus, o' course," said the mayor smoothly. "Not two weeks ago. Helluva thing, it was! We'd just about given up hope, when right on up the street he comes. Baby boy. Bit sickly, truth be told. Hadn't been fed in a while, and look'n more than a mite bit damp. But he's in his lil' blanket—and what's carryin' that blanket but a by-god wolf!"

"A . . ." Beccah was astonished. "A *wolf?*"

"Well, a dog, more 'xactly, but wolf'll read better in th' legends." He smiled broadly. "Young king-t'-be, brought out th' wilderness by wild critters! Can't git more legendary than that." He gestured broadly at the entrance to the book deposi-tory. "Why, there's the fearsome beast even now!"

Beccah stared. Sitting in the doorway of the building was a familiar-looking dalmatian. It wore a collar of what was plainly solid gold, and its harness was studded with precious stones. She took a step toward it, saw its hackles rise, heard the warning growl, and quickly stepped back.

"Service dog, don'tcha know," the mayor continued. "Dead set on protectin' that baby boy. Now, a dog's a dog, but a *service* dog? That's a *perfessional* dog."

Beccah spun on her heels. "You . . ." she spluttered. "You gave the entire reward—fifty thousand in gold—to a *dog*?"

The mayor nodded. "Sure an' certain, ma'am." He paused, returned his hat to his head. "Other fella wouldn' take it."

"The . . . other fellow?"

"Man in blue, with a bullet in his shoulder. Strolled inta town right behind th' dog an' our new ruler. We offered 'im the money. Turned us down flat. Reckoned he didn' deserve it. Dog saved th' king, he said, an' loyalty oughta be rewarded."

The mayor straightened his string tie. "Asked us for nothin' but fer us t' pluck the bullet out of 'im. That and a fresh start. A chance to be a better man, an' t' keep an eye out for young Romulus henceforth. Said he wanted t' pass on a certain gift to him one day, as his daddy did t'him. Asked us for a shot at a new life. A new perfession."

The mayor smiled widely, but his hand went to his hip, where his own sixgun rested. "An' he told us somethin' else, as happens. Told us another certain someun' might be comin' up the road in a couple weeks or so, with a baby on 'er hip. Told us one *hell* of a story, he did." He paused. "Just so happens that same feller's standing 'bout forty feet behind ya as we speak. Just stepped out from behind that grassy knoll over yonder."

Beccah hesitated for a moment, and in doing so, was lost. The mayor's pistol came out, and from every side, she heard the clicks of hammers cocking. "Now, jes' keep those hands free o' that thar rollin' bookcase, young missy. A lil' knowledge c'n be a dangerous thing, or so I'm told."

Beccah put her hands up. She heard the footsteps behind her, and closed her eyes in resignation, not bothering to turn and look. "This man in blue," she muttered. "He calls himself a cop, I suppose?"

"Actually," said the voice from behind her, "these days, they call me Sheriff."

A Unicorn for Rain

Ed Sams

"Be not forgetful to entertain strangers;
for thereby some have entertained angels unawares."

K ing Cole's castle was dry and dusty, but the threshold to the kitchen was spic and span, for its door was ever open to strangers. No beggar passed unfed or traveler unwelcomed. This was due to the hospitality of the cook Bertha and her pet goose Daphne more than to the charity of the king. Indeed had the king learned of such extravagance under his own roof in a time of drought, he would have beheaded the cook and cooked her goose as well.

The drought (and the famine that followed) had been caused by the wickedness and negligence of the old king himself, whose own hard heart, it is said, had dried up all the rain. Two years of failing crops persisted until finally the king was pushed into action. Consulting all his wise men, he convened his court in his dusty courtyard to hear his proclamation. Everyone was there squinting in the hot July sun from Lady Capella and Lord Hamish, the king's lady and the king's hatchet man, to Bertha and Daphne.

"Good people," King Cole began, spitting out a cherry pit as he spoke, "no one regrets the dwindling food supply more than I, and all because of a drought. Digging wells is hard, building dams expensive, and conserving water a bore. Therefore, I have decided the quickest and easiest solution is a symbolic one. I propose that we get a unicorn to bring the rain.

"Therefore," King Cole declared, "I order Lord Hamish to hunt down a unicorn and fetch him here post haste."

"But your majesty," spoke the Lady Capella. "Hamish cannot hope to bring back a unicorn. It is the most ferocious beast alive. A unicorn can only be caught one way."

"By an innocent maiden," Hamish said, lifting his black brows at the king's lady, "and you have none at your court."

The Lady Capella turned her heel on Hamish and explained to the king, "Only a very young girl, a maiden, may touch a unicorn, then only if she be very patient and quiet to sit beneath an apple tree. The unicorn will come and kneel to put his head in her lap. Then if she weaves a garland of wildflowers into a halter, she may lead him wherever she lists. That's the law!"

"Hmmm," said the king rubbing the grizzle on his fat jowls, "Kings can make or break laws; therefore, I decree that henceforth the Lady Capella be the official court virgin. Bertha!" he yelled. "Prepare the celebration."

The feast of ordination lasted from Friday night until Sunday morning. Around noon while the king still snored in his high tower, Hamish led the Lady Capella to the city gates where she was to commence her quest. Though forty years old with dry skin and a rose tattoo on her inner thigh, the Lady Capella was tricked out in white organdy and decked with lilies. The white ass she sat on had been powdered with talcum. Only Bertha and Daphne were there to see her on her way.

Two years passed before Bertha saw the Lady Capella again. Then one day at her kitchen door there came a knock. Daphne waddled over to the open threshold honking urgently. Bertha wiped her hands on her apron and hurried to the door.

"My lady," Bertha said, dropping to one knee.

"Please get up, Bertha. Hello, Daphne." Lady Capella entered in a tattered skirt with red and yellow patches. "I've returned with a friend," she said. Behind her stepped a young man clean shaven with a ring of thick brown hair circling a tonsured head.

"How many miles to Babylon?" he inquired politely.

"He's a holy man," interrupted Lady Capella. "I couldn't find a unicorn, but I did find a holy man."

The young man smiled. "I have enjoyed many long talks with Lady Capella concerning her soul and I have convinced her to accompany me on my pilgrimage."

"We stopped here first," Lady Capella explained. She flung out her hands in exasperation. "I've run out of money, Bertha. I've got to do something. I hate coming back without a unicorn, but enough is enough. I'm well into middle age. I'll not spend my life out chasing unicorns. What am I to do?"

Bertha smiled and stretched out her arms. "Do? Why, do come in. I shall put the kettle on and we shall have tea."

Just then Daphne began to honk furiously. "Hello, hello!" came a cry down the broad road to the castle courtyard. A tall, lean man came pulling a stretcher with a little yellow dog yapping in circles around him. The man wore orange clothing and a pink conical cap. On the stretcher lay a marble statue.

"How many miles to Bethlehem?" he asked.

"You are on the way," Bertha told him. "Enter and meet fellow traveling companions."

The tall stranger smiled and nodded, then pulled his cargo up to the open kitchen door. His little dog ran inside.

Daphne in consternation squawked busily as she ran for shelter beneath a kitchen stool. The yellow dog bounced after her. Curious, he stuck his nose under the stool friendly-like. Daphne shot out her neck hissing at him, waving her white wings and stamping her indignant webbed feet.

"Don't mind Daphne," Bertha said. "Let me find your poor doggie a bone."

Lady Capella leaned out the window. "What's that on the shutter?" she asked. It was a column of marble cut to resemble a knight in armor, whose huge shield covered his entire body.

"It is a knight upon a quest. He can neither eat nor speak until he has witnessed a miracle."

"Poor man to be on a stretcher," Bertha said.

"How do you know all this if he is sworn to silence?" asked the holy man.

"Because he's a fool," Lady Capella said, "because it's a statue!" She stopped short listening to footsteps.

"Who left this junk on the king's doorstep?" called out a loud voice. Through the threshold stooped the giant Hamish, his black brows beetling at the sight of Lady Capella.

"Ah! The official virgin returned at last—oh, happy day! Did you bring a unicorn for rain?"

The holy man stepped between them and held up a hand. "Unicorns, like miracles, are all around, brother; only they pass most people unseen."

"You have to be a virgin to see one," Lady Capella said haughtily.

"I hope for your sake that being a king will work as well," replied Hamish. "I cannot imagine his majesty accepting a unicorn he cannot see."

"He'll see one soon enough," Bertha said waving a soup bone. "Away with you, Lord Hamish. I have the king's breakfast to fix. You may run the castle, but you don't run me. The kitchen is where I rule."

"I shall inform his majesty of your return," Hamish said to Lady Capella. Then with an exaggerated bow he departed.

"Oh, Bertha, whatever shall I do?"

Bertha looked at the bone in her hand and then gazed down at the yellow dog at her heels. "You know, my lady, why can't an official virgin bring back an official unicorn?"

Lady Capella looked at the dog, saw the bone, and caught Bertha's glance. "I sold the donkey, but kept the powder," she said. "It's in my bags outside the door."

"Come here you," said Bertha, grabbing the dog and reaching for her scissors.

The holy man turned to follow Lady Capella, but the stranger stopped him to kiss the hem of his brown habit.

Confused, the holy man asked, "Why do you do this, my son?"

"Because I am in the presence of a pope."

"Because you're a fool!" shouted Lady Capella, then the older woman turned to the younger man. "No offense, father."

The young man laughed. "I am a holy man, I admit, but I am no pope." He told the fool, "Sometimes I think I am very much like your marble knight. I, too, would rather witness a miracle than to go by faith alone." He looked out at the marble knight whose helmet was fixed with a horn of ivory. "Do you know it is said that not even God has made the unicorn. Instead it is told that once the Lord Almighty bid a little star to drop from heaven and fall to earth, but the star was skittish and disinclined. It transformed itself into a wondrous thing, a unicorn, and raced across the floor of Heaven. Gabriel unleashed the hounds of Heaven and some say the geese as well. They chased the unicorn throughout the night until, at last exhausted, it stopped just above the head of a maiden giving birth to a prince."

Lady Capella, listening to all this, smiled fondly, "He was the closest thing to a unicorn I could find."

"Done!" Bertha said, holding up the yellow dog for inspection. She had left the backsides shaggy, but all else had been clipped. The remaining strands of his coat fell down the back of his neck like a horse's mane and his muzzle was trimmed into a courtly goatee.

"Surely you don't expect to fool the king with that," said the holy man.

"Why not?" Lady Capella replied, furiously powdering the dog with talcum.

Bertha dipped the soup bone into a paste of white flour and water. "The king is old and his eyes are bad," she explained fixing the bone to the dog's head.

The stranger nodded at the dog. "He has as it were the strength of a unicorn," he said.

"You see," said Lady Capella. "We have fooled one fool already, why not another?"

"Goodness!" cried Bertha. "The king's breakfast, I clean forgot. I fix it in two ways—pease porridge hot and pease porridge cold, for I never know what mood he'll be in."

As it happened, King Cole was in a particularly foul mood that morning. His foot throbbed with the gout as he limped to his courtyard balcony. "Hamish!" he bawled. "Who left the marble cenotaph on my doorstep?"

Hamish dragged the stranger to the king's presence. "This madman, your majesty."

"It is my friend," the stranger explained, "who could not see a miracle and so he turned to stone."

"He mistakes the statue for an ailing knight who fasts in a vow of silence," Hamish said.

"How many miles to Bedlam, eh, Hamish?" King Cole said tapping his head.

"Exactly, your majesty, and we have other fools as well for this morning's audience. The Lady Capella has returned."

"Capital!" quoth the king, clapping his hands. "Let's see the official court virgin after her long absence."

The Lady Capella and the holy man came forward leading the little yellow dog, white with powder, the soup bone wagging on its head.

"This is a unicorn?" said the king.

"It looks like a mangy cur to me," Hamish said.

"Only virgins are able to see unicorns," Lady Capella answered, "so consider yourself lucky, Hamish, you see anything at all."

"Hmmm," ruminated King Cole, peering out through his red and rheumy eyes at the phenomenon before him. "I am willing to believe, but I require proof." The king clapped his hands. "Bring forth the slops."

From all four sides of the courtyard, minions dragged out tall buckets of dirty water which they poured into a tub in the center of the square. "Here is the foulest water drawn from the deepest cistern in the castle," said the king. "Let the unicorn come forward and charge it with his horn. If the water is cleansed, we might believe."

The yellow dog bolted from Lady Capella's hands and rushed around the tub barking and chasing its tail. The holy man tried to catch him, but the dog slipped under the tub, upsetting the platform it rested upon and spilling its contents. No sooner had the brackish water touched the ground than it turned clear. The holy man reached down to dip his fingers and press them to his lips. "It is sweet," he marveled.

King Cole clapped his hands. "Bring forth the middens!" From the four corners of the courtyard once more came minions hauling baskets of rubbish and garbage and dumping them into the middle of the square. The king spoke. "Here are the chicken bones, potato peels, and apple cores of the castle dump. If here be a unicorn, let him charge this heap with his horn and regenerate it to life once more."

The little yellow dog looked at the king quizzically. He sat down on his haunches and scratched his ear with his hind paw.

"Guards!" the king roared. "Execute that fraud." Hamish raised his hatchet to strike when suddenly from the middle of the trash heap rose a pure white bird flapping its wings. It was Daphne! The cook's pet goose stirred the debris which rose in a cloud above the courtyard, but when it settled, only rose petals and orange blossoms pelted the stone courtyard floor.

King Cole mopped his forehead with his ermine sleeve. "I believe, I believe—if the unicorn could only heal my foot!" King Cole began hurriedly to hop and skip down the curved steps from his balcony to the courtyard below. "Bring me a chair!" he cried and a chair was quickly brought to him. He sat down on the purple cushions and gingerly unbandaged his purple swollen foot.

The little yellow dog watched curiously, then trotted over friendly-like and licked the pustulant crust between the sore and bloody toes. As the dog lapped the pestiferous flesh, the king fell back into his chair sighing, "Ahhh! Ahhh! He is unicorn! I believe! I am healed!"

Wide-eyed and radiant, the holy man turned to the Lady Capella. "I have witnessed a wonder—a unicorn! Forgive me, my lady, if ever I doubted your innocence."

Lady Capella looked into those trusting eyes and sighed. "Oh, your reverence, you were right to doubt me. I am no more a virgin than that is a unicorn."

"What!" said the king rising from his chair on his sore foot. "Ouch!" he cried. "Guards, seize them!"

The holy man turned the lady. "But if not you and not the unicorn, who then performed the wonders we witnessed?"

"I did," said the stranger as the king's henchmen approached. He removed his pink conical hat, and up above his ears shot a halo of light, white and giving heat. "I am an angel," he said.

"An angel!" cried the king. "The angel of rain?" he demanded.

"No," said the stranger, "the angel of death."

Horrified, King Cole dropped into his chair with such force that it fell backward, and his head cracked like an egg on the stones of his own courtyard. All the king's horses and all the king's men gathered round, but there was nothing they could do. Bertha placed a white cambric handkerchief over their dead liege's face and said, "The king is dead, but who will be king?"

"Me!" cried Hamish, brandishing his hatchet. Daphne darted between his feet and tripped him so that he fell on his back. Bertha yanked the soup bone from the dog's head and whacked Hamish on the nose. "Behave yourself!"

Lady Capella threw her arms around her holy man. "You should be king," she told him.

The young man slid out of her embrace and shook his head. "I became a holy man to avoid the world. Don't saddle me with a government to run." Suddenly he shivered, and then he gulped, "Pope?" He turned to the angel, but the stranger was gone. All that remained was the little yellow dog running around in circles barking.

Finally it took Bertha to quiet the little dog. As she was holding him in her arms, the holy man watched and said, "Let the cook inherit the kingdom."

There was a sound like thunder. The earth shook. The large shield had rolled off the marble statue that had been left behind. "It is a sign!" The knight that had lain under the shield crawled off the stretcher and stood on all fours, for wonder upon wonders! Here was no knight in armor but a unicorn in marbled equipage with a war horse's chamfron instead of a helmet. "I never thought I'd see the day that a cook would rule a kingdom."

"I can rule," Bertha said. "I run my kitchen, and so I can run my kingdom."

The unicorn nodded. "It is always a miracle," he said, "when people choose the right one to lead them."

"Only I don't want to rule as a queen," Bertha stipulated. "I want to be a mother to my people."

"Then let me be the first to pay homage," the unicorn replied. He bowed low, touching his horn respectfully to the ground, and rain began to fall.

Curse of the Jackal King

Jenny Perry Carr

Trevor Burton smoothed back his dark hair and swallowed the lump in his throat. He strode into the Cairo hospital ward.

Curious how the medicinal smell brought back so many memories. Times spent in the hospital half a world away where he had visited his dad for the last time when he was ten years old. Aside from palm trees swaying outside the windows, everything was the same—stark white walls to convey cleanliness, stripped gurneys in the long hallway, and the bustle of medical staff saving lives. But not all.

Now, twenty-five years later, he prepared to say goodbye to his grandfather. The Englishman who had raised him alone, who took him on adventures throughout Egypt hunting antiquities, who taught him everything he knew. A man he thought was invincible. His heart skipped a beat.

Inside the disinfectant-laced hospital room, a wall of windows washed the bed in rays of golden sunshine, like Ra shining down on the old man. Only a mere shadow of his grandfather remained. The hiss of oxygen coursed through tubing, and machines beeped his grandfather's heart rhythm. Trevor held his pop's hand. His eyes fluttered open, still sparkling with youth.

Pops smiled. "You're here. Thank the gods." He wriggled to sit. "It's not too late."

Trevor's heart ached. He perched on the edge of the bed. "It's ok, Pops. I'm here."

Like that little boy so long ago, the thought of being an orphan again haunted Trevor. He was a grown man, but being without his pops or any remaining family gnawed at his chest like a gaping void begging to be filled.

The old man strained to open the squeaky drawer beside the bed and withdrew a yellowed cloth-covered item. He folded back the edges of the decomposing muslin. Pops lifted out a solid gold pendant attached to a chain. "This belonged to your grandmother. Passed down for generations." His eyes narrowed. "You must promise to find its secrets." He dropped the weighty necklace into Trevor's open hand.

The yellow gold sparkled in the late afternoon sunlight, reflections dancing along the ceiling. A thick oval of gold encircled carved hieroglyphic symbols. His pulse quickened. "You've never showed this to me before."

Pops wheezed a breath. "It was my burden to carry."

Burden? It's a priceless treasure.

His Pops normally would have been looking to sell to the highest bidder for quick cash. He had taught Trevor well. Had the old man gone soft?

Trevor clutched the gold. "I don't understand."

"You need to go. Find the secret. Something I could never do."

Trevor shook his head. "No, Pops. I need to stay here with you. Until . . ."

"Until I die? No, you won't. Go. Now. Promise me!" Pops coughed from the excitement, doubling over with a raspy wet coughing jag that wracked his body. He gasped for breath, his lip curling. "Do you promise?"

"I promise. You know I'd do anything for family."

TREVOR FIDGETED and drummed his fingers on a stack of dusty leather tomes atop the counter. A maze of floor-to-ceiling shelves blocked out the late afternoon sun from the front windows. The crowded bookshop always smelled of incense and his friend's aftershave. "What do you make of it?"

Hassan scrutinized the gold pendant, turning it over with his thick fingers. "I've never seen such an exquisite piece. Not outside of a museum, that is. Where did your grandfather find this?"

"He got it from his mother, my great-grandmother, Nesu."

"Did he say where she got it?"

"He said it's been passed down in her family."

"But where did they get it?"

Trevor shrugged. "He didn't say."

Hassan cast a disapproving glance. "We need the provenance to assess value. Where was its origin?"

"I don't know. That's why I brought it to you."

Hassan peered over his glasses. "Always bringing me your trinkets to appraise. Selling history's treasures for a quick dollar. When are you going to get a real job?"

Trevor narrowed his eyes. "When are you going to become a real archaeologist?"

Hassan huffed. "When they allow a Palestinian to join a dig. You'd think they could finally let the 3,600-year-old Hyksos invasion go by now. But no."

Trevor scratched his head. "I'm going to pretend I know what that means. What do you think of the piece?"

Hassan pointed at the pendant. "Of course, it's a cartouche. The symbol of the pharaohs. Its shen ring—the oval with the tangent line at one end—is a rope representing the eternal protection of the king. And inside the ring, these hieroglyphs show us the name . . ."

"Which is?"

Hassan muttered under his breath, then spoke with resolve. "The name of the pharaoh is Sabkaref."

Trevor leaned close. "What does that tell you?"

Hassan's eyebrows squished together, and he perched the gold necklace on a piece of red velvet cloth. "Nothing. I have not heard this pharaoh's name before." He retrieved a book from the shelf and flipped through the musty pages.

"How's that?"

"Ancient history is not always clear. There are believed to be around two hundred pharaohs, but they have found only about half of their tombs. And as they dig, previously unknown pharaohs are still being discovered." His finger trailed along the pages as he read.

Trevor's body tingled. His imagination filled with scenes of unexplored tombs, piles of gold and riches. "Are you telling me this cartouche is from an unknown pharaoh?"

"I believe so. I don't see anything in the king lists. I'm sure it will increase your price. But you'd probably have difficulty selling it in respected circles. You're still banned from the Cairo Auction House." Hassan *tsk*ed.

Trevor chuffed. "That wasn't my fault. They assured me the canopic jars were authentic." He picked up the cartouche and examined it. "This is different. I'm not looking to sell this piece."

Hassan gripped his chest in feigned shock. "The treasure hunter who doesn't sell his treasure?" He chuckled.

Trevor studied the floor. "I promised my pops that I'd uncover its secrets."

"Secrets?" Hassan removed his glasses and cleaned them with a linen handkerchief. "Very curious."

"If my grandfather was looking for the secrets of this necklace, I bet he knew there was treasure associated with it." Trevor smirked.

A wide, toothy grin spread across Hassan's face. "Now there is the Trevor I know. Why didn't your grandfather search for it?"

"He got strapped with a sickly ten-year kid when my dad died." If there was any burden, he was the burden on his pops. At least he outgrew his heart murmur. "Pops was a widower and had to raise me himself. And then I guess he just got too old."

Trevor offered the pendant to his friend. "If I could reveal the secrets of this piece, find its treasure, then I'd prove to everyone I'm a legitimate broker of antiquities. That, and become rich and famous. Can you date the cartouche?"

Hassan replaced his glasses and accepted the pendant. "It's quite old, which you can tell by the patina, the discoloration. Clearly twenty-four-carat gold, by the indentations and scratches in the soft metal. And the style is ancient as well. Likely pre-Nineteenth Dynasty."

"Translate?"

"At least three thousand years old."

Trevor's eyes widened. "Wow."

Hassan tugged at his bottom lip. "But the age of the piece doesn't necessarily mean it was created during the reign of the pharaoh. It could have been made later. Meaning this pharaoh could have ruled during the Middle or Old Kingdom, over four thousand years ago."

Trevor stared at the shining gold. "How do we figure out who he was?"

"Let's start with the hieroglyphs. See here?" Hassan pointed to the details of the carved metal. "Four symbols—the jackal, two arms, a mouth, and a horned viper. Each icon represents a sound or syllable, and each can also have meaning. The jackal, *sab*, represents judgement in death. Two arms, *ka*, mean the soul. The mouth, *re*, can be a spoken spell or prayer. And the horned viper is the sound of the letter *f* and often associated with the word *father. Sab. Ka. Ref.* Sabkaref."

"And that tells us?"

"I don't know. I'm thinking." Hassan plucked a book from the stack on the counter and searched through the pages. "I don't recall seeing the jackal in a cartouche before. Maybe there's something there. Symbols hold great meaning to the Egyptians. The jackal was connected with death. They lurked around in the grave-yards, howling, known to eat the dead."

Trevor wrinkled his nose. "Gross."

"The jackal is also tied to the brother gods Anubis and Wepwawet."

"Really? Could this pharaoh be connected to them? Worship them?"

"Very possibly."

"What do we do with that?"

"I suggest we go to Asyut, formerly the ancient city of Zawty. It was the religious center for worshippers of Anubis and Wepwawet."

Trevor raised one eyebrow. "Asyut? That's where my grandmother's from."

TWO DAYS LATER IN ASYUT, Trevor waited for Hassan at the sunny outdoor hotel restaurant perched on the bank of the glassy black waters of the Nile. Swifts screamed overhead as they dove for their morning meal of insects. The clean river scent mingled with that of fruits and fresh-baked pastries.

Trevor pocketed a book of matches from an ashtray on the table. He fiddled with a spoon, then wiped sweat from his brow with his napkin. The temperature had already reached a sweltering 85 degrees Fahrenheit at nine in the morning.

"Sabah al-khayr." Hassan's voice boomed, as rotund as his belly. He took a seat, and a waiter draped a napkin over his lap.

Trevor nodded. "Good morning to you, too."

Hassan leaned forward and whispered. "Do you have the cartouche with you?"

Trevor patted the pendant hidden under his shirt. "Of course. This is not leaving my body voluntarily. I don't trust anyone."

"Indeed." Hassan's eyes brightened. "I have good news. I was able to get us permission to visit the university library today. They have extensive records for the area. They might help us identify our cartouche."

Trevor peeked over Hassan's shoulder at a man peering over a newspaper. They locked eyes, and the man abruptly turned away. "Excellent news. Tell me, Hassan, do you ever feel like you're being watched?"

Hassan looked over his shoulder, following Trevor's gaze. "Not surprising. Locals don't take kindly to strangers."

Hassan reached for the silver coffee pot and knocked Trevor's cup over. Hot coffee sloshed over the marble table and rained onto Trevor's pants and on the floor.

Heat scorched his loins. Trevor sprang out of his chair, shaking the liquid from his leg. His napkin fell to the floor.

"Ya 'iilahi. What have I done?" Hassan dabbed his napkin along the damp table, then stooped to pick up Trevor's napkin.

A brown scorpion skittered across the stone floor and paused next to Hassan's hand, tail hovering over his flesh, poised to sting.

Trevor froze. "Don't move." His pulse beat against his neck.

Hassan's eyes widened as he noticed the reason for Trevor's warning.

Trevor held his breath and slowly raised his foot. He stomped the scorpion with his boot, feeling a satisfying crunch underfoot. He and Hassan sighed and relaxed.

Hassan patted his own chest. "Thank you, my friend."

Trevor dropped into the chair. "Nothing like a bit of bad luck to start the day."

"Spilled coffee is actually a sign of good fortune, which bodes well for us."

"I was talking about the scorpion."

"Indeed." Hassan appeared paler than normal.

In a flurry of clanking flatware and dishes, a troupe of waiters whisked away the spilled cup, wiped down the table, and replaced the place settings and napkins.

One waiter remained and poured fresh coffee. He whispered, "Warnings are all around us. Beware the signs of the pharaoh."

Trevor's mouth twisted. "What did you—" The waiter hurried away before he could finish his question.

TREVOR QUICKLY FLIPPED through the earthy-smelling pages of a history book, perched upon a stack scattered across the wide library table, barely able to hold his attention any longer. He glanced at his pencil drawing of the cartouche on the table. He didn't want to risk flashing the valuable gold relic around town. "There's nothing here. Any luck with digital?"

Hassan turned away from the research computer and pushed up his glasses from the tip of his nose. "Not seeing any signs of this cartouche in the databases."

A librarian with too much eye makeup and salt and pepper hair pulled tight into a bun pushed a cart of books past them to return to the shelves.

Hassan raised a hand to get her attention. "Pardon me."

She paused and raised her eyebrows. She stared with a flat affect, awaiting a question.

Hassan showed her the drawing of the cartouche. "Have you ever seen this symbol?"

Her eyes never left Hassan's face. "No."

"Really?" Trevor said. "You didn't even look at the drawing."

Her words snapped, stern and commanding. "I said I haven't seen it. You need to leave. The library is closing in five minutes." She turned abruptly and disappeared with her cart into the stacks.

Trevor slumped back against his chair. "That was strange."

"Indeed."

A piercing cry of a jackal in the distance drew Trevor's attention, like a lonely howl in the night. He looked toward the now darkened windows. "Did you hear that?"

Hassan stood and adjusted the scarf around his neck. "Hear what?"

"An animal I guess." The sun had set, and wildlife came out at night. Not surprising, Trevor supposed.

He started to close the book in front of him, but a word stood out on the page. *Jackal.* His stomach fluttered. With eyes glued to the page, he motioned his friend to join. "Hassan, I think I might have found something here."

Hassan hovered over Trevor's shoulder. "Oh?"

He traced a finger over the text. "*The Jackal King, son of Setut, pushed invaders out and maintained a stronghold at Zawty to serve as the guardian of the south, protecting Egypt.* Could this be our pharaoh?" Would he be able to fulfill his promise to his pops?

Hassan nodded. "Perhaps." He bent over the computer and tapped on the keyboard. His eyes scanned the screen. "Setut was a pharaoh who ruled during the Ninth Dynasty of the First Intermediate period circa 2150 BC. But no mention of a son Sabkaref."

The librarian appeared, startling the pair, and spoke in a very unlibrarian voice, near shouting. "You need to leave now."

Trevor snapped up and stood by Hassan. He waved at the computer. "We'd just like to print something out first."

She pointed to the door. "Go now."

Hassan patted Trevor on the arm. "It's alright my friend. We can come back in the morning."

Trevor took the drawing.

The librarian ushered them out of the building and slammed the door behind them, the lock engaging with a click.

Trevor rubbed the prickly sensation on his neck. The cool evening air provided relief from the stuffy library and a reprieve from the daytime sun.

As they stepped off the curb, headed toward their hotel, a tall thin man emerged from the shadows. He wore a loose white linen shirt adorned with fine embroidery and walked with a gold-tipped bamboo cane that clacked on the pavement. "Good evening, gentlemen. I hope you acquire a permit before you attempt to dig for anything."

The hairs on Trevor's neck raised. "Who said we're going to dig? And what business is it of yours, anyway?"

The man approached and stood uncomfortably close. He spoke with a crisp voice. "My name is Amir Abdel Khalek, and I work for the Egyptian Ministry of Antiquities, Mr. Burton." Khalek thumped the handle of his cane against Trevor's chest. The ornate golden serpent bared its fangs.

Trevor knocked away the cane. "How did you know my name?"

"It's my business to know. These permits require applications and background checks that take months to process. That is, *if* they're even approved."

Hassan stepped forward. "We're only researching, seeking information."

Khalek ignored him. He peered at the drawing in Trevor's hand and snatched it away. He examined the paper, then locked eyes with Trevor. "There is *nothing* for you here."

He crumpled the page and dropped it on the ground. He turned and walked away, disappearing into the night.

Trevor narrowed his eyes. He picked up the drawing and smoothed out the wrinkles against his chest. "Uh, yeah. I'd say that's confirmation that we're onto something."

"Indeed."

TREVOR GLANCED OVER HIS SHOULDER, then rubbed his neck. The solar streetlamps illuminated the sand-swept concrete, but many shadows remained outside the spheres of light. Clusters of citizens lounged outside in the night air on plastic chairs, visiting their neighbors and smoking cigarettes. It was those he couldn't see—the movements out of the corners of his eyes—that worried him. "I don't think we're alone."

Hassan quickened his pace. "I think you're right. Our hotel is just three more blocks."

"I don't want to get mugged. We can't risk losing this treasure." Trevor gripped the pendant through his shirt. "We're not going to make it to the hotel before they catch up with us. This way." Trevor yanked Hassan down a dark alley.

"Are you crazy? We're most safe on the street."

"Criminals will mug you in broad daylight. We have to outsmart them. After that exchange with Khalek, I wouldn't put it past him to send thugs to scare us off."

"Indeed."

A jackal yipped and barked nearby.

"Did you hear that?"

"What? The air conditioner?" Hassan pointed at a screeching window unit over their heads as they ducked through the deserted alleyways.

"No, the jackal."

"Jackal? I think you're hearing things, my friend."

They spilled out into a lighted residential street. An old man sat on the stoop of a home listening to a radio playing traditional Egyptian music. He nodded a greeting.

Trevor returned the gesture.

"It was probably the radio," Hassan said.

"I don't think so."

Behind them, in the alley, a metal garbage can clanked against a building.

Trevor tugged Hassan's shirt. "Let's go. They're still on our tail."

The pair sped toward a busy restaurant district a block ahead. The glow of colored lights shone over the buildings. Trevor looked back, and three men dressed in full-length gallibaya tunics and white headwraps emerged from the alleyway. Their eyes connected, and the men rushed at them.

The scream of a jackal echoed off the dwellings. A lanky golden-gray canine with erect ears stepped out from the shadows.

Trevor pointed and gasped for air. "*That's* what I heard."

"What?" Hassan panted.

"The jackal!"

Hassan pushed up his glasses and squinted. "What are you saying? I don't see anything."

The jackal sprinted down a cross street.

A gentle tug from within his chest compelled Trevor to follow. "This way."

He took the lead, chasing the creature that Hassan apparently couldn't see. It had to mean something.

The animal turned down another street, then another, winding them through a maze of homes and businesses.

Hassan doubled over. "Wait, wait. I need to catch my breath."

The canine stood by the edge of a building. As if it waited for them. But how long would it wait?

Trevor jogged toward the jackal. "We have to go now. Hurry, Hassan."

His friend followed, lagging behind, but within visual range.

The creature rounded a corner and Trevor followed. The jackal howled. Trevor cleared the structure, but the canine was nowhere in sight on the dead-end street. Trevor dashed between buildings, searching for the animal. Nothing.

Hassan caught up and struggled to catch his breath. "You can stop now. We lost them."

Trevor examined the abandoned two-story building before them, its windows boarded up with sun-faded wood. Sweet-scented acacia trees covered the plaster façade, one growing out of a shattered window. The dilapidated textile factory hadn't seen activity in at least fifty years.

Trevor rubbed his chin. "I think it led me here."

Hassan wiped his forehead with his scarf. "What are you talking about?"

"The jackal led me here."

"My friend, you've stared at books too long today. Your eyes deceive you."

His heart thumped fast against his aching chest wall, a feeling he hadn't experienced since childhood. He rubbed his chest and took a deep breath. *Not now.* "I'm going in."

Hassan grasped Trevor's arm and held him back. "What are you doing? It may be abandoned, but it's still illegal to break in. Let us go back to the hotel. Have a nice cup of tea, then go back to the library in the morning."

Trevor yanked at a rust-stained board nailed across the door. "I'm doing this with or without you."

Hassan's shoulders slumped. "Fine, but be careful. This old building looks ready for collapse."

Trevor heaved the rotted wood, which gave way with a crack and a crunch after a bit of muscle. Plaster from the door frame crumbled like powder onto the stone steps. Trevor reached for the brass doorknob in the center of the massive, teal-painted door, now peeling and chipped.

"It's probably locked," Hassan said.

Trevor turned the doorknob. He smirked. "Or not."

As the wooden door creaked inward, a sandy brown snake slithered out, sidewinding through the opening.

"Whoa." Trevor sprang away from the threshold.

Hassan stepped back two paces.

The snake lingered, two horns protruding from its head, and studied the intruders, flicking its tongue. It slowly opened its jaw, exposing its fangs and hissing a warning. The snake slipped away, disappearing down the street into the darkness.

Hassan blotted his head with his scarf. "Horned viper. Very deadly."

A chill danced up his spine. Trevor nodded, then advanced toward the building.

"Are you sure you want to go in there?" Hassan said.

TREVOR STUMBLED over loose bricks and bumped into a stone vat once used to dye fabric. The orange glow of his match brightened an orb around them, enough to see ten feet ahead. The heat of the match burned his finger. He dropped it on the floor, and it sizzled out.

"Ouch." Trevor sucked on his finger as they stood in the dark. Only a bit of blue moonlight peeked through the dirty glass of the windows.

Trevor struck another match against the hotel matchbook and felt his way along a crumbling inner wall. "I know there's something here. There has to be."

Even in the dim light, Hassan's concern was apparent in his eyes. "You need rest, my friend."

The flame flickered in Trevor's fingers. *Wind.* But there was no apparent draft from the windows on this side of the building. A sensation in his chest drove him forward. "This way."

Ten feet ahead, a square of old boards lay in the middle of the floor, a covering for a cellar, maybe. Trevor knelt beside it and lit a new match. The sulfurous flame danced back and forth, then snuffed out. He held his hand over the wood. Air flow. He lit another match.

Hassan bent to examine the boards. "The wood is old, ancient."

"How old?" Trevor ran his palm over the timbers, then rubbed his fingers together, sprinkling dust onto the ground.

"Old enough to disintegrate. You just might have found something."

"There's airflow. It must be a passageway."

Hassan nodded.

With little effort, Trevor tore back the decaying boards and exposed a staircase, rough-hewn into the stone below, leading into darkness. He lowered his arm into the hole. "Why is this here?"

"As with all ancient cities, they built modern Asyut upon the old. There could be hidden passages throughout the city." Hassan waved his hand in the moonlight. "After you."

Trevor held up the flame and descended. Fifteen steep steps down brought them to a passage cut into the bedrock. He lit an oil lantern that hung on the wall and removed it from its rusted hook. The lamp was old but from the modern era. Trevor shrugged. "Still works."

"That must be more than a hundred years old."

Hassan pointed down the sandy passage. "I get the feeling no one has been down here in ages. But for what reason?"

The corridor ran at least thirty feet before taking a ninety-degree turn. Cool, dry air moaned through the passage, laced with an earthy, woody scent and fluttering their hair. From there, the tunnel angled down, and the walls of the passageway narrowed and continued for at least another hundred feet. They must have been several stories below ground.

Trevor turned a corner in the tunnel and gasped. The passage flared out, ten feet high by eight feet wide, to accommodate a huge sandstone double door. Butterflies danced in his belly.

Hassan held his hand over his mouth.

Hieroglyphics carved into the stone covered the door from floor to ceiling. Loops of dusty ropes tied copper handles together. A round clay seal remained unbroken, affixed to the rope. In the shadowy lantern light, there was no mistaking the Jackal King's cartouche emblazoned on the seal.

"What is this?" Trevor knew, but needed to hear the words spoken.

"A tomb. An unopened tomb. The pharaoh Sabkaref's tomb."

Trevor and Hassan grinned at each other.

Trevor reached for the seal. "We are going to be rich beyond belief."

"Wait." Hassan examined the writings on the doors. "Look at this."

"What does it say?"

"It's a curse."

Trevor chuffed. "Really, Hassan? An old curse is going to scare you off? What kind of archaeologist are you?"

Hassan waggled a finger at Trevor. "A cautious one." He traced his hand along as he read the hieroglyphs. "*Cursed be those who desecrate this tomb. May the scorpion sting. May the viper bite. May the jackal seize them by the throat. May an eternity of torment be cast onto him. Protected are my guardians. Long life, free from disease, shall be bestowed unto them.*"

Trevor wrinkled his brow and mumbled the waiter's words from the morning. "Beware the signs of the pharaoh . . ."

"What was that?"

Superstitions. He stiffened. "Nothing. What does it mean?"

"Curses are rare on tombs, especially during this era. This pharaoh must have had many enemies to go to all this trouble. And perhaps it worked. Here we are at his undisturbed tomb."

Trevor clenched his jaw. "I promised my grandfather I would find the cartouche's secrets. We *have* to open it."

Hassan's eyes sparkled. "This will finally earn me the respect of other archaeologists and scholars."

"Let's do this." Trevor held the clay seal and looked at Hassan, who nodded in agreement. He broke the seal, the pottery snapping apart in his fingers, and paused, waiting for a bad sign. Nothing came. He unwound the rope from around the copper door handles. Trevor inhaled deeply and tugged. They didn't budge. "It's locked?"

Hassan tapped his lip. "There may be a hidden mechanism. Look for a slot or opening in the stone."

Trevor and Hassan scanned the surface of the doors.

"Here." On his knees, Trevor found a slit in one door near the floor.

Hassan squatted beside Trevor. "But we don't have a key."

Trevor sat back on his heels. "We may need to come back tomorrow with tools and break down the door."

A muffled sound carried down the passageway behind them. Unmistakable. A jackal cry.

Trevor glanced over his shoulder, then put his hand to his chest. He withdrew the golden cartouche from his shirt. "Maybe we do have a key." He grinned.

Trevor took off the pendant and slipped the cartouche into the slot. A loud clunk came from inside the door, a thud pounded against the stone, then a series of faint clicks sounded. The door popped open a crack. Trevor raised his eyebrows. He quickly slung the cartouche around his neck and stood.

Hassan smiled. "After you."

Trevor beamed. "Gladly." He swung the heavy door open. The scent of perfumes wafted from inside, with notes of cedarwood, incense, and citrus. He held the lantern high. The glint of gold reflected the light. "I knew it." He pumped a fist in the air.

They stepped inside the intact tomb, a room thirty feet long by twenty feet wide by ten feet tall carved into the bedrock. An enormous, black basalt sarcophagus dominated the chamber. Painted reliefs of figures and animals on bright yellow-gold backgrounds adorned every inch of the room, so real they appeared they could step out of the wall. Artifacts like gold statues, bundles of mummified animals, pots, and jewelry lay piled high in each corner. *Richer than I ever imagined.*

Hassan studied the scenes on the walls, depicting gods and priests and kings preparing for the afterlife. "Fascinating, fascinating." His mouth hung agape. "Here are the two jackal deities they worshipped, Anubis and Wepwawet." He pointed out the tall figures, men with jackal heads, one black, one gray.

Hieroglyphics etched the surface of the unopened sarcophagus. Trevor ran his hand along the cool stone, the carvings like braille under his fingertips. In the middle of the sarcophagus, a familiar cartouche stood out. The cartouche matched his pendant. A jackal. Two arms. A mouth. A horned viper. The tomb of Sabkaref.

Trevor placed his palm against the cartouche. His fingers tingled with electricity, then white hot pain seared across his chest. The lantern clattered to the ground and rolled side to side, its flames casting distorted shadows on the crypt walls. Trevor dropped to his knees and clutched his chest. *Different from before.* The skin on his chest burned. *The curse?* He gritted his teeth.

Hassan rushed to his side. "Are you okay?"

Trevor ripped his shirt open, revealing a patch of burned flesh near his collarbone. "What the hell?"

"It's a brand." Hassan sucked in a breath. "A jackal."

"What?" Trevor strained to examine his scorched skin.

"It's a hieroglyph of a jackal. Like the cartouche."

Trevor rubbed the spot and stood. He righted the lantern on the floor.

Hassan placed his hand on the sarcophagus to steady himself as he stood.

"No, don't." Trevor reached to stop Hassan, but it was too late.

Hassan ran his hand over the smooth stone and the cartouche. "Why?"

Trevor pointed to the brand. "When I touched the cartouche on the sarcophagus, this happened. Why did I get this and not you?"

Hassan tugged at his bottom lip. "Curious. We both touched the sarcophagus. And if it's the curse, shouldn't we both be affected?"

Trevor nodded. "What makes me different?"

Hassan pointed at Trevor. "You said the cartouche was passed down for generations, and it came from your great-grandmother?"

"Yes."

"Remind me, what was her name again?"

"Nesu Saab."

Hassan shook his head. "It couldn't be. Staring at us the whole time. How could I have been so blind?"

Trevor narrowed his eyes. "What are you talking about?"

"Your great-grandmother's name. Nesu. It's an ancient Egyptian name. It means princess. And Saab?" Hassan slapped his forehead. "I never made the connection. Saab is pronounced the same as the jackal hieroglyph, sab. Jackal Princess."

Trevor's heartbeat quickened, and his forehead creased. "What are you saying?"

"You're a direct descendant of the pharaoh Sabkaref. That's how you're different."

Could this be?

"Such a marvelous story."

Trevor whirled toward the unfamiliar voice behind them.

Three men reeking of sweat stood in the doorway. The same men that chased them through the streets.

Trevor's heart raced.

The apparent leader, the man who spoke, wore a navy-blue long shirt that brushed against his dusty sandals. "Too bad your line ends here." He withdrew a dagger from its sheath, his blade swishing through the air.

The other two men, one in a threadbare gray tunic, one in a white tunic frayed at the bottom, flashed switchblades at Trevor and Hassan. Sweat beaded on their foreheads.

Hassan held his hands up. "I think we can come to an arrangement."

The man in gray pushed past his friends and lunged at Hassan, thrusting his knife at his midsection.

Trevor shoved Hassan out of the path of the thin blade.

Hassan lost his balance and fell into the sarcophagus, slamming his head against the stone with a *thunk*. He slumped to the sand-covered floor, knocked out cold.

Trevor swatted away the attacker's knife and swung his fist, connecting with the man's jaw.

The blow threw the man to the floor. He tumbled and crashed into a pottery vessel, shattering it.

An explosion of rope-like contents emerged and enveloped the man.

Trevor backed away.

It wasn't ropes.

It was snakes. *Horned vipers.*

The man shrieked as the vipers' bites sent him into unconsciousness.

Trevor shivered.

The leader's lip curled as he stared Trevor down.

The man in gray craned his neck at the treasures that filled the room. He smirked. "We're going to be the richest men in Asyut. Richer than anyone."

The leader laughed. "Yes, yes, I will be." The tip of his dagger buried into the man's side.

His eye went wide. He clutched the blade handle. Red seeped through his tunic. He groaned, curled over, and collapsed to the ground.

"I will live a life extravagant enough for the *both* of us."

Trevor's stomach dropped. "I can't believe you killed your friend."

"My friend? That was my little brother."

Trevor gasped. *Greed turns men into monsters.* He held up his fists, ready to fight.

The leader's eyes burned with rage. He stormed forward, slashing his dagger through the air.

Trevor dodged the blade once, twice, then a third slash ripped through his shirt-sleeve. He winced. A red line soaked the cloth of his upper arm. He stepped back, deeper into the tomb, blocking the man's advances, until cornered against the back wall.

The man growled and raised his dagger over his head.

A jackal cry pierced the air.

Out of the corner of his eye, Trevor spotted movement.

The jackal guarding Anubis and Wepwawet sprang from the painting and lunged at the attacker.

The same jackal that had led them to the tomb.

It grabbed the man's throat.

He dropped the blade at Trevor's feet and struggled with the beast, who thrashed from side to side, digging its teeth deeper into the man's flesh.

The jackal jerked the man back toward the wall. It stepped into the painting and tugged the man with him. The wall was like liquid, allowing them to pass like it was a doorway, making a crackling sound as they moved through the stone.

Then the man was gone.

The jackal resumed his stationary place beside the gods.

Trevor fell against the wall and slid down. He rubbed his eyes. *Was this real?*

The two men lay dead on the floor.

Trevor's stomach turned. *What will I do with the bodies?*

As if the gods answered, each man disintegrated into dust, the gentle breeze in the tomb swirling them into the sand as if they were never there.

More like them would come.

More like *Trevor* would come.

The treasure was more valuable than anyone would ever understand. They'd tear apart the tomb and scatter its contents around the globe.

After everything he'd seen, it proved the curse was real. If they removed any of the artifacts, the curse would kill them. *But to leave all this treasure?* Dreams of riches gone. His name would be lost to time.

Trevor rubbed his heart, then his hand wandered to the brand on his chest. Maybe the best thing he could do was to protect his great ancestor's secret. The promise of long life, no disease—no heart disease—was priceless. He'd remain a poor man, but there were other ways to make money. At least he fulfilled his promise to his pops. He found the secret of the cartouche. This should have been his grandfather's fate, but he never learned the secret his mother held.

What would Hassan think of this?

Hassan!

Trevor rushed to his friend's side and gently cradled his head in his lap. He patted Hassan's cheek. "Hassan, wake up. You have to wake up."

Hassan took a deep breath, then opened groggy eyes. He rubbed the swollen goose egg on the side of his head. "What happened to those men?"

"You wouldn't believe me if I told you."

TREVOR HELD the last plank in position, and Hassan pounded a nail into the hardwood flooring covering the textile factory. Trevor sat back on his knees and surveyed the open space, now free from the clutter of old dye vats, chemicals, and rubbish. The renovations sped along quickly with Hassan and his brothers' help. First structural repairs, then plaster and paint, now flooring, and soon shelving.

Hassan mopped his brow with a rag. "That, my friend, is a job well done."

Trevor stood and brushed the dust off his trousers. He lent a hand to Hassan to help him up. "Time for a break?"

"Indeed. I'll fetch us some cold drinks." Hassan strolled out of the building, heading toward the street vendors two blocks over.

Trevor grabbed a rickety wooden chair and carried it outside. He placed it in the shade of an acacia tree and plopped down.

Tapping echoed across the dead-end street. *Clack. Clack. Clack.*

Khalek sauntered toward the building, his gold-tipped cane striking the ground with each step.

Trevor leaned forward. "What are *you* doing here?"

Khalek smirked. "Nice to see you, too."

Trevor's jaw tightened. "Should we expect more visits from your goons?"

"Those were not my goons. They were graverobbers. And you thwarted them, I see. Thank you." He bowed. "Some secrets are not meant to be revealed, and the king must be allowed his slumber."

Trevor blinked. "How did you—?

"It's my business to know, Mr. Burton." Khalek tugged the collar of his shirt aside, revealing the brand of a jackal.

A rush of adrenaline coursed through Trevor's body.

Khalek straightened his shirt. "You aren't the only descendant. There are many guardians watching." He pointed his cane at the building. "That's how we knew you put a down payment on the building with your grandfather's inheritance and are opening a shop."

"That isn't creepy at all. Yeah, a bookstore with my friend Hassan."

"Yes, we know."

Trevor raised an eyebrow.

"I'm glad you chose the correct path. What made you decide to abandon treasure hunting?"

"A promise unbroken for over four-thousand years, and I'm going to be the scumbag that betrays it? Not on my watch. I would do anything for family."

"And the family will do anything for you. I'm actually here to deliver this." Khalek passed him a large envelope.

Trevor accepted it. "What is this?"

"The deed to the building. Your mortgage has been paid off, and we've added some seed money to your bank account to help you set up the store."

Trevor rubbed his open mouth. "I don't know what to say. Thank you."

Khalek nodded. "It's the least we can do." He walked away, cane tapping on the road.

Trevor leaned back against the chair. The breeze carried cedar and juniper through the air. The side of his calf tingled, and he glanced at the source. The jackal materialized and lay beside him on the ground. Trevor scratched the canine between the ears.

"Good boy. Anything for family."

EMBER BLOOMS

LAURA HOLLEY

Don't leave him. Watch. Stay alert," Prince Thomas had commanded.

Ember curled her bushy, red tail up and over her snout, tightly closing her eyes. Everything about this room terrified her: the strange, luminescent dahlias and foxgloves on the bedside table, the pulsating, acrid odor, the humid darkness . . . and the king who lay slowly dying in the bed above her.

But Thomas had asked her to stay, so she had been there for hours, silently wishing he truly understood her devotion in doing so.

The king's wet, hacking cough sent a shiver through Ember's spine, and she almost missed it—a creak on the floorboards behind her. Peering out at the enormous floor mirror across the room, Ember's vertically-slit pupils and narrowed eyelids let in just enough light to see clearly in the darkness.

A cloaked figure stood silently beside the bed. How had she missed him coming in? Ember's limbs tingled with adrenaline as she crouched, watching the figure pull out a foxglove flower.

"*Rex purpurea mors statim,*" the figure whispered, dropping the flower onto the king. As it landed, a burst of light like a summer sun blinded Ember. She howled, first with pain, then with anger. Springing out from under the bed toward where the figure had stood, she snapped her jaws in every direction, desperate for her eyes to adjust. Pouncing and gekkering loudly, she felt her teeth scratch through a human calf before finally clamping onto soft fabric. The figure screamed as Ember yanked and pulled, then suddenly fell to the side as the fabric ripped away.

Ember stilled, vision finally returning, and stalked, prepared to pounce at any movement, but there was none. She held her position, glancing at the mirror again, but as undetectably as the figure had arrived, it had disappeared. Frantic, she turned about, honing in her night vision again.

Suddenly the door opened across the room. Several guards and Prince Thomas rushed into the room with candles and torches. Within moments, the room was lit, and Ember's eyes were adjusting again.

"Did you see something, girl?' Thomas asked her.

Ember desperately wanted to help. She sniffed at the floor, trying to catch a scent, but the air had all mixed with the swinging door and the scents were still disorienting.

Thomas turned toward the king and halted, stepping backward and staring at his chest where the flower had fallen. "Guards, split up," he said, turning away. "Follow every hallway and alert those outside the castle. I want every candle lit and every passage checked." But the guards just gaped at the king, one whispering, "His chest . . . burned through . . ."

"*Go to it!*" Thomas yelled, snapping them out of it. The guards scurried about passing orders and organizing themselves. Moments later they had all left and Thomas stood watching Ember in her fury to detect something.

"Nothing at all, Vixen?" His name for her still felt so foreign in Ember's mind, even after so many years. Yet "Ember" seemed to have no foundation in her memory either.

Finally the air seemed to be settling. Ember closed her eyes, honing in her sense of smell. *Foxglove, dahlia, body odor, wine, queen, dust, cloak, guards . . .* wait. The cloak scent matched the taste of the one Ember had held in her mouth just minutes before.

Ember honed her senses directly in on the cloak, negating all else. She followed the scent from beside the bed, over to the corner by the window. There—between the wall and the bench—was a draft, and with it came the earthy, floral scent of the cloak. Letting out a quick bark, Ember turned to the prince, who was already striding toward her. He felt the wall while she sniffed at it and found a small lever between wooden boards on the floor. A piece of the wall opened silently, and the scent of the cloak overwhelmed Ember's senses. She bounded through the opening.

DESPITE HIS BATTLE TRAINING, Ember could hear Prince Thomas's heaving breaths behind her. But she couldn't slow down. Finally the scent stalled, and Ember realized they had arrived at the passage's end. Prince Thomas pulled out his sword and looked down, and Ember crouched, the familiar twitch of adrenaline coursing through her limbs.

As Thomas opened the door, Ember dashed in, teeth bared and ears back.

"Vixen, stop!" Thomas cried. Alone in the middle of the room stood the dark-complexioned queen, her velvet dress failing to cover a bloodied leg. "Mother . . . what? What happened to your leg? Did someone come? Did someone *hurt you?*"

Ember's mind reeled. The queen's leg. Teeth scratches. The scent of the queen, stronger in the kings' chambers than it should've been considering the last time she had come in. And in this room, dahlias and foxgloves glowed ever so slightly on the corner table beside the queen's chair.

A fresh fear swelled from Ember's throat, and she leaped out in front of Thomas, growling and snarling, and preventing him from approaching his mother.

"Vixen, stop it! Vixen, she's hurt! He could still be here!" Thomas entered despite Ember's warnings, so she gekkered again, then barked and crouched, ready to pounce at him if necessary.

"She's protecting you, son. She's a wise friend, your fox," the queen said, quietly stepping backward over a discarded cloak on the floor. "She always was a beautiful, protective creature."

Thomas backed up a step as well. Ember pivoted, watching both intently, prepared for anything. None of it made any sense.

"Ember." The queen's voice had softened as she spoke, and Ember's chest swelled with confusion as the queen's eyes reddened, tears brimming. "It's alright. It's over." She crossed to a table laden with tinctures near the flowers and picked up a small vial.

"Mother, her name is Vixen, not Ember. Ember died years ago, remember? Maybe you should sit down." Thomas turned to get her a chair. Ember growled at him, still too confused to let him move. The queen ignored him, carefully approaching Ember, who was staring back, unblinking and cautious.

"Ember. You know your name, don't you, my dear? I've watched you, all these years. Kept you right here with us so I could keep you safe, watch you grow." She approached.

Ember's mind glassed over. How did the queen know her name? Ember shook her head, trying to clear it.

"Yes, I knew you remembered. But darling, I couldn't let you keep those memories. The horrible abuse. He hurt me too."

Thomas placed his hand on his sword hilt. "Mother, what are you saying?" He was panicked. *"Look at me!"*

The queen held Ember's gaze, stretching her hand out toward the prince. Immediately, the chair he had wanted to get for her swung out behind him, collecting him and wrapping itself around him, then swinging back against the wall they had come through.

Ember's mind was captive; she held no thoughts but a drive to listen to the queen's every word. The queen kept approaching, the vial held out before her. Suddenly she threw it onto the floor at Ember's feet, and it broke, the potion splattering up and onto her fur.

Ember felt her limbs and torso lengthen, a painful stretching and pulling sensation coursing through every bone and muscle. Her head felt as if it would splinter into pieces as it contorted, here shrinking and there expanding. Fur from each of her pores was released, entangling, creating a beautiful red gown that clung to the skin beneath it, and from her head grew long, lustrous red hair.

"You see, my daughter? I've kept you safe from that man, and now that he is gone, we will live together again. We will reign, you and I. We will be beautiful, powerful—*perfection!*" The queen yelled the last few words, light emanating from her as she threw her arms and head back.

With the gaze broken, Ember's mind cleared for a breath's time. The queen glowed, a horrifying, blackened enchantress. Rushed and clumsy in a body she had forgotten, Ember reached over, grabbing the lustrous foxglove vase and throwing it at the queen. It hit her bosom and crashed to the floor, shattering. The flowers burst into a bloom of colorful light, but Ember had prepared for it, her eyes tightly closed.

A moment passed. And then another. Ember listened with what felt like dull ears, but the room was silent. Opening her eyes, she saw only ashes where the queen had stood.

"Vix . . . Ember? Is it really you?" Thomas's chair had released him, and as she turned to look at him, memories flooded back: the two of them playing in the stream in the woods; the queen, her mother, obsessing over her hair and gowns; her father's anger, pulling her through passageways and into his bedroom. Many were painful memories. Yet here stood Thomas, kind Thomas, who had loved her even when neither had known. Kind Thomas, who had kept her safe and cared for her, even thinking that she had died.

"Yes, Thomas. It's me."

Thomas stepped toward her, holding out a shaking hand. She took it, trembling as well, and they embraced.

Just then, the door swung open, guards pouring into the room. "We heard a commotion and . . ." the guard paused, startled and confused to see Prince Thomas and a young, beautiful woman embracing in the queen's bed chamber.

Thomas smiled and took a deep breath. "Guards, meet my long-lost twin sister, Ember."

Delta Oskar Golf:
For the Love of Flora
on a Dead Earth

Jade C. Wildy

Klais ran a hand through his long, dark hair, a legacy from the now long-dead queen. "Oh, come on! There must be something here. I have too much riding on it for another crop to fail." He dug the toe of his heavy work boot into the dark, rich soil, but it turned up nothing. The rows were as empty as the Earth's long-dead landscape that surrounded them. By now, the haizeseed seeds, imported from Poverdant Prime should have sprouted little purple seedlings and become short stalks reaching to Klais' knee.

Klais sat on the ground with his head in his hands, heedless of how the dirt clung to the sapphire embroidery on his robe. This wasn't the planet to be wearing embroidered, royal statement clothes since there was no one here to observe his prince regent splendor besides a few transient scavengers and a lot of farming autobots. He hadn't even been allowed to bring any of his royal house staff. His personal valet would have loved the rugged farm-fashionista look he had going on, but even she remained on Poverdant.

"Failed crops, on a failed planet, produced by a failed prince regent. At least good ol' Klais is living up to everyone's expectations." Even before coming to Earth, Klais had always wondered why no one had tried to clean and terraform the dead planet when its conditions for sustaining life were perfect, right in the Goldilocks Zone; not too close to the sun, and not too far away. He looked at the empty soil. "It doesn't make any sense."

The accumulated junk that littered the planet from centuries of being a dumping ground for galactic garbage was easy for Klais' autobots to sort and recycle. The toxic waste and radiation had been a little harder, but in the two years he had been on the near-barren planet, he cleaned up enough that he had turned his hands to growing things. This was the last hurdle to overcome. Nothing had taken.

A breeze picked up, tickling Klais' hair across his face. He considered the Trayback, complete with its harvest equipment, seed canisters, and planting bots ready to sow another crop if this one had taken.

He tucked a long strand of hair behind his ear. "No point even trying." The darkening clouds over the royal bunker where he lived matched his mood as he wondered for the hundredth time over the last two years if he should just pack it in and go home with his tail between his legs. "It's what my dear old father, Emperor King of Absolutely Everything expects, isn't it? Who wants to become King-in-Waiting of an entire galaxy anyway?" *Someone who wants their family to pay attention to them!* Klais pushed the thought away.

The communicator at his wrist chirped, reminding him of the messages he had been ignoring. "Oh, yeah, my conniving sisters, that's who would like to rule the entire galaxy." He turned his attention to the communicator and grudgingly tapped its screen.

The voice of Donna—the older of Klais' two sisters—filled the air. "The king wants productivity reports on the planetary reclamation progress and how the seeds allocations from Poverdant Prime have been put to *good* use." Donna was all about the galaxy's fiscal policies and economic state.

Klais screwed up his nose. "Hey, Klais, how are you?" he said to himself, mimicking Donna's voice. "I've been worried about you down on that dead pile of toxic rock they call Earth. Everyone at the royal palace on Poverdant misses you, and we wish we were there with you." Klais kicked at the barren farm soil. "Not likely." If Klais failed, it was one less sibling for Donna to compete with for the throne and rule of the galaxy.

"Ah, Sister, you probably have calculated the costs of having me assassinated and decided it made more financial sense just to wait and watch me fail." He took a handful of the empty soil and let it filter out between his ringed fingers. It trickled to the side as the wind picked up. "Probably a safe approach." He dusted his hands off and played the next message.

"Klais, it's Agneta. Father has said colonists have started heading to Earth. I hope you know what you are doing." Agneta was called "The People's Princess" by the galaxy-wide media, who showed her holding fundraiser balls and walking the slums of Poverdant, where all the dregs of the galaxy seemed to hang out despite it being the galaxy's capital homeworld. And, oh boy, she did so much slum walking! If Donna was about the profit, Agneta was about the people, or at least she pretended to be.

The wind was picking up almost as if Klais' mood were controlling it. "Great. The last thing I need is people flocking to the planet expecting to survive." He considered the messages. With two messages from his sisters, he had an inkling the terms of his King-in-Waiting arrangement with his father had been the topic of conversation. It didn't take a genius with an education costing the price of a medium-sized moon (like Klais had), to guess who the third message was from. He groaned and hit play on the comm watch.

"A message from the Galactic Emperor King Zan to Galactic Prince Regent Klais," came the voice of one of the king's many advisors. "Message reads: Prince Klais, I remind you of the terms of our *mutual* agreement."

Klais paused the message and took a steadying breath. "How could I forget? It was broadcast to the entire galaxy." Klais mimicked Agneta's voice. "'It will renew the people's interest in the ruling family.'" He snorted. "Well, lucky Donna found a way to capitalize on it and set up a system where the richest family in the galaxy can fleece the poor—oh I mean supporters can make donations. That's better than the galactic government picking up the tab!"

He unpaused the message. "You have been apportioned three years in which to complete the task that you have been assigned, which involves proving viability on the planet Earth concerning food, shelter, and resources; one to which you readily agreed. You have received provisions and support and yet the Galactic Empire has yet to see you bear fruit. You have one final year left to demonstrate the qualities of a King-in-Waiting. The king reminds you that succession is decided by the capability and suitability of a galactic prince or princess to the required tasks of running a galaxy. If the planet is determined to be unviable, you will return to Poverdant Prime and will publicly renounce your claim to the galactic throne. You have twelve months left." The message clicked off.

"And there it is," Klais said to himself. "Execution by public humiliation where all my misdeeds are laid bare like the crops I couldn't get to grow. No doubt the publicity stunt was Agneta's suggestion."

Klais let his hand drop to his side and considered the empty dirt and rock around him "The entire project is a joke. You never expected I could change this lump of polluted long-dead rock into somewhere people could live, did you, Father? Just a convoluted plot, keeping your least favored progeny out of the public eye until you can formally denounce him."

He stood, stomped the dirt off his boots, and shook his bangled hands to clear some of the familiar tension that messages from his family always brought. "I can rule a galaxy, I just don't have the rabid royalty gene Donna and Agneta possess. And I am not the worthless dandy who isn't even worth considering." He smoothed his hands over his robe. "Even if I do talk to myself."

Head high, Klais trudged over his newest batch of hopelessly failed crops toward where he left the farming Tray-back. The large-wheeled, silver vehicle had a cabin that could fit two people and a large open tray for moving equipment. It was loaded with soil samples, seeds, and expensive, automated farming machines and bots covered with a heavy canopy. A dark looming storm was brewing in the direction of the royal bunker.

"Oh, this looks lovely to drive in. Something to cap off this stellar, successful day."

As if to make its point, lightning flashed overhead, and a deafening thunderclap rumbled into the distance.

"Great, just great. Not only am I going to die on this stupid planet, there's a storm between me and the royal bunker." The royal bunker, just visible in the distance, was a series of concrete rooms repurposed from who knew what that Klais had decorated as expensively as possible to annoy Donna. In the face of the storm, its best attribute was that it could withstand a nuclear bomb and had an exquisite barista machine.

Klais broke into a run toward the Tray-back. It could move quicker than Klais could, but he wished he had brought his fancy purple Sports Speeder instead. He put his hand on the gear stick and hovered his thumb over the acceleration button. The ferocious storm was rolling in fast. There was no way he was going to make the royal bunker without getting caught in it.

With a deafening clap of thunder and a flash of lightning, the storm broke. Klais threw the Tray-back into reverse, turned away from the bunker, and drove across the empty fields toward the rocky outcrops of nearby hills, which he hoped might be hiding shelter.

"Running away again, Klais?" His sarcastic tone was tinged with a pitch of fear. "That doesn't sound like you!" His breathing became rapid. "Then again, I'm driving with no idea where I'm going and no idea what could possibly be out here. Oh, completely clueless Klais, there you are. I missed you." He flinched at another clap of thunder. "Here's hoping we find some shelter from the storm and don't make the fam happy by dying."

The rain pelted down on the front windscreen of the Tray-back. Klais squinted, trying to make out some strange humps up ahead that looked vaguely familiar. "Oh, please let it somehow be the bunker and my coffee machine—" He slammed on the brakes and skidded to a halt. "You've got to be kidding me!"

The square boxes Klais had mistaken for the bunker were flimsy cargo container pods, the kind that rich companies sent down to planets when they had no intention of retrieving them. Klais' terraforming, farming equipment, and even the Tray-back had arrived in similar pods.

"Oh, no, no, no!" Klais tightened his fists on the wheel. It was a small colonists' camp using the pods as shelter. People scurried between the buildings tying things down. They couldn't have been there long. The very worst of the storm had yet to arrive, but it was getting nastier by the second. He let out a strangled groan, threw open the door of the Tray-back, and leapt out into the storm.

"Hey!" He waved at the first person he saw, his soaked robes clinging to his arms. His dark hair whipped backward and forward across his face.

A red-haired woman in a grey jumpsuit spotted Klais next to the Tray-back. "Prince Regent Klais?" Her eyes widened and she dropped the ropes she carried onto the ground. She ran toward the rest of the group shouting, "Everyone, everyone! It's Prince Regent Klais! Right here in our camp!"

Klais balled up his fists. "No, this is not a time to get starstruck by royalty." A deep rattle of thunder drowned out his words as he danced from foot to foot, eager to get away to some kind of safety. "Oh, come back!"

He groaned, then ran after the woman, following her into one of the larger cargo pod dwellings. A communal gasp from the group of twenty-five or so miserable and bedraggled people inside greeted his entry.

"Prince Regent Klais . . . in our camp?" A grizzled old man with gnarled, worker's hands struggled to his feet.

Klais gestured dramatically with his hands. "Hello, I'm here. Yes, I'm Klais. That's great, isn't it? Now, I don't know where you're from or what you think you're doing out here, but there is a very mean storm coming. And I'm not sure that you're going to be okay in these pods. You need to go."

No one moved, then a younger man with fair hair fell to his knees, clasping at Klais' soggy robe. "My name is Francis, and I knew it. I knew that you would be the king to follow. My family has come to this planet because we believe in you. We believe in your vision. We are indebted to you and your presence in our humble—"

"Enough." Klais hated how much he sounded like his father. "Let me be clear." He spoke slowly, gesturing with his hands like he was addressing children. "Big, big storm. Coming this way. Little camp. Not going to survive. Colonists need to go."

The wind and rain howled, and the sides of the small dwelling started to rattle as various bits of rubble and rock—and probably people's possessions—were thrown against its side.

"We have nowhere to go," the jumpsuit woman said. "Everything we have is here."

"Merrin's right," the old man added. "We've been here less than a week. We don't know this terrain or any of the dangers. We're better off staying here. Unless . . ." He looked at Klais. "Do you know a place that we could shelter?"

"Well . . ." Klais looked from face to face, twiddling one of the rings on his fingers. "I was planning to head for the hills."

"That's good enough for old Carl." The old man crossed the pod and picked up a backpack. "Everybody, grab what you can. Don't bring anything that isn't integral to your survival, or of extreme sentimental value. Someone, do a headcount of the children. We're going to have to move quickly and evacuate the area, as per our king's decree."

"Whoa, whoa, whoa!" Klais waved his hands. "I am *not* the king."

The colonists ignored his protests as they scrambled to grab blankets, food, and cute little toys.

"My father is going to have me beheaded if he thinks that I've been using the title 'king' before he said I could," Klais said.

His day was getting worse, but it was nothing compared to the weather they faced when they threw open the pod door.

"We can't travel in this!" Merrin shouted over the wind.

"There is no staying here!" Carl shouted and moved into the torrential rain.

Klais waved the colonists, each with a bag of meagre possessions forward. "Follow me!" It occurred to him that he wasn't just telling them to evacuate, he was *leading* an evacuation. *That's great! A life and death situation with me being responsible for people when I wasn't even allowed to have pets!* The savage irony weighed heavier than his soaked robe.

They reached the Tray-back and Klais turned to the nearest colonist, the blond man called Francis. "Hey, gather up people who can lift very heavy things." *And provide witness protection when my sister finds out what I'm about to do to several billion credits worth of farming machinery.*

Klais yanked the canopy back. "Unload everything off the tray."

"Where do you want to put it?" Francis asked.

Klais' snorted, which he regretted instantly as a large quantity of rain went up his nose. "I genuinely don't care. On the ground?"

"But this stuff is worth billions of credits!" Carl's mouth hung open as he looked over the machinery. "And half of it is brand new. You can't just dump this out."

Klais clenched his fists as the rain turned to hail. "I don't care about the farming equipment. We need the space, or you die. It's up to you."

That spurred the colonists into action. Very quickly, the expensive farming supplies and machinery were dumped in the rain, and the colonists were safe underneath the canopy.

Carl did a quick head count and gave Klais a thumbs up. "All here!" He closed the canopy.

That was enough for Klais. He launched himself into the driver's side of the Tray-back, slammed his foot on the accelerator, and sped over the rocky ground almost as if he could outrun the storm.

"What are you doing, Klais? You are driving blind, through rain, in an area you completely ignored and didn't survey because it wasn't immediately useful. You have no idea what's in front of you." He tapped his ringed fingers on the steering wheel as the hail rained down. "And now you're looking for a magic cave in the middle of nowhere because everybody has always given you anything you ever wanted except love and acceptance. You somehow believe that because you want it, shelter will materialize directly in front of you. That's grand. That's not going to end up with everybody killed and be all your fault. No problems. Definitely King-in-Waiting qualities." His knuckles were white. It was the most responsibility he had ever had in his life.

The terrain became rockier, causing the Tray-back to bounce, which was terrifying given the ferocity of the storm erupting around them. Klais could feel his hands shaking as he squinted, trying to peer through the battering of hail. Up ahead, something rose out of the haze of the storm. He assumed it was a rock until the clean lines of a structure came into view.

Something hit the windscreen and a large crack appeared. The wind buffeted the side of the Tray-back. "We're here!" he shouted to the colonists as he climbed out of the cabin.

The front of the large structure supplied mediocre shelter from the hail driven like buckshot by the wind. Directly in front of Klais was a large, heavy metal door, but a dimly lit panel on one side drew his attention.

"Does anybody happen to read Ancient Human?" There was no response. "Oh, just me then." Klais' Ancient Human knowledge was sketchy, but he thought it read "Password". He let out a whine of frustration. "Can't anything be simple!?" He tried a combination of random digits and the panel flashed red.

Carl, sheltering his weathered face from the onslaught of rain and hail, came up next to Klais, along with Francis. "Is this it?"

"Guess so. Did I lose anyone?"

"No, my King we're all here," Francis said.

Klais ignored the title as the door panel rejected another password attempt. "Cool. Well, I don't know where we are. I don't know what I found. But it looks like shelter if we can get those," he pointed to the doors with both of his fingers, "open".

"Francis," Carl said "go get the pickaxes from my pack, we'll need them."

Klais blinked. "Of all the things that you decided you desperately needed to take with you, you brought pickaxes?"

"Son, you never know when you're going to need a good pickaxe."

Klais stood there for a moment, his mouth hanging open. "You know that's true. I don't know when I would need a good pickaxe." In fact, he had never really considered when he would *ever* need a pickaxe, good or otherwise.

The pickaxes arrived, and Francis and Merrin pried the huge doors open. Klais and the colonists dashed into the structure, and they let the doors close on the storm, leaving a small gap that Klais put his eyes to. As the icy wind whistled through, he thought could see the Tray-back rocking violently, and even the heavy doors had an alarming hum. Klais turned his back on the scene. They had been incredibly lucky.

"Okay, so what do we have here then?" The shelter was little more than a reinforced box, slightly bigger than the Tray-back. There were no windows and nothing that suggested its purpose.

Klais straightened his sopping wet cloak and smoothed his hair, hoping to appear a little bit more regal. Inside, he was freaking out. *Klais, Prince Loser, the least desirable offspring, is leading a group of living, breathing people. I don't want to lead a group of people any more than the galaxy.* He almost told them that, but in each terrified colonist's face, he saw the hope and trust that they put in him. He groaned. Something heavy rattled against the doors, making everyone flinch. Klais hoped they would be safe in the box, but he didn't want to stay. Who knew how long the storm would last.

Klais spotted a panel like the one outside "Okay, we can do this." He tapped on it and it lit up, words flashing across the screen. Then the floor underneath everyone's feet bounced, and they started descending.

The platform came to a juddering halt, and the door opened to a dark room, deep underground. The air smelled stale, full of electrical decay and ancient dust. They couldn't even hear the rage of the storm anymore.

Klais stared into the eerie, gloom. "Righto, Everyone, follow me." *And I hope you don't die doing so.*

Lights flickered on revealing a common area mixed with a command space. There were little signs of past habitation in the room: the wear and tear on the tables and couches, something that may have at one point held some kind of plant, and several empty cups.

On one wall was a series of blank screens. Scattered around them were strange paper notes. Klais looked at one taped to the computer screens. "Foxtrot Lima Oscar Romeo Alpha? Humans were weird." He flicked his hand over the panel which, like the door panel, sprang to life. The wall-mounted screens showed live feeds of what appeared to be a large, underground complex. Klais turned to the colonists to remark on it to find that every single one was waiting for him.

He gestured at the chairs and tables. "Just chill, relax, sit down."

"My king?" Francis looked incapable of relaxation.

Klais pointed at him. "And stop with the king thing. I am not the king. I am just a rubbish prince regent whose father will kill him if you keep calling him 'king' before he's crowned."

Ironically, it looked like Francis was willing to argue the point, but at least the little group of people seemed to relax. Their adrenaline was probably ebbing in the same way it was for Klais. He felt wet, cold, soggy, and exhausted, but at least for the time being he was safe from the weather.

Carl had come to stand next to Klais. "So, what's this all about?" He gestured at the screens.

"Ancient Earth stuff." Klais pointed at the first screen showing heavy rain and the blurred edge of a flat roof. "Well, there is the little surface building we pickaxed our way into. It looks like it's got photovoltaic shingles and a couple of broken turbines still hanging in there. So that's probably where the power is coming from." Klais gestured to the second screen. "That's probably a memory core full of computer banks since Earth never developed sonic ribbons for storing information . . ." His words dribbled to a halt at the look on Carl's face.

"What?"

Carl scratched at his chin. "How d'you know about all this?"

The color crept into Klais' cheeks. "School." He had learned about the galaxy's roots in his private, tutor-led history classes. It was an education very few could afford. "They called Earth the 'Cradle of Existence' because all the galaxy's population stems from this one planet."

"That's hard to believe given there is nothing alive out there now. I would have liked an education like that for my kids and grandkids." He swept his hand toward a group of children huddled together. A woman Klais hadn't met was reading to them. "Perhaps they'll get one here on Earth."

"The galaxy's credits have to come in handy somewhere." Klais swallowed. They wouldn't get anything if he couldn't make the crops work. "Fortunately, this is one of the many human languages drummed into my head."

Carl frowned. "One of?"

"Earth didn't have one standard language like the rest of the galaxy has now. My . . . ," Klais paused to count, "great, great, great, great, great whatever Grandmother was the one to make sure that only the language she spoke was the one that was spoken in the galaxy. My family have always been super accepting of differences." He smiled sarcastically. "But there are planets that have local dialects based on other Earth languages. So dear old Father made us learn them. Most of our names for foods, animals, technology, and the like, come from Earth even if they are nothing like whatever the original was."

"I'd love to know more sometime." Carl pointed to the next screen. "Now what's those?"

Klais peered at the screen Carl pointed to. "Stasis pods?"

"I can't imagine there'd be many stasis pods that would have survived since the Earth civilizations, even with those fancy power generators." Carl gestured to the screen showing outside the complex. It was now completely blurred.

"Well, it'll be a bit of a shock if they have. A lot's changed around here since they were around." Klais turned his attention to the last screen showing a room with a door. "Oh, cool. A closed door. That's definitely worth watching. I love the closed-door channel."

Carl chuckled as the sounds of the colonists making themselves comfortable and chatting reminded Klais how much he was an outsider.

"All right," Klais said. "Well, sitting around and doing nothing is not something I'm capable of right now because I'm too stressed and worked up. So I'm gonna go check out . . . ," he looked from screen to screen, "the weird pod room."

Carl arched an eyebrow as if seeing his eccentric "king" for the first time. "Probably good to assess your assets."

"Absolutely," Klais said, not sure—nor caring—what the old man meant.

KLAIS FOLLOWED the corridor to a door that slid open as he tapped the screen next to it. Flickering dim lights sputtered to life. Inside were sixty or so grime-covered cylinders, tilted back and lined up in two rows facing each other. His footsteps echoed and the chill seeped through his wet clothes into his bones as he approached the first pod. It was dark and covered in dust. Klais wiped his hand over the glass. It did little but smear the dirt from one side to the other, but Klais thought that he could make out the vague shape of a human, a very *dead* human.

"Oh, ew! Well, it might have been a stasis pod once, but we won't be getting any tips on Earth farming anytime soon." Klais made his way along the row, pausing to have a closer look. Halfway, he realized that there were names on the top of each pod. "Botanist: Emily Tudawali. Agro-ecologist: Thomas Graham. Regeneration Expert: Sami Leung." They all had something to do with the planet's botanical properties and ecology.

Klais shook his head. "Sorry, guys, whatever your specialties were, it didn't pan out. This lump of rock is *dead*." He flinched then over his shoulder to make sure that none of the colonists were within earshot. Their improvised camp was the type that people created when it was a one-way ticket.

Klais was three-quarters of the way down the line of pods and about to turn back to announce to the colonists that this room was a tomb and only people who had very particular tomb-walking hobbies should come in here, when a slight glow at the back of the gloom caught his eye. At the very end of the pods, there was one final pod that was different from the others.

The pod was smaller, and while the other pods in the room were upright, it was horizontal. The hair stood up on the back of Klais' neck as it occurred to him that it could be a child or a baby. He wasn't sure how he felt about gazing at something like that, even if they died hundreds of years ago.

"You should go back, Klais. Get someone qualified to check this out. Get a margarita. Put your feet up. Catch up with all the latest goss about who's done what." Instead, he reached out and wiped the dirt from the top of the faintly glowing pod, revealing a label. "Flora? Why would you put a plant in a pod?" Klais took a breath, hoping the sight wasn't too grisly, and leaned over. Inside was not a plant nor was it a child, or even a human. It was a perfectly preserved, medium-sized shaggy dog. "Oh look!" Klais' heart melted. "A human's best friend." Klais ran his hand over the pod as if he was petting the dog itself. "Hey there, fuzzy thing," he said, then leapt back as the dog's tail began to wag.

The top of the pod slid open, and the furred head popped up out of the stasis pod. The dog leaned down and yet let out a large-jawed yawn as she stretched, then jumped out of the pod. She turned toward Klais and her speckled brown tail swung backward and forth, creating a slow drumbeat against the side of the stasis pod. Her head came up to his knee and her coat was a strange mix of patches of black, white, and light brown speckles. She had a green collar around her neck. She sat at Klais' feet looking up at him, then she offered him her paw as if she wanted to greet him with a handshake. Klais had pressed against the stasis pod across from hers and gave an involuntary shudder as he pushed himself away.

"Hey. I'm Klais." He moved closer to the dog. "I wasn't allowed to have a dog even though I begged my father, because galaxy forbid I have anything under the royal roof that might actually like me, so I don't know proper doggy protocol." He dropped to one knee and held his hand out. "Please don't rip my face off, okay?"

The dog glanced at Klais' hand, then put her paw in it. Klais shook her paw, and she licked his face.

Klais giggled. "You may be the single most wonderful thing to happen to me on this planet, but that's gross." He gently patted her head then he reached for a disk that was hanging from her collar. "F. L. O. R. A." Klaus puzzled over the ancient human letters. "Oh, your name is Flora?"

The dog's tail started drumming a faster beat on the floor.

"That makes more sense than preserving plants." A slow smile spread across Klais' face. "I've got a dog!" He jumped to his feet, heedless of the wet slap of his robes. "Come on, girl."

Flora let out a yip and raced at Klais' side, back to the colonists in the common room.

"Hey, look what I found," Klais said as he bounded back into the common room. "They *were* stasis pods, and all the others were full of humans more dead inside than my sisters, but I also found . . . Flora!" He held his hands out to the dog.

As if understanding her introduction, Flora's tail wagged.

"I know she may not help with our current predicament, but that doesn't matter because I've got a dog. And look what she can do!" He knelt and held out his hand. Flora placed her paw in it, and they shook hands.

"And she's certainly taken a liking to you," Merrin said. "Does she eat soup? This is yours since I thought you would be as cold and hungry as the rest of us." She handed a bowl to Klais. "But I can make her another." Merrin smiled at the dog.

"I . . . have no idea," Klais said, taking the bowl as Merrin set about making a bowl for Flora. The soup was bland and watery but made with care and thought. It was probably the kindest thing anyone had ever given him. He sat on the couch as the colonists settled around him. Flora scoffed down her bowl, then made her way up onto one of the couches and curled up, nose to tail next to Klais. Within a few minutes, she was snoring softly.

With the warm dog by his side and the bowl in his hands, Klais felt a sense of disquiet. Here he was, rich beyond all belief (at least until his father threw him out), and these people were sharing their dried fruits and broths with him. Even though he knew of this kind of food, it was the first time Klais had eaten it. His sister, Agneta— the People's Princess—talked about how much she hated what she called peasant food and how disgusting it was. He didn't think it was that bad.

Klaus listened to the chatter around him, realizing the colonists were a family of circumstance rather than relatives, coming from different planets and orbital stations but all trying to make a go of it together. Some of them were criminals, which was a little concerning, but Klais could see that they were also people. *Real* people. With one hand resting on Flora and his clothing starting to dry, he found he was enjoying himself.

Yet it came with a small sense of sadness. *Nobody cares about me the way these people care about each other.* He glanced at his watch. There were no messages, but then again, it was possible that messages wouldn't reach this far down. He shook his head. "Maybe Agneta will notice I've gone missing," he told his dog, hoping that the colonists wouldn't hear. "But then I'm more like her publicity project than her brother. Certainly, Donna would prefer I just winked out of existence. She just sees me as a drain on the government coffers." He hugged Flora close to whisper to her. "At least I have a dog now."

Flora licked Klais' face, then snuggled up in his lap.

Carl came and sat across from Klais. He nodded at the bowl in Klais' hands. "Merrin makes a good soup. It's all freeze-dried, but she can work wonders with it." The old man smiled. "Freeze-dried *for now*. I'm sure with all that fancy farming equipment you have, she'll be cooking up a storm of fresh food before too long." He winked.

Klais shifted uncomfortably in his seat. "You seemed to know a lot about the equipment on the Tray-back. Were you a farmer?"

"I worked the hydro-crops on the satellites around Garlotte. Even did a couple of rotations on Poverdant Minor A. The conditions there are much like Prime."

"Is that so?" Klais enjoyed talking to someone without feeling like they were plotting to use him. "What did you grow?"

The old man scratched his stubble. "Ah, I was mainly in the procuring of seeds and crops and other materials, but I did pick up a thing or two."

Klais considered the machines he used to sort and recycle junk, and the autobots he used for farming. "I wish I had someone with experience instead of autobots." Klais meant it to sound light, but it probably came out bitter. This man probably knew far more about terraforming planets than he did.

"Well, there is always tomorrow. What have you planted?"

Klais tried to sound casual. "Oh, you know. I have most recently been trying my luck with haizeseed. It's such a nice breakfast and the bold purple looks great in a vase with some accent flowers." In truth, the seeds were selected by his father, like most of the other materials and equipment sent to the planet with Klais, including several manuals of Poverdant farming practices. His sense of unease grew as a deep furrow appeared on Carl's forehead.

"Haizeseed, you say?" Carl shook his head. "That would be a hard one to grow here. I've only done a bit of scanning for interest's sake, but as far as I can tell, Earth doesn't have poverdantite. It's everywhere else in the galaxy, but not here."

"Poverdantite?" It rang a bell, but Klais couldn't say why.

"It's a semi-acidic substance that's in all the soils, and it softens the nutrients so the plants can absorb them. I can't imagine any plant native to Poverdant Prime, like haizeseed, would grow on Earth." His eyes flicked to Klais. "But I'm sure you've thought of all of that and fixed the problems."

"Oh, for sure," Klais lied.

Carl smiled. "Alright, I still have some people to check with before we turn in." Carl held out his hand to Klais who shook it. The old man smiled and walked off, whistling an old nursery rhyme.

Klais sat stock still and stony-faced. There was *no way* any of his crops were going to grow. Poverdantite was why no one could make Earth viable again. The planet was in the Goldilocks Zone, not too close to a sun, not too far away. The gravity wasn't too high because the planet was too big. Nor was it too low because it was too small. Complete environmental collapse had driven the ancient humans away, but it wasn't what prevented them from coming back. Biological incompatibility was.

Klais' head swam. As if sensing it, Flora pressed her head against his leg and let out a soft whine like she was worried about him. "It's okay Flora," he said, but really, nothing was ok. He placed a hand on her head. She made him feel slightly better about the situation, but he was going to have to tell these people the planet was doomed and would stay that way.

"Um, King Klais?" A small boy with a mud smear running from his nose to his ear came up to Klais. There was another boy and two girls in various degrees of muddiness a little way behind him like they were afraid to approach.

"Oh, hey . . . small people." Klais looked around for the adult supervising the children and then realized *he* qualified as an adult. "Did you need something?" *Like an adultier adult, maybe.*

"Can we play with your dog?"

Klais looked from the children to Flora. "Oh. I guess. If Flora doesn't mind?"

"Come on, Flora!" The boy ran to the other children.

Flora wagged her tail, then shot off after the squealing kids.

Klais surprised himself by laughing, then realized Merrin was watching him.

"What? Have I got something on my face?" He brushed his cheek to find it smeared with dirt, but then so was everyone's.

Merrin smiled. "You're not really how I thought a king would be."

Klais held up his hand. "Not a king. I am just the family's disappointment."

"Okay," Merrin said, looking unsure. "But it's not that. I mean, in the broadcasts with the royal family, everybody seemed so . . ." She paused and seemed to be choosing her words.

Klais tilted his head. "Stuffy, snobby, wooden, unapproachable, terrifying, horrible?"

Merrin tucked a curl behind her ear. "I was going to say obsessive about the galaxy. You just seem so . . . normal. You talk to us like we are *people*." There was an odd murmur of agreement amongst the other colonists. "We are grateful for your leadership and ensuring our small family's safety." Merrin smiled.

"And for saving us in your underground complex," Francis called from the other side of the room. He was standing with Carl next to the screens.

"Oh, that's fine. Don't mention— Wait, *my* complex?" Klais frowned.

"Well, isn't this part of your terraforming of Earth plans?" Francis asked, gesturing around the room. "You seemed to know so much about the place, and with all these plant pictures and things written in languages you understand, I just assumed it was part of the plan."

Klais went to the computer terminal, stepping around the children who were playing some kind of handshake game with Flora. The screen showed different Earth plants from various biospheres. Flora's tail began thumping as she watched Klais, while still playing with the children.

"These are different parts of the planet, right?" Francis looked from Klais to the screen.

The man was so hopeful that Klais was almost willing to let him believe it, but despite what Klais' family said, he wasn't a liar. "Probably. But I'm sorry, guys, it's not part of my terraforming, or probably anyone's." He clicked through the screens hoping for some kind of explanation. "The files seemed to only be the list of pictures. They might just be some old human's happy snaps."

Francis looked disappointed. "I hoped they might be places we could go."

The old man scratched at the stubble beard on his face. "I suppose that's possible. But I don't know, something about this looks like some kind of inventory. Can you read anything since you have that good education of yours?"

Flora left the children and came to Klais, as if to check what he was doing. "Well, there's words like *tree* or *biosphere* or *atmospheric conditions* that leapt out, but there isn't much more besides the photos. "If there is any more info, it's stored somewhere else." Klais stared at the screens showing the memory banks, pods room, and the random closed door for some kind of inspiration. His eyes flicked to one of the pieces of paper stuck around the screen and picked up the strange note with the word list: Foxtrot, Lima, Oskar, Romeo, Alpha. No help there." He tried to stick the note back where he found it, but it dropped to the floor where Flora picked it up.

"Oh no, that's not for eating." He took the note from the dog's mouth, shoved it in his pocket, gave her a scratch behind the ear and returned to the screens.

Francis and Merrin moved in close. "What are those?" Francis asked, pointing to a column next to the list.

"They're numbers," Klais said.

"Like a stock inventory?" Merrin tilted her head and squinted as if she could make herself understand. "It must be wonderful to receive such an exotic education." She stared wistfully at the screen.

Klais had hated the information and facts crammed into his mind by his tutors. The colonists would know how to pilot a shuttle and tetris a cargo load, but they wouldn't know about the Venusian Opera that originated on a planet close to Earth, or even about the territorial feuds over the iridium pits of Garlotte. Klais felt a little bit ashamed as the gulf between him and these people seemed to widen.

"It's a mystery," he mumbled as Flora pressed her head against his leg. He kneeled next to her, scratching behind her ears and making her collar name tags jingle. "Oh, how I wish you could tell me what it is all about."

Flora's tail wagged, but the mystery, the storm, and the huge gap between him and this loving little family were all a bit much for Klais. He needed some space. He glanced up at the screen that showed the strange heavy door. "You know what, I think I'm going to investigate that." Klais pointed at the screen.

"If you're talking about that big heavy door," Francis. "We tried to pry it open with the pickaxes, but it wouldn't budge. And nothing we did to the panel seemed to make a difference.

"We were wondering if you knew how to open it, but I guess not if this isn't your complex?" Carl phrased it like a question as if he expected Klais might still know the answer.

"Well, I'd best go and investigate," Klais said and headed off toward the door with Flora at his heels.

As KLAIS ARRIVED at the heavy door, Flora sat next to him and offered her paw to shake. "That's cute, but probably not going to help right now." Her tail wagged, and she laid down and set about chewing at her feet. Klais wasn't sure if that was an okay thing for a dog to do, but it didn't seem to be harming her.

He spied the wall panel the colonists mentioned. A word flashed up on the screen that said: "Password?" Klais tried typing "password" into the screen, which, like the door into the complex, flashed from green to red.

He tried "password1234". Again, the panel flashed red and then returned to green. "Dammit. Well, I hope I didn't just arm some kind of self-destruct," he said to Flora, who paused in her paw chewing and looked up at him, tail wagging. "What were your humans trying to do here?"

The dog's ears pricked up, and she tilted her head as if to say, "I don't know either."

"There is something big here, something that I'm missing," Klais drummed his fingers on the wall. "But without knowing whatever fancy word or random string of digits the humans used, I'll go mad trying to figure it out." Klais shivered. "Unless I die of cold first. Let's head back to the room with the comfy couches."

The colonists had spread out, making use of the chairs and couches.

"We saved you a spot," Francis said, pointing to a pile of cushions.

"Thank you." Klais sat on his cushions with Flora and fiddled with a gold ring on his finger as he watched the screen that showed outside. It was black, but that may have just been the night rather than the storm. *At least, I hope it is and we haven't been snuffed out of existence.* He curled up next to Flora and fell into a deep sleep to the background noise of the colonists talking about what damage the storm may have inflicted.

KLAIS WOKE to the sounds of the colonists stirring. The screen showed a cloudy, but not stormy, view of the outside. Klais felt a pang of sadness as the colonists started preparing to leave. It worsened when Carl hefted his pack onto his back and said, "Lead the way, my king."

There it was. Klais was no longer one of the survivors who had weathered the storm and shared tales and food together. He was back to being their royal regent prince and child of Galactic Emperor King Zan (who may very well kill Klais for treason if these people kept calling him king!).

Flora wagged her tail. At least she liked him. No matter what anyone said, he had decided she would be coming with him to the royal bunker. She would be his consolation prize for having to go back. He rode the elevator in brooding silence. The scene that greeted them above ground was staggering.

While there wasn't much to begin with except dirt and rocks, the storm had changed the landscape. The hills that were sitting behind the bunker seemed to have several dark smears that suggested landslides, a thick layer of mud had built up against the doors, and pools of dirty water speckled the landscape.

Flora let out a joyful bark as she raced around the colonists, churning up the ground and adding to the mess of black, muddy muck. It even had a slight smell of rot, but that didn't seem to deter the jubilant hound. With a start, he realized the ground was covered in bits of metal that might hurt Flora.

"Flora!" The dog paused then raced straight toward him and sat at his feet. "Good girl." Klais scratched her under the chin. "Glad I didn't spend the night out here."

Merrin covered her mouth as she took the scene in. "Do you think we would have survived if we had reached the hills?"

"No." Carl shook his head. "Something drew us to the bunker." He turned to Klais. "You and your Tray-back saved us."

"The Tray-back . . ." Klais looked around for the vehicle. "Can anybody see my truck?"

Among the colonists, there was a murmur of no's and head shaking.

"Is that it?" Francis pointed to a mound of twisted metal wrapped around one of the few rocks that dotted the area around the complex. It did look like it could have once been Klais' Tray-back. If they had remained in it, they would have died. *I wonder how long it would have taken my family to notice . . .*

Klais' shoulders sagged. A part of him wanted to turn around and go straight back into the bunker, and yet he still had to face the music with his father. He started trudging in the rough direction of the royal bunker, Flora at his side. As his boots crunched over the rubble and bits of metal, Klais realized there were footsteps behind him. He glanced over his shoulder to find that the colonists were following him.

"I'm more or less heading back to the royal bunker," he said over his shoulder.

"As good a destination as any," Carl said. "Our camp should be in that direction too. We can walk together and then you can take your leave of us." The old man smiled.

It was supposed to be reassuring, but Klais' heart sank. He and the planet he had tried to terraform had nothing to offer these people. Nothing he had tried to grow had succeeded and now he knew why: the Poverdant plants were completely incompatible.

Klais looked over at Carl. "You know, it's going to be a while before this place is all set up with condos, a shopping mall, and a day spa or three."

"We will manage. We've still got some basic supplies at camp. And we've got enough favors between us that we can call in for some extra tools and food. We'll be okay." He smiled affably at Klais.

"I'm not so sure, Carl." Francis pointed ahead. The colonist camp was a field of wreckage.

The square container pods lay in pieces, like some evil giant had picked up the entire camp, shaken it and scattered it for miles. There may have been some salvageable items, but the colonists would have to search far and wide for them.

Klais stopped walking and let the colonists continue forward. Flora whined by his side as they exclaimed over the loss of this and that. A weird sensation settled in Klais' stomach. Somehow, he wanted to share their loss, to be a part of them, to be a part of their family, which was nothing like his.

Almost as if someone had heard, Klais' communication watch started a continuous chirping indicating an incoming call.

He moved away from the camp so the colonists wouldn't hear him and answered the call.

"Where have you been?" Agneta snapped.

"Oh, the People's Princess, you know, in the middle of a massive killer storm thing, so I had to go and hide in a bunker I didn't know about, full of ancient human stuff, the regular old thing."

Agneta scoffed. "Well, I've been trying to get in contact with you. Father is approaching. He wants a tour of all your *accomplishments*." There was a note of sarcasm in her words.

Oh, darn it! Did a whole year go past in the bunker? "Okay, no problem." He hoped he sounded as nonchalant as he needed to. "Oh, and guess what? Good news for the Galactic Empire. There's a bunch of colonists here and they know loads about growing things and can give me a hand."

Agneta paused as if taken aback at his words. "Klais, you shouldn't be encouraging this. It's lovely that you've made some little friends, but Father won't let them stay on the planet when you return."

He knelt to pat Flora. Her presence was reassuring. "What makes you so sure I'll be returning?" When his sister didn't respond, Klais' eyes narrowed. "Agneta, what do you know?"

"Klais, we already know that Earth's not viable. Father's been scanning the planet and everything you've been doing for the past two years. It's sweet that you cleaned up and recycled a bunch of the junk, and that there are areas that can be walked around without a hazard-zone suit on, but it's clear you haven't achieved anything and that you're not going to achieve anything."

Klais felt a wave of suspicion. "Everyone is so certain, are they?"

Agneta sighed. "Father said Donna and I were not to breathe a word, but he's coming now to throw you on a ship and take you back to Poverdant."

Klais' entire body felt heavy, almost as if the rain had dumped a second load upon his shoulders. "Well, there's no time like the present." He mimicked his father's voice —if not his words—saying, "Klais, I will give you this opportunity to prove yourself. If you can terraform a planet and make it habitable, I'll make you King-in-Waiting, but really, I'm going to sabotage you in every single way. Then I'm going to give you a dressing down, humiliate you in front of the galaxy and tell you you're out of the royal line, which is what I always wanted."

"Klais, that isn't fair. Father believes in galactic rule and ruling properly."

"Really? Ruling properly? Is that abandoning your son on some forsaken, polluted planet, saying, 'Here's a bunch of credits, go terraform it,' and then keeping tabs on him while he's thwarted in every single way?" Klais kicked at the mud, spraying water into the air.

"How have you been thwarted in every single way?" Agneta shot back.

"Do you know about poverdantite?" Klais asked. Again, there was silence on the other end of the line. "Well?"

Agneta sighed. "It's an element in the soil of most planets that allows seeds to grow. It's not present on Earth, and even if you provide it, the interaction with Earth's solar radiation fields means it will break down immediately. Nothing that needs it can grow on Earth."

"Cool." Klais bit off the word. "So you did know about it. There is absolutely no way I can make things work with the crops, seeds, and materials I was sent here with."

Agneta's silence gave Klais his answer.

"So Agneta, why *are* you calling? Is it to tip me off about dear old Father coming down to humiliate me, or was there something else you wanted? Maybe you'd like to have a crack at your own humiliation of me?"

"Shut up, Klais. I was going to offer you a lifeline."

Klais had to bite his tongue from saying something nasty and caustic. "Oh?"

"I can have my ships there before Father arrives. You can board them and disappear off to Hollandulu or Kalacatchone or whatever other dive planet you like. Father won't have you physically there to be able to publicly humiliate you. He'll just have to enter it into the record without making a big official song and dance. I mean you *are* my brother."

"So it's all about *your* public image?"

"Klais—"

"There are people here, Agneta! I can't just skip out saying, 'Sorry the planet's dead, but I'm off to go and party on Hollandulu. Enjoy your brief and probably starving life.'"

Agneta's tone changed to one she used to talk to the people in the slums. "I feel for you. I truly do. And I know just how hard it is to not put the people first."

Klais rolled his eyes. "Sure."

"But those people made their decision to follow you down there and there's not much either of us can do about that."

Klais thought about it. *King Klais.* That was what the colonists were calling him. They didn't believe the king's rhetoric. They believed in *him.* He watched the group as they placed all they could salvage on a piece of cargo pod wall to keep it out of the mud. They were strong. Resourceful. But even those qualities would only go so far on a dead planet. "I can't do that to them, Agneta."

"So you're really going to sit there and face the music waiting for Father to come and demonstrate what a useless king you would be on a public broadcast?"

Agneta's words hurt. "What's the difference?"

Agneta snorted. "Must you always be so adversarial? Do you have any idea what this little experiment has cost?" It was remarkable how much Donna seemed to come out of Agneta's mouth.

"I don't know. I guess it cost as much as Father threw at it trying to humiliate me in the first place."

He could almost hear Agneta shaking her head. "I guess Donna was right about one thing, you really don't care how much time and credits you waste."

There was a click and Klais glanced down at his wrist. Agneta had ended the communication. "Miss you too, sis. Yeah, I'm okay. I almost died in that storm. Good chat."

Flora, who was sitting by his side, tilted her head.

"Yeah, I know. I talk to myself a lot. It's what happens when you grow up completely alone surrounded by people."

He took a deep breath and watched the colonists picking over the wreckage. It looked like most of their possessions were damaged or destroyed. Even if they could scrounge up enough of their meagre food supplies, it was a good chance that they wouldn't be able to turn them into anything edible.

He smoothed the tangled mess of his hair. "Alright, everyone. Let's head back to the royal bunker. I might be able to replace some of your supplies from mine."

It was a strange moment as the colonists turned to look at him and the tears and despair on their faces became expressions of appreciative hope. Merrin smiled and mouthed the words, "Thank you." Klais had never seen anybody look at him that way.

One by one the colonists picked up whatever possessions they had gathered, slung them into their packs, and started the long trek to the royal bunker.

As Klais led the colonists through the heavy doors into the main lounge of the royal bunker, it struck Klais that Agneta had been right about one thing. When he arrived on the planet two years prior, he had wasted no time spending copious amounts of his Father's credits, much to Donna's disgust, out of pure spite.

The lounge was decked out with emerald marble. Fresh trees in hues of pink and purple and yellow in huge artist-made planter boxes from his home planet of Poverdant sat in every corner, bathed in a gentle glow of artificial Poverdant sun. Lots of ridiculous unimportant things were scattered about, like expensive teacups that Klais never used, a collection of limited edition huggable pet plushies, and so very many clothes.

"Oh, you all help yourself to those," Klais called to the colonists as Francis picked up a pair of green pleated slacks. "I have heaps." It felt nice to share what he had.

A large fountain sitting to one side of the couch-filled room was surrounded by colonist children. It had an extravagant half-man, half-horse centerpiece firing an arrow that formed a stream of water running into a small pool with little fish in it. The children giggled and squealed as the fish darted about.

Klais had to admit it, he *had* always played with credits. It wasn't until he saw the wide-eyed expressions on the colonists' faces and the big gasps as they pointed out exquisite paintings from the outer rings and his collection of singing crystals that hung along one wall that he felt ashamed. He almost saw himself the way his father did: as a wastrel; somebody who was more concerned with pretty things than the galaxy.

With a sinking feeling, he realized it was a horrible backdrop for the news Klais had to give them. "Okay, everyone I need you to gather round." Like obedient subjects, they all shuffled about to sit in the chairs. These people would hang on to his every word and it killed him. "I know you guys followed me across the galaxy to a dead rock because you thought that I could make a new planet for you . . ." Nausea rose in his gut. *Here it is, the moment of truth.* "Well, it's not going as great as I could have hoped."

Wrinkles of concern appeared on people's faces and the sickness in Klais' gut grew. He dropped into one of the chairs, leaning his elbows on his knees to put his head in his hands.

"Truth is, I'm sorry, guys. I screwed up. I screwed up badly. It all seemed so fun and so easy. I'd just come to a planet, terraform it, and people . . ." He gestured around the room at the colonists. "People like you believed in me. But the truth is, I let you down."

"What do you mean?" Francis asked.

Carl nodded. "Nothing can grow here, can it, son?"

Klais swallowed rising nausea. "No crops. No vines. No . . . whatever plant produces wine. Nothing. It's a dead rock. I've spent two years cleaning it and trying to grow stuff. But nothing grew. I failed." He couldn't even look at the colonists.

"But isn't there something we can do?" Francis asked. "You're going to be the king."

"No. I'm not. Not even close. Only Earth plants will grow on Earth, and no level of super-stylish, rich, powerful royalty can reset a planet back to its pre-damaged state."

Francis looked from face to face. "But—"

"Francis," Carl cut him off. "There isn't a future for us here besides starving as our supplies run out." Stunned silence hung heavy in the room as reality set in.

"The king's fleet can evacuate everyone. I'm so sorry, guys." Klais brushed at the tears that threatened to fall as Flora placed her head on his knee.

Merrin stepped forward and touched his shoulder. "It's not your fault. You had a vision. We took the risk, knowing it wasn't a done deal." Some of the others murmured their agreement as she turned to Carl. "We'll have to contact the others."

Klais sat up. "Oh, okay . . . What others?"

"We were just *one* family ship," Merrin said. "There are at least three or four other larger ships that have either touched down somewhere else on the planet or are still on their way."

"Oh, cool. That's really great." Klais tried to force a smile as his head spun. "Well, everyone can stay here, until . . ." Klais couldn't finish his sentence out loud. *Until I tell Father I give up and he comes and gets me.* "Mi casa, su casa."

The colonist turned to discussing the situation while the children went back to playing, the gravity of their future going over their heads. Klais walked over to the singing crystals so the would-be colonists couldn't see the tears that despite his best efforts had dribbled down his cheeks. It wasn't about his pride anymore. It was about people, and it tore him up.

Merrin came to stand next to him and lightly touched his shoulder. She smiled as the children played. "Your bunker is beautiful. Do you live here alone? I mean, I thought you would have staff."

Klais arched an eyebrow. It seemed a light topic given the bombshell Klais had dropped on them, until he realized she was changing the subject. "Oh, my father said I needed to stand on my own feet. It's all autobots that cook, clean, and farm. It can be lonely." He set the crystals playing with a strum of his fingers. "I never would have found Flora or met any of you if I stayed on Poverdant, though. I kinda wish we were all back in the vault." He tried to laugh, but it sounded bitter.

"That's a funny way of putting it." Merrin was transfixed by the crystals.

Klais brushed the tears from his eyes. "What is?"

"A vault. It was almost like a vault, wasn't it? Like someone's treasure vault with a heavily armored door to keep thieves away from jewels and other rich people things."

"Somehow, I don't think the humans were hiding treasure and singing crystals." Klais ran a finger over the singing crystals again, starting a fresh melody. "But you're right. The big heavy door was almost like a vault. Were they trying to keep something out? Or something in? Or neither? Or both? I wish I could ask Flora."

Klais looked around. The children were still giggling, but the dog had disappeared. "Flora?" It came out almost like a shriek. "Please don't let anything take my dog away!"

"Klais," Carl said. "Flora is over there." The old man pointed to the other side of the lounge.

Flora was sitting *in* his fountain. There was a moment of silence then a grin spread over Klais' face. The fountain cost as many credits as one of the farming auto-harvesters and there was his mud-smeared dog, paddling in it to the disgust of his fish. He let out a bark of laughter. "Father would be so proud." He started to giggle, laughing with the kind of hysterics born of broken tension.

The laughter proved infectious. One by one the colonists joined him while Flora danced around trying to catch the streams of water. She was in doggy heaven. A couple of the colonists had filled up their bottles from the streams of water. It had never occurred to Klais to drink the water; it was always just there for looking at. Then he remembered who he was, where he was, and what he had to offer.

"Oh my gosh! Who's hungry?" Klais shouted. "You fed me, I feed you!" He went over to his buffet. "Choose whatever you want." He had no idea how it worked, only that he selected things from a menu and the machine made it. "Enjoy, press all the buttons. You can't break anything. If it could break, I would have done it ages ago. Have fun!"

Klaus's wrist communicator began chirping as the colonists lined up and made their selections then spread out around Klais' lavish lounge. He couldn't decide if he was just being flashy, but it felt good to share his stuff with people who didn't look down on him, even if they were disappointed.

"I will be right back," Klais said, ignoring the angry chirping as he retired to his bedroom. The room was larger than the entire colonist's camp. His bed itself was the size of the Tray-back, positioned in front of a huge computer screen so he could watch his favorite space soap operas. He threw down his mud-splattered, tattered robe, lamenting the damaged hand-stitched embroidery, followed by his other clothes on the carpet and took his time selecting a new outfit of black cargo pants and a lilac silk shirt, while his wrist communicator screamed at him. Eventually, he couldn't put the call off anymore.

This time it was Donna.

"Klais—"

"Hi, Donny!" he said, with false excitement.

"How much will it cost?"

"Oh, the cost of a summer's day, and the musical note of C minor." Klais didn't bother asking what Donna was referring to. He waved to Flora as the dog made her way into the room. "Checking up on me, sweetheart?" he said to the dog who curled up on his discarded clothes.

"Don't you 'sweetheart' me!"

"As if I would," Klais muttered, picking at his sleeve.

"And I'm not checking up on anyone," Donna snapped.

"Why are you calling then?"

"How much will it cost to have you abdicate?"

Klais sat up straight and stared at his wrist. Donna was talking like Klais was an actual threat to her becoming queen-in-waiting. *Does she not know that everything's rigged? She is more cluey than Agneta.* "What makes you think that I'm about to abdicate?" he asked, hoping he sounded casual.

"Father is heading toward Earth. He said there's some kind of advancement that you've made or some big discovery, but I've had enough of you playing games. I'm sick of wondering whether my complete fiscal management of the Iredion Sector will be overlooked because my wayward disgrace of a brother has managed to somehow trick his way into becoming galactic emperor king!"

Suddenly he smelled a rat. He needed time to think. "Hang on, Donna. I can't hear you. I'm putting on pants." *What discovery? What has happened in the last couple of hours that could have gotten Agneta so riled up? What do they know that I don't?* Klais drummed his fingers on the bed. Flora sniffed them and tried to shove her nose underneath his hand.

He ruffled the hair on the speckled dog's head. "What can you tell me, girl?"

"What?" Donna said.

Klais answered anyway. "Look, it's clear that something is going on. If Father has decided to accelerate his trip to Earth by twelve months, he wouldn't have done it unless there was an urgent good reason. I want to know what that reason is."

"Klais, I have worked too damn hard, studied too many fiscal policies, and worked at squirrelling away too many credits for my idiot brother to—"

Klais ended the call. Donna didn't know anything. Something had happened in the last twenty-four hours to spur his father into sudden action, and whatever it was hadn't been shared with his sisters. *Was it the storm? Has it revealed something?* He crossed his room and clattered away on his computer, trawling through his data about the geology and topography of the local area. "Nothing interesting there, but Father's scanners can see deeper than mine. Maybe he's found fuel deposits. Or a rare gem that Donna can use to exploit millions of credits out of the galaxy." He turned to his dog. "No, he would have told her so she could crunch the numbers."

Flora had snuggled deep into the clothes on the floor. She watched him over the edge of his robe, and her tail started thumping on the floor.

"You're very friendly, aren't you?" Klais said to her, crossing the room to sit with her in the clothes. She turned big brown eyes to look at him. "Whoever your long-ago human was must have been pretty special. I guess it was one of those botanists or ecologists or conservationists that are now dried-out husks like the rest of this planet. I'm sorry you lost the people who loved you, but I hope to make up for them."

He rubbed her tummy as something Merrin said flared up in his mind: *The door reminded her of a treasure vault.* "Scientists, ecologists, and plant scientists were preserved in the complex. Knowledge is preserved in the complex. Father can scan deeper than I can . . . Flora! Father knows what's behind the complex's locked door, and I'll bet it's something that I can use to make this planet viable and beat the old man at his game."

Flora's tail wagged, echoing Klais' excitement, and she snuggled closer to him. "But I can't scan that deep and it's password protected." He chewed his lip as his gaze settled on the dog. "*Flora* was preserved in the vault. She *is* special, special enough to be placed in stasis with the rest of the people . . . but how does it all fit together?"

Klais' wrist chirped once. It was a message from Agneta. "Father is in orbit. Enjoy your remaining time on the planet, you self-absorbed little rat!"

"I love you too, sister."

Klais picked at his embroidered robe, surveying the damage to the delicate motif on the pocket. The slip of paper with 'Foxtrot. Lima. Oskar. Romeo. Alpha.' written on it that he had found in the complex fell from the pocket. Flora put her head on his knee.

"Wait a minute." Klais reached around the dog's head for the disk on her collar. "F. L. O. R. A." He surged to his feet. "I've got it!" he shouted. Flora began barking excitedly as he ran for the lounge.

"Merrin?" Klais ran into the lounge realizing he probably sounded like a madman.

Merrin looked up from a plate of what looked like sautéed lobster in Mole Poblano sauce—Klais' favorite. She had gone for the luxury dish. "Is everything okay?"

"Foxtrot. Lima. Oskar. Romeo. Alpha! It's not just a weird jumble of nonsense words." He handed the paper note to her. "The first letters are on Flora's collar. It's not just her name. It's the letters of the password to the vault." As Klais said it out loud, he knew the absolute truth of it. His head spun with the possibilities. "Oh, oh." Klais hopped from foot to foot. "We gotta get back out there. I think I know what my father's trying to stop me from discovering in the vault. It's why he wants me out of here right now."

"Are you sure?" Merrin's lobster was forgotten.

Klais pointed toward Carl, Francis, and Merrin. "Come with me. We've got a vault to go visit and a king to annoy!"

KLAIS, Flora and the three colonists piled into his flashy purple Sports Speeder and zoomed across the ground in a much smoother ride than the Tray-back had provided. Despite enjoying the luxury, the three colonists seemed nervous. Klais suspected it was the possibility that their resettlement on a viable planet wasn't doomed as much as it was the possibility of upsetting the actual emperor king of the entire galaxy. They made it to the complex within a few minutes.

"Hi, honey, I'm home," Klais sang to the empty common room. "Did you miss me?" He made his way over to the computer screens showing the different parts of the vast underground complex, including the mysterious door.

There was the slightest pang in his stomach. *What if I'm wrong? What if I open the vault and find furniture, or some serial killer's taxidermy collection?* He wasn't going to alarm the colonists by saying what he thought, so he flashed them a glitzy smile and made his way to the vault door with the three colonists and Flora in tow.

Klais knelt by Flora and checked the word on her collar. "I really hope your last owner loved you as much as I think they must have, and I'm on the right track."

Flora barked and held up her paw.

"Sure," Klaus laughed. "I'll shake on it." Then he stood and punched the letters into the password screen. For the briefest moment, nothing happened, and then the panel turned green, but the door didn't open. Instead, a box appeared on the screen.

"What does that mean?" Merrin asked.

"I . . . I don't know." Klais' hopes sank. "I was sure I was right." He turned to look at Flora.

Francis was kneeling next to the dog, patting her head. Flora was offering him her paw.

A slow smile spread over Klais' face. He crossed the floor, picked up Flora and took her to the panel. Without hesitation, she placed her paw in the box. The panel turned green and as Klais placed the tail-wagging dog back on the floor, there was a heavy grinding sound. Klais' heartbeat quickened. The vault door opened, revealing a huge warehouse filled with immense boxes.

"They look like our camp cargo pods," Francis said. "How many do you think there are?"

"I have no idea." Each box was twice Klais' height, and they were stacked at least twenty-five high. As he walked between them trying to calculate how many stretched off into the distance, a screen on one of them sprang to life. Klais punched the air and let out a "whoop!"

Displayed on the screen was the full truth of what his father had been trying to hide.

"I was right," Klais said. He spun around with his arm spread wide. "The secret to terraforming Earth is all here! The ancient humans stored it all away because they knew that everything they had done was going to destroy the planet." He ran up to Carl, Merrin, and Francis. "But somebody back then made the right decision."

Merrin laughed as Carl shook his head.

"Spit it out, son!" Carl said. "What have we found here?"

Klais was grinning from ear to ear. "These are organic stasis cargo containers. It's a *seed* vault."

"A what?" Francis looked about to burst into tears.

"A seed vault. A repository of seeds. And there are so many here!" Klais spun around a second time. Flora joined him with excited barking.

"Does this mean we don't have to leave?" Merrin asked.

"Yes. All I need is one more year of Earth seasons. With the right place, clean soil, and no junk, I think I can make this work." He gestured to the containers.

"But how do you know these seeds will work when the best plants in the galaxy don't?" Francis asked.

Klais grinned. "These are *Earth* seeds. These are the seeds that *Earth* plants grow from. They are for this planet." Then his expression darkened. "And my father knew it. This is why he suddenly wants me off the planet. It was fine when it looked like I would just fail, and he could sweep me aside." Klaus made a shooing gesture. "Off you go, embarrassment to the royal household, we will definitely forget you."

Francis stared at the screen. "So, you will become King-in-Waiting and go off and learn how to rule the galaxy?"

The thought hit Klais with the full, dizzying force of a Tray-back. "I guess so."

Carl had continued along the line of cargo crates, turning on screens and checking the contents. "There's so much here. This is more than just creating a basic farm for food." He pointed to the pictures on the nearest pod. "There are hundreds upon hundreds of plants, trees, grass . . ." He crossed to a different crate. "And here there are soil microbes, organic matter, mycorrhizae. There is far more here than our family can help with. We'll have to get word out to the others." Carl nodded to himself as he continued checking the crates.

"Klais, this one has flowers," Merrin said.

Francis tapped on another screen. "And this one has something that looks like a little bushel of berries that can be fermented. Maybe it makes wine?"

"We're planting that one first!" Klais pointed toward Francis's cargo crate. "We better get back and give the others the good news."

They made their way back toward the lounge.

Klais glanced at the lounge's screens and froze, staring at the one that showed the outside the complex. "Either someone's a snitch, or my father didn't trust me."

A royal shuttle from the king's fleet had landed outside the doors.

With Flora and the three colonists behind him, Klais trotted out of the vault complex's doors. Two lines of armed guards dressed in royal copper livery greeted them. Drones hovered overhead, but they weren't military drones, they were recording. *Here to broadcast my humiliating, tantrum-filled, evacuation from the planet.* He rolled his eyes. *They were probably Agneta's doing.*

One of the guards stepped forward and placed a projector unit on the dirt. "Galactic Emperor King Zan," she announced. The unit flickered and a life-sized image of the king in his regal golden-yellow robe appeared. Klais' sisters were standing behind him.

"Hey, Father. You came to see me? I'm honored." Klais curtsied. "Beloved sisters, how are you?"

"Enough of your antics," the emperor king said. "I want you and those people you involved in your mess on the shuttle immediately."

Klais glanced at the recording drones, crossed his arms over his chest, and addressed the entire contingent, not just his father and sisters. "Oh, I don't think I'm going to do that because here's the thing. I figured out your little secret and why you wanted me off the planet so quickly. See these?" Klais gestured toward the door behind him. "This is the lift to a big complex that holds a whole lot of *Earth* seeds." He spoke slowly, enunciating every word. "Earth seeds that will *grow* on *Earth*." He held up a finger as if he was a schoolteacher. "*Not* like the seeds from Poverdant, which can only grow if they have poverdantite, which Earth *doesn't* have. You know, like the ones I was given by you to make this planet viable again."

Donna stepped forward, looking every bit the royal cutthroat economist in a severe blue suit-dress. "Klais, heed Galactic Emperor King Zan's words! You are only making yourself look foolish in front of the entire galaxy." She was choosing her words for the camera.

Klais was having none of it. "Bite me, Donna! This vault has *everything* I need to make this planet work. I've cleaned the soil. The atmosphere is breathable. The planet is still in this solar system's Goldilocks Zone. Everyone said the planet was just dead, but nobody thought to check any of the useless boring architecture that the humans left behind. What would Earth humans know? They're just a pack of backwoods savages that wrecked a planet and moved on to populate the rest of the galaxy. They couldn't have left anything useful, could they?"

Agneta, in a flowing, fairytale pink gown, darted forward to whisper in the king's ear. It was all about image with the People's Princess.

"Don't even think about cutting the broadcast," Klais said, fixing Agneta with a hard stare. "You'll only make yourselves look worse." Judging from the sour look on her face, it was exactly what she was thinking. He addressed his father again. "Did you know about the seed vault all along?"

The emperor king glared at him. "No. If I had thought there was even the slightest chance that you might succeed and become King-in-Waiting, I never would have sent you. We were scanning for your remains after we detected the storm and picked up traces of organic plant matter in stasis."

"My remains . . ." Klais shook his head. "You knew there was a storm coming and you didn't bother to tell me. Instead, you hoped it would sort out your problem for you. Really nice move from my loving family. Well, the legally binding, quite publicized details of our deal were that I have one more year." He looked toward the media drones and flashed them a dazzling smile and a wink. "And given that I think I can prove the planet is viable, I'm going to take it. What do you think my chances are in that time, Father?"

The king looked like he had swallowed several rocks. "The planet will take at least ten years to sustain a small population."

"Oh, I'm guessing from that estimate you can see that cleaning the planet up and planting Earth seeds means that this planet *is* now viable." He fixed his father and sisters with a hard stare. "That means I fulfilled my side of our agreement."

There was a stunned silence among royalty and guards alike, then Agneta and Donna darted forward to whisper to the king. Klais waited to see how the next scheme was going to pan out.

The king took a deep breath and rose to his full height. "It does. I, therefore, declare you King-in-Waiting. You may return to Poverdant Prime and start preparations for your precoronation."

"What?" Klais blinked. "Just like that?" He expected his father to at the very least demand Klais finish terraforming Earth. His sisters didn't look unhappy enough either. There was something else afoot. He shook his head. "You'll get me back to Poverdant, and then you'll find some way of saying I never did what I was supposed to, so the planet isn't terraformed in twelve months, and I won't have fulfilled my end of the agreement. Not a chance."

Donna's face hardened. "Galactic Emperor King Zan has already declared you King-in-Waiting."

"So he has." Klais considered his fingernails. "But I haven't accepted."

"It's what you wanted, you little turnip!" Agneta's fists balled up. "It's what everything was all about!"

Klais stared at them. "You still don't understand. It was never about the galaxy; it was about proving I wasn't a wasted drop in the royal gene pool. It was about having someone who wasn't disappointed in me. I don't want the galaxy, like some consolation prize for winning a game."

"What do you want?" The king's voice was icy.

Klais looked at Carl, Merrin, and Francis standing behind him, representing the people back at the royal bunker and who knew how many other people warping their way toward Earth. He looked down at Flora, whose tongue lolled out of her mouth as she offered her paw to shake. *This* was what he wanted.

"What I want, if not the whole galaxy . . . ," he addressed the recording drones and everyone in the galaxy watching through them, ". . . is this: I will abdicate my right to become King-in-Waiting and let my sisters fight it out on one condition." He turned back to the king, gratified by how his father's mouth hung open. "That condition is this: Earth remains under my jurisdiction rather than the galactic king or queen or whoever. This will be my planet. Not yours to exploit. Not my sisters' to sell off or set up some token galactic orphanage or prison in a big charity gesture. *Mine.*"

Gasps came from behind him.

"Would you really abdicate the throne to the entire galaxy to be king of one small, dead rock and a handful of dreamers?" Donna asked.

"For the people who took me in and showed me what real people caring for one another looks like? Absolutely." Klais felt mildly dizzy, wondering if he was making the right decision. "But also, for my dog." He smiled down at Flora.

The king stood taller. "Done."

Donna darted forward. "Father the economic benefits of a viable planet, far—"

"Enough," the king cut her off. "By the royal decree of the Galactic Emperor King Zan. I declare Earth as solely under the jurisdiction of Prince Regent Klais."

There was an odd sadness in his eyes. "If only you had demonstrated this leadership sooner." The projection flickered and the royal family were gone.

Six Earth months later, Klais stood with his growing team of colonists, surveying the autobots as Carl guided them to plant a new forest from various saplings grown from Earth seeds native to the region. The harsh, bare earth was now dotted with small spots of green that would grow and spread. So far, Klais' growing team had set up nine farms on various parts of the planet that were producing food for those locations. They were now turning their hands to repairing other ecosystems. Flora sat next to him, her tail thumping in the turned-over, fertile soil. No one could take her away from him.

"You know, girl," Klais said, dropping to one knee in front of his dog. "I might have given it up and gone back to Poverdant if it wasn't for you. You helped us open the seed vault, but with each tail thump, I felt like somebody believed in me. You helped me out. It's not going to be easy, girl. But together we will help every single person who comes to call Earth home. You saved me. You saved the colonists, and you saved the whole planet. Not bad for one happy, loving dog."

There's a Wolf at the Door

John Steckley

The boy ran into the kitchen, where I was peacefully having my second coffee of the morning. "Mister Fred, there's a wolf at the door."

I wanted to say to him, "But you're the prince of this fair land, and you will always be wealthy. There can't be a wolf at the door." But I didn't. He was royalty. When would he have ever heard people talking about poverty and wolves?

I stood, and the prince took my hand and walked me to the front door as if I didn't know where it was. Opening the door would be a stupid idea, so I pushed the curtain aside that covered the taller-than-wider window to the left of the door. Sure enough, there was a wolf at the door, standing still and staring in our direction. It looked rather like a show dog, but with a more intense look in its yellow eyes, often described as "honey eyes" but without any sweetness. To my imagination, now running a little wild, it looked like there was fire in its eyes.

As much as I wanted to go outside to see what the wolf would do, I had to remember that Prince George and I had had to do a lot of convincing to get the queen to let him go to the small but regal cottage with only one servant to protect and take care of him.

Prince George began to open the door, saying, "Come on, Mister Fred. Let's go outside to get closer to the wolf." After all, the royal family crest was the head of a wolf. He wore an expensive shirt with that insignia on it.

While I stared, the boy prince finished opening the door and was halfway outside. A servant should never grab a member of the royal family, no matter how young he or she might be. I had been reminded of that fact just before we left for the cottage. It was written down on my sheet of instructions.

But what do you do when a member of the royal family is in great potential danger? All I could do at this moment was shout, "You are in great danger, Prince

George. That animal can cause you great harm. Come back into the cottage, young sir."

George stopped all forward motion but did not turn around. The wolf stopped its own motion away from the cottage, staring into the eyes of the young sir.

What could I do? The beast had some kind of supernatural hold on the boy. I had no choice. I had to do something drastic. I grabbed Prince George by his shirt sleeve, careful not to touch him, as that would be wrong.

I turned him around, whereupon he shook his head as if suddenly waking up. The wolf turned his eyes upon me. I lost all sight except for those glowing yellow eyes. I grabbed His Highness by the arm, then turned him around to again face the wolf. Neither of us flinched at the touch.

The wolf stared into our eyes as it backed away slowly. We moved forward, following it. It followed a path of its own through the woods, avoiding bushes and tangles of brambles. We followed the wolf a few strides behind, unable to do otherwise.

After a few moments, the wolf stopped and turned to face us. It blinked a few times, and the spell over us released. The prince and I shook ourselves free of the wolf's hold, then walked back to the cottage.

We were shocked by what we saw. Two men stood beside the building, both of them carrying a brightly burning torch in one hand about to light the cottage on fire.

With my toughest, meanest voice, I yelled, "Hey there, you fellows. What do you think you are doing?"

They paused, eying us. Their torches wavered toward the cottage.

We didn't see them, but we heard the growling from a pack of wolves. They were led by our friend, who had lured us from almost certain doom.

The two men dropped their burning torches and ran away. The torches fizzled out on the dampish sandy path.

When I turned back to the wolves, I hoped the look on my face would be seen as a way of saying thanks. They dipped their heads, then turned to gallop back into the woods.

I spoke to the young prince in perhaps the most commanding tone that I had ever used. "You must never tell anyone of this experience."

He nodded his head ever so slightly.

"But be glad and proud that the insignia that you wear is of the noble animal that just saved our lives."

He looked down at the wolf head on his shirt. He smiled the biggest smile I had ever seen cross his young face.

A RIGHT ROYAL REWARD

DJ TYRER

Sergeant Axel wasn't sure he held with kings. Human ones and most definitely *elven* ones, that was. Dwarven clan-holds had kings, of course, but that was different. Dwarven kings were more mine foremen and chief sanitary engineers than the fancy, frivolous folk who inherited their positions rather than being appointed based upon their qualifications and a rigorous examination process. Frankly, he was glad he lived in a city with—admittedly imperfect—civic authorities put in power by a mishmash of popular elections and appointments.

But today, he had to attend upon the monarch of a Sylvan realm. King Senallion Memethress Oakenbrow, if you could credit the name. The elf was giving him an award.

And Spot.

As he made his way through the gold-leafed gaudiness of the Civic Palace, Spot padding softly along at his side, the dwarf watchman considered that he wasn't sure how he felt about that.

It was good to have his work, and that of his canine companion, recognised;—too often it was overlooked, unless someone made a complaint—but, being lauded by an elf felt unnatural. It was well known throughout the world that elves and dwarves were barely one step removed from being enemies, even if nobody could remember any longer the reasons why. Axel's father had mumbled something vague about "beards". He ran his fingers through his own at the memory, when he'd once asked him about it, but Axel had never managed to get a clear answer. Who knew? It wasn't as if people seemed to need much reason to hate one another.

But still, as ridiculous as it was, it did make him feel a little uncomfortable. A pair of guardsmen in brightly coloured and overly baggy pantaloons and shirts stepped smartly apart to allow him to pass, bringing their glaive-guisarme-voulge-spetums—as

Axel was fairly confident they were listed in *Madwell's Book of Polearms*—upright into a salute.

He nodded and passed them, and a pageboy—less baggy but with ludicrously long bobble-tipped shoes—opened the doors to the audience chamber for him.

A similarly dressed trumpeter blew a sharp note, and a page—with even longer and larger-bobbled shoes—held forth a scroll and announced, "Sergeant Axel of the City Watch and . . . Spot . . . also of the City Watch."

Axel and Spot advanced into the room where the chief of the City Watch and Lord Mayor flanked a tall and imperious-looking elf. Behind them were a gaggle of elven lords and ladies and city flunkies.

The chief ruffled his feathers. A griffin standing upright was almost twice the height of the Lord Mayor and his plumage was most imposing.

The Lord Mayor may or may not have been wearing a baggy outfit. It was difficult to tell given his girth--the result of many civic luncheons—and whilst his shoes were shorter than the page's in length, they were no less impressively bobbled at the toes. In his red velvet cloak, he was as imposing as the monarch beside him.

The elven king was tall, albeit not as tall as the chief, though the antlered crown he wore brought them closer in overall height. He was dressed in robes of emerald and gold that somehow seemed to resemble a forest despite lacking anything that Axel would have called leaf-like.

Axel halted before them, commanded Spot to sit, and saluted.

"At ease," said the chief between clacks of his beak.

Axel relaxed into an only-moderately tense stance.

Beside him, Spot made a low, agitated sound and started to stand.

"Sit," he hissed at the dog, who uneasily complied.

Axel wasn't sure that he blamed Spot for his discomfort. Their place was in seedy taverns and dirty alleyways, surrounded by crime, not here in the corridors, or rather reception hall, of power.

The elven king raised an eyebrow slightly. "I was under the impression the dog I was here to bestow an award upon was spotty," he said softly, aiming his words at the Lord Mayor. "This one is brindled."

Before he could reply, Axel spoke up. "I named him, sir, er, Your . . . Worship?"

"Majesty," hissed the chief, making them all jump.

"Er, Your Worshipful Majesty," continued the dwarf. "Raised him from a pup and trained him, too," he said proudly. "Anyway, Spot is the traditional name for the dogs guarding the gates of dwarven strongholds—they're usually spotted, you see—so, well . . ." He spread his hands, as if running out of explanation.

"It sounds a lot fiercer in Old Dwarvish," he added.

"I can believe that," said the elven king.

"Er, shall we continue?" said the Lord Mayor.

"The dog seems agitated," said King Oakenbrow.

It was true. Spot had half-risen and was making a low growling sound.

"Spot, will you please just sit?" said Axel.

The dog ignored him and—barging past the assorted nobles and flunkies—advanced upon where a tray sat upon a low stool. The tray, Axel could see, was lined with red velvet and held a pair of golden items that, to eyes unfamiliar with woodlands, he could only assume were intended to be deformed bats. They were actually the oak leaves and acorns badge of the Sylvan Order of Merit.

The Lord Mayor sputtered. "I must apologise, Your Majesty! Sergeant, that dog had best not eat those awards!"

"Spot, come here!" Axel hurried after him and caught his collar. The dog whined.

"Unless they're made of sausages," he said, "he won't."

He tried to tug the dog back past the outraged gaggle to their position before the king, but Spot was having none of it.

"I thought the dog was supposed to be highly trained," said King Oakenbrow. "The dwarf, too."

"He is," said the chief. "They are, I mean. And Sergeant Axel will get in position unless he wants to be reduced to latrine duties for the next ten years."

Axel gulped. He didn't doubt the veracity of the threat.

"I'm sorry, it's most uncharacteristic of Spot," he said, as he finally hauled the dog back into position and one of the elves picked up the tray and held it before the king so that the ceremony might proceed.

"You see, normally, he'd only behave like this if he'd scented something, such as unicorn horn or fairy wings or some other controlled substance."

The elven king gave a mirthless chuckle as Axel fixed him with a hard stare.

"I trust, Sergeant, you are not accusing me of smuggling in some illicit horn; after all, your foiling of the abominable trade is why we are here today to present this award."

He reached for the oak leaves.

"Don't!" cried Axel.

"Sergeant, you are no longer on thin ice," hissed the chief, "you are falling through . . ."

"No, sir, I'm not. What I mean is, Spot is also trained to detect other substances, such as the exploding powder the alchemists make for use in fireworks and the watch's handguns."

The Lord Mayor snorted. "Are you saying someone has planted barrels of exploding powder here? Don't be silly—the palace was thoroughly searched prior to the king's arrival. We take the safety of all our guests most seriously. No assassins hiding behind the drapes, no exploding power beneath the seating, nothing at all."

"Maybe," said Axel, as Spot continued to growl, "but we had a guy incinerated by a fake dragon egg not so long ago, or so I heard."

"I," King Oakenbrow said, regally, "am well warded against all magical threats."

"Maybe," said Axel, "but Spot is trained to detect the scent of one or two other dangers, one of which is," he said, just a moment too late, for the exasperated Lord Mayor had reached for the awards himself, "mimicry beasts . . ."

The Lord Mayor's hand brushed the awards, and both it and the awards vanished. The oak-leaf awards vanished because they had transformed into a pair of slobbering, fanged creatures like large, ugly, and angry puce-coloured toads. The Lord Mayor's hand, however, had vanished because it had been bitten off and swallowed by one of the mimicry beasts and its owner was now howling and waving about a stump. The elven king's robes were going to be ruined.

Spot leapt forward without waiting for a command and Axel followed a moment later as the two little monsters jumped off of the tray, still held by a startled elven lord, and went for their target, King Oakenbrow.

If there was one problem with being invited to an awards ceremony at the Civic Palace, it was that even watchmen weren't permitted to bring weapons within the presence of the great and the good in case they were plotting an assassination, which, in the current circumstances, Axel considered ironic.

All he had on him was his shield, the symbol of his office. Luckily, it was a full-size shield and could serve quite well as a weapon, which Axel again considered somewhat ironic given the reasoning that had banned his actual weapons.

He unslung the shield from his back and swatted one of the mimicry beasts with it, sending it with a loud *splat!* into the wall. The chief quickly dealt with it with his wickedly-sharp talons.

Axel turned and saw that Spot, never bereft of weapons, had the other one in his jaws.

"Assassination averted," said Axel just as the palace guards finally ran in, waving their unwieldy polearms about ineffectively.

"Will somebody please assist the Lord Mayor," said the chief wearily, gesturing at the man who had half-fainted from his injury. Several flunkies ran to do their best, which—Axel considered—wasn't that great. He hoped there was a half-decent cleric of healing in the palace somewhere. At least most of the room's decoration was red to begin with.

He turned to the elven monarch, who looked a tad less impressive now that his robes were in a messy state.

"You're welcome," Axel told him.

The elf laughed. "It seems that now I must return to bestow upon you not only the awards you and Spot were due to receive today, but further ones for your deeds now."

"If it's all the same to you," said Axel, "a simple letter of recommendation would suffice, and maybe tickets to that new play."

King Oakenbrow laughed again, but Axel had turned serious.

"Now that Spot has finished, er, disposing of the threat, we need to discover who was behind this." He glanced to where one of the city flunkies and a couple of elven lords were attempting to slip away unobtrusively. "And I think I have a fair idea."

Spot was also looking in the same direction, sniffing. They doubtless had traces of mimicry beast scent upon them.

"Sic 'em, Spot."

The dog charged across the room, once again making people of rank scatter, and grabbed one of the elves by his cape, pulling him to the floor.

In spite of his short legs, Axel wasn't far behind.

"Halt, or I'll jolly well smack you over the head with my shield!"

The flunky took him seriously and turned, hands raised. "I surrender."

"Good." Unfortunately, the second elf was making a run for it.

Axel took aim and cast his shield like a discus. It was chunky and heavy and he hadn't tried throwing a discus since he was a young dwarf competing in the Pan-Mountain Games, but it flew straight and true and clonked the elf in the back on the head, knocking him to the floor.

The dwarf jogged over to him and picked up his shield and gave him another bash, right over the head, just to make sure.

The chief had taken charge of the flunky and the elf that Spot had pinned to the floor and was busy reciting their rights when Axel returned, dragging his unconscious prisoner with him. The Lord Mayor had been hustled away, which was probably a good thing given his flunky's involvement in the affair.

"Second cousins," said the elven monarch with an aggrieved air. "Such treachery pains me."

"They'll rot in Hellgate Keep," the chief assured him.

"Good. Now, how does one go about purchasing tickets to a play? And what reward does a dog desire?"

Axel grinned. "I can explain the former, and—as for the latter—it's simple enough—sausages!"

THE OMEN

KEVIN WASDEN

ONE

E ager to escape the biting cold of late autumn, Sarah descended into the subway station at the corner of Cortlandt and Church. It was two-o-five in the morning, and the weariness of a long day weighed on her. She hurried through the clicking turnstile, then ran to catch the Brooklyn-bound R train currently at the platform. She slid between the closing doors and grabbed a hand hold as the train lurched into motion. The car was empty except for a solitary passenger—a woman with black hair, stunning dark skin, and a provocative red dress that seemed sorely inadequate for a cold night in November.

The woman in red appeared to be crying, her delicate features obscured by trembling hands. Sarah, caught between sympathy and apprehension, opted for caution and found a seat at the far end of the carriage. She pretended not to notice the weeping stranger but couldn't help casting furtive glances, her mind teeming with curiosity about the stranger's circumstances. Lost in speculation, Sarah's gaze lingered for an instant too long, only to be met by the woman's piercing ice-blue eyes that stood in such contrast to her dark features. A shudder crawled along Sarah's spine when the woman's voice sliced along the length of the compartment, "Got a problem, princess?"

Perplexity melted into embarrassment as Sarah realized the reason the woman called her princess—a forgotten tiara sat on her head and heavy black eyeliner accented her eyes, remnants of the Cleopatra costume she wore at work. Tearing off the adornment and tucking it into her handbag, Sarah offered a hurried response, "Er, sorry. No. Just admiring your dress."

"Yours is a lovely shade of blue," murmured the woman before descending into sobs once more.

Sarah, not yet fully touched by the callousness of the city, rose from her seat and approached the grieving woman, rummaging through her handbag to retrieve a package of tissues. "Here," she said, as she extended the plastic-wrapped offering. The woman took a tissue and dabbed away the mascara streaks from her cheeks.

"You have the most beautiful eyes," said Sarah as she settled into the seat next to the stranger.

"Thank you," responded the woman, smiling sincerely.

"Can I help in any way?" asked Sarah with concern.

"No," said the woman. "I'm not sure I'm meant for my line of work. I messed up tonight, and someone else paid the price for my mistake."

"If it's that bad, can't you just find a different job?"

"It's not that simple," said the woman. "My controller would never let me walk away."

"Oh, you have that kind of job," said Sarah. "I totally get the dress now."

The woman's expression became a mixture of embarrassment and frustration. "No!" she exclaimed. She nervously smoothed her dress, as if brushing off the misconceptions that plagued her. "Why does everyone assume that?"

Curiosity sparked within Sarah, prompting her to inquire further. "Then what is it that you do?"

The woman hesitated, then revealed, "My controller dispatches me to pursue individuals."

Sarah tried to draw parallels. "Like a bounty hunter? Do you track down criminals and bring them to justice?"

A shadow darkened the woman's gaze. "I find the guilty, and I punish them."

Caught off guard, Sarah struggled to find words. "Oh," she said. "Um . . ." She turned her attention to the flickering interplay of darkness and sporadic light bulbs passing outside the train's window, searching unsuccessfully for something to say.

"This is my stop," the woman announced as the train eased into the Atlantic Avenue station, one station prior to Sarah's intended destination. She approached the train doors, pausing to acknowledge Sarah with gratitude. "Thank you for the tissue," she expressed softly before stepping off the train.

Minutes later, the train pulled into Union Station, and Sarah stepped out onto the platform, her mind still entranced by the enigmatic woman with piercing pale blue eyes. Climbing the stairs up to the street, she couldn't shake the lingering unease that had settled within her. Inside her handbag, her fingers found some solace in the presence of a can of Mace nestled within.

As she began the five-block journey from the station to her apartment, Sarah's senses remained heightened, and every sound caused her to jump. Behind her, she was sure she heard a faint noise resembling the soft padding of dog paws on the pavement. She glanced over her shoulder, searching, but she found only empty streets.

Two

ON THE ENSUING NIGHT, Sarah pulled her coat tight against the piercing chill as she left work, beginning her walk to the Cortlandt Street subway station. She couldn't kick the sensation of being followed and quickened her pace. Arriving with a few minutes to spare, she studied the advertising posters and distanced herself from the few commuters scattered across the platform. In due course, the R train clattered into the station. As the doors breathed open, Sarah entered the first car, closest to the conductor, and took a seat.

"Well, well, if it isn't my favorite princess!" Taken aback by the unexpected voice, Sarah looked up—there, holding a hand strap across from her, stood the woman with the pale blue eyes and black hair, still wearing the same red dress.

"I play Cleopatra off-Broadway," said Sarah with a hint of defensiveness. "And technically she was a queen."

The woman's lips curled into a knowing smile. "Ah, you're an actress," she remarked. "Let me guess, you come from the west," she said with a dramatic gesture, "embarking on a pilgrimage to New York in search of fame."

"Yeah, well, so far this whole pilgrimage thing isn't exactly going as planned," Sarah lamented, her voice inflected with disappointment.

"What do you mean? You've landed the lead role in *Anthony and Cleopatra*. That's quite an achievement."

Sarah's voice held a hint of embarrassment as she confessed, "Oh, it's not Shakespeare. When I said off-Broadway, I meant way, way off. I perform nightly in a melodrama at the Dora Hand Dinner Theatre in SoHo, and when I'm not on stage, I serve burgers."

The woman laughed. "Well, it could be worse. You could be burdened with an eternal curse inherited through your family's bloodline."

Confusion etched across Sarah's face as she processed the woman's words. "I'm sorry, what?"

Abruptly, the woman rose from her seat as the train rumbled to a halt at Atlantic Avenue. Seizing the opportunity, she swiftly exited through the sliding doors. From the platform, she paused, and her gaze fixed on Sarah. With determination in her eyes, she spoke solemnly, "I made a mistake last night, and an innocent life was lost. I promise you; I won't let the same tragedy happen to you." And just like that, the woman was gone, leaving Sarah bewildered and frightened.

At the next stop, Sarah exited the subway, and the uneasy click of her footsteps echoed as she briskly strode along Fourth Avenue beneath the feeble glow of the streetlights. She veered left on First Street, and then halted abruptly. From the shadows of a dilapidated warehouse across the road emerged a colossal black dog. It watched Sarah intently but kept its distance. At first Sarah was sure it was a wolf, only to dismiss such thoughts as preposterous within the confines of Brooklyn. It had to be some domestic stray dog, albeit an unusually large one. She kept a watchful eye on the animal. If need be, she could use the Mace on the dog as effectively as she could on a person. But there was no need; the animal disappeared into the shadows just as silently as it had appeared. With her heart still racing, she hurried the rest of the way home.

THREE

THE SUBWAY RIDE HOME the following night was quiet, devoid of the presence of the woman in the red dress. Despite the unsettling encounters, a strange yearning had gnawed at Sarah's thoughts, a faint hope that she might cross paths with the enigmatic stranger again. But tonight, she was left disappointed.

Wielding the can of Mace like bug spray aimed at a hornet, Sarah marched home from the subway station with as much confidence as she could muster. The black dog was waiting for her on the corner of Fourth Avenue and First Street, and she stifled a small scream when she saw it. It sat motionless, patient, and partially obscured by shadows.

With steady determination, she skirted past the creature, carefully keeping her distance along the opposite side of the road. A whispered reminder resonated in the depths of her mind, "Don't run; it will chase you if you run." The animal did not move until she had passed, then it left the shadows and followed her home. It trailed her every move, maintaining a calculated distance of half a block, a persistent shadow on her journey. Yet it never moved closer, its intentions shrouded by distance and darkness.

Sarah turned her attention to the gate of her building, her fingers trembling as she fumbled with the lock. As she opened the gate, she glanced again over her shoulder. The dog was gone. She exhaled, her heart still fluttering with anxiety, and hurried into the protective embrace of her apartment.

FOUR

SARAH, plagued by the haunting image of the black dog every time she closed her eyes, found it impossible to sleep. Frustrated and weary, she gave up around nine in the morning. By noon, she had arranged to meet her best friend, Tess, at a sandwich shop nestled along Seventh Avenue.

As Sarah entered the shop, she spotted Tess seated near the window, staring intently at her phone.

"Hey, Tess," said Sarah.

Tess looked up, smiling in recognition, but quickly furrowing her brow as she took in Sarah's disheveled appearance.

"You look like crap," said Tess with her usual candor.

"Thanks for the compliment, Tess. Your honesty is truly a gift."

Tess leaned forward, her tone shifting to genuine worry. "No, seriously, are you all right? You look like you haven't slept in days."

Sarah confided in her friend about the black dog and the strange occurrences that had plagued her. She poured out her fears, hoping the conversation might lead to some sense of understanding.

Tess listened attentively, her eyes widening with each passing revelation. "You have to be careful, honey," she cautioned. "My boyfriend, Tony—the cop—he's been talking about a serial killer on the loose in Brooklyn."

Sarah nodded. "I've heard about it," she admitted. "But I'm talking about a dog, Tess, with four legs, a tail, and teeth that send shivers down my spine. It's like a wolf somehow snuck across the Hudson, and it's utterly terrifying."

Recalling *The Hound of the Baskervilles*, Tess mused, "You know, in stories, black dogs are often seen as omens of doom," but when she saw Sarah's fearful reaction to her words, she quickly backtracked. "Oh, my goodness, I'm so sorry. I mean, I don't believe you're about to meet your maker or anything. They're just old tales, make-believe. I know you're telling the truth, that there's a dog out there. I'm not saying that it's supernatural or anything. Just super creepy. I'll mention it to Tony, I promise."

FIVE

SARAH WAS RELIEVED to have the night off work. Tonight, cast B would be performing *The Pirates of Verona: Romeo and Juliet on the High Seas*. She was happy to be free of both the dog and the play.

Before bed, she diligently completed her ritual of securing her apartment. She double-checked the outer gate, ensuring it was closed, and meticulously locked the two deadbolts on her front door. She was grateful for the sturdy iron bars that adorned the ground level windows of Brooklyn brownstones. In the living room, she hesitated momentarily, her hand hovering over the curtains, before finally summoning the courage to part them for one more check. There, sitting just outside the window, was the black dog, its form illuminated by the soft glow emanating from her apartment. This time, there was no mistaking it—it bore the undeniable likeness of a wolf. Sarah let out a cry as she leaped backward, colliding with the living room lamp, causing it to topple and shatter upon impact, throwing everything into darkness. Sarah was left standing there, trembling, vulnerable, and alone.

SIX

IT HAD TAKEN every last bit of courage for Sarah to go to work that evening, and the return home was the hardest thing she'd ever done. The night air seemed colder than normal as she emerged apprehensively from the subway station, her senses on high alert. Almost immediately, the presence she had come to dread materialized before her, sending a chill down her spine. With slow, measured steps, the wolf advanced toward her, its head lowered, teeth bared, and a guttural growl reverberating through the night air. Sarah's heart pounded, consumed by an overwhelming terror that defied reason or sanity. She ran along Seventh Avenue, desperately trying to evade the relentless pursuit of the wolf. But it matched her stride, its unyielding presence shadowing her every move.

As she turned the corner onto First Street, she collided with a tall man in a dark winter coat and black beanie.

"Excuse me," the man's voice cut through the chaos, tinged with a hint of annoyance. "What's your hurry, miss?"

Sarah's voice quivered as she pleaded for aid. "H- Help me, please. There's a wol- . . . a dog chasing me." She pointed frantically toward Fourth Avenue.

"Wait here." Without hesitation, the man disappeared around the corner before Sarah could utter another word. Gripped by a paralyzing sense of guilt, she berated herself for potentially leading an innocent soul to his demise.

"I didn't see anything." Sarah jumped at the sound of the man's voice as he came back around the building. He chuckled. "Whatever's got you so spooked, ma'am, I'm pretty sure it's gone. Can I walk you home?"

"Yes, please," Sarah said, relieved. "Thank you."

"My pleasure." The man took her wrist firmly and began to pull her in the opposite direction.

"Hey! What are you doing?" said Sarah.

"I said I'd walk you home, and that's exactly what I'm doing." His grip tightened, and he seized her throat with his free hand. "But if you scream, I swear, I'll end you right here and now."

Sarah pulled futilely at the man's arm, trying to force him to release his grip on her as his fingers dug into the sides of her neck. Panic welled up in her. She searched for some glimmer of hope. And then, over the man's shoulder, her gaze met the piercing stare of the black wolf once more. Time seemed to distort, elongating each passing second as the predator crept closer. And for the first time, as the tentacles of death slowly enveloped her, Sarah realized that the wolf had the most amazing pale blue eyes.

Then the world regained its tempo and Sarah's voice erupted into a primal scream, defying the man's threats. The man did not see the wolf, but he heard Sarah's scream and squeezed harder to stop it. Black spots filled her vision. Fierce growls filled the air.

SEVEN

SARAH AWOKE IN THE HOSPITAL, greeted by flowers and a "get well" balloon. Tess, busy texting on her phone, sat in a chair in the corner of the room.

"Hi Tess," said Sarah, feebly, pain tearing along her throat.

Tess jumped up. "Sarah!" She rushed to grasp Sarah's hand.

"What happened?" whispered Sarah.

"Don't you remember?" said Tess.

"A man grabbed me and . . ." Sarah stopped before mentioning the wolf.

"That dirtbag almost did you in. They think he's the same lowlife that was preying on women in Boerum Hill for the last ten months. They say he might even have killed that woman earlier this week."

"They get him?"

Tess hesitated as if wondering if it might be best to wait, but she must have seen how desperately Sarah needed to know what happened because she said, "He's dead, honey. Someone heard a scream and dialed 911. When the cops arrived, the guy was dead, and you were out cold."

"Dead? I don't understand?"

"Everyone figures you managed to kill him, in self-defense, of course," said Tess. "But I talked with Tony, you know, the cop I'm dating, and he wasn't supposed to say anything, but he told me that the guy's throat was completely ripped open, like . . ." Tess hesitated for a moment, her eyes widening in realization, before she finished, "like a dog got him."

Sarah shuddered at the memory.

Tess continued at full speed. "Tony said there wasn't a drop of blood on you. No DNA under your fingernails, or anything. Tony said that's one of the first places they check. But zilch. It's the weirdest thing he's seen in a long time, and let me tell you, Tony's seen some crazy stuff here in Brooklyn."

Sarah fell silent and shuddered, recalling the wolf with the mysterious blue canine eyes. She couldn't shake the sensation that something or someone otherworldly had rescued her that night, that the black wolf truly had been an omen, not of death, but of deliverance.

"Oh, I almost forgot. Some woman dropped this off for you." Tess handed Sarah a plastic crown and a folded paper.

Sarah took the tiara from Tess, unfolded the note, and read, "I've got your back, princess. Never give up on your dream."

"You all right, honey?" said Tess, noticing Sarah's distant gaze.

Sarah whispered hoarsely, "Yes. For the first time in a long time, I feel like things are going to be okay."

BLUE BEFORE DAWN

DARREN LIPMAN

The Blue Wind will claim Him in twenty years.

A large weight pressed against Daugg's back. He rolled over on his bedroll to face the stone-grey wolf leaning against him. The wolf swung her head around and their eyes met. The hairs along his arms stood up as he felt the wolf's worry.

"The Blue Wind?"

The demon of old, Memet said to him, *the one who shall not be named.*

Daugg was no expert in ancient monsters. Memet's words confused him, but he felt the wolf's urgency and sat, running his hand through Memet's coarse hair as he yawned.

"Who?" he said, then added, "Who will it claim?"

King Dorian, Memet answered.

Daugg's blood ran like ice through his veins. He straightened his back, eyes suddenly sharp, then shivered.

"How do you know?" There was a sting in his words.

Stirrings in the earth. Memet's eyes peered deep into Daugg's. He shuddered as his whole body tingled. *Old dark ones are rising, ancient seals breaking. The earth knows this; she cries in terror as she watches.*

Daugg reached for his fur breeches and pulled them on, belting them at the top, then crawled through the small, earthen space toward an opening. He emerged into the forest, the sun trickling through gilded leaves. Memet crawled after him. When she stood to her full height, she shook her whole body. The rustling fur sent a wind upon Daugg.

"May I ride?"

As always.

He gripped her fur and swung himself atop the giant wolf, pressing his body flat against her back and neck. Her fur smelled of springtime grasses and moss. He closed his eyes as he savored the rich aroma.

Memet leapt into a run, dashing between the trees with controlled abandon. Hardly half an hour passed before she slowed, then spun in a circle to bring herself to a full stop. Daugg sat up and let himself slide to the ground.

They stood before an archway formed by the curved root of a great tree. A doorway had been built into it. Daugg knocked three times in the pattern of his people. A light-skinned boy, his skin still smooth with youth, opened the door and bowed.

"Welcome home, brother," he said.

"In kindness," Daugg said before he ducked through the small opening. He dropped a few feet onto the compressed ground and was able to stand comfortably. When the door shut behind him, walling off the light, crystals embedded in the walls glowed with faint purple light. Mushrooms running the length of the tunnel on either edge of the path glowed with soft green spots. Daugg bowed his head to the boy then started walking the tunnel.

Perhaps a hundred paces ahead, he emerged into a grand chamber lit by the crystals and mushrooms around the circular walls. A scant line of light from far above fell upon the king, a burly man with skin the rich brown of summer tree bark. He had one arm wrapped around a woman while his other wrapped around a young man still coming into his fur, his legs hirsute but his chest bare. Daugg bent his knees and bowed to them.

"Rise, my boy," King Dorian said.

When Daugg stood, Dorian rose as well, spreading his arms. He took a few steps forward. Daugg closed the distance. As the king's thick arms closed around him, their lips met in a sustained kiss. Dorian had raised him into manhood; his heart throbbed with the honor and love he felt toward his king.

When they parted, Dorian's eyes glistened in the purple and green light like the shiny black seeds of apples, ready to blossom at a moment's notice.

Daugg turned away. "My lord," he began "Memet warned me the Blue Wind will claim you in twenty years." Daugg sighed, his heart heavy in his chest. When Dorian said nothing, he added, "What is the Blue Wind?"

"A demon once called Tehelet." Dorian turned to the woman and young man and waved them off. They bowed and scurried into another tunnel on the far side of the chamber. "When the Garden was broken, many monsters were born in the aftermath. Over time, they were banished and slain by Children of the Gods, but they were still part of Creation. Some believe they will yet return." Dorian swallowed. "If Memet is right, then it is true. They will return."

"And the Blue Wind will kill you."

Dorian waved his hand through the air. "Death is only another step in life, and besides, twenty years is a long time."

Daugg shook his head. "You aren't worried?"

"Why should I worry, my boy?"

Daugg's heart raced; he feared Dorian would hear its drumming thunder. "There must be some way to stop it."

"Oh, yes." Dorian drifted back to his cushions and sank down onto them. "I suppose, when it returns, it must be banished again. Let me remember the stories . . . Won't you lie with me as I think?"

Daugg nodded, biting his lower lip. He crawled next to the king and nestled himself beneath Dorian's arm. The older man hugged him tightly. Daugg closed his eyes and breathed in the thick, earthy musk of the other man; he had not realized how deeply he longed for his smell.

The next he knew, Dorian shook his shoulder. Daugg stirred with a yawn.

"I remember now," Dorian said. His hot breath on Daugg's cheek made him shiver. "Tehelet was bound by tying the wind, though it is a rare soul who may weave the wind. When the time comes . . ." Dorian tapped his hand against Daugg's chest three times. "I hope you will find the one who may bind him and watch it be done."

Daugg sat, his hands finding Dorian's. "What did the demon do?"

Dorian's face sank. "It stole your breath while you slept. At night you would lie down in peace. When the Wind passed over, you were blue before dawn."

Daugg's skin prickled at the thought. The only thing worse would be the death of his king.

"Fear not." Dorian squeezed Daugg's hand. "Twenty years is a long time."

Dusky shadows fell through the canopy when Daugg emerged from the king's dwelling. Memet stirred, lifting her head and staring at Daugg with yellow eyes.

He has been warned?

"Yes." Daugg clenched his hand into a fist. "But he doesn't seem to care. The Blue Wind will kill him in twenty years, yet he is unafraid—he seems to ignore it entirely." His fists trembled as he walked toward the wolf. "I will not allow him to die by this demon. I must stop its rebirth and ensure it never touches Dorian."

Daugg patted the wolf's head. "Memet, can you listen to the earth and tell me what else she says? I know too little."

I will carry you home. Then we may listen together.

Daugg climbed aboard and relaxed into the wolf's mane as the wind whistled past. Soon they were crawling back into his small home beneath the earth. He sat cross-legged on his bedroll, Memet curled in a tight circle before him.

The earth knows all that is, all that was, and all that will be, Memet said, *but all this knowing is one thing, and the earth cannot always say in which direction she speaks.*

Daugg nodded then waited for Memet to go on.

The closer one comes with the Wild, the more they may hear the earth. Humans rarely think to listen, and many forsake the practice before they understand what they hear. However, if you wish it, our bond may allow you to listen through me.

"I do," Daugg said. "I will not let the Blue Wind claim him."

Very well. Then come to me; hold your heart against my breast.

Daugg crawled toward the wolf and nestled himself inside the curve of her body. He rested his head upon her fur and wiggled deeper into it. The rich scent of the forest overwhelmed him, and he closed his eyes, breathing her in deeply. He heard her heartbeat like a distant drum, its vibrations cresting gently across his whole body.

Listen . . . listen and hear the earth speaking.

Daugg strained, but this only caused his ears to ring. He settled himself, as if he were trying to calm himself for sleep. Memet growled low, sustained like a long roll of thunder. He focused on it, imagined himself sinking below the wolf and melting into the earth.

At first it felt like swimming, except instead of the cool embrace of water, he felt the warmth of the earth around him. Colors, muted and dark, flashed before his eyes. When he tried to chase after them, the feeling started to slip.

Listen, Memet said. *Allow the earth to lead you.*

Daugg relaxed, releasing his urge to follow the lights. The warm fingers of the earth tightened around him. He saw the forest floor through pulses that washed like surf over him. He saw the distant ocean in the east and felt the towering mountains in the west as wind swept over them. He sank deeper into the earth. The hand around him became soothing fire. He kindled like embers, filling with life.

He whispered into the flames, "Tehelet."

The memories of the earth shifted. Cold air tangled his body. A blue figure reached through windows, leaving the dead in its wake. He saw a knotted rope and knew it was woven of golden hair, a single blue thread at its core. He saw a boy with a bow. Heard the wailing of mourners whose loved ones had been left breathless. He saw the white walls of a great city, saw a princess round with child, saw himself offering her the blue thread. This was what would be; this was how he would save his king.

"MEMET, WHAT IS THE BLUE THREAD?" He touched her paw.

It is from the shroud, the burial cloth of the demon. Look, I shall guide you.

Daugg nodded and leaned into the wolf again. Opening his ears to the earth was easier this time; the plunge into its warmth devoured him, at once he felt part of everything. This time, he felt Memet beside him, the wolf leading him to ancient memories. The images blurred, foggy through the expanse of ages. He saw the threads flying through the air, a whirlwind of blue. Wings flapped furiously; feathers cut through the swirling wind. The forming shroud sucked taut around a humanoid shape with limbs too long to be normal. It drew Daugg close, his breaths labored, every inhalation a rasp, each exhale pulled swiftly from his lungs. Suddenly he felt teeth wrapping around him, his consciousness pulled upward, back toward his body.

He gasped as he woke, flinging his body forward to catch his breath.

"What happened?"

The demon yearns to breathe again, to kill again. Memet shook her head, then licked the side of Daugg's face with a coarse tongue. *Even now, it stirs, eager to escape.*

Daugg shivered. "What if trying to keep the demon bound is what releases it?"

Memet did not answer.

A cold feeling settled in Daugg's spine. "What if retrieving the blue thread is what breaks its binding?"

THE NEXT MORNING, Daugg stirred with a yawn. When he looked over his shoulder for Memet, the wolf was gone. This was not terribly unusual; she was one with the wild, after all. He dressed and crawled from his abode. Rain splashed on his head. Leaves curled tightly to guard against the water. A cold wind blew.

Daugg closed his eyes and reached outward. At the edge of his senses, he felt Memet running with the other wolves. He sensed the forest through their eyes, the trees racing by, the chill of the puddles they leapt through, their glee as they shook their fur dry. Daugg opened his eyes. Small rivulets ran down his chest, his arms, his legs. He shook himself like the wolves and laughed.

Memet had forbidden him from earth-listening after their last foray, but he yearned to know where Tehelet lay bound so he could retrieve the blue thread to save his king. But first he had to find the woman from his vision.

Daugg wound his way through the rain to King Dorian's door. He knocked before thinking not to.

The young boy opened the door and welcomed him inside. He followed the glowing mushrooms and shimmering crystals back to Dorian's chamber. Today he was alone, eating berries from a wooden bowl resting on the floor beside his cushions.

"My boy," he said and smiled, though as Daugg walked closer, the smile faded. "What troubles you?"

"The Blue Wind." He felt his heart racing and wrung his hands together. "I'm afraid taking the thread to bind it is what will wake it—"

King Dorian silenced him with a raised hand and bid him to start at the beginning. When he finished, Dorian stroked his chin with thick fingers. "Retrieve the thread, and worry not about what may happen. The Wild will as the Wild wills."

"How can the earth know the future, if the Wild wills?"

The king shrugged. "All life is like a great river, and like any river, there are eddies where the detritus can get caught for a while before it spills ever onward. Some events are like these eddies: no matter the small differences or the great, a leaf upon the surface will always find them." Dorian smiled. "Perhaps the Blue Wind's waking is one such eddy, and no matter the path we choose, it cannot be stopped. But perhaps, if you retrieve the thread, then a second binding can be assured; otherwise, it will terrorize us forever."

Daugg nodded. "I hope you are right, though I wish I knew where to find it."

Dorian raised an eyebrow. "You do not know? Heh. That I can help with."

Dorian waved him closer, leaning over the compacted dirt floor. He drew a number of circles, which Daugg realized were trees of the Great City. He had been there only once, and his welcome had not been warm. The city was Sadrian, her court did not look kindly upon Dorian's kind, the Sironen. For as long as the Forestlanders had lived, the two factions were at odds, one pledged to Order, the other wed to the Wild.

"The Blue Wind is but one of six great malevolent beasts." Dorian said. "The early Sadrians led the battle against them. After being defeated, the six, bound each in their unique way, were entombed beneath the Great City, right here." Dorian pressed his nail into the edge of one of the circles, forming a cross in the dirt. "The chamber is guarded, but perhaps you may find a way inside." He patted Daugg's shoulder. "You were a clever boy. Are you yet a clever man?"

Daugg laughed, his mind already turning over possibilities.

NIGHT LAY OVER THE FORESTLANDS. Daugg perched in the lower branches of a tree in the forest surrounding the Great City. Unlike the Sironen who lived beneath the roots, the Sadrian lived in towns built upon the upper branches of the towering trees. Guards in emerald and sapphire and ruby tunics patrolled the forest floor, their steel-tipped staves at the ready. Daugg had been watching the tomb's entrance for two days and nights.

The tomb's guard—this one wearing blue—waved a salute to her replacement, a guard dressed in green. They shook hands then walked in opposite directions around the base of the tree, the only time the tomb's entrance was ever unguarded. Daugg dropped from his perch and rolled toward the entrance. The tree's bark twisted into an archway, the wood beneath carved to form a passageway. Daugg plunged into the opening, then down steps carved in a constricting spiral. The walls changed to dirt. The light faded as he moved slowly down the steps, his eyes adjusting enough to barely see the outline of a stone door as he reached the passageway's end.

He searched for a hold to open the door and found a seam running up and down the middle with a lock tying them together. One touch told him the lock was enchanted, magic tightly woven to keep the doors shut. He swore under his breath.

He closed his eyes, holding the lock in his hand, and wondered what the earth would say. Memet would not approve, but if he could not retrieve the thread, the king would soon be dead. Daugg would not let that happen. He nodded, reassuring himself, and tried to quiet his mind.

He did not know how much time passed before he finally felt his mind start to meld with the earth; without Memet guiding him, it was harder to feel the undulating current of thought pulsing through the planet. He tried to direct the flow toward the lock in his hand, but trying brought him closer to the surface. He settled himself again, allowing the earth to take him. He saw the roots of the forest, the tendrils of mycelium woven all through them, sending signals back and forth like messenger birds. He saw a young tree sprouting beneath a patch of sunlight, saw it grow buds and bark and branches. He saw the ancient Sadrians weaving the wood with their magic, splitting it to form a tunnel into the earth. He saw the dirt melded together into stone doorways, saw the lock that tied them together, woven like a cord, knotted upon itself.

But there was something else. Its voice came like a serpent, soundless, slithering. Daugg saw through the stone door to the other side. Six stone-grey caskets arranged like the spokes of a wheel. A blue light gathered around the third one on his right side. His mind drifted closer. Empty lungs crying out for air rattled inside. He heard a new voice, flickering like fire, from the second casket on the left. Soon they all stirred, cachinnating echoes, claws upon stone covers. The image whirled, the earth trembling as the demons fought to break free—

A burst of wind threw him backward to land crumpled on the steps. He sat, his body aching, and saw the shattered lock and the open doors.

Daugg turned his head to listen and stayed still for an entire minute, but no guard came, no other sounds echoed in the tunnel.

He got to his feet, then stepped past the stone doors. The chamber was dark and silent; the stirrings he heard were deep within the earth, not here, not now. But he had seen enough to know which casket held Tehelet. He approached the bland stone box and gripped its cover. He exhaled as he lifted and pushed it forward. For a moment he feared what was inside—cobwebs and spiders, snakes with venomous fangs, or even just the body of the demon itself, ready to swallow him whole. A long moment passed before he was able to steel himself and reach inside.

His fingers brushed against rough fabric. What lay beneath was clearly dead; it held no warmth and made no movement as he placed his palm against it. A rattling voice in the back of his mind begged him to listen to the earth, but he knew if he did, the demon would be there, unbound and ready to steal his breath. He would not allow it. He was here to save the king, and to do that, he needed a single blue thread from the shroud. One binding to another.

He moved his hand along the demon's wrapped corpse, until his fingers came to the shroud's edge, just starting to unravel after centuries entombed. He gripped the longest thread between his forefinger and thumb and pulled. The thread came loose, then broke away. It was twice the length of his forearm.

The thread he saw in his vision was shorter, hardly a few fingers long. But that was a question for another day; now he had to escape.

Daugg coiled the thread and stuffed it into a small pouch, then pushed the casket's cover back into place. He returned to the tunnel and started climbing, crawling up the stairs as silently as possible. He paused at the top, waiting until the guard was out of sight.

He closed his eyes and reached for Memet. The wolf was about a mile away with her pack, circling the Great City. The man summoned his urgency, shaped it into an impulse to act.

The first wolf howled. The others took up the cry.

Daugg waited. As the howls came closer, the guard shook and trembled. The wolves loped into view. The guard ran.

Daugg ran from the tree, climbing to the perch he had used before. He touched Memet's mind and shared calm. The wolves stopped howling and ran into the forest away from the Great City. A few minutes later, the guard returned to her post, but it didn't matter now. Daugg had what he needed.

MEMET PACED, her hair bristling. *You were foolish, Daugg, foolish and foolhardy.* She stopped bothering to use words, using instead the many variations for stupid and idiotic the wolves used amongst themselves. He hung his head, waiting for the barrage to end, but it kept coming as she circled him, her anger growing.

"If I hadn't listened," he said, his voice a bitter growl, "then I never would've gotten in."

The Blue Wind almost claimed your soul when you were with me. Why would it not try again when you were alone? It almost took you!

Daugg did not want to admit it, but he knew the demon had. A great wind had broken the lock, and had it not snapped Daugg out of his trance, the demon would have killed him.

"I won't do it again," he said, his voice level now, "not without you."

Memet continued to pace, but the sting in her thoughts ebbed. *You have the thread, isn't that enough?*

"No," he whispered. "Not yet: we still need to find the woman."

I shall look then. The demon cares not for wolves—but you? You it seems to hunger for.

Daugg shuddered.

I HAVE SEEN THE WOMAN, Memet said some time later. *The earth stirs around her.*

Daugg sat up. They were enjoying the sunlight on an outcropping in the forest.

"Do you think she's the one?"

Possibly. The woman we seek will be a noble, of a northern kingdom. This woman appears to be such.

"Let's go then," Daugg said. He stood by Memet's side, waiting until the wolf gave him permission to ride; it seemed a long delay until she acquiesced. Then they were off, the trees flying past. A day and a half they traveled until they came to a small fiefdom. They stopped at the edge of the forest where the fields began.

"Show me her, then I'll go ahead."

Memet conjured an image of the woman. Daugg saw her clearly in his mind's eye. She was lithe and beautiful, young but old enough to be wed.

He dismounted and kissed Memet on the forehead before running off. A small town surrounded the keep. Though he drew some strange looks, no one paid Daugg much attention. Still, he glanced over his shoulder frequently, surprised when he reached the towering wall around the keep unquestioned.

He followed the wall until he was alone, then he studied the walls, noting where the stone was chipped or the white bricks were slightly misplaced. He climbed to the top, pressing his body flat against the stone as he stared across the other side. There was a garden, short hedges cut in distinct rows like a labyrinth. Near their middle, a maiden read a scroll on a stone bench. Daugg swung his feet over the wall and lowered himself as far as he could before dropping. He landed in a roll, unscathed save for a few spots that might bruise.

The woman looked up from her scroll as he approached. He stopped mid-step. He had seen the woman eye-to-eye when listening to the earth with Memet, yet this girl was not the one. Her face was too narrow, her hair too dark; even the look in her eyes spoke more of fear than the wonder he had seen in his vision.

When she screamed, he ran. He bounded over the low hedges, quickly spotting a gateway through the wall. Guards on either side turned toward him and signaled to close the doors, but Daugg dashed faster and threw himself between the narrow gap. The doors shut behind him. He didn't stop running. He gasped for air when he reached Memet and didn't wait for her to give permission before he slung himself across her back.

"We were wrong," he panted after the town was a smudge upon the horizon behind them.

Then we shall try again.

"We must," Daugg said, thinking of King Dorian. Every day wasted was one less he had to save the king from the Blue Wind.

A FEW WEEKS passed before Memet announced the earth had shown her another noblewoman. Once more, they raced to a small kingdom, only to discover she was not the one either. Time and again, they ventured to the northern kingdoms, fought their way inside, only to have their mission end in failure. A few times Daugg could not tell if the woman he found was the one he sought or not, so he gave her a small snippet of blue thread. Perhaps his first vision had shifted over the months; there was no way to know.

A year passed, and then another. It seemed there was no end to the women who might be the one, nobles whose children might slay the Blue Wind. Soon the thread dwindled to shorter than the length of his right hand.

"We can't go on like this," he told Memet, pacing back and forth before the wolf.

We shall go on as long as we can, and what is done, will be done.

"The Wild will as the Wild wills," he repeated. He wished he were holding something so he could throw it on the ground and smash it, but his hands were empty.

Perhaps his entire fight was futile; perhaps there was no way to save Dorian from his breathless fate.

No, he would not stand for that. He could not.

He sank to his knees, looking at the wolf with pleading eyes.

"Find another," he said. "We will find them until there is no more thread." Then all that would remain would be the hope that he had done enough.

On the morrow, Memet said. *You must rest sometime.*

Daugg rolled his eyes. Still, he saw the truth in her words. The wolves were always the wiser, it seemed. It was early afternoon. A walk would clear his mind.

"I'll be back," he promised before striding into the woods.

DAUGG HELD the last sliver of blue thread clenched in his hand as Memet carried him one final time. The town surrounding the castle looked as all the rest. He ran through it as quickly as he could. He entered a courtyard lined with hedges and saw guards at the doors.

Daugg shouldered past the guards and pushed through the ornate doors; it wasn't the first time he had forced his way into a palace. At once the chatter halted and hundreds of nobles turned toward him, gasping at his bearish appearance. One woman fainted.

Daugg ignored them as he walked toward the room's center. He spotted the princess in her white gown. She set her jaw and clasped her hands together as he approached. When they were two steps apart, their eyes met. Daugg's breath caught in his throat. Her blue eyes, framed by golden locks, were the same that he had seen when listening to the earth.

"Lady," he said, "I bring a warning and a gift."

"What do you want of me?"

It was as though they spoke only to each other, as if everyone else had vanished.

"The demon Tehelet stirs." Daugg watched her eyes widen at the name. "When the time comes, send your son, your dearest son, to slay him."

Her lip trembled. "How?"

Daugg held out the blue thread. "Weave this thread into a rope made of your hair, and it shall be the rope to bind the Blue Wind."

She reached for the thread, but he pulled it back.

"I need your word, Lady."

He held her gaze until she nodded.

"My word," she said, blinking, "I—I promise."

He offered the thread again. "Do this, and your land shall be blessed."

Daugg turned and strode from the palace. He had done his part; now the Lady must do hers, and when the demon was slain, his king would be saved.

Outside, riding Memet back to the forest, he shared his elation with the wolf that they had completed their quest. "She was the one. I recognized her the moment I saw her."

Will she do as instructed and give the rope to her son?

"She must and I think she will. The earth says it will be so, so it must be."

Then you may rest at last. Her progeny shall slay the Blue Wind when it rises, and King Dorian shall be spared.

Daugg did not speak, but prayed the wolf's words would prove true.

SEVENTEEN YEARS PASSED SLOWLY. No one noticed the broken lock upon the tomb. Inside, in the third casket on the right, a shroud unraveled, spurred by a single stolen thread. The demon within spread its wings. A great gale shattered the stone covering, and four pale blue, six-fingered hands gripped the casket's cold edges. Tehelet pulled himself out of his tomb, limbs too slender, too long to be human. Around him, the other caskets trembled and shook, but it was not their time to wake.

For now, Tehelet walked alone, his ghastly body as translucent as air.

Step by step the skeletally thin specter climbed to the top of the tunnel. With a single touch upon her shoulder, he stole the life of the red-robed guard: She fell to the ground with lips as blue as the night sky.

Tehelet spread his thin, tattered wings and shot forward like a blue wind. There was one he hungered for, one he had ever so briefly tasted in memories only barely his own, enough of a taste to leave him wanting, craving more. Soon he found the hole hidden beneath a curving root and flattened himself to crawl inside.

Memet rose from her slumber, standing as tall as the small space would allow. A thick growl emanated from deep inside the wolf. Daugg stirred in his sleep, but did not wake.

Tehelet's four hands descended upon the great wolf. With a yelp, she fell.

Memet's body thudding to the floor finally broke Daugg's slumber. He leapt up, not seeing the demon, and crawled to his companion's side.

"Memet," he cried, "Memet!"

Tehelet spread his wings. A flash of blue lightning lit the small enclosure.

Daugg whirled, his eyes wide. "Demon! You've awakened."

Tehelet pinned him; two hands held Daugg's arms to the ground, while the other two cupped his face. Daugg writhed but the demon easily overpowered him. Tehelet brought his face closer, breathed in the rich breath of life inside the man.

DAUGG'S back pressed into the ground as the demon towered over him. He struggled against its weight, but the beast kept him pinned. Its mouth came closer, and it inhaled. Daugg's life force began slipping out; he shut his mouth to hold it inside.

This close to death, the earth opened to greet him: He saw his whole life in heart-beats, saw the princess he'd given the last shred of blue thread. The earth shifted to show her future: two sons, one with a golden rope, the other with a bow. They would track Tehelet and slay the demon. More than bound, it would be broken.

Daugg's eyes flashed open.

"You will not win! A hero will rise to slay you. I made certain of that."

The demon inhaled again. The light in Daugg's eyes began to fade.

He foresaw the demon leaving his home, facing Dorian's, drawn toward the king for the very love Daugg felt for him. But the demon would turn away, sensing the tangles of thread scattered through the land. Thread from his shroud, thread that would bind and break him.

Daugg had saved Dorian and countless others, though he could not save himself.

Yet even as the demon left him, there was a smile on his face.

THE WORLD OF WULDOR

KAREN KEELEY

Aye, me laddie," said the master. "He be a good pup, I grant you that, and from a good bloodline. But look at him. He be waggin' his tail, for Chrikeysakes!" Canine Master Galbraith was eyeing me alright. I didn't like the look in his eye. He was a big man, barrel chested with bandy legs, flaming red hair, his beard braided with beads.

The boy, maybe twelve, bit down hard on his bottom lip. I sat up straight and stopped wagging my tail, trying for a look of courage and good breeding. The master was correct in his assessment. I did come from good stock, my ma'm and my pa both champions with impeccable pedigrees.

We were the last to be seen, the master having reviewed the other dogs along with their handlers, the inspection order ranked by seniority, me being the youngest.

"He be sharp eyed," continued the master. "I give him that, with a look of intelligence. But that grin on his face and that floppy ear makes me be thinking, he'd be listening with only half an ear."

I made every effort to get my floppy ear to stand at attention without success. The silly ear had a life of its own—or rather, no life at all. As for the grin, it was something to do with my overbite.

"I be hearing his first time out, he be failing in his duties," stated the master.

"With respect," said the boy. "He was sent on patrol in error. He's just a pup without proper training. He didn't know nor understand his duties." The boy was a slight lad, a copper hue to his ginger locks, with soulful eyes like my ma'm, the reason I liked him so. That, and the fact he'd been with me since my birth.

Canine Master Galbraith pulled on his plaited beard, rubbed an ear. "True, a mix up with his name—dispatch be thinking they deployed his pa." He tugged at the hem of his gold-threaded tunic. "His rambles were recorded. Holographic images which be offering up nothing useful. A mere pup following his nose, scampering up one hill, down another, and then scurrying across some flamin' creek."

The boy said nothing. But me? I wanted to give a quick yip! It was a lovely meander under the warmth of our two suns, the morning mist lingering over the creeks where I happily chased my beloved hummers. The master was now using words like *foolhardy* and *reckless,* words I had yet to understand but my chi was willing. It mattered not that selective breeding led to a retriever's ears standing erect, like the shepherd and the husky, with additional selective breeding allowing for tails that didn't wag. What mattered was our willingness to serve and protect.

"Only those dogs with second sight are chosen to be members of the match," said the master. "He be showing no sign of that during his travels."

The boy nodded, stayed silent.

"Without second sight, he can't be unmasking the enemy," explained the master. "Can't fight what can't be seen."

"But he's the nose of a bloodhound," said the boy, giving his own freckled nose a thorough rub. "Isn't it possible his extraordinary sense of smell would compensate for his lack of second sight?"

Canine Master Galbraith sighed, pulled on a bushy eyebrow, squinted at me. "It takes more than the ability to be sniffing out a fishmonger rat," he said. "Return him to the kennels. I'll do me some thinking on the matter. He be what now—close to five stone in weight? Much like his pa despite his age, not quite full grown."

The boy nodded, took up the leash. I trotted alongside, my tail somewhat droopy, trying to show the master it didn't necessarily wag of its own accord. How to make the canine master recognize my full potential?

THE BOY and I slept in Daisy's stall. She was a gentle giant with limpid brown eyes ringed with dark lashes, two erect ears despite her age, and hairy fetlocks which tickled my nose. After the boy gave Daisy a good brushing and her nighttime oats, we bedded down, the two of us curled together on a lumpy layabout bed. The boy wasn't supposed to stay. I knew he should'a been home with his pa, but given we received no word from Canine Master Galbraith, I knew the boy was worried. Word came late the following day. The master had made a decision.

The boy brushed my bronzed coat until it shone as lustrous as my m'am's. He then tethered me to my leash. I trotted at his side, doing my best to keep my tail from wagging. We entered Master Galbraith's domain. He sat in his grand chair carved with images of masterclass dogs.

"Time be of the essence," he said. He then indicated the holographic map behind him which outlined the Ch' karrie infestation to the north. They were ugly creatures, no larger than an Old Earth mouse, eight-legged like a spider with many golden eyes which hypnotized their victim before striking. "We be deploying all good dogs and their handlers as we speak."

"And what of us?" asked the boy.

"It be against my better judgement," said the master, "but I be allowing him to continue with his training what includes an arduous journey to the farthest region of Wuldor, to the Q'ang Doong Cave. There, he will learn what the inflicted have suffered, allowing his chi to blossom, giving him the wisdom to be tapping into the second sight."

The boy fidgeted, pulled at a loose thread dangling from his own tunic. He then stammered, "His handler, who would that be?"

"Why, you, my fine young lad. You be the one looking after his care, you be the one to teach him the second sight."

The boy offered a respectful bow. "I thank thee, Master. The pup and I will not fail you."

"Two fortnights," said the master. "I suggest you be using the time wisely."

The boy bit down hard on his bottom lip. My tail wagged but given the boy's lack of enthusiasm, I sensed not all was as it should be. What if I failed? What would become of us? Outcasts, stripped of our citizenship, adrift as beggars? Perhaps being a member of the watch wasn't such a good thing. I then remembered what my ma' m told me. Failure was never an option.

THE FOLLOWING day we began in earnest. The boy's pa, a quiet man with ginger curls and thoughtful brown eyes, permitted the boy to use Daisy to haul our gear: bedroll, clothing, grub-in-a-tub for my welfare, extra oats for Daisy. Once Daisy's packs were full, we began the trek north.

At first, the villagers were wary of our approach. Was my presence a threat? A weapon to be used against them? It had long been common knowledge dogs were bred solely for the royal court or as members of the watch. Soon their thinking shifted when I wagged my tail and licked their hands, and oh! The joy of it! To interact with others, to engage in their activities. Word soon spread and the children raced down the dusty laneways and across flagstones to greet us with affection. The boy, too, took much joy from our encounters.

A week into our travels, we left Daisy in the care of a local blacksmith and continued our journey. The air became colder, the ground harder, the path we tread, rockier. Soon my paws took a beating. The boy outfitted me with leather booties. After a sharp command to stop shaking them loose, we carried on. The booties felt awkward but I soon came to appreciate their protection from the sharp rocks.

The boy took to wearing three woolen jumpers and a knitted tam pulled over his ginger locks that kept his ears warm. At night he built a fire. When he fed me, I had little appetite being so far from home and all that was familiar. When we slept, we curled together for warmth, comforted by the flames of our wee campfire. While never completely dark, the smaller of our two suns emitted a faint glow in the south, that glow offered no warmth. The lack of sunlight left us sluggish despite our few hours of sleep. Gone was our jaunty step. I had no desire to wander and explore the land. It held no interest. We saw no animals, no birds, no insects—not even my beloved hummers.

The entrance to the Q'ang Doong Cave came into view long before we reached it, so vast and grey and desolate was the land. There was no movement except for the wind.

The day we entered the cave, I held back, wanting no part of it. I pulled on my leash, whining my distress, but the boy's stout mettle kept him focused. With my tail tucked between my legs, we entered the cave. Our footfalls echoed—a distorted sound which tumbled and doubled back on itself. The boy carried a torch, the flame emitting a faint glow despite the size of the wick. Suddenly the torch spit and sizzled and died. If this was total darkness, it was too horrific to describe! I shivered, not from the cold but from something far greater—a sense of loss. My heart could not contain such sadness.

The boy trembled. He knelt in the dirt, holding me close, struggling to hold back his tears. He eventually found the matchsticks and with shaky hands set to lighting the torch. Again and again, he struck one matchstick after another, to no avail. Oh! The horror of it. To be forever trapped, unable to find our way out. But then, success! The torch was lit and we hurried back the way we had come.

When we cleared the cave's entrance and once again stood in muted daylight, the boy knelt and wiped the tears from his cheeks. "You now understand why we must not fail," he said. "That feeling inside the cave, that is what befalls those poisoned by the Ch' karrie—their chi, their lifeforce, sucked out of them."

I whined my understanding. I did not like the cave. I did not like the darkness. Within the darkness, I smelled fear, my own, and that of the boy, coupled with a terrible sense of loneliness, my heart fit to breaking.

The boy then told me, "So many lost to the darkness. Thus, the need for second sight. You must tap into your chi and look past what is in front of your nose. Remember what the master said, it is much more than the ability to be sniffing out a fishmonger rat."

I pondered what the boy shared with me during our return trip, learning the Ch' karrie carried no scent, which made it impossible to know when and where they would strike next. Stealth and trickery were their weapons of choice, thus the reason for second sight.

WE RETRIEVED Daisy from the blacksmith, offering him a shilling and a sixpence as payment. Later at sunset, the boy, having hobbled Daisy and now making haste to build a campfire, allowed me the freedom to wander the hillsides, searching for my beloved hummers. I then caught the scent of a skeetercat, them what preyed on the fishmonger rats. That discovery led me to a Ch' karrie den, the cat most likely ignorant of the fact the vermin next door carried no scent.

I began to dig, frantic to make amends for my poor performance in the cave.

Soon I exposed the den, where two of the filthy vermin leapt at me. I dug deeper, dirt flying, partially blinding me. The boy, hearing my yips and barks, rushed to my side, prepared with his nets and portable flamethrower.

One of the Ch' karrie breeders attacked, gnashing its teeth, clawing at my pelt with its deadly claws. I shook it free and grabbed it in my fanged jaws, snapping its neck. It exploded like an overripe Arabis orb, the disgusting fruit eaten by the Fishmonger rats, that thing what gave the rats their foul-smelling stench. The boy dispatched the other breeder.

He then captured the filthy Ch' karrie maggots in the netting and set it alight with the flamethrower. We watched as the vermin squirmed and writhed, each maggot popping like a punctured boil, dying before our eyes.

I sat back, depleted. If this was victory, why did I feel so empty? I gazed at the boy, he too confused. I intuited regret and disgust, despite the knowledge the Ch' karrie must be destroyed. But this! Engaging in warfare with flamethrowers and bloodlust did not seem the answer.

TWO DAYS LATER, we happened upon a village far to the east which offered no hospitality.

"Be off with you," one man shouted, waving his arms in anger. "You and your kind, you not be welcome here. What good be you? One boy and a mere pup." A wee lad stood at his side, the child a bedraggled ragamuffin, hollow-eyed, thin as a reed.

"He be in training," hollered the boy. "We've just come from the Q'ang Doong Cave."

The man made a terrible sound, a rattle in his chest meant for a scornful laugh.

Others had joined him at the edge of the village. The women, wrinkled old crones with tangled, matted hair, and faces like prunes, picked up an assortment of rocks and threw them at us. One shouted, "Here be our yearly tithe! You be taking that to the master. Tell him, this is what remains of our village, nothing but rock and rubble befitting nobility who care nothing for the welfare of their citizens. The Ch' karrie have infected the best of us. You with your pup! You be too little, too late."

The boy offered no rebuttal, certain the woman spoke true.

WITH HEAVY HEARTS we returned home, steering clear of any remaining villages. Only by luck had I discovered a Ch' karrie den, no indication I'd been blessed with second sight. Upon reaching our village, we eventually stood before the door what led to the master's inner sanctum. He bade us to enter. He perused one of the holographs taken during our travels. Behind the holograph was the contour map of Wuldor, the Ch' karrie infestation having grown worse during our travels.

The master pulled on his red plaited beard. "What's that he be doing now?" he asked.

"Playing with the children," said the boy, eyes downcast. "At the start of our travels, we encountered those willing to offer us respite within their village. The pup was overjoyed, especially with the children. Once he gained their trust, many of the little ones shrieked with laughter as he chased his tail. It was our only bit of joy during the weeks we were gone."

"Joy," huffed the master. "What be the use of joy when the Ch' karrie continue to poison our good citizens, all left to suffer in darkness and despair."

What the boy wasn't saying—we too, had experienced darkness and despair during our foray into the Q'ang Doong Cave, our hearts too, filled with sadness at what had befallen those we could not help, and me, showing no aptitude for divining the second sight.

The master sat back and stroked his beard. "You be leaving the pup's fate with me," he said. "Now, be off with you."

AT WEEK'S END, a great hubbub arose within the Great Hall, an impromptu gathering. Late-comers pressed against the massive oak doors, eager to gain entrance, many arriving from the outer fringes. Men carried short swords, waving their weapons without regard to life or limb. Women clutched carvings of their loved ones, seeking retribution for those lost to the Ch' karrie, former shells of themselves lying comatose on straw beds. Children huddled in groups, the smallest of them sucking on a thumb. I wondered what was to become of them.

There were shouts, "The ruling class be failing us!" Similar to what the northern villagers shouted that day we came upon their poor wretched existence. Perhaps they too, made the trek from the farthest region of Wuldor to descend upon the Great Hall. I looked about, wondering, would I see the old man and the wee lad?

I pressed close to the boy, not wanting to lose him in the crowd. The boy's pa walked ahead, shoving his way through the ensuing bedlam, slowly making his way toward Canine Master Galbraith's inner sanctum. When he reached the master's door, he banged heavily upon the oaken door with an iron fist. He was presently told to enter, whereby informing the master what was taking place beyond his quiet sanctuary.

The master rose, straightened his gold-threaded tunic, and took up his own short sword, shoving it into the hilt of his leather scabbard. He strolled forth with a determined step. "I knew this day be a'coming," he said. "Wuldor's day of reckoning."

He then thrust his way through the crowd, eventually standing behind the balustrade that ran the length of the Great Hall. Wuldor's massive oak shield hung at his back. It depicted Wuldor's coat of arms: the head of a golden retriever and

Wuldor's two suns. Written beneath the crest was an Old Earth motto: *Loyalty, Truth, and Courage.* The master held up his hands, shouted for quiet. Those in the front rows obeyed; others toward the rear did not.

One man's voice rang out, "We be paying our taxes and yearly tithe, and still nothing is done. The watch roots out the Ch' karrie but they continue to breed and infect our loved ones. Whatever you be thinking, Canine Master, you be thinking wrong!"

Those around the man shouted in agreement.

A second voice rang out, informing the crowd it was common knowledge dogs had been bred as a status symbol for the ruling class, only those in power allowed to keep a dog within their midst. So far, not one from the ruling class had been infected, not one member of the elite taken and made to suffer. What secrets did they possess?

Canine Master Galbraith stroked his red plaited beard. "It weren't serendipity what gives Wuldor two suns," he shouted. "It was foretold long ago. Old Earth seeded Wuldor as a land of wisdom and of light. Darkness is not inherent in our collective wellbeing. We be a happy folk by nature, content and hardworking."

The boy and his pa nodded in agreement. The crowd quieted, most wanting to hear what the master had to say.

Just then a great upheaval came from beyond the doors of the Great Hall, a hubbub of noise, much shouting and mayhem followed by the heraldry of trumpets.

A voice rang out, "Behold, the king has come! His Grace has come to our village!"

Everyone in the Great Hall fell deathly quiet, all eyes turned to the rear of the building, the oak doors having been thrown open, secured by their leather hinges. Moments later, King Leopold entered, resplendent in his royal purple robes, a white musk-mink encircling his broad shoulders, gold chains about his neck, silver brooches pinned to his expansive chest, his red beard plaited with many colourful beads.

Two of his hounds strode with him, magnificent beasts half the size of Daisy—wolf hounds originally from a land known as the Green Isle, the dogs bred solely for the royal court.

The women of the village curtseyed, the men bowed, children stood in awe, the youngest of them hiding behind their mother's skirts. None raised their eyes out of respect for the king's authority as divine ruler of Wuldor. Many trembled in their boots.

King Leopold strode forth, the cleats on his riding boots tapping the floorboards, his golden spurs jangling. The pair of majestic wolf hounds led the way. As the crowd parted, he presently climbed the spiral staircase and approached Canine Master Galbraith. The master surveyed all before him, the captain of a sinking ship.

I whined my discomfort, smelling the fear coming from those around me. The boy quickly hushed me, him now giving me the evil eye. I sat and watched and kept my tail from wagging. This was no wagging matter.

Canine Master Galbraith then knelt before the king, welcoming him to the Great Hall. "Your Grace," he said, taking the king's hand and laying a kiss upon the royal ruby signet ring.

The king turned and addressed the crowd. "Word has come to me of an uprising. Do you refute the leadership of those who have ruled Wuldor for centuries?"

"No, no," shouted the throng before him. "Never," came a shout from the farthest reaches of the hall, followed by another, "We only be asking for an accounting, our loved ones taken from us, the Ch' karrie stealing their lifeforce!"

"An accounting, you say?" bellowed the king, his voice resonating deep within his barrel chest, a sound like thunder. He turned to the master. "And what of you, my good man? Is this a day of reckoning?"

"It is exactly that, Your Grace. It be Wuldor's day of reckoning."

The king parted his lips in what was meant for a smile. "I bid you to carry on. I be here simply to observe, nothing more." He now stood off to the side, one hand stroking the great shield that held Wuldor's coat of arms. The two hounds with him took up their position on either side of the king, each resting on its haunches. They too, looked upon the crowd, tongues lolling, eyes watchful.

Canine Master Galbraith, clearly shaken, once again addressed all those in attendance. He pulled on his plaited beard, rubbed an ear. "We be thinkin' dog and handler could root out the Ch' karrie through bloodlust and battle," he shouted. "But we be thinking wrong. I now be thinking second sight is not the answer."

The master turned and bowed his head, perhaps an apology in the making?

The crowd stood in stunned silence.

"What if it be joy?" he shouted, his voice too carrying authority. "Unbridled joy what frees us from the filthy vermin." Smiling, he glanced at the king, then slapped his knee and broke into joyful laughter. His barrel chest rolled under his red plaited beard, making the ornamental beads jangle. My tailed thumped the floorboards.

"I be seeing a pup, a fine young fellow with a floppy ear, making merry with the children. All these images captured during his travels to gain second sight. In that merriment, the children's chi came alive. Lit up with the divine light of love and happiness."

It appeared the Canine Master had tapped into a different kind of second sight.

"I decree this day, in the name of His Grace, King Leopold, reigning Grand Duke of Warrington and Lord Baron of Jericho, we be freeing the dogs. No more kennels, no more keeping them solely as a status symbol for the elite or as members of the watch. We be setting them free to chase their beloved hummers, and by crikey, yes! They be wagging their tails!"

The crowd cheered. Women offered heartfelt hugs to the children. Men danced the jig of merriment, slapping their thighs with unbridled enthusiasm.

"And we be needing pups, lots of pups," shouted the master. "Soon we be seeing the love of a dog in every household, our best defense, a strategic offense. You be bringing a dog before the afflicted, and they too, will reap the benefit of canine affection. The filthy Ch' karrie will soon be dropping like flies, their husks withering in the dust."

The master then fell backward, landing hard upon the gilded chair what bore the brunt of him, without collapse. He gave the boy and his pa a wave of his hand, a sure sign of dismissal.

"Be off with you, all of you, and be doing what I ask. By crikey, we be seeing the last of the Ch' karrie or my name isn't Mortimer Hamish Galbraith!"

The king too, was smiling, clearly in acceptance of the master's decree. He nodded most solemnly to his Lord High Commissioner, who ran the length of the hall, instructing the trumpeters to herald the decree into law. As the trumpets sounded, the boy's pa hurried to the kennels and threw open the cages, freeing the dogs. He and the dogs and their handlers raced back to the Great Hall, everyone caught up in frenzied hysteria.

King Leopold, having left the balustrade, now stood in the center of the Great Hall, taking much pride in the showing of his massive wolf hounds to peddler and farmer alike.

He laughed, he smiled, he shook hands with some of those he recognized as couriers to his kingdom, them what brought news from all corners of Wuldor.

Dozens of dogs, members of the watch, leapt onto those kneeling before His Grace, wriggling into their arms, licking their faces. I too, joined in the merriment after the boy bade me do so, taking pleasure in the company of the children. I accepted their belly rubs, licking their wee hands with delight. I then spotted my littermates with my m'am and my pa, their coats brushed to a polished bronze and ebony. We greeted each other with playful yips and banter, all the while knowing it was a great day for dogs, all dogs. We would keep a faithful watch over the people of Wuldor while happily wagging our tails.

Through the Mud I Dug and Dug, Until I Found My Master's Hand

Akis Linardos

I've always been a loyal wolf to my master, my king.

Beneath the shadow of the great tree, the wet, burning mist glued fur to my skin as I scooped mud with my right leg—my left hanging powerless and limp, aching me still. My muzzle caught the sweet scent of raw animals shaking on the ground beside me, and my mind demanded I pounce and devour. But I gritted my fangs and resisted its pull. A hungry wolf is a sad thing, but a wolf without the king he bonded with, vowed to protect, a wolf without a forest is sadder still.

The hole grew large. The hole grew deep. Mud dripped from my paw.

A single thought gripped my mind and pushed me onward.

I've always been a loyal wolf. And I will find you my master, my king.

Even if I have to reach the darkest bowels of the Earth.

ONCE UPON A TIME, my master lived in a palace within a giant tree, within a forest, within a kingdom he called his own. The faeries loved him, as did the nymphs and jackalopes and all the creatures sheltered by the warm embrace of the canopy. My king loved them all back, not just the creatures but every branch and leaf and stone, because his heart was big and strong.

Yet of all the living things, none cherished him as much as this wolf's harkened heart.

My master wrested me from my mother's belly, as maggots feasted on her dead flesh. He cradled me, my muzzle digging in his rough beard that smelled of pinecone. He played with me, tossing deer bones in the air for me to leap and snatch. And he shared secrets with me no other creature of the forest knew.

Among the things he told me was what lies beyond the trees, at the border of the kingdom. Tall towers of obsidian and magic, conjured by a witch who used to be his wife. A witch vowed to protect him from the dark things lurking even farther, within the thick mist that had swallowed the rest of the world. My master told me these things because he knew I lacked the voice to share them with other forest creatures. He wished solace in their souls, which the blissful ignorance offered.

My master also told me these things because he needed to share the love of this witch with someone. Her absence prickled his heart like the thorny stem of a rose swelling from within. So before his heart could burst, the king chose to redirect his love to me and to the vast forest. To make her sacrifice matter.

The witch loved him too, and never stopped holding a place in her own heart for him. This the king believed deeply.

She was a brave soul that sacrificed her youth, her being, for him and for the forest. She was the barrier between the devouring fog and this last refuge of life.

She was the warden of the light.

ONE DAY, a crow fluttered through the orange sky, carrying a cloak of smoke upon its feathers. This upset my king, and he told me it could only mean one thing.

That the barrier had been breached.

My king bid me to lope as fast as my canine legs could take me, beyond the forest glades and beyond the prairie fields of hunting where jackalope and deer roamed. Beyond the golden river at the border of the forest. Beyond, beyond, beyond. Until I reach the looming blackness of her towers.

"And if she's wounded, my loyal friend," he said. "Carry her on your back and bring her home to my palace within the tree."

There was a scent of mixed emotion in his breath as he told me this. Worry and hope. Worry for his witch's safety, hope that he'd see his wife again.

My master embraced me, and I sniffed the pinecone of his long beard, the sweet maple of his weathered shoulders. And once we parted, I leaped away from the palace, out of the tree, and through the vastness of the forest.

I RESISTED my urge to hunt as I loped across the prairie fields, and I didn't halt to drink fresh water from the golden rivers of the glades. In the thickets, branches whipped at me, but I kept on, tearing apart the vegetation that got in my way with my fangs and the force of my body. In the swamplands, I leaped over the gnarly branches of the willows and waded through the thick murky waters with all the power I could muster in my legs.

And once the swamp was behind me, the trees were suddenly taller. Gigantic. Trunks dark like midnight and branches bare of leaves. Then I realized these were not trees but the conjured towers of my master's witch. But what was beyond these towers made my spine shudder like a crushed centipede.

The fog.

A swirling gray mist that unleashed biting snakes of smoke, sending cascades of dust flying off the ground like waves on a restless sea. And once the smoky snakes touched the branches of her tower, lightning sparked and sent them back. There was an overwhelming scent of decay that made me—by pure instinct—keep my muzzle low and whimper through my fangs.

The closer I got, the more powerful that scent got. I'd smelled rotting corpses before, but this was something else. Something more *sinister*. If there ever was a smell with intent behind it, this would be it. It was not just decay but a will to pull, to absorb, to vanquish.

My gaze now shifted to one of the towers, one that was smaller than the rest, like a tree struck by lightning. Its branches desperately reaching out to clutch the sky as the fog bulged and thrashed violently around it, carrying waves of earth to crash against it. It was a wonder that the mist had not overwhelmed it yet. But when I sniffed and narrowed my eyes to look closer, I realized why.

The witch was there.

Arms held up high, her tattered sapphire robes and hat thrashing to the maddened wind, by will of magic she kept a barrier that shoved the waves of earth back, keeping a clear area around her, letting only the tiniest slivers of smoke escape. Smoke slivers that took the form of crows and flew through the trees into the forest.

I leaped through the swirling mist, feeling its burning, stinging bite at my own skin, and the taste of charcoal on my tongue. I had touched fire before, and this was no different, save for its greater hunger. Dust and dirt flew around my legs as I stepped closer. Now the witch was in front of me, her eyes as blue as her robes, her skin was wrinkled and pale, and when I approached I saw the unnatural fissure spreading from the corner of her left eye down to her bosom.

For a moment the witch lost her focus, her attention caught by my presence. The fog flared around us and she kneeled, revealing a footless leg that had shriveled and turned pale brown, connecting to the earth as if she were not human but a witch-shaped little tree.

Her hands clutched the air and twisted like they were grasping a membrane, and the fog leaped back with a loud *woosh*.

"*He* sent you, didn't he?" she whispered. Her voice like drizzle on a lake.

I came closer, sniffed the crippling touch of age on her bones. And a whimper escaped me because I realized this was not the scent of a woman that could hold a barrier to protect the wall. Not the scent of a warden that stood vanguard against the darkness.

This was the scent of a woman that was soon to die.

"Don't cry for me, dear wolf. Cry for the forest, and for the snuffing of the light. But don't cry for this old woman. I will not come with you. My duty is still here, no matter how feeble I have become or how flimsy my barrier. If only to save a few more hours of light before the ending of everything. If only to allow another jackalope, fairy or nymph to be born and glimpse the sunlight."

I craved so much to shape words and cursed my canine tongue for allowing me only to howl, to raise my voice to the skies in mournful acceptance. The fog was creeping closer. And now shapes formed in the mist. Shapes of bipedal creatures with feathers and pale bony heads with long beaks, snapping at the air, with loud *sharp* noises. My heart pounded and my mind demanded I cower before them. But I resisted, and bared my fangs at them instead.

A swarm of crows flew past and crashed against the barrier, sending a fountain of black feathers flying up. But one, two, four made it past, into the forest.

"This old witch can hold little longer, dear wolf. Please, run back to the king. Stay by his side. Stay and enjoy what life there's left. Tell him . . ." She chuckled mirthlessly. "You can't really tell him anything, can you? Instead, put your muzzle into his beard, and lick his cheek with your warm tongue. He should understand."

A whimper escaped me again. My king had said to bring her with me, if she was wounded. That fissure spreading from her eye . . . it cracked her skin as if she were not human but a piece of land divided by earthquake. But her will was strong, refusing to give in to her wounds, and if I removed her from this position, the swelling fog would swallow us all.

None of this was fair. Why did the dark hold such vast power before us? Why was it so inevitable, the dying of the light?

"Go now, brave wolf. Go back and be free. Go and be by the king's side. So that hope might still linger, perhaps to make a kingdom smaller still."

The mist now inched closer. The beaks grew longer and the cackling sounds they made came sharper. The earth swelled and waves of dust and dirt came hurling at us.

"Go now. Go. *Go!*"

And now I was leaping away, trying hard to dispel the sight of the long beak snapping at her arm, taking a part of her with it.

Trying hard to convince myself I was not a coward.

THE EARTH QUAKED BEFORE ME. Once I reached the golden river, a wave shuddered the earth below my feet, and I found myself stumbling into the water. Then I was back on my feet again, shaking to spray away the wetness, leaping onward, refusing to look back. Through the prairie field, through the thickets, until the great tree where my king's palace nested was in front of me. The earth quaked louder now, a painful groan as if the land itself was pregnant with something terrible.

Once more, I stumbled, tasting the dirt and grass. The jackalopes, the deer, and the nymphs ran past me, the wind hissed and sent thick dust flying over me and—no longer able to resist—I turned my head and saw it.

A tsunami of gray fog.

I AWOKE from a terrible dream to a terrible pain in my leg and a heavy, wet burden all over my body. I shook, scattering the mud that covered me, feeling now the familiar burning sensation of the swirling mist around me. Ahead, brown leaves rained down from what remained of the tree that once housed the palace. The door to that palace had vanished, and the tree seemed smaller because the earth had swallowed most of it.

I limped ahead, aching to touch my front left leg to the ground. The grass had turned ashen, and it crumbled to dust as I passed over it.

As I approached the tree, I saw jackalopes limp and shaking on the ground, fur dissolved to bald spots and bone showing through the skin. Perhaps my own skin, a wolf's skin, is stronger. Perhaps a wolf can survive the devouring mist and witness the ending of the light.

Perhaps a wolf is made to suffer.

I reached the base of the tree, sniffed the earth, now wet and thickened by the mist. I shoved my right paw into it and began digging.

THE HOLE GREW LARGE, the hole grew deep. And I reminded myself that I'm a loyal wolf. Always been a loyal wolf.

My paw had grown numb from all the digging, and the mist hurt my skin, searing me like the faint touch of embers. I was, at first, vaguely aware of the beaked creatures rushing by me, leaving a trail of black smoke behind them, stooping over the corpses of the forest to devour them. And although they were all now distant shapes above the hole I dug toward the base of the tree, the bone-snapping, flesh-tearing sounds could still reach me.

The burrow of the tree—the gate once leading to a palace—was slowly revealed, and the sight of it spurred me to dig faster, aching to find my king. Until eventually, I scooped enough dirt for four of his fingers to emerge, smelling of sweet maple.

I dug deeper, now gently to avoid hurting his frail form.

And when the hole was deep enough, his body fell over my back, and I nestled him beside me. His eyes were distant, glazed with paleness, and his beard was caked with bits of mud. I sniffed over his beard, taking in the scent of pine cones.

And then, as the witch had bid me, I placed my muzzle close to his face, and licked his cold and weathered cheek.

A REQUEST

If you liked this anthology, please take the time to leave a review on the site where you purchased it and/or on one of the social media reading sites like Goodreads. Tell your friends that you enjoyed it. Suggest it as reading for your local book club. Request it at your local library (or more than one local library). This helps others learn more about the book and gets the word out. Please use the #dogsavethekingantho and #hemeleinpubs tags.

Thank you for your time, and thank you for reading this book!

Find more exciting books to read at hemelein.com.

HEMELEIN PUBLICATIONS

About the Contributors

LEE ALLRED is the award-winning author of several dozen fiction stories for professional markets such as *Asimov's Science Fiction* and *Pulphouse* magazines. His works are found in dozens of book anthologies. He has also scripted comic books for Marvel, DC, IDW and Image Comics, including such books as *Batman '66, Batman Black and White, Fantastic Four, FF, Bug! The Adventures of Forager,* and *Dick Tracy.* His novella, "For the Strength of the Hills", was named a Sidewise Award for Alternate History finalist.

A great love of history and historical detail infuses all of his work, whether he's writing steampunk, vampire tales, alternate history, or military sf. Allred served three rotations in Iraq as part of Operation Iraqi Freedom for the United States Air Force. After retiring as a Master Sergeant, he settled down to a writing life. Learn more at leeallred.com.

JENNY PERRY CARR is group vice president of scientific services for a medical communications company by day, budding sci-fi/fantasy/horror writer at night, which sounds much like the beginnings of a superhero's bio. But alas, her only superpower is remembering random facts, like the human body contains trillions of microorganisms that outnumber our own cells by 10 to 1!

She has a PhD in molecular neurobiology from Yale University that influences much of her speculative writing. She's a Minnesota native living in North Texas with her husband. She has been published in *Dark Recesses,* the anthology *Murderbirds* by WonderBird Press, and *Troubadours and Space Princesses* from Hemelein. She is currently working on a sci-fi trilogy.

She can be found on her website, jennyperrycarr.com, or @JennyPerryCarr on Facebook .

JALETA CLEGG was born some time ago and has filled the years since with plenty of make-believe. She writes science fiction adventure, fantasy of all flavors, and silly horror. When not writing, she enjoys playing with yarn, cooking weird vegetables, designing costumes and quilts, and generally messing around.

She has published eleven volumes in her Altairan Empire series, has written many short works and has multiple collections collecting them, most recently *Waiting for Elephants*. Jaleta is co-editor of the LTUE Benefit Anthologies series.

Inspired by the works of Robert E Howard, Ray Bradbury, J.R.R. Tolkien, H.P. Lovecraft, Edward Abbey, Clive Barker, and various piles of cassette tapes, random pulp novels, blues records, and B-movies, indie author D. S. COLEMAN writes wild tales of horror, fantasy, action, revenge, and redemption.

His adventurous life as a whitewater guide, trucker, casino dealer, trail cook, musician, artist, and storyteller bleeds into his work like oil bleeds from a 66 Dodge. Raised in the haunted woods and fields of the Mississippi Delta, Coleman was fascinated at an early age by ancient history and mythology. His musical tastes grew from his childhood, and he still draws inspiration from his love for blues, jazz, classic rock, pirate metal, Norse/Celtic folk, and other music.

After decades of wandering throughout North America, he currently resides on a sagebrush-covered refuge on the Lake Bonneville shore, with his inexplicably patient wife and countless deer, rabbits, and coyotes. *Like Sunshine,* book 1 of the genre-bending Song of Grace pulp cosmic horror fantasy adventure series, debuted in the summer of 2023.

STEVE DUBOIS is a high school teacher from Kansas City and the author of over thirty pieces of published fiction, poetry, and drama. He has been shortlisted for the James White and Baen Adventure Fiction Awards. Find out more on his author site at stevedubois.net.

ANGELIQUE FAWNS is a Canadian speculative fiction writer. Her very first sale was to *Ellery Queen Mystery Magazine*. You can find her work in *DreamForge, Allegory, The School Magazine,* and two Third Flatiron anthologies. "The Last of the Gen Xers" is a 2022 Tangent Online Recommended Read. Learn more at fawns.ca.

Born in Palo Alto, California, JOE FICKLIN was abandoned by his parents at birth and then raised by engineers in the wild. He has spent a lifetime gathering experiences as writing fodder. He's sailed on both east and west coasts, flown a jet over Texas, skied the Sierras and the Rockies, swam in the South China Sea, spent 6 months working inside a certain mountain in Colorado, operated a food truck for several years, and done many other things, most of which he survived with only minor injuries. Occasionally, he writes.

His stories normally focus on how emergent technologies change social expectations and interactions in the near future. He should write more stories, but he's also busy with a full time job (still!) while renovating his house, destroying his backyard (so he can save it), and writing and performing filk music in his copious spare time. That last bit was sarcasm, DYK.

He lives in Provo, Utah, with his wife of mumble-mumble (>39) years, one cat, and possibly the largest collection of *Star Trek* books in Utah.

JENNIFER LESH FLECK has stories published or upcoming in *MetaStellar, Gamut, If There's Anyone Left, Heartlines Spec, Flash Fiction Online, Cosmic Horror Monthly,* and the 2023 Shirley Jackson Award winner for best anthology, among others. She lives with her family near Portland, Oregon, in a home that's a dead ringer for the *Amityville Horror* house, though repainted a cheery jade green.

She's a 2024 Writers of the Future finalist and a grateful recipient of the 2025 Superstars Expanding Universe scholarship. Her two dogs, Olive and Frankie, are among her best friends. Find her @mettle.and.metal (Instagram), @jen_lesh_fleck (X), and jenniferleshfleck.com.

Max Florschutz was born in the wilderness of rural Alaska and survived there for two decades before moving. A long-time lover of sci-fi and fantasy, he published his first book in 2013, and since then has continued to thrill and delight audiences with unexpected adventures and delightful characters. He runs a weekly writing advice feature, "Being a Better Writer," at his website, maxonwriting.com.

David Hankins writes from the thriving cornfields of Iowa. His writing journey began years ago in Germany as he made up stories to convince his daughter to go to sleep, which always backfired. Those midnight ramblings developed into a passion for creating new worlds while exploring the idiosyncrasies of this one. He has two novels out: *Death and the Taxman* (2024) and *Death and the Dragon* (2025), with a third forthcoming.

Laura Holley is an aspiring writer and voice narrator, who also loves spending time with her husband and five kids. She weaves deep and rich stories both on stage and on the page. When not holed up in her she-shed writing, she also really loves writing and arranging music, gardening, acting, and failing to make sourdough bread (someday she'll get it!).

Rhys Hughes is a writer of fantasy and magic realism who often uses comedy and absurdism to examine philosophical issues. He writes short stories, novellas, and novels, and (to a lesser extent) poetry and nonfiction. He sometimes says that writing is the only thing he's good at. While he tries to make that sound like a joke, his passion for writing keeps growing stronger!

He was a writer from an early age. He completed his first proper short story when he was fourteen, "The Journey of Mountain Hawk", and still remembers what it was about even though it no longer exists. His earliest *surviving* short story dates from 1989, and since that time, he has embarked on an ambitious project of writing a story cycle consisting of exactly 1000 linked tales.

AKIS LINARDOS is a writer of bizarre things, a biomedical AI scientist, and maybe human. He's also a Greek who hops across countries as his career and exploration urges demand. Find his fiction in *Apex, Uncharted, Heartlines, Gamut*, and more at https://linktr.ee/akislinardos.

DARREN LIPMAN is a high school math teacher and writer in Milwaukee, Wisconsin. His fiction has appeared in the *Eastern Iowa Review* and *Literally Dead 2: Tales of Holiday Hauntings*. He is a member of DreamCasters and Wulf Pack Writers.

One half of ROBERT F. LOWELL'S brain has authored, edited, or contributed to fourteen books and numerous articles and papers on terrorism, nuclear proliferation, and chemical and biological weapons. The other half writes about swords, sorcery, unicorns, and magic birds and has earned Honorable Mention three times (so far) in the Writers of the Future short story contest. Both halves live together in California with Robert's wife and at least one dog.

KAREN KEELEY has published short fiction in more than a dozen anthologies: literary, speculative, and crime. She is a member of the Short Fiction Mystery Society (SFMS) and Sisters-in-Crime, Canada West. Now retired, she divides her time between friends, family, the outdoors, and writing—not necessarily in that order. Find more about her writing at karenmkeeley.blogspot.com.

HANNAH MARIE grew up in several western states, her imagination fueled by the rainforests of Washington and the deserts of Utah. After discovering as a child that her imagination could be written down and shared, she started writing and has not stopped. As an adult, she traveled to the UK and lived as an ex-pat in South Korea, collecting freckles and experiences. When she is not reading, writing, or working, she enjoys biking, spending time with her family, and dreaming up fantastical worlds.

JOE MONSON loves reading, books, and butter mochi. He has worked at a couple dozen different jobs during his life. In his current job, he valiantly battles worms, trojans, viruses, corruption, hardware, and updates to keep computer systems running.

He has co-edited multiple anthologies with Jaleta Clegg in the LTUE Benefit Anthologies series, and he's the series editor of the Legacy of the Corridor publication series from Hemelein Publications. His most recent anthology, *The Horror at Pooh Corner,* was a successful Kickstarter and was released in bookstores worldwide in 2024.

Joe writes short stories and is outlining a space opera adventure series. He collects science fiction and fantasy art, but not as much as Paul (as if that was even possible). He lives in the tops of the mountains with his thoroughly amazing wife, three miracle children, and their pet library.

DALE PARNELL is an author (and sometime poet), writing mainly fantasy, science fiction, and horror. He has self-published three short story collections, a full-length sci-fi novel, and is featured in over fifty excellent anthologies.

FRANCES PAULI writes award-winning animal stories. Her fantasy worlds feature snakes, spiders, horses, and very rarely, the occasional human. She is a member of the Furry Writer's Guild and lives in Washington State with her family, pets, and a ridiculous amount of houseplants.

Originally from England, and having lived in several countries, RICK A. PEARSON now resides in New Mexico. His fiction and poetry can be found in various anthologies and magazines. He can be found on Instagram.

ED SAMS is a Californian writer whose award-winning fiction has been published in regional and national publications. *Pigeon Review* published online his story "The Mad Spells of Miss Wycherly" (October 2021), and "Shuis Slo Slumus Sheen" appeared in the anthology *Tales from Fiddler's Green* (Spring 2021). His short story "Among the Fairies" was anthologized in *Santa Cruz Weird* (2018), and Main Street Rag published his novella *Wicked Hill* (2012). Every year, he recites "The Raven" at Poe Fest, San Jose State University's celebration of Edgar Allan Poe at Halloween. More information can be found in Wikipedia under the entry "Ed Sams".

JESS SMART SMILEY is the bestselling creator of over twenty books, including picture books, hidden object books, chapter books, and graphic novels. He has helped more than two thousand children, teens, and adults around the world in creating their own comics, and he's always looking for opportunities to connect and create with other artists, writers, and storytellers.

What Happens Next: Talent Show Troubles and *What Happens Next: Science Fair Frenzy* are his two newest books, both interactive graphic novels from Macmillan's First Second imprint. *Let's Make Comics* is an activity book published through Penguin Random House, which debuted at #1 on Amazon in four categories and has been celebrated by students, parents, librarians, educators, and comics professionals.

EMILY MARTHA SORENSEN writes clean fantasy adventures with clever characters, fun plots, and lots of humor. Her bestselling book is *Dragon's Egg*, about a baby dragon and his human parents. Her second-most popular book is *Black Magic Academy*, about a good witch who gets sent to a school for fairy tale wicked witches. She also draws two comics and loves talking the ears off anyone who happens to be nearby.

JOHN STECKLEY is a retired community college instructor who began writing short stories upon his retirement in 2015. He has published twenty-seven nonfiction books plus one nonfiction book—*Stories for Mia*—on the subject of his four-year-old granddaughter's imagined future life. The subject of most of his nonfiction books is usually the Wendat/Wyandot people, their language, culture, and history.

When not out exploring the universe, CHRISTINA TANG-BERNAS lives in Southern California with her family. Her work has appeared in *Radon Journal*, *Strange Constellations*, *Twist in Time*, and *And If That Mockingbird Don't Sing*, among others. Find out more at christinatangbernas.com.

DJ TYRER is the person behind Atlantean Publishing and has been widely published in anthologies and magazines around the world, such as *Winter's Grasp, Tales of the Black Arts, Pagan, Misunderstood, Sorcery & Sanctity: A Homage to Arthur Machen, Fantasia Divinity, Broadswords and Blasters, BFS Horizons*, and *Tales from the Magician's Skull*. He has a novella, "The Yellow House", available in paperback and in ebook.

KEVIN WASDEN is an artist, storyteller, poet, and educator. His artistic journey began in childhood, sketching comic book heroes and doodling for friends. Mr. Sylvester's 6th grade art class at Fillmore Middle School flipped a switch. There he discovered the magic of light and shadow, forever altering how he saw the world.

He went on to study at Utah State University, where mentors such as Glen Edwards and Gregory Schulte helped hone his drawing and painting skills. His quest for artistic excellence led him to study figure painting under Andy Reiss in Brooklyn, New York. As a professional illustrator and designer, Kevin created art for numerous book, periodical, and game publishers, including Avon Camelot, Baen, Fantasy Flight Games, and Alderac Entertainment Group.

Kevin played a pivotal role as the creative director at Alinco Costumes, where he helped guide the creation of many famous mascot characters and costume designs for the Chicago Bulls, the Arizona Diamondbacks, the Oklahoma City Thunder, and others.

Throughout his career, Kevin has felt a deep desire to share his knowledge and skills with others. For many years, he served as a private art instructor and high school art teacher. In 2023, Kevin turned most of his creative energy toward making more personalized artwork for shows and galleries. He is currently an exhibiting artist at Urban Arts Gallery in Salt Lake City. He also participates in numerous local and state art shows. Learn more at kevinwasden.com.

JADE C. WILDY is a South Australian writer and a member of Wulf Moon's Wulf Pack and David Farland's Apex Writers. She has had short stories published in several anthologies including *Stories of Survival* (Dead Set Press) and *The Clockwork Chronicles* (Madhouse Books).

Holding bachelor's and master's degrees in visual arts gives her a flair for culture, and she returned to creative writing in 2020, concentrating on speculative fiction but branching out into fantasy, science fiction, and horror. Through her writing, Jade addresses themes like climate change, mental health, and being different, and delights in slipping in the unexpected. She believes in the power of storytelling as a motivator for change, and her writing has been included in numerous publications internationally.

A self-confessed wallflower, Jade acknowledges the traditional custodians of the Kaurna Lands where she lives and can frequently be found writing or drawing in the local cafes.

Additional Copyright Information

The following was used as the ornamental break:

The following were used in creating the cover:

www.ingramcontent.com/pod-product-compliance
Lightning Source LLC
Chambersburg PA
CBHW021502110726
47899CB00001BA/261